MW01125382

STRONGHOLD

By

Skip Ball

*"We are hard pressed on every side, but not crushed;
perplexed, but not in despair; persecuted but not abandoned; struck down, but not destroyed."*
2 Corinthians 4:8-9 NIV

A story inspired by actual events and real people.

IN DEDICATION

—∿—

This story is in memory of my mom, Luona Ball who trusted God with the life of her son and believed enough to simply pray that this day would ultimately come. One day we'll meet again and I'll tell her my story from cover to cover.

ACKNOWLEDGEMENTS

This story is not mine alone. It belongs to my three sons, Chris, Dan and Jon, who love me more than I deserve. You've made my life rich beyond measure. It belongs to my dear friends like Dave Sorensen, Rick Shurtz, Jim and Kristina, Tom, Nigel and a host of lifelong friends in England. You encouraged me to keep going and not give up. You've made me richer still. It belongs to my mentor and brother Bill Myers, who prayed, agonized and gave me the freedom to dream. You've made my heart prosper. And to my editor Alton Gansky who held me to a course and challenged my precepts and believed in the story. And to my closest friend, Curt Brock who held me up when I was weak and was my voice when I could not speak and gave me the reassurance that the path to God is worth following no matter what. You've made me a wealthy man. This story belongs to the people of God.

FORWARD

—ᘺ—

W e writer types are a dime a dozen. Some of our stories are good, some of them stink, and some are somewhere in between. A story is only a story. But man, now there's something worth talking about. And a good man, well, that's worth writing a Forward about.

I've only walked with Skip through a portion of the times in this book. I've prayed with him, I've rejoiced with him, I've cried with him. But during those times, I've never once seen him lose his integrity. Even when broken, I've seen a man of God with a heart wide open to help and serve others. I don't know what he was like before he fought this battle. But I tell you, the strength and metal he is made of now, is an example for the rest of us.

He's disguised this story as fiction, for reasons I'm still not sure of – probably to protect the identity of some folks, probably because others wouldn't believe him, anyway. I'll let him answer your e-mails about which is truth and which is fiction. But I'll tell you this . . . if you walk away from this story with the same truths I've received from knowing Skip, then the book will have been "worth its tree." Truths that talk of fighting a spiritual battle. Not playing some game, not toying with some hobby. But fighting. And real fighting is costly. Real fighting faces fierce opposition. (I'm afraid in our zeal to bring others to Christ, we've glossed over that fact). Yet the treasures won in the spiritual wars that Skip has fought have brought a transformation of character in his life and in others that is worth every scar. Skip Ball has scars. Skip Ball is also a mighty man of God who has received treasures upon this earth as well as in Heaven.

My prayer is that "Stronghold" will have the same impact upon your life as knowing Skip has had upon mine. Yes, we can sit on the sidelines, fearful of investing our talents, focusing upon our families and ourselves, refusing to do battle . . . and indifferently watch the world slip into Hell. Or, as Skip, we can press in, take the heat, and fight the good fight. Does it cost something? Yes. It costs our lives. Do we receive something? Yes. We receive God's life. And we don't have to be nuclear scientists to know which we'd rather have, the hay and stubble of our own lives, or the imperishable gold of His.

Blessings,
Bill Myers
www.Billmyers.com

PROLOGUE

—◊—

Frigid rains swept the crest of Kingsbridge hill, backed by biting north winds. The desolate day wore a shroud of pewter gray as an old priest shuffled in front of a lonely casket carried by four hired pallbearers. Beneath the lid of the casket were the remains of an old, legless woman. A small arrangement of white lilies and baby's-breath drooped on the lid of the rain-drenched casket. The procession moved toward the outskirts of the graveyard, to the section reserved for commoners.

Two figures dressed in black mourning clothes followed the casket. Neither the man nor the woman acknowledged the other's presence. They walked with heads bowed in a state of mournful repose.

Middle-aged and fleshy, the woman wore her dark, gray streaked hair pulled back and pinned beneath a hat. Black leather gloves ran beneath the sleeves of her long winter coat. The black hat with a wide brim and a beaded floral pattern rested squarely on top of her head. A heavy ebony veil concealed her face.

The man was in his mid seventies and dressed meticulously, as if he had just stepped from one of London's prestigious banks. He wore a black pinstriped suit beneath a tailored cashmere overcoat. His shoulders stooped, and a bowler hat held thin wisps of white hair in place. Rimless spectacles clung to the bridge of his nose. His hands bore the unmistakable scent of Pears Soap, as though he had scrubbed them a dozen times that morning. In his pocket rested an ironed ten-pound note, sealed in a folded white envelope, and a final receipt from the Kingsbridge funeral home.

The priest stopped and turned as the casket drew near to the six-foot deep void—a hole freshly dug for Maggie Trick. Father Mahoney wore his wool vestments, visibly thread bare around the collar. The incessant rain and soggy grass now soaked the hem of his wool cape.

Mahoney had long ago grown accustomed to the pervasive smell of wet wool and mothballs at winter funerals. He shivered as he stood waiting for the pallbearers to suspend the casket over the ground's gaping maw. A raindrop trickled down his neck. His thoughts slipped to a hot cup of tea with a touch of whiskey and the cozy fire waiting for him at the vicarage. He wondered about the size of the honorarium he would receive for his services rendered for Maggie Trick, the mistress of a local banker. His mind wandered from the cup of tea, the shot of whiskey, and the honorarium to the corpse before him.

What favors did Maggie offer to this old man to make him so devoted even in death? What would possess a man to pay so high a price and risk so much, to house a woman of ill repute in the same community where his wife and children lived? What will become of the ill-famed Erindale Cottage, now that Maggie is dead?

To Mahoney, Erindale was synonymous with fornication, and terrible deeds done in darkness. He blushed as he recalled the fleeting temptation he had years ago to visit Maggie's home. He never did. Avoiding eye contact with the mourners, Mahoney directed his stare beyond the mourners to the church tower a short distance away.

"We are gathered here today to show respect for the life lived by our deceased sister Margaret Regina Trick. May God be praised." He began to read from the Book of Common Prayer.

"Mankind that is born of a woman hath but a short time to live, and is full of misery. He cometh up, and is cut down, like a flower; he fleeth as it were a shadow, and never continueth in one stay. Yet O Lord God most holy, O Lord most mighty, O holy and most merciful Savior, deliver us not into the bitter pains of eternal death.

"Thou knowest, Lord, the secrets of our hearts; shut not thy merciful ears to our prayer; but spare us, Lord most holy, O God most mighty, O holy and merciful Savior, thou most worthy Judge eternal, suffer us not, at our last hour, for any pains of death, to fall from thee."

*   *   *

The woman winced at the words, "'The Lord knows the secrets of our hearts." *There were plenty of secrets of the heart in Mother's life. Sadly, I am one of them.*

She shifted her considerable weight from one shoe to another, as her eyes peered from behind the draped veil toward the casket. A nagging feeling of shame and a genuine sense of loneliness flooded her soul once again. She abhorred what her mother had been: a mistress, a whore, and an immoral woman. It had been revulsion of her mother's lifestyle that forced her to the life of a spinster. Long ago, she had given up hope for someone to love her, to care for her as a mother should have, or a father, or, God forbid, a husband. She hid her pain beneath the veil and stood alone.

*   *   *

The old man stood at a chilly distance from the woman. He shielded his eyes with his black umbrella. As the rain continued to fall, it gathered in large puddles and ran down a ridge of the umbrella onto the man's hand-stitched Italian shoes. His selective vision allowed him to focus on the casket alone. Over the years, he had hardened his conscience to regret. He had learned to live for the day. His only loyalty now was to finish the job, pay the bill, and get on with his life. He had long ago ceased to care about Maggie. The cost was staggering in return for what little gratification had ever been his. He would soon be finished fulfilling his vow to provide for her.

With uncertainty, he gazed out of the corner of his eye toward his estranged, illegitimate daughter whom he had seen only at a distance. Through the black veil, he could clearly identify her rounded cheeks and the slight line of her chin. Herbert quivered at the sight. He recognized Maggie's face in her daughter's profile. He returned his eyes to the coffin.

* * *

"Amen," Father Mahoney muttered, and looked down in silence for the briefest moment.

Her father stepped to the priest and shook his hand stuffing the folded envelope into his pudgy palm, thanked him then left.

Margaret merely nodded to the cleric and turned to slosh through the puddles. She would shed no tears, but sadness flooded her heart like a rising sea. She knew she would feel it for the rest of her life. She watched her father walk down a small path and away from her forever.

* * *

Three days later, Herbert listed Erindale Cottage with *National and Provincial,* a real estate agency, handed over the keys, and wiped his hands of Maggie Trick for the last time.

CHAPTER ONE

―∿―

Twelve months later

"Incredible, this is *too* good to be true. Lisa will be over the moon." Clutching a piece of paper, Pastor Jacob Knight rushed from the real estate office toward an ancient Ford parked at the curb a few yards north of the office. The skies had grumbled earlier and now rain pelted the ground in big drops that splattered the sidewalk and splashed against shop windows. Jay's hair flattened against his scalp as he hurried. He hoped his wife would be excited and see this as God's provision. *How could she not?* He knew how. Sometimes she missed the potential he saw in things.

Potential. That's what this was all about. It boggled the mind to think that he and Lisa could actually own a piece of British real estate, rich with primordial history. Jay was dizzy with excitement. He'd read of England's colorful history. *On this island in lifetimes past, ancient warring races fought bloody battles.*

The rain fell harder and Jay quickened to a trot, rushing past the market stalls until he pulled open his car door and folded his long legs into the driver's seat. It chugged to life with a stutter and idled with a familiar wobble. The wipers click-clacked back and forth, leaving two eyebrows of smudge across the windshield.

Jay wiped the condensation from the window until he could see enough to navigate. His head buzzed as the Ford chugged up the lane toward home. This Roman village had remained the same for centuries. Green belt boundaries, limited expansion, and a townspeople who held no desire for extensive real estate development kept the area pristine and uncluttered. The provincial atmosphere of this village offered a security that few cities in England could equal.

In twelve months, the town would be celebrating its nine-hundredth anniversary as recorded in the Doomsday Book, but today was just another business day full of shoppers and merchants and the usual rainstorm. Jay glanced again at the real estate listing, now damp and puckered with raindrops. He'd laid it on top of his frayed Bible which rested in the front passenger seat.

Executives from Liverpool and Manchester were snatching up the nicer properties in Kingsbridge. People would give a lot to own property here in the heartland of Cheshire.

Jay's imagination took hold as he envisioned what kind of house awaited them. The flier lacked the usual photographs and details were sketchy, but it was the cheapest house in Kingsbridge and it had a history all its own.

"Everything has potential." The words bounced off the windshield. He shoved the gear stick into second and slowly gained speed.

He, Lisa, and the three boys had lived in England for nearly nine years, ever since the Lord had moved him and Lisa a world away from Los Angeles. Their three sons were born on British soil, making them subjects of the Queen. They'd always lived in a church-owned property, the manse. His father had done the same his entire career. Somehow, Jay wanted better. Was that so wrong? He wanted the great

American dream of home ownership. He felt called to England to plant a church and offer the hope of salvation to those who had never heard the Good News. It was Jay's passion, a passion set in stone.

He had contemplated the idea of purchasing a home for a long time. He was thirty-eight. If ever they would be eligible for a first time mortgage, it would be now. Of course, they had only two thousand pounds in savings. Not much of a down payment. He would figure that out later. Lisa would be quick to express her doubts about their ability to afford such a purchase. He would have to convince her. He could already hear her protestations.

"You're a dreamer, Jay. Not *everything* has potential. Be realistic. Her exasperated stare would only make her more alluring. Lisa looked cute when she was mad. He chuckled as he steered the car up another lane. The optimist in Jay often clashed with the realist in Lisa, but their differences had a welding effect and made them stronger.

Jay had learned early to make something out of nothing. That was his missionary attitude. They graciously received cast-offs and willingly accepted secondhand furniture. Here was a next to nothing house, a fixer upper, a home no one else seemed to want. Whatever it was like, he could transform it. No, he would transform it. Somewhere between the real estate office and the manse, resolve forced its way into Jay's head. He would buy this house and Lisa and the lads would love it.

Jay made a right turn on Overton Road and shifted gears. Suddenly, a car roared up behind him on the narrow lane, its daytime lights glaring in Jay's mirror. The heavy rain blurred Jay's vision. The driver hit the horn three times and then pulled menacingly close to the rear of Jay's Ford. In a split second, on a blind turn, the car roared past. The driver leaned on the horn again then flashed a rude hand gesture. It fishtailed down the lane leaving a blur of red lights.

Anger flushed Jay's face. "What an idiot! He must have a real problem. He could have killed me." Jay didn't have patience for ignorant drivers. As the rear lights disappeared, Jay forced a laugh.

"Sorry, Lord. The guy's probably got a bad case of the runs." Jay laughed at the joke and pressed the Ford to a quivering 30 mph. An earsplitting crack of thunder shot from the sky and rumbled through the sedan. The rain became a pummeling downpour. He tensed but not even rain, thunder, or a mindless driver could dampen his spirits. He thought of the house and the iron keys in his pocket.

How should he break the news to Lisa so she would see it as good? He'd been very clear on the phone with Miss White, the estate agent. "We're looking for an inexpensive property as an investment." More like a gamble, he had thought, but since missionaries don't gamble, *investment* seemed more theologically appropriate. "We are first time buyers and willing to look at anything."

Jay had gulped at the price tag of twenty-four thousand pounds, yet he knew the asking price was dirt cheap compared to most houses in town. Considering everything, this one-hundred-year-old cottage was a bargain. According to the leaflet, the original owner had been Lord Chumley himself, who at one time had owned much of Cheshire. Surrounded by woodlands, the location sounded idyllic. This chauffeur's cottage, a part of a large manor estate, was an incredible opportunity. Why someone hadn't snatched it up already was beyond him. The agent had mentioned one other interested party, but didn't appear forthcoming as to whom it was or if they remained interested.

"Just a crackpot. Not a serious offer." She changed the subject to the adjoining forest.

Must have been saved just for us. That's what he would tell Lisa.

Jay sped into the driveway bottoming out on a bump in the pavement. He hit the brakes, shut off the ignition and bounded out of the car. Another piece of rust fell from the doorframe as he slammed it. It took two attempts before the door finally latched. He flew into the kitchen with all the excitement of a lad winning a soccer match. His well thought-out explanation dissolved into an emotional jumble of exhilaration.

"Look at what I've got, sweetie." He dangled the keys in front of Lisa's face then gave her a kiss. Before she could respond, he took her in a tight squeeze and swung her around.

"Keys to a vault, I hope. The Lord knows we could sure use some cash." Her eyes were the color of cornflowers and seldom failed to twinkle. "Take off your wet jacket. You're making a mess on the floor." She knew how to use her dark lashes to great advantage, sometimes enticing, sometimes teasing Jay to absolute distraction.

The short English days had quickly given Lisa a soft cream-colored complexion with the natural rosy cheeks of a bride. With the exception of her California accent, Lisa was often mistaken for a local.

She grimaced as she glanced at the iron keys. "They look more like keys to a dungeon."

Jay read from the soggy flier, smoothing it out on the countertop. "You won't believe this. Listen: two bedrooms—one bath, kitchen with sink—living room with fireplace. Great potential—possible gas available—one third of an acre—surrounded by pristine woodland."

Her slender brows met together. "Potential? Let's see the photo." She leaned over his shoulder.

"Sorry, no photo. I guess we'll just have to go see it." He raised an eyebrow. "This cottage was once part of Erindale Manor house."

Lisa looked disappointed. "See this mess? It's Michael's. I'm tied up right now cleaning it—" Tipping her head, she said, "Let me see that flier." She grabbed the paper and read it through. "Look here." She pointed to a phrase. "This says 'Possible gas available.' Don't they know if there is gas or not? It's like saying, 'Possible roof included.' Either it has gas or it doesn't." She hand the flyer back.

"That is kinda dumb." Jay rolled his eyes. "You would find the inconsistencies."

"Somebody's got to." Lisa scooped up a handful of flour and water paste. She tossed it in the garbage and headed back for more.

"Hey, did I tell you about the forest? For the lads?" He didn't wait for an answer. "I've got to return the keys before closing." He rattled them in front of her again, all but dancing in the tiny kitchen.

She shooed him with her hands and took the towel off her shoulder. "You go look if you want. Come back and tell me about all its potential."

Lisa wanted a house of her own too. She had said so a number of times, but he had watched her resign herself to living on someone else's goodwill as long as they were missionaries. Her practical attitude toward life would have never brought them to England, he knew that very well. Jay had to admit her practicality balanced him. He was like a helium balloon, willingly carried into the unknown, while Lisa kept her eye on the earth and her hand on his string.

"Possible gas. Humph! Go, but be back for supper."

"Thanks, Mum. Yes, Mum. Be back soon, Mum." Lisa threw the dishtowel at him.

"Go, and please make sure it has a roof. And make sure there are no ghosts hiding in the closets. I've heard stories about these old English houses. Whoever wrote that flier must have been smoking pot."

Jay was out the door before Lisa could exhale. The rain had slowed to a drizzle, leaving small breaks in the clouds where sunlight peeked through. From the flier, he learned there were several ways to get to Erindale. For now, he would go on foot. He could approach the house by a path not far from where they lived. He had neglected to mention the lack of vehicle access to Lisa. He wondered if any of this was important to her. Of course it was. It must be. For months, he had questioned whether they had a right to lay up a little treasure in this life. He concluded that most of his colleagues back home had already bought houses, RV's, time-shares— all those things they had chosen to leave behind. Was he chasing a dream that should never be?

Caution rose in his heart as he hurried down the road. "Make sure there are no ghosts." Typical Lisa sense of humor about all things British. "Family skeletons everywhere," she often said.

With his stomach churning with anticipation he moved on easily locating the beginning of the wooded footpath. *Everything has potential, gas or no gas. Lisa would see.* He was certain of that.

We could buy an oil heating system or a solid fuel boiler. Fireplaces are cozy. He pressed on, a grin pasted to his face. *The Knight family and the ghosts will have one big tea party.*

CHAPTER TWO

—w—

The rain had gone but saturated trees continued to water the already damp ground of the woods. Fresh sunlight streamed through leaves and branches pushing back the shadows. Trees arched high above the ancient footpath forming a cathedral-like ceiling.

Jay moved quickly through the woods, stepping around puddles and hopping over the roots that crisscrossed his path. Excitement churned in his stomach. Jay peered through the foliage, eager to get his first glimpse of the cottage.

Ahead shadows filled the forest narrowing the path into a long dark tunnel. It wasn't until Jay's fingers began to tingle that he realized how fast he was breathing. *Calm yourself, man.* He slowed and forced himself to take measured breaths.

In the thick of the forest there seemed to be no evidence of civilization beyond the worn footpath. The hush of nature muffled the distant street noise. A wren flitted past with a single chirp. A red squirrel leapt through the tangled branches and stopped to study the stranger. Jay felt he was in a mysterious medieval forest with trees that whispered secrets to the wind. For a moment, he felt consumed by the solitude.

The forest erupted into a conflagration of noise: a flock of birds flapped away and crows cawed high above. Through the trees, Jay saw something charging his way. He slowed and tensed. A woman moved toward him in a forced march. A dog on a leash pulled her along as she struggled to stay upright. Her skirt flashed in bright Bohemian colors. As the dog towed her along, Jay could see the woman mumbling. She had olive skin and high cheekbones that gave a hint of another culture, foreign, almost earthy. A wisp of gray hair danced across her forehead. The dog was a gritty animal and tugged hard at the leash as it forged ahead. When it saw Jay it stopped and emitted a low menacing growl. Its ears flattened and the hair on its back bristled. Jay tensed. With a snarl it lunged forward nearly yanking free from the woman's grip. Jay jumped back and goose bumps chased down his neck.

"Randolph...heel. Heel!" Her voice was gravelly. The dog ignored its master's commands determined to sink his fangs into Jay's leg. The animal's neck muscles bulged. "STOP, RANDOLPH." The woman shrieked and grabbed the dog's collar. "Randolph...Randolph...easy, easy." When her voice dropped to a whisper, Randolph finally obeyed. The dog put his tail between his legs and cowered close to the ground. The woman stood and studied Jay for a minute. "Sorry about Randolph. He's usually friendly to strangers. I can't imagine what set him off."

"He's probably hungry." Jay smiled and quickly looked away. This woman was strange in a way that unnerved him. His throat went dry.

The woman smiled.

The dog growled again.

"Well, I must be on my way." He rattled the keys; he struggled to control each breath. "Good-bye, Randolph."

"Are you all right?" She took a step closer. "You look rather pale."

Jay stepped back. "I'm fine thanks. It's the animal. I'm a little nervous around dogs." True as that was, the woman made him more nervous and he didn't know why.

The woman blocked the path. "You look so familiar. Haven't we met before?" She glided closer in a bold, sensuous move.

"No. I'm sure we haven't." He wasn't convincing.

While the woman studied him, Jay broke out in a cool sweat and he prayed for strength. It took an act of God to break loose of her gaze and he took one-step after another focusing his eyes on the path ahead. "I'm in a bit of a rush. Good-bye."

Confusion swept over him but slowly dissipated with each step he took. *That was weird. Whoever she is, she's trying to rattle me.* He rushed through the forest and wished Lisa had come along. He glanced back to be certain the woman and her dog were not following. It was four o'clock and daylight would soon fade to darkness. Jay started to jog and wondered if the dream house really existed. In his moment of doubt, Jay came upon a clearing in the trees where he could see the unusual slate green roof tiles of an old house. The path was elevated so that the view of the cottage and the entire estate stood below him. He caught his breath.

The building was the most beautiful cottage he had seen. He moved closer. The garden was overgrown, the windows boarded up, and trash littered the property, but the front porch had been made of solid oak, hand-carved with a sea crest over the entrance and the walls were fashioned in vintage brick-work. Jay's artistic eye converted the dilapidated cottage into a pristine country home. *Even Lady Haversham would be delighted with this place.*

Jay headed toward the gate. The cottage percolated character and oozed promise, as if waiting for someone to reclaim it. From the sugar-twist chimneys of spiraled brick to the green gradient slates, the house had possibilities. A little repair, a little paint, and this cottage will be the envy of the neighborhood. The yard tiered downward, but waist high nettles choked what little growth remained. It looked huge, larger than the typical English garden, and he knew the lads would love it. "This is a Godsend."

Along one side of the house, a magnificent evergreen stood like a forty-foot sentinel. Red and pink rhododendrons grew wild along the garden wall. The flier explained Erindale Cottage's legacy, built and owned by a Lord.

From his position, Jay could see the peaks and chimneys of the manor house directly behind the cottage. It stood elegant in park-like surroundings, creating by contrast, an orphaned cottage.

"I can do this. I can make this beautiful." He moved closer to the front gate. It was solid oak and hung on a single arthritic hinge. It creaked in complaint as he unlatched it and pushed it open. The sandstone steps were concave, worn by a hundred years of passing. Three steps down and his feet rested on a herringbone path of red brick that invited him to the front door. No matter how tarnished, this home was a treasure.

A pile of rubbish by the front door did not deter him; neither did the nettles and the repulsive smells of mold and mildew. Suddenly, a pair of cat eyes blinked at him from between the weeds. The scrawny cat yowled and dashed between Jay's legs.

Jay stared at the carved insignia of an anchor over the porch. "My anchor is Jesus," he reminded himself. Caught in the dream of it all, he saw the crest as a witnessing tool when visitors came. *This place could be our home forever. The boys could play in the woods, the big oaks for climbing, and that tall acacia would make a great swing tree.*

The difference between Jay and Lisa was simple: he saw the cup half-full while Lisa saw it half-empty. At times, the dissimilarity frustrated them. Jay looked at the dilapidated house and visualized the windows with fresh paint, the garden full of roses, and the hinged gate repaired, but he knew what Lisa would see: a house in ruin.

Several rusted padlocks secured the front door. Jay pulled at one trying to determine which key would open which lock. Several minutes later, the last padlock scratched open and Jay gave a hefty shove at the door with his shoulder. It squeaked inward.

He walked into the blackness and clawed the cobwebs from his face.

*   *   *

After the American had left the office, Marianne White placed the detailed file of Erindale Cottage on her desk. She sat and flipped through the thick folder. By late afternoon, with half a dozen interruptions, she was still reading the stories of Erindale. She found a full ledger of everything bought for the cottage, from wallpaper to laundry detergent. Herbert logged all his expenses in light of Maggie Trick's fleeting favors.

Marianne grew up hearing the stories of Maggie and her secret escapades. Herbert had housed the woman and paid her a modest income for fleshly favors. The town gossips had gathered torrid stories of Herbert and Maggie and the wife and kids he left home. Over the years, the affair turned bitter as forbidden love always does. Herbert called it off when his wife threatened divorce and promised to take his children away. That was more suffering than he could bear.

Then there was Margaret, the illegitimate daughter that he quickly put in the Methodist orphanage. Never adopted, both parents abandoned her. Maggie's brokenness caused her to die alone and forsaken, leaving behind a legacy of pain for Margaret. When Ms. Trick died, the local paper filled in the gaps on Maggie's life, sad shameful gaps that left young Margaret to live in the shadow of her mother's shame.

Marianne thumbed through the receipts. The agency had paid for the removal of mildewed furniture, boxes of rubbish, and newspapers saved over ten years. They removed old stoves and washing machines, lined up in front of the house like a row of rusty tin soldiers. They replaced the kitchen door that had become the escape hatch for trash. The years of discards thrown into the back garden created a mound of refuse that stood like a six-foot monument. They were left-overs of a lifetime fulfilled with a thousand stories no one would ever hear.

The minute hand clicked on the wall clock. It was four-thirty. Marianne pulled a newspaper clipping from the file. It told of Maggie Trick's fate. The old woman's mind had snapped like a summer twig. Alone in a dark, damp, unheated house, her body deteriorated along with her surroundings. Gangrene claimed her feet, then her legs. Crawling from room to room, Maggie finally gave up the fight for life and died in her upstairs bedroom. Alone. Painfully alone.

Marianne shuddered as she closed the file drawer and sat in the growing gloom. It was now four-forty-five. In fifteen minutes, she would lock up and leave, key or no key. She would be very surprised if the American was seriously inter-ested in Erindale. Only the very desperate or very rich would take on a project like that.

* * *

The house smelled like mold and urine. Jay groped his way forward. *Why didn't I think to grab a flashlight?* He clicked the light switch, but it was dead just as he expected. Determined to investigate, he propped the door wide, and moved deeper into the room until the blackness swallowed him whole. He felt like he was in a burial chamber.

"Maybe it was a good thing Lisa didn't come on this first visit." He waited for his eyes to adjust to the dark. The floors were made of quarry tiles in red, black and white geometric patterns. The tiles were damp, uneven, and loose. Something scurried into a corner making Jay jump. *Probably a mouse.* The walls had peculiar patterns where pictures had hung for years without change. He touched a square, then pulled his hand back in disgust. Caked in the picture frame patterns were the remains of insects.

The living room was small with wide sculptured door-frames thick with layers of murky green paint. An old fire-place with broken tiles had been the room's only focus of attention. Everywhere plaster had worked itself loose. Cracks were visible across the ceiling and a broken light fixture dangled from a rusted chain. The place was eerie.

Jay opened a door under the stairs and was astonished to find another door on the opposite wall. It was made of heavy steel rusted almost black. It made Jay think of a prison door or a concealed entrance to a hidden chamber. With great effort, he lifted the heavy latch and opened it wide. The hinges spat out rust as it moved. "Wow, it's been bricked up from the other side. What a strange thing to have beneath the stairs. Wonder what's on the other side?" He frowned, confused at the many mysteries this place presented. He backed out of the closet and headed for the kitchen.

The kitchen was grim and Jay wrinkled his nose. It was long and narrow with a high cracked ceiling, glossed in a sickly cream paint. A clothes rack suspended by ropes and pulleys hung from the ceiling. A large fireplace over-whelmed the constricted room. Jay walked to the sink and shook his head. Furry mold covered handles and spout. A web stretched from the faucet to the drain with its resident spider dangling in place.

Jay forced a chuckle. "Lisa can't even stand a fly on the loose in her kitchen." A plate and cup lay on the drain board. Red glossed cupboard doors hung from broken hinges, exposing pipes wrapped in old socks. At the window, ragged curtains hung limp like resting bats. Greasy slime layered the walls. "I must be crazy to think this could ever work."

Crazy or not, his mind raced thinking of all the possibilities this deal could offer. He struggled with a desperate determination. "Somehow, someway I'll do it." He wanted to make this a happy place for his family.

Erindale Cottage had a mystery about it that piqued his curiosity. *This place has a look and feel of being...haunted, spooky. But history does not control the future. Only what we do today can determine what happens tomorrow.* Their lives were in the hands of God. He had led them to Kingsbridge. Couldn't this be a part of His provision?

A pantry opened off the kitchen with a small, unboarded window that opened through the backside of the cottage. The window looked onto the courtyard belonging to the neighbor next door. Jay had read a small blurb on the flier: Builders had converted the connecting stable and garage into a tiny dwelling, making this a one-of-a-kind duplex. The houses were back-to-back, with no shared entrance. The units shared the kitchen wall.

How had these neighbors viewed this derelict side of their dwelling? Any improvement would increase the value of their property. Having a happy family as neighbors would be a plus.

He headed upstairs. The first room he came to had a curved walled entrance. "Incredible. I won't find anything like this back home."

The front bedroom had exposed beams at angles above with a dormer ceiling. The boarded window was low and wide. Gaps between the boards let enough light in for him to see. It surely would reveal the forest's beauty in seasons once the boards came down. He imagined Lisa and him lying in bed, watching the leaves grow golden as autumn approached. *Why were all the windows boarded up? Paranoia can make lonely people do weird things. Maybe that's it.* For Jay, the cottage produced more questions than answers. He wanted to get more than beneath the wallpaper, he wanted to get beneath the soul of this house and discover the mystery of Erindale Cottage.

The curved bedroom wall became a sculptured convex wall on the other side, opening into a spacious bathroom. The white enameled claw foot bathtub was a sorry sight with cracks and chips of rust exposing iron bones. The sink was angular and boxy with rusty veins and fissured corners. The old flush toilet was carefully coordinated with an equal amount of cracks and stains.

"Perfectly matched bathroom suite. I must tell Lisa." He laughed. The laughter sounded good in this place.

A window on the upstairs landing had been left uncovered. Dust billowed as he shoved the curtains aside. He could see the neighbor's courtyard below. It consisted of a slab of tarmac. A Volvo station wagon was parked at an angle, as if it had veered in at high speed. Next to it was a tired-looking, orange Volkswagen van. Next to the garage he could see an old, dappled mare with a sagging back. Jay was unimpressed, but curiosity made him wonder who these people were.

Jay's eyes moved to the manor house itself. "Wow. What a beautiful place." The gardens were magnificently laden with roses and sculptured hedges. Stained glass windows and doors embraced each entrance and rich fascia boards graced the eaves of each dip and rise in the roofline.

So that was Lord Chumley's house. Fantastic. Chumley, old chap, we'll take this humble cottage if you don't mind. Just don't expect me to call you Lord. I reserve that for someone far greater. His mind flew to the Scriptures. "For there is only one Lord, one faith, one baptism…" He let the curtains fall back into place.

Jay pushed open the last upstairs door to discover a back bedroom with a floor that was about six inches lower than where he stood. Unprepared for the discrepancy in levels, he stumbled into the bedroom but managed to stay on his feet. The hardwood floor echoed his footsteps as he approached, then peered through yet another north facing window. Jay realized that the neighbors were now below him. Somehow, the upstairs extended over the entrance of the neighbor's front door. *The upstairs is larger than the downstairs.* This room was light and airy and would work fine for Nathan, Michael, and Joey. He discovered that this Victorian house did indeed have a form of central heating. Each room, including both bathrooms and the kitchen, had its own fireplace. The variation of each mantel gave a touch of beauty.

Jay headed down the stairs and stood in the silent living room. Faint light pressed through the open door. Columns of dust hung in the still air.

The door creaked then groaned, and began to move on its stiff hinges—moving of its own accord. He felt no breeze and the dust in the air gave no sign of wind. *Must not be hung level.* Jay put his hand on the doorknob—

It slammed shut; the noise filled the room.

Jay's heart rattled like a machine-gun.

The room went pitch black. "What's going on here?"

He heard the latch click shut. Jay lunged for the door in the dark. "Who's there?"

Clink…snap…clink…snap…clink…snap.

Someone had locked all the padlocks. Jay hammered on the door. "Hey. This isn't funny."

Silence.

Something changed. Something about the room. It felt as if the air had gone out of the place. Jay gasped and beat the door with his fists, "Open this door." He heard footsteps recede in the distance. "I said, open this door!"

No answer.

"If someone thinks they can scare me away from here, they're greatly mistaken." His words echoed in the empty room.

Groping along the wall, Jay found the boarded window. He felt the glass and then the lock. He unlatched it, but the window was stiff and probably swollen in place. He tried again. Then again. It took several attempts before it moved a crack. He probed the narrow opening for the boards and then took a half-step back to get leverage. He raised his foot, kicked the boards hard, but they refused to budge. He kicked again and then again, until he heard the screech of nails and the muted thud as the boards fell away. Jay climbed through the opening and stumbled into the evening air.

"It had to be some punk kids," he mumbled as he did his best to replace the boards using a rock from the yard as a hammer. He had to move quickly to get home before it was completely dark. There would be no need to tell Lisa. *I'll tell her all the good news. I'll make this place beautiful. I can do this.* The kids will love this place. This must be God's provision.

Dusk settled around the cottage, the sun marching toward the horizon. By the time he exited from the tunnel of trees, the sky was black broken only by the solitary light of the North Star.

CHAPTER THREE

"Well?" Lisa stood framed in the study doorway with her hands planted on her hips. "Tell me." She blew a stubborn strand of hair from her face.

"Tell you what?" Jay acted dumb. He'd been stalling, slipping into his study through the side door. Once at his desk, he fumbled through a pile of papers before he gave up trying to look busy and surrendered to Lisa's stare.

"The house, of course."

"You won't believe what an incredible find it…"

Lisa broke in. "Do you have any idea what time it is?" She was angry.

"Yeah, it's…." He looked at his watch. "Wow, apparently not. I *am* sorry." He scrambled to his feet, knocking a stack of papers to the floor. "I had no idea." He scooped up some of the papers and dropped them back on the desk. "I guess the time got away from me."

"Jay, you're absolutely hopeless." She shook her head and bit her lip, something she did when fighting back tears.

Shame warmed his cheeks. He and Lisa were experts at pushing each other's buttons.

"Sorry I'm late." He gave a weak smile. "I'll help get dinner on. I'm famished." He swiveled his chair ready to stand again.

"Too late. Dinner is finished." Lisa's voice was flat.

"Then I'll wash the dishes." He stood attempting to prove his sincerity.

"They're done." She crossed her arms. "Jay, you're an hour and a half late. What's wrong with you? Not only is dinner over, but the dishes are washed, the kitchen is clean, and the boys have had their baths—everything is done." She balled her hands into tight fists. "We waited for you. I'm so angry at you right now, I could...I could..." She glanced around the room, pulled a book from a nearby shelf, and threw it on the floor. "...scream." It was a single volume of *Matthew Henry's Bible Commentary.* It landed on its side and made a loud slap. Jay jumped.

"It's one thing missing a meal for ministry reasons, but a stupid house? I can't believe you did this." Lisa's shoulders drew tight and a crimson flush crept up her neck. She shook her head again and marched from the study. "Your dinner's in the oven and probably fossilized by now."

Jay flopped in his chair. "I'm sorry. That's all I can say... I'm sorry." He called out, but there was no reply. *I can't believe she did that. Man, I hope the kids didn't hear it. In this tiny house, they must have. Jay, you're digging your own grave. You had better shape up while you can. You've definitely lost the first round.*

He rose, moved to the commentary on the floor, and slowly retrieved it. It was a massive volume. He studied it for a minute before sliding it back on the shelf. He headed to the kitchen where he found Lisa staring out the window into the darkness. The dam had broken—she'd been crying. In the small room, in the dark of the evening, she looked so delicate.

"Isn't there anything I can do to redeem myself?" He hovered at the kitchen door, daring not to get too close.

Lisa didn't move except for the nervous dance of her right index finger taping on the countertop.

"Anything?"

Her voice was low and uneven. "It's too late for that. Just leave me alone." Then she added, "The lads are upstairs waiting. At least read them a story." She didn't turn; didn't move.

"Sure." The word was almost a whisper. He slipped from the kitchen doorway and headed for the stairs. He hated disappointing his wife. Jay climbed the stairs one plodding step after another. Pausing at the door that opened to his children's bedroom, he took a deep breath, plastered on a smile, and then popped his head into the room. "Hey guys, you wanna hear a story?" The room smelled of freshly scrubbed kids and clean sheets.

The boy's excitement buoyed his sagging ego. He plopped on the bed and they clambered all over him, wrestling him until they rolled onto the floor in a heap. Huddled together, Jay began to whip up a story of adventure. He could dream them up as fast as the boys could devour them.

"Once upon a time, there was a family in search of a new home. They set sail for England because they heard many legends of brave knights who defended their king." Jay paused to think of where to go with the tale. "But the journey was long and hard. Warriors had invaded their country and they feared for their lives yet they continued on because they believed God was directing them." Joey wriggled his two-year-old body into a comfortable position beside dad and popped his thumb in his mouth. "They believed God would lead their family to a new home in England…somewhere deep in the mysterious woods of…Sherwood Forest."

"Cool, Dad." Nathan grew excited. "Was Robin Hood around then?"

"He sure was, but no one knew him yet. He was just an average thief and hadn't done anything special to become famous yet."

"How did he get to be famous?" Michael was on the floor, lying on his stomach, his blond hair still damp around the edges.

"Well, he defended poor people. He took money from the Sheriff of Nottingham and gave it back to the peasants."

"I'm going to be famous when I grow up," Nathan said thoughtfully.

"And how are you going to do that?" Jay lay on his back.

"I'll start by being an average thief." He grinned at his dad.

Jay ruffled Nathan's hair. "Funny guy."

The boys crowded around Jay. The hall light bathed them in a soft glow. "The family sailed for days in wind and rain. Sometimes the waves nearly sank the ship, but they trusted God to save them. They believed God had a plan for them, and they knew that anything was better than nothing, which is all they had."

"Why didn't they have anything?" Michael asked.

"Well, let's see." He paused. "Invaders came and ransacked their homes and burned down their villages."

"I heard about them at school," Nathan said. "My teacher said they were called Vikings and they sailed big long ships and they wore horns on their helmets." Nathan held his fingers to his head like horns.

"You're right, kiddo, and some of them were a mean bunch of guys, too."

"I wouldn't be afraid of them," Nathan said.

"Me neither. I'd punch them in the belly and then tie them up." Michael tried to look mean.

"I guess we'd all be safe with you guys around. You're a tough bunch. Well, this family hid in the woods when the raiders attacked their village. It was before they sailed, and all they could do was watch from the forest as the Vikings burned their house to a crisp."

"Like toast," Michael said.

"Like toast." Jay grinned.

"Burnt toast," Michael added and giggled.

"They left their home to sail to a new place. After many days of sailing they were hit by a terrible storm on the North Sea."

"Where's the North Sea?" Nathan wondered.

"It's between England and Ireland. We've sailed across it many times. Once we took the ferry to Ireland. You guys remember that?"

"I remember," said Michael. "We all puked on the floor."

"Yup, Mikey. You never forget the important things, do you?" They took turns making heaving sounds. "Okay, okay you guys. Let's get back to the story." Jay settled back against a pillow. He let his mind float, allowing the story to take shape. "It was rainy and cold and the waves kept crashing over the boat. The captain warned the passengers to take cover. Then the ship hit something hard. The captain shouted, 'Every man for himself. The ship is sinking.'

"The ship heaved forward, and the passengers slid all over the deck. Some people jumped overboard. Some screamed, and others prayed. 'Save us God. Please save us.' Then lightening struck and hit the mast. The tall mast cracked and fell into the sea. Everywhere, people were splashing in the water. This family grabbed pieces of the boat and held on for dear life. God came to their rescue and helped them get safely to shore. When morning came they saw all the destruction and knew God had rescued them." Most of Jay's stories finished like a sermon. *Everything in life should have a moral to it.*

After a pause, Jay said, "God always comes to our rescue when storms happen. Storms are terrible things that we can't control. Can you guys think of any storms that have happened to us?"

Nathan raised his hand as if in school. "Dad, I know, I know."

"Okay Nathan, what do you remember?"

"When Michael couldn't breathe, and we had to take him to the hospital. That was scary."

"It sure was," Jay said, looking at Michael. "Do you remember that, Mikey?"

Michael nodded. "I remember. God made me better."

Jay combed his fingers through Michael's hair. "God is always close when we're in trouble." Jay was silent for a moment. "That is really special Michael. God is our protector, isn't He?"

"Yes." Their voices were hushed, caught up in their own story. "Yes He is," they whispered. "Yes...."

In an instant, Jay's disagreement with Lisa paled. How could things get so out of proportion? "Okay kids, enough for tonight."

"No, Dad. More. Tell us more. What happens next?" Michael and Nathan pleaded. Joey had fallen asleep and lay with his head on Jay's lap.

* * *

Lisa shoved a stack of linens in the hall closet and tried to shut the door. *Why can't Jay be on time for once in his life?* The stack of sheets wouldn't fit. *Why is he so impulsive, so determined to get his own way?* She pushed harder to force them in, but the stubborn stack tumbled to the floor. She ground her teeth forcing pain to shoot up through the roof of her head. Already her headache was stabbing her with pitchforks. She was too tired to fight anybody, anything. *There's no excuse for Jay to be so late. Why should he please himself while I'm at home taking care of the house, the kids, the laundry, everything?* She got on her knees and started refolding the stack. She could hear the kids chattering. *Jay acts like nothing is wrong, as if everything is cheery and nice. How can he pretend like that? It's totally unfair.*

After refolding, she shoved them back into the linen closet. Before she turned away, they fell on the floor. Nearly in tears and exasperated, she carried them into their bedroom and slid the closet door open. She stuffed them onto the top shelf. They fell again. *I hate this house.* She swiped up the sheets and wadded them into a ball. *There's no room in this house to store things. It's not big enough to raise three kids.* Sometimes she wished she were back in California where there was room to live and play and life was more relaxed. "Stupid house." She hated it when she felt like this. She always ended up crying. She wondered why she was so angry. Was it Jay's irresponsible behavior, or because he wanted something so badly?

Defeated, she turned to head down stairs, but stopped outside the children's room. Leaning against the wall, she listened to the tender responses of the children—so young, so full of wonder. A tear slipped down her cheek. When Jay finished his story and suggested they pray, Lisa slipped into the room and sat on the floor beside them. Jay gave her an affectionate smile but her response was weak. After they prayed, Lisa picked Joey up from the floor and settled him in his crib. Nathan and Michael climbed onto their bunks and let Lisa tuck them in.

"I love you, Michael. I love you, Nathan. Sleep well tonight." She kissed them then stepped back and studied the boys. They were such small bundles of life. *So innocent. Why do I get so worked up over so little when I've got these great kids?*

* * *

43

Jay moved from the doorway to let Lisa pass. He reached out to touch her but pulled his hand back. She hesitated for a second and headed down the stairs.

"Dad?" Michael raised his head from the pillow.

"Yes, Michael?"

"Are you going to tell us about the house you found?"

"Tomorrow, son. I'll tell you about how I found it, and about a secret iron door that leads to a hidden room."

"Cool." Michael's sheets rustled as he rolled over. "I'll bet the house has got lots of spooky ghosts, too."

"Could be," Jay whispered. "Now close your eyes and go to sleep. I love you, cowboy."

Nathan lay still with his eyes closed. Jay caressed his head. "You're a good boy. Don't grow up too fast. I love you so much."

Without opening his eyes, Nathan said, "I love you too, Dad." He rolled on his side and tucked his knees tight to his chest.

* * *

It was almost midnight and everyone in the house was asleep—everyone but Jay. He'd eaten the charcoaled dinner in the oven and survived. Lisa had made a point of going into the guest room to sleep. The rejection stung. *Am I the cause of all this, or is something else going on with her?* He determined to be more disciplined with his time and not let this happen again. To be more empathetic; pay more attention to her needs and wishes. Still, he was sure the house was God's provision. It couldn't be anything else. He rolled on his back and stared at the ceiling. He had hurt Lisa with his indifference and felt completely irresponsible for not getting home on time. What had he been thinking?

A small knot grew in the pit of his stomach. He shifted to his side to ease the discomfort. He rolled over and hugged his pillow wishing Lisa were beside him. He prayed for sleep to descend.

*   *   *

When Jay awoke the next morning, Lisa was busy downstairs. He could hear the kids chattering away in the kitchen. Nathan was describing how big dragons could grow. Jay pulled on a pair of jeans and a white T-shirt. Still barefoot, he headed down to join the family. He kissed Lisa on her cheek. She turned away refusing to make eye contact.

"Do you want coffee or tea?"

"I don't mind. Whatever you've got." After tousling the kid's hair, Jay pulled up a stool and sat beside them.

"Coffee or tea." She raised her voice slightly. "I have both." The boys stopped talking and looked at her.

Her tone startled Jay. "Sorry. Tea, I'll take tea please." He paused to take the cup. "I guess we need to talk." Lisa didn't respond.

"Michael, you're finished, go up and brush your teeth and tie your tie. You too, Nathan." She collected their dishes and carried them to the sink. "Make it quick or you'll be late."

As Nathan walked past his dad he whispered, "Mum's still mad." Then he scooted up the stairs.

"I'll take the lads to school." Jay looked at his watch and glanced out the window. "No rain, so we can walk."

"Thanks. I'm going to take a shower and try to get rid of this migraine." After putting the lunches on the table, she headed upstairs.

*   *   *

Jay settled in his home office and scribbled a couple of notes before he began studying. Twenty minutes later, he pushed his glasses up on his forehead and rubbed his eyes. He'd been reading in the gospels, identifying some points for his studies, when he remembered a request to pray for the Thomas family. Bryan Thomas had a severe drinking problem and it caused a lot of anxiety with Kate and the children. Although Kate never said so, Jay suspected her husband became violent at times. He definitely wasn't happy that Kate attended church.

The phone rang. Jay wasn't surprised to hear Kate's voice. She sounded alarmed. After a brief exchanged, Jay said, "I'll be right over."

He darted from the office. "Lisa, I just got a call from Kate. It's Bryan again. He's gone missing." He began to change clothes. "I don't know how long it will be. If it's more than an hour, I'll give you a call. Otherwise, I'll pick up the groceries after and be back before lunch."

Lisa was moody and silent. She let Jay kiss her on the cheek. "Give her my love."

"Will do. I love you, sweetie." Jay waved as he went out the door and hurried to the car. Lisa's silence and worry over Kate's family wearied him.

I hope Bryan hasn't done something stupid again. If he doesn't get help he's going to drink himself into the grave. Last month, the courts had placed Bryan in the county detox facility for a twenty day stint, but he'd left after five. He'd climbed out the window wearing only pajamas and slippers and walked the five miles home in pouring rain. Jay was familiar with the two sides of Bryan. The sober Bryan was gentle and intelligent; the drunkard was abusive and cruel. Jay worried about the safety of Bryan's wife and two sons.

When Jay arrived he saw that Kate was exhausted. She wore no makeup and her mousy hair hung limp around her shoulders. "Kate, any word?"

"'None." She invited him in. "He didn't come home last night and his boss just called and said he hasn't shown up for work for two days." She twisted a tissue in her hands. "If he loses his job, I don't know what we'll do." The rims of her eyes were red. "He's going to lose his job. I'm sure of that."

"You've got lots of friends at church. We'll take care of you and the children," he said reassuringly. He sat on the worn and faded sofa. He patted a spot near him and she sat.

"I get so exhausted, never knowing what he'll be like when he does come home. When he's missing, I worry. When he comes home, I worry. I'm afraid for the children. He uses what little money we have for drink. They kick him out of the pub every night. I'm exhausted, and I'm worried about what's going to happen to me and the lads."

Jay had to ask the dreaded question. "Kate, has Bryan ever hurt you?"

Kate tugged so hard on the tissue it tore. "Let me put the kettle on, Pastor. I'll make a brew." She shoved the remains of the tissue in her pocket and headed to the kitchen.

Jay followed her. "Kate, I know this is hard for you to talk about, but I need to know." He had to be sure. "Kate…?"

"Oh Pastor, you know my Bryan. He makes a lot of noise but he never does much. He's usually too drunk to know what he's doing." She checked the electric kettle to see if it was full and plugged it in. Immediately it began to hiss and she stood there waiting.

"You haven't answered my question. Has he hurt you or the lads?"

Leaning against the kitchen counter, Kate began to sob. Tears spilled easily and she lowered her head in despair. The kettle whistled for attention. She didn't move. Jay reached over and unplugged it.

"Please don't make me answer that, Pastor. They'll lock him up if the authorities find out. I don't know how I'd cope." She pulled another tissue from a box and blew her nose. "I seem to be using these things all the time. You'd think I'd run out of tears eventually." She tried to laugh but couldn't.

"So he *has* hurt you." Jay studied her. "Are those bruises from him?"

Kate wrapped her arms around herself but she didn't answer.

"Kate, you don't need to be ashamed. Bryan needs serious help and you can't do it. He needs professional help. But you and the lads need protection or your family won't survive. One day, he'll go too far. You won't be able to stop the authorities from taking him away."

"What should I do?" Another flood of tears washed down her cheeks. "I love him, Pastor. Turning him in would be just like betrayal. I could never turn him in."

"Kate, I know you love him. But what if he harmed one of the lads and you hadn't notified the authorities? That would be far worse wouldn't it? The consequences would be devastating." After a few moments of silence, Jay asked Kate, "Can I read something to you?"

"Sure." She daubed her eyes with a fresh tissue.

Jay pulled a small Bible from his jacket pocket and flipped through several pages until he found what he was looking for. "Listen to this, 'No discipline seems pleasant at the time, but painful. Later on, however, it produces a harvest of righteousness and peace for those who have been trained by it.' Kate, I know this is difficult and I certainly don't have all the answers. But I know what alcoholism can do to a family. It can shred your life." Jay lifted his head and waited for Kate to look at him. "I had an uncle who was an alcoholic. His family paid the price for his drinking."

Kate stared at Jay. "What happened?"

"Six months before he died of alcohol poisoning, he became a Christian."

"God forgave him?" She brightened. "Then there is hope for Bryan."

"Yes, there's hope. There's always hope in Jesus Christ. But my uncle wasted a life for drink. His children's lives

were devastated. I can't tell you what you should do..."
Suddenly, Jay paused, wondering if he had just nurtured fear
and despair instead of hope. Then he remembered it was
about what Jesus could do for them, not what he could do.
As a man, he could not offer Kate and Bryan anything.

"What was that verse you read? I want to copy it down."
Kate got a pen and note pad.

"It's Hebrews, chapter twelve." Jay stood. "I didn't mean
to give a negative picture, Kate. Not every alcoholic ends up
like my uncle. God doesn't give up on us."

"Thank you, Pastor." Kate followed Jay as he moved
toward the door. "You're right. I'll call the police and give a
missing person's report on Bryan."

"Thanks so much for coming. I'll call you as soon as I
know something."

"Good. Please call anytime. I'll be praying." He slipped
out the door, and then headed to his car.

When Jay pulled away from the curb, he slapped the
steering wheel. "I'm a jerk. I shouldn't have offered such
negative information to someone in her condition. I might
have just sent Kate over the edge." Jay shoved the gear
into second and hit the accelerator. The car crept forward,
choking, and sputtering, making its way toward town.

Jay drove into the Sainsbury's parking lot and finally
found a parking spot. The supermarket was new and seemed
to have almost everything, except peanut butter. As he
headed to the store he had a strange sensation that someone
was following him. He glanced over his shoulder, but saw
nothing unusual. Once inside, Jay glanced over his shoulder.
There was a guy standing near Jay's car, a cigarette clenched
between his lips. He seemed to be studying Jay's car. Jay
chuckled to himself. *There's nothing in there worth stealing,
except my Bible Pal.* He flicked the cigarette butt into the air
and headed around the corner. Jay was tempted to go and ask
what he wanted, but decided to leave it alone.

* * *

The hot shower felt good against Lisa's scalp and neck. She could feel the tension ease. Her headache had lasted for two days and she couldn't bear to have it continue. She feared it might turn into a weeklong migraine if she didn't get a handle on it. If the migraine became full blown, she knew she would be able to do nothing more than draw the blinds and go to bed. It would wipe her out for days. It had happened before.

Lisa lathered her hair messaging her scalp slowly, methodically. It was relaxing. She was tired of this conflict with Jay. Earlier that morning, while Jay walked the boys to school, Lisa had made a quick call to her mom in California. Jay and Lisa had agreed not to make international calls unless it was an emergency—today felt like an emergency.

"I just needed to hear your voice, Mom." She listened to her mother's sympathetic words. "Yes, I know. It's nothing major. We're just arguing over small stuff and Jay is getting on my nerves." She listened. "It's so tempting to just hop on a plane and come home for a visit. I know you'd pay, but I couldn't. We're just having communication problems. It will pass." Lisa heard the sound of an engine out front. "I've got to go, Mom. I love you too. Bye." Lisa put the receiver down and peered out the window. It was just a neighbor.

That was a half hour ago. Now she let the shower relax her muscles and release the tension. She'd stay there until the hot water was gone.

* * *

Jay wandered through the supermarket. He used Lisa's list and filled the cart with corn from Israel, plums from France, fresh bread and scones from the village bakery, and an assortment of cereal for the children's breakfast. When he returned home, he made three trips in with bags of groceries. Lisa sat on the sofa sipping a cup of tea and reading a book of devotions.

"Uh oh, I forgot coffee." He said as he walked through to the kitchen with his arms full.

"Don't worry. No rush. We're not completely out."

Jay came back in with the final load of groceries. In one hand he carried a bunch of brightly colored flowers. Lisa looked up. The coal fire crackled and popped, sending sparks up the chimney and filled the room with a pungent aroma.

"And who are those for?" Lisa quipped. She put her book down and followed Jay into the kitchen.

"They are for the fairest lady in the land but..."

"But what?" Lisa reached for them.

He pulled the flowers just out of reach. "They come with a condition attached."

"And what condition would that be?" Lisa stood on tip-toe to reach them. "They must be a peace offering?"

"Kinda." He lowered the flowers and handed them to her. "I'm sorry for being such a jerk. Will you forgive me?"

She studied the flowers and finally looked up. "Well, you're kinda forgiven then." She started to turn to the sink when he stopped her.

"How about a kiss to make up?" He studied the depth of blue in her eyes.

"How about a hug?" She let Jay hold her briefly but turned her face away when he tried to kiss her. "Just give me some time and space on this one. Okay?"

"Okay," Jay replied, but still felt the bitter edge of rejection. "I don't like us being at odds with each other."

"Me neither. We've got to do better at communicating." Lisa finally turned back to the sink to find a vase for the flowers.

"Lisa?"

"Yes?" She turned her head his way.

"Can you explain to me what you felt I did wrong?" He swallowed. "So I don't make the same mistake again."

"Okay." Lisa whirled around and laid the flowers on the counter. She pulled a vase from the cupboard and filled it with water. "You're impulsive, inflexible, bullheaded, and narcissistic. I think you're too much like your dad in those areas. You're mulishly loyal to causes rather than people." She paused. "Apart from that, you're not such a bad guy."

Jay was stumped for words. He felt the blood drain from his face. "Where did you come up with all that?"

"You asked. That's the way I feel."

"Oh." The harsh words baffled him. "Is there any hope for me?"

"Barely."

Jay studied her face hoping to read the truth in her expression. He scratched his head and stood mute.

"By the way, thanks for the flowers, they're beautiful."

"You've got me totally confused."

"Well, we've been married for ten years now. I should know some things about you after all that time." Lisa carried the vase of flowers into the dining room and set them at the center of the table. Jay followed. The spring colors brought life to the cozy room. She rearranged a stalk and then stood back to admire them.

"Is there anything else you want to say?"

Lisa pulled up a chair and sat facing Jay. "I have a problem when you plan something without discussing it with me. I feel like you're just covering yourself when you notify me of what you've already decided on."

"Do I do that often?" Jay was sincere.

"Yes. And it's hard for me to make up my own mind because I feel you've hoodwinked me into doing what you want."

"Thanks for explaining yourself." Jay sat in a dining chair and sighed. He studied his hands. "So, what do you suggest I do to change?"

"I don't know. Talk to me before you make a decision, I guess." Lisa picked up her tea and took a sip. They sat staring at each other.

"Okay. I'm talking to you. I won't bring up the cottage idea again, for now at least, but I would really like you to see it." Jay raised his brows. "Can we agree on that?"

Lisa remained silent. She kept sipping her tea and staring at her cup.

"Say something." Jay squirmed. "Just answer, yes or no."

"I guess. But don't push me on it."

"Okay." Jay's emotions sagged, certain of her final answer. *To get to this point took an exceptional amount of work. If she sees the house the way it is now, I'll never be able to convince her it's worth buying.* He had to find a way to impress upon her its value to them as a family. That certainly wouldn't be controlling the situation.

* * *

That afternoon Jay went back to the realtor's and asked to borrow the keys to Erindale Cottage again. When Marianne White seemed curious, Jay said he couldn't see much in the dark. This time he would take a flashlight.

"Well, that makes a lot of sense. Sure, take your time and you can drop the keys through the letter box if the shop is closed."

With keys in hand, Jay made his way back to the cottage. Once inside, he moved cautiously going from room to room, letting the light hit corners and crevices he'd missed on his previous visit. The air had a distinct smell of rot and the walls had large age spots where plaster had cracked and crumbled. Jay's flashlight sliced through the darkness like a blade of steel, cutting it into a patchwork of shadows. He could hear the scratching of rodents as they scurried beneath the stairs.

The emptiness of the place made it feel like a burial chamber. *If I can clean this place up a bit, it won't spook Lisa so much. Somehow, she's gotta see its potential.*

Jay headed back to his car and gathered the cleaning items he'd brought along. For the next two hours, he brushed away cobwebs, swept dirt, and carted bags of trash outside. He shook out dusty curtains that hung in the living room. He removed three dead mice and a stack of newspapers piled in a corner. The kitchen smelled of cat urine. From an outside faucet he filled a bucket with water and mopped the tile floors.

Jay worked frantically cleaning one room after another. Finally, he'd filled five bags full of trash which he tossed in a shed around back. *What if Lisa still doesn't like it? This behavior must be what the shrinks call obsessive-compulsive disorder.* Dust and sweat covered him as he made an umpteenth trip carrying trash around back.

When Jay called it quits, he gathered all his cleaning tools and shoved them into the trunk of the car. He knew these were desperate actions, but he was a desperate guy, and to his knowledge he hadn't done anything illegal. He'd just improved "'curb appeal" for his wife.

Lord, am I wrong in wanting this? How can I convince Lisa? If you help us to get this, I promise I will... He paused in the shadowy doorway, his own thoughts shaking him. *What in the world am I doing?* The words of Scripture filtered through his thoughts, "Who is this that darkens my counsel with words without knowledge?" *Can a man bargain with God?* Yet, desperation rose and begged, *Just this once, Lord.*

As Jay worked himself out the front door with broom and dustpan, he felt a presence. He glanced over his shoulder but saw no one. The memory of being locked in the cottage returned to him and brought a chill with it. He worked fast to finish when a shadow passed the entrance. Jay swirled around but no one was there. He saw only the gnarled arms of the oaks reaching for him. He had a vague sense of something nearby.

After walking the circumference of the property carrying his broom like a battle axe, he gave up the hunt. There was no one. *This is stupid.* Jay finished and then turned and locked the door. The night was drawing in when he looked at his watch. His heart thumped. *Lisa wants dinner at five. I've got fifteen minutes to get home. I can't believe I'm repeating the same mistake. Why am I so lame?* Jay stomped his feet frantically. He brushed his clothes and hair to get rid of loose debris and cobwebs. *This is crazy. What's got into me? Why am I doing this again?*

Jay climbed into the car and drove directly to the realtors where he shoved the keys through the letter box while the car idled at the curb. Inside he sensed a nagging guilt. *Why am I feeling guilty?* But his heart knew. His guilt came from a well of desire so deep that he feared he might compromise something precious to get what he wanted. He had four minutes left. The car chugged up the hill and dread filled his heart. He would not speak of this again until the dust had really settled.

CHAPTER FOUR

—〰—

J ay had started his sermon preparation on Tuesday morning, but his mind kept wandering. In his study, he'd pinned the real estate flier to his wall as a prayer reminder, but instead, it distracted him. He turned his back on the flier and tried to focus on his work. He thought all the more about it. Finally, he grabbed the flier and stuffed it between the leaves of a book and then he shuffled the books around on his shelf so he couldn't easily find it again. The more he tried not to think about it, the harder it became to think about anything else. He could not discipline his thoughts against his obsession. Late that night, he rifled through the shelf of books until he found the flier. Marching to the kitchen, he crumpled it up and stuffed it in the wastebasket. Before he turned off the light, he pulled out the coffee filter still full of grounds and held it over the wastebasket. He hesitated.

Just one more look.

That night, Jay thrashed in bed, plagued by dreams. When he awoke around 2:00 a.m., the only comfort he felt was in holding Lisa tight. Her steady breathing calmed him into a deep sleep.

On Wednesday, Jay had several people to visit; an elderly man in the hospital, a young couple who'd recently visited church, and a family whose teenage daughter was behaving strangely. Lisa had slipped back into her usual loveable self. She had asked for space to work things through and Jay honored that. The tension was gone and even the children seemed more relaxed and happy. Jay was enjoying being back in Lisa's favor. It wasn't long before he began to show signs of a love sick man. He couldn't get enough of her.

Around ten, Jay kissed Lisa goodbye and headed to work. After his first two visits, Jay drove to the Raines home to discuss their daughter Maria. The couple had started coming only months after the church was established. They grew in their understanding of salvation, and one day they made a public declaration of their faith in God. That's when their problems started.

Geoff and Brenda were consistent in their church attendance. They were quiet and kept to themselves in a typical English fashion. But the daughter was something else. Jay had learned a bit about her outlandish behavior from the youth group. She was the talk of the town in some circles, and it eventually passed Jay's hearing. From all reports, Maria was hostile to the Christian faith. She'd even changed her name to identify with her rebel heart, Sabrina.

The Raines house was a two story brick duplex that sat on the edge of town. Their half of the duplex was neat with white and gray trim. Their garden showed signs of meticulous care, neatly trimmed with a row of rose bushes already pruned for the autumn. Jay pulled up in front and parked at the curb. He wondered if Maria would be there today. He'd met her at school when he spoke to the Christian union. She was a rebel, plain and simple. Her pimpled face held defiant eyes. Although she wore the gray and blue school uniform, all her accessories were in black with white makeup that gave her the desired look of the walking dead.

Jay knocked on the door and waited. He heard some scuffling in the house, a shout, and an interior door bang. Finally the door opened and Sabrina stood there in all her glory. She wore a tartan plaid mini-skirt, three chain belts, and Doc Martin calf-length boots. Her hair was right-out-of-the- box midnight black and her face was bone white with black lips and eye sockets. She wore a nose ring and studded eyebrow. Jay tried not to stare.

"Hi, Sabrina."

Sabrina glared at him. "Oh, it's you." Her voice was flat. "I presume you didn't come here to see me." She wiped her nose with the back of her hand. "They sent for you, didn't they? My parents want to tell you what a bad girl I am." She pushed past Jay and headed down the path. "Well Vicar, whatever they tell you, it's probably true, all of it. Ta ta."

"Come in, Pastor Jay." Brenda was wringing her hands and fidgeting with her wedding ring. "I'm so embarrassed at Maria's behavior. We just had another shouting match and now she threatens to move in with her boyfriend. She's only sixteen and still in the middle of her sixth form."

Jay stepped through the doorway. Geoff greeted him and led him into the sitting room. "Have a seat pastor," Geoff said. Brenda had retreated to the kitchen. When she returned she was carrying a tray of fine china tea cups. She had a plate full of pastries and biscuits. Brenda set the tray down on the coffee table and began to pour steaming tea from an ornate Spode tea pot. "You take milk for your tea, don't you?"

"Yes, thanks Brenda." Jay watched as his hostess handed a rattling cup to him. After taking the cup and setting it down, he took Brenda's shaking hand and held it quietly with his own. "Brenda, relax, it's just me." He forced a smile. Slowly, her shoulders sagged. "I understand about conflict in the home. It winds us up like a top." A wispy image of Lisa's face flashed in his mind. Jay blinked.

"We're so worried about our Maria. We just don't know what to do. We can't communicate with her at all. She hangs around with some very unhealthy people."

"Unhealthy?" Geoff said. "Brenda you're far too kind, their just a bunch of freaks and weirdoes. And we get strange phone calls night and day." His voice rose. "Last night the phone rang at three in the morning. Maria must have gotten it on the first ring. I would have given them a piece of my mind. She's definitely involved in something dark."

Jay reassured them. "I know you're anxious, but it's probably a cult fad she's going through. She dresses to impress, it's everywhere in London. They call it the punk look. Life is confusing for teens these days. They're trying to find themselves apart from their parents. I think your daughter is waiting for a prince to come and rescue her." Jay studied Brenda's face. "She just might be looking for boundaries, hoping that if she pushes enough, the boundaries would be set for her."

"Maybe I should strap her in at night and nail all the windows and doors shut." Geoff rolled his eyes. "How about those boundaries?"

"Stop it, Geoff," Brenda said.

"What else do you think she's involved in?"

The father's voice tightened. He looked at his wife and then took a deep breath. "I'm afraid to say."

"Afraid of what?" Jay inched forward.

"Afraid of what might happen to Maria." His voice trailed off into a whisper.

"Is her life in danger?"

"If not her life, her soul certainly is. But, yes, she's playing with fire." His wife nodded. "I believe that whatever is happening is connected in some spiritual dimension that I don't fully understand."

Jay furrowed his brow. "Are you speaking of something demonic?"

Geoff looked desperate, but said nothing.

Brenda took the lead. "We've received a letter of warning not to interfere, or something terrible will happen to Sabrina, our Maria." She struggled and her eyes reddened. Between sobs she said, "Sometimes she disappears at night, and comes back just in time to go to school. She hardly eats. It's making us sick with worry. We can't sleep or eat or concentrate on anything." Brenda stood up and walked to a small desk. She opened a drawer and pulled out a letter. "This warning came last Friday. God alone knows if we've just put our lives in jeopardy by telling you. But we had to tell someone."

Jay took the letter and read it through. "No name, no address, no signature, and no clues. That's a recipe for cowardice." He rubbed his forehead. "I'm so sorry you've been carrying this burden alone. First, whatever you've said to me will remain absolutely confidential." He reached out and put his hand on the father's shoulder. "Second, I'll support you throughout this ordeal. Remember that we have confidence that in spite of the powers of darkness, we know that God's power is greater."

"What can we do for Maria?"

"You are already doing it. You're love for her is evident. She can't escape that. She can run but she can't avoid your love forever. And your prayers for her have great effectiveness. Sometimes that's all we can do until the storm blows over. If you'll give me permission, I'll call the church prayer team to start praying for Maria. I won't give them her name or any details. Their prayers will be a powerhouse for you. God can deliver Maria no matter how dark or how deep her problems are. Remember, you can call me anytime, night or day." Jay leaned forward and spoke softly. "The devil is scheming to destroy anyone who will pay attention. We must put on the armor of God and fight." After praying together with the Raines, Jay left and headed home.

That visit was Wednesday and Jay had played it over in his mind a dozen times, trying not to assume anything as sensational as the parents seemed to imply. He hoped the Raines wrong in their assessment, but he feared they might be right. Sabrina was certainly a desperate girl. He'd seen a lot worse in L.A. *But the enemy is crafty and deceptive in all he does and intends to trick us one way or another.*

Jay navigated through the remainder of the week with his focus on Sunday worship, but underneath he felt restless, and he knew why. At times he wished he'd never stopped at the realtors and wished he'd never seen the flier or looked at the house. Why couldn't he let it go? He found it hard to concentrate. He wished he had someone he could talk to, but there was no one. He was the shepherd and shepherds usually worked solo.

The week hobbled by and Jay kept busy, but when it came time to focus on the Scriptures or prayer, his mind flew in a million directions. *What's wrong with me? That cottage can't have this much control over me.* He thought about his encounter with that strange woman in the woods. Did Sabrina have any connection to her? After his thoughts had spun themselves out, he calmed himself by reflecting on Jesus and His words. It was comforting to know that even when the world is in chaos Jesus never changes.

By Thursday, Jay had only discussed the cottage once with Lisa. He had however, mused over it; wrapped it into the plots of his bedtime stories, and stopped at the window of the real estate agency more than once. But he had kept his promise not to push Lisa into this. He wondered if she had given it any thought at all.

* * *

Friday morning came and the clouds were bruised and swollen.

"It's going to rain," Lisa shouted as she ran out the door. "I'll be right back."

"Want some help?" Jay called from the kitchen door.

"It's only a few things. I've got them."

"Wow, you've got this down to an art." He stepped back as Lisa rushed through the door with an arm full of still damp laundry.

"Whew, just in time. Here it comes." She exhaled and dropped the load on the counter. Jay started folding towels. Right on cue, the skies opened up, throwing down buckets of rain. The leaves on the shrubs and trees turned glossy as the rain splattered them, making each leaf quiver and dance. "I think I've missed my calling. I should have been a meteorologist. I think my prediction rate is at least twenty percent higher than BBC's weatherman."

Jay snickered. "Mr. Rodgers? He's always giving us wrong information. You'd think that here where rain is a daily occurrence he could be at least right half the time."

"Maybe it's just that we've lived here long enough to know that it rains every Thursday and Friday, whether we order it or not."

"I really don't mind the rain. It's calming to me." Jay stopped folding and gazed out the window.

"Don't stop helping me now. You just got started." She threw a towel at him. "If you stare out the window long enough your eyes will glaze over."

"You know me too well, Lisa Knight." He paused and took a tentative breath. "I was wondering." He smoothed the already folded stack of towels, "Maybe we could take a look at the cottage tomorrow."

"Tomorrow? Don't be silly. Tomorrow is Saturday and you're usually working until midnight either on your sermon or music or something."

"You're right. What was I thinking?" He went back to folding while Lisa separated the children's clothes into three piles.

"Obviously, not much." She grinned. "Monday."

"Monday what?" He folded a pair of Nate's pajamas and put them on a stack of towels.

"To see the house, goof ball." She looked at Jay. "Isn't that what you've been planning for days now?" She picked up the folded pajamas and put them with a stack of Nathan's clothes.

Jay brightened. "Yes, I mean, sure. Monday would be great." Jay was suddenly bursting with exuberance. He threw the towel in the air and grabbed Lisa, giving her a swing. "Wahoo!"

"Calm down, cowboy. It's only a look." She tried to break loose of his hold. "I'm not promising anything."

"I know. I know. But Lisa, it could be a great house for us. It just needs some work, and I can do it all." In an instant, Jay had boundless energy. He hoped he could channel it correctly to get through the weekend without becoming obnoxious.

"You're such an overgrown kid." Lisa grinned and picked up the towel. "I'll finish these. Get back to your sermon."

Jay's eyes sparkled with mischief. "I've just had an inspiration, Lisa. Obviously, it must be from the Lord." He said with a pious tone. "I think I should change my sermon text to Luke 6."

"Jesus' parables, right?"

"It sure is." He grabbed a Bible from the coffee table and flipped it open. After running his finger down the chapter headings he stopped and began to read. "I will show you what he is like who comes to me and hears my words and puts them into practice. He is like a man building a house, who dug down deep and laid the foundation on rock..." Jay cocked his head to one side. "Yes, I hear you Lord. What a great idea. I'll begin with an illustration, laying a row of bricks. The congregation will love it. People will probably want to sign up to help in the renovations."

Lisa took one of the folded towels and threw it at Jay. "You're impossible Jacob Knight. You're such a schemer. You've been plotting all week, haven't you?" She grabbed another towel and threw it so that it landed on his head. Jay looked silly and Lisa got into a laughing fit. "I've heard of guys wearing towels on their heads, but now I've got one in my own family. I wish I had a camera."

"Now you're in trouble." Jay pulled the towel off and took both ends, flipping it over her head and around her waist. "Hey, you're mine now." He pulled her close. "This comes in handy when a cowboy's got to get his girl. He pulled her against him. After an impassioned kiss he shouted, "And the winner is—me! I got the girl." They teased and laughed until they ran out of energy. Lisa kept giggling over Jay's turban. It sounded like music to Jay.

* * *

When Sunday arrived, Jay was on such a roll that Lisa feared he might not stop. At breakfast, he talked endlessly.

"Jay, what have you been eating? Slow down before you give yourself a heart attack."

By the time the worship team had warmed up and the service started, Jay had sped up the beat until they were nearly playing double time. Lisa worried that someone or something just might explode.

She looked at the folks next to her. They appeared to enjoy the worship. She glanced over her left shoulder where she knew Joe and Maggie would be sitting. The elderly couple waved and began clapping in time with the others. Across the room, some people stood in worship. Lisa scanned the crowd and every person she saw appeared absorbed in the joy of celebration. In fact, the crowd was larger today than it had been for a long time. And there were new faces, too.

In spite of all the emotion and energy, Jay appeared to remain in control and reverent. Lisa was bewildered. *Maybe it's me.* When the Scripture was read and she was confident

Jay had not rewritten his sermon to incorporate real estate slogans, she slowly relaxed and allowed herself to worship.

Lisa immersed herself in worship. In these moments she knew they were in the center of God's will. Issues come and go, but God remains the same. *Lord, forgive my stubborn heart. Help me accept Your plans for our lives.*

* * *

Bang. Bang, BANG.

Jay shot up in bed. Sleep drained from his head in an instant. "Lisa, someone's at the front door." They heard a crash. "I better go check."

"It's two o'clock. Sounds like someone's trying to break in." Lisa clutched the sheets up around her.

Jay pulled on a pair of jeans and a tee shirt, slid into slippers and headed for the stairs.

"Jay, be careful." She looked around the room and then grabbed an iron bookend on her bedside table. "Here, take this."

"What am I supposed to do with this?"

"That's the closest thing we have to protect ourselves."

"Don't be silly Lisa. Go into the boy's room and lock the door. Just in case." He moved down the stairs and peered through the peep hole. "It's Bryan. He looks drunk. He's bleeding."

* * *

Lisa had locked herself in and listened from the boy's bedroom door. She heard Jay and Bryan talking downstairs. Bryan's voice was booming and angry. *At least he knew where to come for help.* "Is everything all right down there, Jay?"

"We're fine, Lisa. I'm going to drive Bryan home. He's cut his hand, but I'll fix it."

Lisa slipped from the boy's room and moved to the top of the staircase. She peered around the corner trying to stay out of sight. Jay appeared at the foot of the stairs. He'd put his coat on and held Bryan's shoulder to steady him. "There is a broken beer bottle outside the front door. I'll clean it up when I get back. Go back to bed. I'll be back soon."

Bryan looked harmless enough and didn't appear bothered by his wounded hand. Lisa waited until she heard Jay lock the front door before venturing out of her children's room.

She went back to bed, but didn't find sleep easy to come by.

*   *   *

Something woke Lisa from her sleep. One glance at the clock and she realized that Jay had been gone for more than two hours. She shivered and felt her stomach sour. Trying not to be anxious, she prayed. *Lord, be with Jay. Protect him. Whatever he's going through right now, give him wisdom. Watch his back.* She wondered if she should call Bryan's home, but decided to wait it out. Jay should be back anytime now.

Any time now.

*   *   *

"Bryan, don't do this." Jay's back thudded against the kitchen wall. A thin sheen of sweat covered his forehead. "Bryan, you're drunk and you're not thinking straight."

Bryan stood hunched, his shoulders tight against the base of his neck. His eyes burned beneath his brows as he held a 12 Gauge shot gun at Jay's chest. "You been talking to my wife, haven't you?" His knuckles whitened. He took a step closer.

"Yes, Bryan. I've talked to her. You've got her worried sick because of your drinking." Jay stiffened.

Bryan's finger tightened on the trigger. "Don't move, preacher man. I'll shoot you down like a jack rabbit."

"I'm not going anywhere, Bryan." Jay looked over Bryan's shoulder. "Where are Kate and the lads?" He looked toward the stairs. "Have you done something to them? Have you hurt them Bryan?"

"None of your business, preacher." The barrel was now in Jay's face. "I wouldn't hurt my wife or kids. Never."

"You've been hurting them for a long time." Jay kept his voice calm. "Your drinking has robbed Kate and the kids of their father and husband." Jay gave a slight nod. "Bryan, where is your family?"

"They're not here, so shut up. They left me. Went to her mum's. And don't go laying that guilt trip on me." Bryan's eyes watered.

"Then who's to blame, Bryan? Kate? Your parents? Or are you blaming God?"

Bryan growled and shoved the muzzle against Jay's forehead until his head whacked the wall. His vision blurred. Bryan continued yelling, his words jumbled as he digressed into a stupor. After an hour, Bryan sat on a kitchen chair and propped the rifle in front of him.

"What good is this going to do?" Jay stood stiff, aware that the slightest provocation could bring his death. He was a stationary target and at close range. One shot would blow his head off. He prayed hard and felt a calm wash over him. "For the sake of your family, give me the gun."

"Stop talking. I can't think."

Jay didn't stop. Slowly he talked Bryan down, calming him, reasoning with him. "Bryan, you can put the gun down and walk away from this mess. The police won't have to come and take you away. Your wife and sons will come back and you can be forgiven for everything in your past if you turn to Jesus. Only He can help you now."

"Stop. It's too late. I've ruined everything." He choked up.

Jay kept eye contact with Bryan. It was now or never. Anticipating the worst, Jay slowly reached up and took hold of the muzzle. Without a word, he guided the barrel away from his head.

Bryan didn't move. He didn't speak. He only cried.

"Let me take that, Bryan. This isn't what you want." Jay held the barrel but kept eye contact.

Bryan let go and suddenly sunk to his knees and began to sob. "I hate what I do, but I can't stop."

Jay opened the chamber and dumped both cartridges on the floor. He kicked them out of sight and breathed relief. Placing the shotgun behind the kitchen door, he knelt beside Bryan and wrapped his arms around him. Through sobs and stuttering phrases, Bryan confessed his shame and cried for help from God. He was a broken man and by daybreak he'd finally found some peace to hold on to.

Jay called home. "Lisa, I'm okay, but it's been a rough night. I'll be home soon and tell you everything. I've got a pretty nasty headache and I think I'll need to use some of your make up on my forehead. I'll explain later."

Next, Jay called Kate, who promised to come back right away. Bryan was now sleeping off the remainder of his hangover.

CHAPTER FIVE

—⟋⟍—

Being up all night left Jay exhausted. Once home, he told Lisa the story then crashed on the sofa and fell asleep in minutes. His forehead had swollen into a black and blue egg. No amount of makeup could disguise it. Jay didn't stir when the phone rang or Joey cried. He slept through the clatter of dishes and the smell of burnt toast.

Lisa let him sleep until one in the afternoon before she woke him. "Okay, big guy. Wake up." She tugged at his arm. "Come on. Get up. Let's take a look at your cottage. I'll drive."

Jay jolted upright, which made his head thump. He wiped the drool from his face. "Really? I'll be ready in a minute." Twenty minutes later he was giving directions as the car wound its way through Kingsbridge. They turned up Carriage Drive until the road came to an abrupt end. Lisa turned left onto a small dirt track, drove a hundred feet, and parked the car. Ahead was the path that led to the gate of Erindale Cottage. The path bordered the forest on their right. The trees were dense and hung like a cloister over the narrow path. Jay had Joey asleep in a back carrier. Taking Lisa's hand, Jay led her up the path toward the cottage.

"Thanks, Lisa. Do you still think this is a bad idea?"

"Does it make any difference?" Lisa studied Jay's face. "You've already got your mind set on this don't you?"

"What's wrong with wanting our own house?"

"Nothing's wrong with that. You're just so impetuous, so reckless. You jump in with both feet without knowing all the facts."

"Reckless? That's a new title for me. How am I reckless?" His hands grew sweaty. "I've taken calculated risks, usually when I believe something strongly enough. We took the risk to leave everything behind and move to England, didn't we?"

"Yes, Jay. Coming here was a big risk. But it was right."

"So, how is this different? Maybe this is right."

"And maybe it's wrong."

"Maybe so, but we'll never know unless we first consider it." Jay held back a branch so Lisa could pass ahead of him. "It's just up to the left." Jay felt nervous, fearful of pending disappointment. "This house has great potential and it's the cheapest place around. It needs a lot of work but it's solid." They were almost in sight of the cottage. "Don't jump to conclusions until you see everything. Okay?"

"We'll see." They walked a few more steps until the front of the cottage came into view.

"This is it. Erindale Cottage." Jay watched her. "I know I can make this beautiful, Lisa. I think—"

"Stop. Don't say anything." Lisa stood frozen. Sunlight and shadows danced across the front of the house.

"But Lisa, I...."

"Stop." Her stare remained fixed on the cottage. Behind them the forest was alive with bird-song. Before them stood a century old cottage that had been severely neglected for a quarter of its life. Modernization had passed it by.

"Lisa, let me ex—"

"I don't want to hear it." She stared him in the eyes. "You've wasted all this time and energy to bring me to this dump, this trash heap?" Lisa's fist balled up. "This place is disgusting! It's creepy. It looks haunted." Tears reddened her eyes and she turned away.

"Lisa. Please give me a chance. That's all I ask." Jay's voice calmed. He took hold of Lisa's arms and turned her to face him. "Look at me a minute. I've asked you to look before you make an instant decision. Now, at least give me the chance to show you everything and explain what I think I can do with this place."

"Do you really expect us to live in this pigsty?"

"No, I don't. But this house is restorable. It is worth saving and could become a beautiful home."

"Jay, think." She was working herself into a frenzy. "This place is not like a soul to be saved or a life to be spared, it's just a pile of rubble only worthy of bulldozing over."

Jay studied her eyes for a long moment without speaking. "That's your opinion, but not everyone's." He let go of her and walked to the front door and unlocked each latch. "You agreed to look at this place, so let's look and then we can talk."

"The children wouldn't survive in this hell-hole."

"Let me show you the house." Jay pushed open the door and a wave of stale air met them. "You'll need this flash-light to find your way around. Follow me." Lisa shivered and wrapped her arms tight around herself. She hesitated in the doorway. Eventually she stepped over the threshold and into the shadows of the cottage.

Jay led her through the labyrinth of rooms and doors, but she didn't say a word. He described the cottage's uniqueness and pointed out the peculiarities of concave walls and cast iron fire grates. Lisa didn't react. He showed her where they could remove walls and windows could frame the beauty of the forest. He tried to describe how the kitchen would look with new oak cabinets. They could put sliding glass doors here, a wrap around patio there. Lisa listened but appeared unmoved.

With little optimism left Jay said, "Now, there's some-thing outside I want you to see. Follow me." He led her back out the front door where they stood, this time facing the forest. It spread up a great hill that seemed endless. Autumn leaves had fallen, leaving the forest floor full of color. Beyond the gate were magnificent oaks that extended their arms toward them, as if they were guardians of time. A wall of rhododendrons in pink and lavender bordered the cottage. Birds flitted and chirped from branch to branch. Jay and Lisa stared at the forest in silence. The image was breathtaking.

Lisa finally spoke. "You've got my attention, Jacob Knight. What's your plan?"

CHAPTER SIX

—∿∿—

The lawyer stared out his office window, studying the troubled horizon. A storm brewed over the Atlantic and small fishing vessels bobbed in the water like toys. He watched as the Belfast ferry pulled from its dock and headed toward home. Fog was rolling in; soon it would consume everything.

Philip Gentry's chair squeaked as he settled back and surveyed the stack of legal documents that crowded his desk. He'd worn his gray suit which he'd worn yesterday and the day before; always clean, always pressed. He adjusted his wire rimmed glasses and then set to work on his files.

Although Gentry's law practice prospered, he took his own calls and typed his own reports. Polly, his receptionist, was there to file paperwork. After an hour of mind grinding concentration, Gentry looked up and called, "Polly, can you bring me the Hugh's case file please?"

"Here you are, sir." A pleasantly plump woman of fifty something placed the file on his desk and retrieved another stack of papers from his outbox.

The phone rang, stirring Gentry from his concentration. He picked up on the third ring.

"Hello, Mr. Gentry," the line crackled and the caller was decidedly American, "My name is Jacob Knight. I'm a pastor in Kingsbridge."

"Kingsbridge? Kingsbridge Massachusetts or Kingsbridge, South Devon...or... "

The caller laughed. "Sorry, Kingsbridge in Cheshire, just down the road."

"Your accent caught me off guard. So, Mr. Knight, how can I help you?"

"I got your name through Reverend Victor Trinder. He speaks very highly of you."

Gentry laughed softly. "Victor speaks highly of almost everyone. He's the greatest diplomat of all time." He pulled out a legal pad and began scribbling notes. "So, you need legal advice?"

"Yes sir, we do. We need advice on how to purchase a house." There was a pause. "I presume foreigners can purchase property here."

Gentry grinned. "If you have the money, then you can spend it on anything you wish. The British economy is not so flush that we won't take money from Americans."

"I guess you're right. But we don't have any money, or at least we don't have much. Victor suggested that I call you. We want to know what's possible." The caller paused to catch his breath. "My father was a faithful pastor for over forty years and he retired with little more than the shirt on his back. They never owned a thing. I'd like to do better if it's at all possible. Do you think you could help us?"

Gentry hesitated. Of course he wanted to help this man. "Why don't you tell me what you've found and how you think I can be of help to you?"

"Mr. Trinder appointed my wife and me to start a church in Cheshire. He helped us plan the mission to evangelize three communities. But when we got to Kingsbridge, we just knew God had led us there. It was pretty challenging at first. We've been in Kingsbridge now a couple of years, and we've been amazed at how God has worked in people's lives. We've got a great group of new believers. We're already considering building a worship center."

"So, a church has been born in that dark place. That's wonderful."

"Absolutely. We started reaching a group of teenagers, and then it spread to their parents." Jay's voice suddenly became animated. "I think young people are tired of tradition for tradition's sake. They're rethinking their values and we've already raised enough money to get a good start on a building program. I don't know much about Kingsbridge's past, but it seems ripe for the gospel. God is doing some incredible things here."

Gentry closed his eyes as he listened. "This is exciting. Kingsbridge has been in the grip of darkness for centuries."

"How's that?"

"It's a Roman town as you probably know. I'm a bit of a history buff and enjoy reading through old, dusty books. Kingsbridge was actually founded by a Roman battalion who camped there for a winter. They discovered a group of people living in the forest that practiced witchcraft and called themselves Druids. After the Romans invaded Briton, Christianity was introduced as traders and soldiers brought their personal faith with them. It grew quietly but steadily yet faced fierce resistance from pockets of Druid's across the island. Christianity never did fully conquer Druid practices and they insist they still hold claim over many places in England. Kingsbridge is one of them." Gentry opened his eyes and stared blankly at the wall. "Have you felt their presence yet?"

There was an uncomfortable pause on the other end of the line. When he spoke, the pastor's voice had lost some of its vitality. "I'm not sure I have. I guess, I hadn't considered such a possibility, not in this day and age."

Gentry closed his eyes again and furrowed his brow. His voice was soft and pleading. "Pastor Knight, please be careful. You're working in the devil's kitchen. England is a hard place to grow a church. There are so many ancient claims on the land." Gentry hesitated. "I hope you'll consider what I'm saying. I don't mean to discourage you."

"Oh no, not at all." But Jay's voice trembled as if the comment had knocked the wind out of him. "I just hadn't considered…"

Gentry felt a twinge of guilt. *I should have been more tactful.* "Reverend Knight, you've got my full support and prayers. It sounds like God has called you to Kingsbridge for such a time as this."

Jay eventually brought the subject back to the cottage, describing what he had found and the poor condition of the home. "Regarding an application for a mortgage, can you advise me on applying for a home loan?"

"Certainly I can. I've got connections with the Burnley Home Loan Society. Let me get an application and together we can get the process rolling. How much cash can you put down as a security?"

"Only two thousand pounds."

Gentry knew he'd already discouraged the poor guy with his little lecture, but two thousand pounds wasn't much of a down payment.

"We generally require twenty percent down payment for first time buyers, plus the costs of repairs if the house is as bad as you say. They won't advance the money until all the required repairs are completed. You'll probably need an extension request to allow the work to be done before payment is made from Burnley."

"I didn't know how it worked. I guess I can do that. My only hesitation is coming up with the cash to buy materials. I'm pretty experienced at fixing things and learning how to make do with whatever is available. I'll take that as a challenge."

"I'm afraid that is the case. Burnley will send out their regular inspection team to ensure the work is proper. The lenders need to have assurance that the property is worth the money they are investing in the place."

There was a long silence on the other end of the line.

"I can't guarantee you a loan, Reverend Knight, but I'll give it my best shot. I'll prepare the documents and send them to you. I'll need your signature and that of your wife. When you return everything to me, it could take a week or two before they confirm a loan. Let's wait and see my friend, and pray." Gentry replaced the phone in its cradle and stared at it for a long moment. This would take a miracle.

CHAPTER SEVEN

—⟋⟍⟋—

In the British mind, the only proper place to worship was in a consecrated chapel or cathedral. Anything less was not proper. It just wasn't normal. And people in town were quick to voice their opinion. Such talk could hinder the work, or it could stir interest and create curiosity. In Kingsbridge, it did the latter. Nothing about the gathering was normal. The music was energetic with a rhythmic beat that stirred teens. The message was hopeful and relevant and as always, the gospel was free. These were new believers who reveled in the freedom the new church offered. Sunday evening, with its vibrant singing and deep Bible study, became the favorite time to worship. Such freedom seemed almost heretical compared to the typical Church of England gathering. This church was vibrant and very much alive. These new believers were passionate about their faith, and some considered that a threat to their community.

The week started bright, but soon became overcast with steel-gray billows. They hung heavy and low, and the village atmosphere turned melancholy. By 6:10 Sunday night, the wind had whipped past the windows and under the doors, howling a lament. The rain was perpetual. The service had taken off and was in full swing when a teenager appeared at the back of the room. Jay hadn't spotted him until the crowd sat down. He stood there watching. His appearance was dark, even morose. Jay saw rage in the kid's face. Silently, he prayed for wisdom. Eventually, the kid slouched down in a chair, folded his arms, and stared at Jay. His eyes were like black holes boring through him, and it chilled Jay, rattling his composure.

Jay glanced at Ian, the band leader. He seemed composed, but definitely not himself. Jay didn't know what brought Trevor Chernik to the service that night, but his presence stirred an unholy dread.

When the evening ended, Jay felt like he'd been pushing against a stone wall. He was wrung out. This troubled kid had disappeared as abruptly as he had arrived. As the winter rain continued to pelt against steamed windows, a group of teens stayed behind after the service to talk to the Jay. Lisa took Michael and Joey home, leaving Nathan with his dad. While Jay said good-bye to the rest of the congregation, Nathan stacked the chairs and slid them into the corner.

Six teens sat in a small circle drinking coffee while talking in subdued tones. Jay pulled up a chair and joined the group. Nathan studied his dad's face until Jay motioned for him to sit beside him. Ian Davis was talking. Ian was not only the worship leader, but the best guitar player this side of the Mersey River. He was also mature and discerning regarding spiritual matters. Ian had been a believer for two years now, but was already considering a ministry to France. Ian's spiritual stamina was forged in fierce ridicule he'd weathered at the hands of a domineering, agnostic father. It took time, but Ian eventually won his respect.

"Pastor Jay, it seems everyone is upset that Trevor Chernik was here tonight."

Jay was not surprised.

Karen, Ian's seventeen-year-old sister chimed in. "It's bad enough facing him at school. He puts down Christianity all the time." She looked at the others. "I don't know about you guys, but he gave me the creeps tonight. I just couldn't concentrate."

Loren sat next to Karen. "I've known Trevor since I started school, and quite frankly, he's always been strange. I can't believe he is really interested. I mean, with his mother, and what she does, how could he?"

Jay was startled. "What about Trevor's mother?" No one wanted to speak. "Okay gang, you know something and are not telling me. What's the secret? Is Trevor involved in something?"

No one spoke.

"If there is something I should know, then someone please tell me."

A motion and the sound of the door opening startled Jay. Someone had been listening just outside. Sabrina stepped into the room and stood with her arms folded. "So this is what Christian's do to people they don't like." Her lips turned up in a smirk. "They tear them apart." She stepped closer in defiance. "You people think you have all the right answers. I know Trevor and I know his mother. They are very nice people. Trevor's mother has been a high priestess in a witch's coven here in Kingsbridge. Everybody likes her; she isn't dangerous. She only performs white magic; no sacrifices or evil stuff." Sabrina's face hardened. "Your judgment of Trevor is wrong. And you're wrong about his mother, too." She glared at Jay. "I thought Christians were supposed to be different. Obviously, I was wrong."

Sabrina's surprise visit left them dumbfounded.

"You're all a bunch of hypocrites. You make me sick." She ran out the door into the drenched night.

* * *

Lisa hummed a tune as she cleaned, enjoying the moment. Jay was in his office looking up a reference when she popped her head in the room. "How about a cup of tea?"

Jay jumped in his seat. "You scared the dickens out of me." He frowned. "I hate it when you do that."

"Okay, Mr. Grump. So you don't want tea?" She gave her best innocent smile.

"Sure I do. Just don't keep trying to scare the jibbers out of me."

"Okay, Captain. One cup of tea coming up."

Lisa filled the kettle and sat it on the cold stove. She smiled and waved at Michael who was playing outside. He was climbing through the maze of openings in the little plywood fort Jay had built last year. Michael's face peered through a window at the top, his imagination lost in a make believe world. Lisa grinned as she watched him fighting an invisible enemy. He sliced at the air with a stick and jabbered away. Giving a yelp, he shoved the wooden stick into the ribs of his unseen opponent, then in a dramatic lunge he moved forward, lost his balance and went flying through the air landing in the bushes a few feet below.

"Michael! He's had another fall, Jay." Lisa ran to the rescue and found him entangled in the middle of a Copper Beech shrub. He shrieked as its spiny branches skewered his tender flesh. Within minutes Lisa had him back in the kitchen with colorful band aids and a plate of cookies and milk, the kettle momentarily forgotten.

Jay walked into the kitchen. "Michael, how ya doin', partner?" He tousled the boy's hair. "You're a tough cowboy. I think you'll live."

The doorbell rang. "I'll get it." Lisa headed for the door and brought a visitor into the living room. Jay moved from the kitchen into the larger room. "This is Amber Page and she has a special message for the two of us."

Amber walked with a cocky step. She was a pretty teen with a creamy complexion and striking red hair.

"Hi, I'm Jay, and this is Michael." Michael proudly held up his battle scars but the visitor didn't seem to notice. Jay motioned for her to sit down. "Make yourself at home." She looked familiar but Jay couldn't place her. Her sea green eyes seemed distant.

Lisa returned to the kitchen to check on the kettle. Michael immediately scuttled after her.

Lisa called out, "I've got the kettle on. Tea will be ready in a minute." A few moments later, she stepped back into the doorway to listen to Amber.

"What brought you here today?" Jay asked. He made the comment with a slight grin. "Have we won the lotto?"

When the girl began to speak her prettiness faded. Her complexion became putty-like and her words wooden.

"Jacob and Lisa Knight, I've got an urgent message for you. It's a matter of life and death."

In the kitchen the kettle began to squeal. Lisa stood frozen in the doorway. "Life or death? That's pretty serious. What's this all about?" The kettle screamed but Lisa ignored it.

"You've got to get out of town. Fast. Before someone gets hurt."

Jay stood up. His face had paled to gray. "Why in the world would you come to us with such a message? It doesn't make sense. We're no threat to anyone."

"Hey, I'm just the messenger. Don't blame me."

"I'm not attacking anyone. But I'm concerned that someone has asked you to deliver a threatening message to us. Why?"

Ignoring the question she turned to Lisa and smiled. "I'm sure ready for that cup of tea, Mrs. Knight. My mouth is parched."

"What's going on here?" Jay said. "I'm completely confused."

85

Lisa scurried back into the kitchen to brew the tea. Within minutes, she'd collected china cups on a tray with tea and biscuits and carried them into the lounge. She looked at Jay as she placed the tray on the coffee table.

Jay had composed himself. "I remember where I have seen you before, Amber. You've come to our Sunday evening service a couple of times. Isn't that right?"

"Once. Just once," Amber responded as she stirred her tea. "I didn't come because I'm religious." Her laugh sounded brittle. "I don't need religion. I need power."

Jay said, "We've got lots of young people like you who are searching for significance in their lives. And knowing the truth gives us freedom. Knowing Jesus Christ…."

Amber jolted up straight at the mention of Jesus Christ. She nearly knocked her tea cup to the floor. "I wasn't looking for any personal relationship. I don't need anyone. It's power that I wanted."

"Then you've come to the right place." Jay picked up his Bible from a side table.

Amber pulled back. "I don't need that. I don't want that stuff. I found the power I need. That's why I'm here."

Jay frowned in confusion. The girl's behavior was odd, almost schizophrenic.

Lisa had to ask. "Okay then, Amber, you tell us what you came here for. We're dying to know."

Amber's mood changed again. "I went to a weekend conference held in the ruins of Beeston Castle. They designed it to attract young initiates, people like me. It started with lectures on the history of Britannia. They showed artifacts, gave demonstrations, performed rituals and held séances. They revealed the religious history of Kingsbridge before the Romans contaminated it. They performed ceremonies of the Druids and ancient Celts."

Lisa kept her eyes fixed on the strange young woman. "Ah, but that's religion too and you said—"

86

"There's a big difference." Amber hunched her shoulders, eager to tell everything. "This is the true religion of the earth. It's…it's…"

Jay interrupted. "It goes far deeper than the earth, Missy. It comes from the pit. You're talking witchcraft."

Amber blurted, "Christianity is the usurper. It creates war and poverty everywhere it goes."

"I'll have to admit, you're gutsy to come into our house and tell us we're wrong," Jay said. "Who told you to come here?"

Amber's eyes glazed again. "Jay and Lisa Knight, today you've been warned. I've been assigned to tell you that you must leave this place. Get out. Take your children and go. You're not wanted here. And if you refuse to leave, then you will pay dearly."

Lisa turned angry. "Who says? Who gave you this assignment? And what gives you the right to come here and tell us?"

"It was a voice in my dreams."

"So you don't know?" Jay said. "Maybe you just made it up."

"The voice said he was, Lucifer." With a sudden look of innocence, Amber faced Lisa, "It's a cool name, but I've never heard of it before. Who's Lucifer? I'm a bit embarrassed. I think it's someone I should know, but I don't."

Lisa's teacup rattled, slipped from her fingers, and dropped to the floor. It shattered, spraying shards of fine bone china into the air. Hot tea splashed across the coffee table pooling into small puddles. Lisa sat there in stupefied silence until Jay came to her rescue.

"Don't worry. I'll take care of this." Jay reached down to pick up the pieces as Lisa and Amber stared at each other. Lisa recovered enough to bend over and pick up broken shards of a once exquisite piece of china. She wondered if this was a portent of things to come.

CHAPTER EIGHT

—◊◊◊—

Suzanne Liermann was excessively round and low to the ground. For a middle-aged woman, her long ginger hair threaded with gray seemed somewhat inappropriate. Her tresses draped over her naturally padded shoulders, giving her an appearance of a female Viking warrior. A breastplate of steel armor would have seemed more fitting than the cotton pinny, she usually wore. But Suzanne was still a pretty good soul, and her recommendations were generally worth some consideration. So when Suzanne called the manse Tuesday morning spot on nine o'clock, Jay listened.

"Pastor Knight, did you realize that there is a two-acre parcel of land near Fox Hill that might be for sale?" It was typical of Suzanne to charge right into a conversation with no introductions.

"I certainly did not, Suzanne. Tell me about it." He settled into an easy chair and listened as Suzanne chattered away.

The church elders had searched relentlessly for a property to lease or purchase. The local town Council's suggestions were useless. "Do we really need another church in Kingsbridge? Aren't there enough empty churches in this town? Why build another one?"

Their attitude was typical. To the locals vacant churches represented a dying religion filled with superstitious rituals.

To them, church buildings were nothing more than wasted real estate that should be used for office complexes, housing developments, and retail shopping districts.

The church elders thought they had left no stones unturned. They settled on the community center for the time being, knowing the town couldn't turn them away. The small but energetic congregation consisted of tax-paying members of the Kingsbridge community.

Suzanne continued her chatter, and Jay recalled his frustrated efforts. He remembered the day when he drove to the crest of Kingsbridge hill. The view from the top was breathtaking. Kingsbridge looked so idyllic, like a sleepy English shire. Church steeples pointed skyward. Rooftops bore colorful gingerbread fascias. A faint mist drifted up from ornate chimney pots creating a lazy haze across the valley.

Jay loved this place. In the four years, he and Lisa had truly made it their home. They could live here forever. Their lads loved it, but he had not found a single plot of land where they could build a church. Jay pleaded with God. "Lord God, You called us here to serve you and we've done that. The work is growing and we're running out of space. So where do we go from here?"

No sooner had the words left his lips, when a strange sensation came over him, as though someone else had listened in on his prayer. It touched the nape of his neck. It traveled down his spine, through his shoes, and into the ground. The air grew cold, yet Jay broke into a sweat.

"Helloo! Are you listening to me? Is anyone there?" Suzanne squawked over the phone.

"Oh, yes . . . sure . . . carry on. So the property is up for sale?"

"As I was saying, Pastor," she paused to make her point. "I'm positive the owner wants to sell this parcel of land. You can see it from the main road and it has three old barns on it."

"I can't picture where it might be."

"Councilman Clary owns it. He wants to dump it because his own council refused to rezone it for residential use. I guess they thought he was rich enough." Suzanne released a strange little laugh.

"You're a jewel, Suzanne." Jay smiled. *You're also a nosy parker.* "I'll take a look today. See you on Sunday." He set the phone down and shook his head. After all his personal searching met with nothing but frustration, God used nosey Suzanne to find a plot of land with no effort at all.

Three hours later, Jay drove up the back road toward Fox Hill. He made a right turn and followed the lane toward an imposing two-story farmhouse. Opposite the farmhouse stood a gate, and beyond it were several barns. Jay pulled his car into the driveway and parked. This had to be the place Suzanne described. There were three barns and a field that must have come close to two acres. The two stone barns were in disrepair, their roofs having fallen in. The third barn appeared more substantial and looked solid. It was built of red brick and had windows and doorframes supported by concrete lintels.

Jay got out of his car and jumped over the gate like a cowhand. One glimpse and he had no doubt: God was in this. *This is a prime piece of land, and I hadn't seen it.*

He prayed as he walked. *Is this the land you promised us, Lord? Why did you let me drive past this for so long without even a whisper as to its existence?*

Jay walked the perimeter of the land, offering every square inch of it to the Lord. He studied the walls of the barn and prayed over them. "Lord, by faith I claim this land and this barn for your use in the Kingdom of God. May this be the place where hundreds find the peace that passes understanding and the forgiveness of sins through Jesus Christ. Let it be so, Lord."

This barn, its location, and boundaries were more than any in the church had dared dream. He sat down in the middle of stale hay in wonder. He was stunned. *Could this really be God's provision? Lord, your blessings always surprise me, but they shouldn't. Because you promise to give until it overflows. I'm ashamed of my weak faith.* Jay stared out an open doorway onto a neighboring field and watched as the breeze rippled the wheat across the landscape. It was ready for harvesting.

Jay seldom succumbed to overheated zeal. And the one significant time he was certain of God's specific direction was his calling to go to England. From then on, it was usually a quiet inner assurance that he was in the center of God's will. But this place, this provision stopped him in his tracks. He listened carefully, believing that God was in the midst of doing something beyond his dreams. He was certain God spoke.

Jay, there was no room for Me in the inns of Bethlehem two thousand years ago. Kingsbridge has shut me out for far too long. I used a cowshed to introduce My Son to the world and I will use this barn as a place where men and women can meet my Son and fall in love with Him. Nothing shall stop this from happening, because I am the Lord God.

"Then Lord, show me what to do next." Jay took spiritual authority over the land in a simple act of faith. Whatever claims or strongholds that had been associated with this land were severed. God was free to do with this as He chose. A quiet confidence blossomed in him. God would work out His will. Next Jay must present this suggestion to the elders for prayer and consideration. Elder David Thatcher was first on his list.

* * *

In their early thirties, David and his wife Rachel had made a sacrificial choice to move from their Liverpool family home to be available for ministry in the town of Kingsbridge. The Knights had met them several years earlier, and their friendship riveted them together. Mercedes-Benz employed Dave as a specialist mechanic. His rough hands bore the signs of a grease monkey, and that is where he felt most at home. He spent his life under the hood of some mean machine, except when he and his son Jason got together for fencing lessons or to watch a local auto race.

The Thatchers were young enough to be adventurous, and believed that God had freed them to move out, set up their own garage in Kingsbridge, and minister to a community that needed Christ. Jay felt privileged to have them on his team. People like them were rare.

* * *

Jay sat in the kitchen, spilling out the story of discovery to Rachel and David. He'd finished his second cup of coffee and started on his third when Rachel stopped him.

"Pastor, you're not going to overdose on me are you? All that caffeine."

"No fear Rachel. I'm immune to the stuff." Jay warmed his hands around the steaming cup.

Rachel smiled and noticed that David's cup was untouched. "David, you haven't touched your cuppa."

"I'm thinking." David leaned back in his chair rubbing his chin. After listening to the pastor's account, he hadn't said a word. "Hmmm."

David seldom said much, but Jay had learned over years that the man's brain ran at full speed. Whatever David had to say would be worth the wait. "Very interesting." He sat up straight, letting his chair settle on all fours and looked at Jay. "That's a significant piece of Kingsbridge property. What's in our building fund?"

"Not enough. I know what you're thinking, but I have a question for you: Where does faith fit in? Faith depends on invisible evidence."

"It's bad stewardship to jump into something without the funds to back it up."

"I agree in developing a financial plan, but without the critical element of faith, the whole exercise is pointless."

Jay understood David's intent was not to discourage the work, but to be certain it would not backfire. Still, David's cautious approach frustrated Jay.

"Have you always been this slow at making decisions?" Jay grinned. "How long did it take for you to propose to Rachel?"

"Pastor," Rachel said rolling her eyes. "I decided for him. After three years of wondering, I gave him an ultimatum. It was now or never."

Jay hoped an ultimatum wouldn't be needed.

* * *

The day finally came when Erindale cottage was theirs and Jay's energy soared. The Knights were dumbfounded to find that both the sellers and lenders gave the extraordinary permission to begin repairs before the monetary transaction was complete. This had to be God's doings. With the transfer of two thousand pounds and a signed contract, a piece of ancient real estate now belonged to an American couple.

It was a cool morning and clouds mottled the sky. Lisa shooed Jay off with her blessing and a packed lunch. After loading supplies in the back, Jay climbed in the Ford and headed to Erindale Cottage. She reminded him, "Remember, I am not the renovator, I'm the mum." Jay was okay with that.

He drove to the end of the dirt track, braked quickly, and hopped out. He gathered his tools and headed toward the small home. *Lord, You're so good to us. Thank You. I know I've been a real pain, but You tell us to ask, and so I did.*

His fingers worked quickly to unlock the front door. Twenty minutes later, he had torn the panels from the downstairs windows. The wash of daylight dispelled all spookiness and transformed this dungeon into a dusty cottage. Jay yanked back the curtains and studied the stained wallpaper. Disgusting! With a flourish, he pulled at a strip of mildewed paper. Ribbons of paper flew off the walls until he had strewn the floor.

He hadn't noticed that the front door had swung closed.

He didn't hear the gate creak on its hinge.

He didn't detect the sound of footsteps coming toward the house.

So immersed in his own adventure, Jay had not heard a thing until something slammed against his front door.

Fists crashed against the wood causing the door to shake. The door shuddered as a heavy foot kicked it. A man's voice boomed with rage. "You piece of trash! Stinking scum! Get your fat rear out here." Jay's heart throbbed out of his chest. His head pounded.

"Get out here, scumbag." The door heaved inward as the man rammed against it with his body.

Jay shook and cold sweat oozed from his pores. He grabbed the knob and opened the door.

The man stood dead center in the doorway. He was short and wiry with neck muscles that bulged like an ape. His gray hair was bristly and he stood with his legs spread and fists bunched tight. His knuckles were bloodied. Jay stumbled backward and lost his balance.

The man cursed, spraying spittle in Jay's face. "You're pathetic," he sneered.

Jay scrambled back to his feet and they stood face to face. The man's eyes startled him. They blazed with rage. Cataracts had dulled any remaining color from them. Jay steadied himself against the doorframe. The man roared, "You're not wanted here. Take your family and bugger off." He lunged forward, swiping at Jay but hitting only air. "I'll make you wish you'd never seen this place. I'll make your life a living hell."

Jay staggered. "I don't even know who you are. You've got the wrong man."

"Wrong man? Wrong man? You're that preaching American sponger, grabbing up whatever you can get your dirty little hands on. You and your little snot-faced family. Get out of Kingsbridge you freakin' scum bucket."

"I've done nothing to you and I don't intend to. So I'm asking you politely to leave. I've got work to do." He took a step toward the man. His hands shook, but he stood his ground. "Please leave now or I'll call the police." Jay was terrified, but was determined not to let this monster intimidate him.

"Oh, you've got me really scared." He shivered in derision. "You better keep your kids on a leash because if I ever see them, I'll teach them a lesson they'll never forget." He raised an invisible knife into the air and pretended to skewer something. Jay understood exactly what he meant.

"Get off my property. I refuse to respond to your threats. And if you ever lay a hand on my family, you'll have me, the police, and God to face."

The man hocked a wad of spittle at Jay's shoes. "God? Ha. He's not powerful enough for me. Just be sure of this, if you ever cross my path, you're a dead man." He turned to go while screaming, "You're a dead man. A dead man, you pervert." He slammed the broken gate and was gone.

Jay nearly collapsed. He held onto the doorframe to keep steady. He shook his head at such unbelievable behavior and finally muttered, "What have I got myself into?" He stared out at the woods and shivered. "God help him. God help us."

CHAPTER NINE

—〰—

Richard and Jean McGregor had dreamed of one day owning a home in the country. Richard had worked for twenty years in a fast paced environment and had reveled in competing for the top rung of the corporate ladder of Lion's Snacks Limited. For the past ten years, he had been their best rep and was beginning to feel jaded. No one wanted to take him on, and he despised the apathy he saw in his colleagues.

Feeling restless, he turned his attention elsewhere. This was the perfect time to discover what country living was all about. Kingsbridge suited the McGregor's just fine. They had only been in town for six months, and Richard embraced the challenges of home repair and improvements, enjoying his own castle. Jean felt ready-made for rural life. The pair had been delighted to discover an old farmhouse situated within the green velvet ribbon known as Fox Hill. The house had been part of a small holding owned by Councilman Clary, who first attempted to have the farm rezoned for small industrial use. When the council rejected that, he tried residential zoning which went down in defeat immediately.

Richard was satisfied with purchasing just the farmhouse, at least for the time being. But satisfaction was so elusive. On one particular morning, Richard and Jean were sitting in their kitchen mulling over the land next door. "Thank

God," Richard, who didn't have a clue whom that might be, said. "That Clary's request for residential rezoning was shot down. I didn't come all the way from the big city to live next to a pig farm. I can't imagine the smell."

Jean said, "That's part of rural living."

"Pig smells were never a part of the bargain." He lifted the tea cozy and poured himself another cup. As he sipped, he peered out the kitchen window. "Those dilapidated stone barns are eyesores. If those barns were gone we could see right across the estuary where the Mersey River runs into the sea. That would double the value of this place overnight." He paused. "I could tear those down quite easily."

"They must be twenty feet high. How would you do that?" She squeezed his biceps playfully. "Superman?"

"It would be easy. A one man job. I'd remove the roof tiles and battens, and then swing the beams around to balance along on the piers. It would be easy enough to topple the beams." He stood and walked over to the window. "I'd chip out the mortar at the base of each column, tie ropes around the top, and hook it to my hitch. The rest would be easy. I could do it at night and nobody would be the wiser. Can you imagine what the neighbors would think the next morning?"

"I have no doubt that you could pull it off. But we've got our hands full now with restoring this place."

Richard agreed. "At least I can pipe dream, and I don't even smoke." He hee-hawed at his own joke.

Their new move had brought some unexpected changes. There was a new loneliness to rural living. In the city they frequently entertained or went to the theater and fancy restaurants. There was always something going on. Their two sons were now on their own, only coming for brief visits. Jean and Richard's greatest fear was living without purpose. There was comfort in the familiar— laughing with old friends and dreaming about tomorrow. Without their dreams, what remained?

* * *

The phone jangled on the kitchen wall, adding one more task for Lisa as she corralled Joey into a corner, his fingers working hard at opening drawers. "Hello, Knight's residence. This is Lisa."

"Hello Lisa, this is Jenny. Hope I'm not disturbin' ya."

Lisa brushed the hair from her face and laughed. "Not at all Jenny, I'm just trying to focus the energy of one wiggly boy into something less exhausting. How are you doing today?"

"Fine love, thanks. Ray and me, we would like to invite everyone to our home next week for the Bible study. Our house is still unfinished, but actually, we just got new carpet and we would really enjoy havin' everyone here."

"That would be wonderful, Jenny. I'll have Jay announce it on Sunday. Why don't we have a couple ladies bring coffee and biscuits?"

"Just a jug o' milk and some biscuits would do fine. I have everything else. Well, thanks then. It'll be fun havin' everyone at our house for a change instead of always at the manse. You've got your hands full enough with the children. Besides, I have somethin' I want to share with the group that's very excitin' to me. Ray said that I should just go ahead and share it with everyone. "

"You've got me curious already. I'll arrange for someone to mind the children so I can come. I hate to miss anything. Thanks Jenny. See you Sunday. Whoops, I gotta run. Bye and God bless." Lisa dropped the receiver as she lunged for Joey. He had just discovered how to turn the knobs on the gas stove.

Wednesday rolled around and twenty-six adults gathered in the tiny living room of Jenny and Ray Orsen. Cars lined the roadside, and more kept coming. Jenny kept the kettle hot, brewing new pots of tea and cups of coffee as others arrived. The tiny room became stifling as the crowd grew. People were sitting wherever they could find a spot. Ray bussed drinks back and forth as people chatted. As usual, there was the anticipation that God would speak and instruct these new believers. God never failed to show up.

Jay was teaching through the book of Acts. Tonight, studying Acts 12, they marveled how Peter was miraculously set free from prison while the disciple James, John's brother, was brutally beheaded without any intervention from God.

"God allows different events, some good and some bad, to happen to his people for a purpose which we mortals seldom understand," Jay said. "The whole story presents a tapestry of life which can't be seen or understood while the threads are being woven into place. Only as the tapestry is completed, and one stands back through the distance of eternity, can one see the whole picture. The cross is the center of our faith. It reminds us that God Himself suffered so that we might live."

The dialogue on pain, suffering, and God's will was good. When Jay came to a good stopping point, he invited the group to pray for each other and for God's work in Kingsbridge. The prayer time was tender, caring for each other's burdens. Their worship permeated the room like a sweet scent, and together they offered themselves to the Heavenly Father.

Finally, Jenny cleared her throat and asked to share an insight that came to her in a night vision. Jenny opened her Bible and flushed with a nervous excitement. "It's in the book of Haggai."

"Wow, Jenny. You do dig in deep, don't you?" Jay laughed.

"Before last week I didn't even know this book existed. But I got so excited when I read this verse. It seemed clear that this was written just for us here in Kingsbridge."

Jenny had uncovered an obscure verse written hundreds of years before Christ walked the earth. The message came from a prophet who witnessed the destruction of Solomon's temple and now was a part of the returning exiles to Jerusalem. Haggai's message was a call for obedience. He challenged the people to rebuild the house of God. When the people put God first, they would be blessed rather than cursed. As a young believer, Jenny took the Scriptures at face value.

Jenny read slowly in her lilting Liverpool accent. "Go up into the hills and bring down timber and build the house so that I may take pleasure in it and be honored, says the Lord." Jenny looked at Ray, waiting for his nod. When he smiled Jenny continued. "Ray and me have been working so hard on our own little house we haven't had much time for anything else. It dawned on us that we needed to concentrate on God's house instead." She glanced around the room. There were still unfinished sections of their tiny terraced cottage.

"We have made a decision about this house. But now, we need a house for the Lord. We don't know where that will be, but we want to help, so that God will be recognized as Lord in Kingsbridge." Jenny paused a minute and then continued. "Ray and me, well, we have decided to give somethin' of ourselves so that a proper church can be built. We went to our bank, you know, *The Westminster*, and asked for a second mortgage on this house so's we can give it to the Lord. Here's a check for 14,000 quid, er I mean pounds, toward the purchase of a piece o' land for the Lord."

Everyone gasped with surprise, and finally a cheer went up, and then clapping until it thundered in the room.

Jay was speechless. He had not seen this coming. Finally he spoke. "Jenny, Ray, I had no idea you were even thinking of such a thing. What a wonderful gift. I can't think of the words to say. I'm dumbfounded."

"That's a first," Lisa said with a smile. "He has nothing to say."

Jenny continued. "The Lord's asked us to do this beyond our regular givin'. We're not doin' it to be praised, but to be obedient. The darkness has held claim to Kingsbridge for too long." She handed the check to Jay, who shook his head in grateful silence.

David leaned toward Jay and whispered something in his ear. Jay looked at his watch, nodded, and finally stood up. "This has been a wonderful night. But there is still more to this story. Tonight we are seeing God work beyond our expectations. No one knew that Ray and Jenny were planning this, but the elders have met to discuss a piece of property that has suddenly come on the market." Everyone held their breath. "It sits at the foot of Fox Hill and has two acres of prime land, which face the main road through town."

Several people gasped.

"Now folks, this is the amazing part. The listing price is—14,000 pounds." He held up the check for everyone to see. "We have exactly fourteen thousand pounds." Jay purposely looked at David and their eyes locked in confirmation. Jay mouthed, "The money's in the bank."

As the meeting came to a conclusion and prayer sealed the night, Jay felt a deep sense of God's presence and he was sure the others felt it as well. Outside, the wind whipped up dust rings on the pavement as friends said good-bye with hugs and hearty handshakes.

Jenny handed Jay a note with Haggai 1:8 written on the bottom. She'd drawn a simple church by a hill with the words, Kingsbridge Fellowship over the top. "Go get the wood pastor. Let's start building."

CHAPTER TEN

—〰—

I t was Friday afternoon and McGregor decided to take advantage of his flexi-hours to avoid rush hour traffic. It didn't matter that everyone else in the city had the same brilliant idea because Richard treated traffic like he treated his business associates: subdue and conquer. Violating all driving courtesy, Richard dashed, weaved in and out, and sped along exit lanes to cheat others of their space.

Dusk was settling when he climbed out of his Mercedes. He grabbed his briefcase and headed toward the back door, when a motion across the street caught his eye. A paper was flapping in the wind. Curiosity made him walk across the lane to see what it was. Someone had posted a notice on the door of the old barn. It was a procedural document declaring the intent of a local church to gain legal permission to build on the site. McGregor groaned. He squinted as he read the fine print.

"I can't believe this! A church? Houses okay, pig farm maybe, but a church? There is no way that I am going to let a church come along and build a monstrosity across the road from me. Absolutely not." He ripped the document off the door and carried it with his briefcase into the house. Richard's voice boomed when he got excited. "Jean, where are you?" Before she could answer, he found her in the sitting room. "Look at this." He shook the notice in his fist. "I'm not going to stand by and let this happen! We're not going to live next door to a bunch of holy rollers. All those religious nutters do is play bingo and hold rummage sales and say "Hallelujah" to everyone, and fill up their cemeteries with dead people. Never!" Richard could feel the heat of anger redden his balding head.

"Calm down love. It's not good for your blood pressure."

Richard paced the floor. The move from the city was not turning out quite like he had planned. As the night drew in, Richard ate his supper of pot roast, and talked about his concerns regarding the church proposal. He stayed up late writing.

No, sir, no church is going to destroy my plans.

* * *

The restoration of Erindale Cottage proved a monumental undertaking. Of course, anything would be an improvement. Cleaning didn't involve much expense, just plenty of elbow grease and time. Jay found the work exhilarating; to Lisa it was a necessary chore.

They chipped away old plaster on the first floor walls while Joey slept upstairs in a bedroom wrapped tight and snug in winter clothes.

When the time came to pick Nathan and Michael up from school, dust covered Lisa and Jay. Exhausted, they sat on the living room floor and laughed at each other. They'd gotten a lot done and were pleased with their progress. To Jay, it felt like they were finally in agreement that God had provided this home. They locked up and set off down the lane like a couple of school kids, chattering about their plans for tomorrow.

Jay was beginning to feel good about things again.

* * *

Jay knew how to find things free, or at least cheap. He learned how to repair things on the run. Asking questions and experimenting gave him an edge on the building trade. He taught himself how to trowel concrete, put the finishing skim on the new plastered walls, and build a brick fireplace from the ground up. He rewired the house, installed new plumbing, and laid flooring throughout downstairs.

The gardens had been landscaped with the help of a backhoe. One thousand squares of sod yielded an instant lawn. One thing remained a mystery. It ate at Jay: no one knew what was behind the bricked up doorway under the stairs. There was no evidence of it on the legal deeds. It said nothing about another room or extension. Faced with more work than he could handle, he decided it would remain an unsolved mystery, at least for now.

After wrangling with the county, a disgruntled committee gave approval to widen the footpath into a driveway. This was a major breakthrough, and the Knights began to feel that perhaps they might complete most of the work in time for Christmas.

The gas board solved the enigmatic phrase, "possible gas." They flushed the lines and activated a meter outside. On the first cold winter day in November, the heat was turned on and the cottage breathed with new life.

* * *

Noel Dungess grew up in County Cork, Ireland. His father was the village drunk who eventually killed himself in a potato field three miles from home. It changed little in Noel's life. Long before his father checked out, he ceased being there for the family. If it hadn't been for Noel's older brothers, they would have starved. The town came to know the Dungess family as the "rag and bone" people. Each day one of the brother's would head to town with a horse and wagon, picking up scraps of metal, wood, clothing, and left-over food. They used everything but the bones. Dogs followed wherever they went, yapping until the brother threw a bone their way.

Noel's mother was a bitter woman. Although life had cheated her she determined to beat the odds. So she schemed to put one of her sons in a place of power. Priests lived well and had great authority. If one of her sons were a priest, she would be taken care of in her old age. This had nothing to do with God and everything to do with her. She would be somebody. Noel was her pick.

*   *   *

Dungess had an impressively long driveway that ended in disappointment. His home was the size of a postage stamp. Each evening after work, his painter's van creaked up the driveway and rattled to a stop. Noel would drag himself out of the van and head toward the house. His fifty-eight-year-old body ached. He deserved better than this.

Today, like every day, he was haunted by his mother's condemnation. "Noel, you're worthless. I wish you'd never been born." He'd joined the Royal Navy and was stationed in Italy. Then one day he went AWOL and was missing for two years. When he returned, he was dishonorably discharged.

Elda waited for him, poised like an iron cannon in the kitchen doorway, arms triggered at the hips. She bellowed as he climbed out of the van, "Get in here, you snake. What's going on next door? Didn't I tell you to take care of them, you sniveling idiot?"

"Shut up, you old cow." Dungess stared at her. The cow and the idiot stood their ground; each determined not to be the first to yield.

Elda's straggling gray hair blew around her head like a tornado, and her darkened profile was menacing in the kitchen light that glared behind her. Noel's resolve evaporated in the heat of her stare. He was too tired to fight. He backed down and turned to the garage in retreat. He knew her pattern, and eventually she would run down, allowing Noel to enter the house and regain control—so he hoped. Noel hated the woman and he knew she despised him. Together their world consisted of random blasts at anything that moved into their sights. Elda pointed the gun and Noel pulled the trigger.

An hour later, Dungess successfully entered the house, changed clothes, and made his way to the kitchen. Elda banged plates and cutlery onto the table, and offered unsolicited information. "Those people next door are stupid. This morning they had two blokes on the roof chipping out the old mortar on the chimney. It was a mess. Chippings were flying everywhere, even down onto *our* driveway. Those blokes couldn't be union men, they're too stupid."

Dungess stared down at his empty plate.

Elda droned away. "I got 'em back good, I did."

"What did you do?"

The woman boasted, "I threw stones at the blokes until they stopped. They almost fell off the roof. I guess they whined to that stupid Vicar. When the American came over, I told him he had to sweep up our driveway or I'd call the police."

Noel showed no emotion. "What did he do?"

"He swept the driveway clean and took the rubbish away with him. He even swept up the horse droppings."

"Curse that man. He's trying to use Christian hocus-pocus on us." Dungess said. "We've got to teach him a lesson or two." Noel gazed out the window with a determined stare. He'd fix this guy somehow.

CHAPTER ELEVEN

—〰—

From the Cheshire plain, one could easily recognize the communities of Kingsbridge and Tarnum by the three prominent hills that embraced the valley below. Tarnum, a Saxon village, had the greater hill which rose with a rugged rock face that resembled the profile of a man's head. Kingsbridge hill was lesser in height and Fox hill was a graceful two-mile stretch that married Kingsbridge and Tarnum. Rich vegetation covered the hills and offered an illusory sense of security as if they were the ramparts of a medieval stronghold.

Behind these hills, stood miles of countryside blanketed in a rich forest of tall pine, holly, laurel, and bracken. Residents knew it as Dunstin Forest. On weekends, regardless of the season, Dunstin Forest was the playground for families living in the city. Picnic sites dotted the small rises along meandering footpaths.

Jay had been feeling like a yo-yo for weeks. It seemed that some personal blow followed each ministry success. After each conversion came some form of antagonism. The church was growing, but so was the opposition. Amber, the young witch initiate seemed to have disappeared completely after delivering the curse, but Trevor kept busy, poisoning the pot, stirring up hostility among the youth. Sabrina continued to provoke her parents, which seemed to deepen their faith. It was not surprising that Jay felt yanked between hope and despair but he had no intention of surrendering.

Winter had come with a cold blast. There were no snow blizzards, just the damp cold that chilled to the bone. The days were short and nights long and the skies provided miserable company.

Jay had been trudging the streets of Kingsbridge, witnessing from door to door. Sometimes people were curious, but to others the message of hope seemed too good to be true, and faith too hard to come by after generations of unbelief.

Jay was nearly finished for the day. His fingers were numb with cold. As he walked toward another front door, he noticed movement from behind a curtain. Before he could knock, the door sprung open. A heavy busted woman shot out the door like a bat out of hell.

Her voice boomed. "How dare you come to my front door?" She shook her fist causing a tremor throughout her body. "Get out of Kingsbridge," she bellowed. "Nobody wants you here in England." Her nostrils flared.

Startled by the outburst, Jay stumbled backward nearly falling down the porch steps. When she stopped to take a breath he replied meekly. "I'm sorry if I offended you. I just want to tell people about the good news of Jesus."

"Get out of town, you Pied Piper. You're ruining my husband. He's been a minister here for fifteen years." She reached inside and grabbed a broom and rushed down the steps toward Jay. "Get out. Get OUT." She smacked his head with the broom and chased him down the sidewalk. A few yards from her home she screamed a profanity, rushed back inside, and slammed the door.

Jay felt embarrassed by the woman's outburst. She'd scratched his face with the broom and he felt the sting. The sting inside was worse. Neighbors peered out their windows.

As he headed home, he remembered the words of Jesus, "If the world hates you, keep in mind that it hated me first."

"Forgive them, Lord." Jay headed home.

* * *

Lisa heard the car in the driveway and the crunch of gravel as Jay walked to the house. A moment later he crossed the threshold. The sight of him made her pause. "Jay, what happened? You're bleeding." She helped him off with his coat and checked the scratches on his cheek. "Who did this?" She sat him down and began to clean his scrapes.

"I'm not sure." Lisa stood back and watched Jay's face as he talked. "I just had a run in with a woman. She chased me off with a broom."

"A broom?" It sounded funny. Lisa tried to hold a straight face but couldn't. "She really chased you with her broom?" She broke into laughter. Soon they were both laughing until the tears came. "Did she fly away on it?"

"Isn't it silly? I wonder what the Lord must think." Jay's shoulders sagged.

"I'm not laughing at you."

"Yeah, yeah, I know the line." Jay grinned then abruptly changed topics. "Are you up to a hike in Dunstin forest?"

"Well sure, I guess so." She looked at her watch. "We'll need to head out there right away before it gets dark." She moved into the kitchen. "I'll put some snacks together if you'll bundle up the kids. They're in their room, probably building something with the Lego set."

Jay rose from the sofa and started for the children's room. "Kids, do you want to go to the forest?" Their joyful squeal was all the answer he needed.

The drive took only ten minutes and soon the family was stretching their legs as they headed into the forest. Joey rode in his dad's backpack and jabbered with excitement. Michael and Nathan couldn't wait to explore the woods. The rule was to stay together and not to wander out of their parent's sight. It was a rule the children constantly tested. A brisk breeze surrounded them with the clean smell of pine. It seemed the Knights had the forest to themselves.

Lisa took hold of Jay's hand and inhaled deeply. "Thanks for the suggestion. We need these times together, Jay." She smiled. "And you know, this is the one, only one mind you, redemption about buying the cottage."

"What's that?"

"That we'll be living on the edge of this great forest. It's a grand playground for the lads."

"I'll remind you of those words on moving day."

"I guess I can live with the mess of the cottage if we can walk out the front door and into the beautiful woods anytime we choose. I just wish the work was finished and we were already in. I dread moving day." She kept her eyes on the boys who had run ahead. In the backpack Joey fell silent, watching the movement of the trees and flitting of the birds.

"There are not many homes that open onto such a forest. I'm sure the kids will love it there. Eventually, I want to build another tree house for them."

"Eventually? You've got so many dreams: England, planting churches, the cottage, a new church building. Your dreaming never stops."

"That's who I am, Lisa. God wired me that way."

They walked in silence for awhile; the beauty of the forest recharged their spirits. Lisa had lost herself in the sounds and smells of the magical environment before something snatched her back to reality.

"Where are the lads?" She felt alarmed, her eyes scanning the forest around them. "Where are they? I can't see them." Before they could call, Nathan came running toward them.

"Dad. Mum." Nathan was frantic. "I can't find Michael! We were playing and then he just disappeared." He sobbed.

"I tried to keep an eye on him. I turned around and he was just gone!"

"Calm down, kiddo." Jay sounded confident but Lisa sensed it was an act. "He can't just disappear. He's probably hiding behind a tree." Jay patted his shoulder. "Show us were you were playing."

"Over there." Nate pointed and then ran to the area. "We got right here and then he was gone." Nate started crying again.

Jay and Lisa took turns calling Michael's name. But the forest gave no answers.

"What do we do, Jay? I'm worried." Lisa had turned pale. "What if we don't find him?"

"We'll find him. Please Lord, be our helper." He looked at his watch. Night would come soon enough and chances were slim of finding him in the dark. "We should have brought a flashlight."

*   *   *

Michael had slipped down a prickly slope. The brambles snagged his jacket and had pinned him on his back so he couldn't move enough to sit up. His face and legs stung. Above, clouds clustered and a distant rumble shook the ground. Michael called out for his brother, but his voice was small in the forest and only the wind replied. The forest grew darker. Michael's stomach fluttered. Everywhere he looked, he saw shadows, shadows that moved and swayed.

"Help me, Mum, Dad." The shadows crowded shoulder to shoulder. Michael's teeth chattered. The shadows bent over him and Michael felt his heart would shoot through his chest. One shadow blinked. Michael let out a shrill cry. It moved closer, its eyes staring intently at him.

"Help!" Michael cried weakly. Fear had knocked the breath from his lungs.

From the shadows, a hand reached toward him. Then there was a face—a woman's face coming close, her breath hot, and her eyes cold like a snake.

Michael struggled to untangle himself from the branches. "Mum! Dad! Help." His wriggling only tightened the grip the branches had on his winter jacket.

The woman stared. "Hello there." Her voice rose as if she took pleasure in his predicament. A long finger touched Michael's cheek and traced his face and neck. He flinched in response. "You're scared aren't you, little rabbit? Your heart's thumping wildly." Her fingers wrapped around Michael's small wrist and tightened like a vice. "You would break so easily," she hissed between her teeth.

"Stop, you're hurting me." Michael was scared. He could feel a warm sensation, trickling down his pant leg. He whimpered.

"Shush. Shush. Don't make a noise."

"I want my mum and dad." Above, Michael heard someone call his name. He looked up. "I'm here! Mum and Dad! Here I am. Down here. Help!" There was noise and then he saw their faces peering down the embankment.

Their sudden presence startled the woman; she straightened and retreated a step. She called up to them, "He's down here." She waved and then turned back to Michael. "You brave little soldier, let me help you up. Here, take my hand." With a theatrical flair the woman pulled the child free.

Michael felt a rush of relief when his parents arrived at his side.

"I found him here. What a brave boy you have." The woman attempted to give him a hug but Michael wanted none of it. He recoiled at her touch and clambered into his mother's arms. "I want to go home now. Please, can we go home?"

"You're safe now, cowboy." Michael felt his father's arms wrap around him and his mother in a hug. He couldn't remember anything feeling so good. "You sure gave us a scare."

Michael began to cry. "I'm sorry." He felt the wet of his pants and cried more.

"You don't need to be sorry." His father's voice sounded calm and reassuring. "You've done nothing wrong. Let's just make sure you're okay." Michael let his mother lower him to the ground and held still while his father looked him over. "Hey kiddo, you've got a couple scratches, but you're fine." He pointed to his forehead then to his own cheek. "We both got a scratch today. Matching battle scars."

Michael watched as his father stood and appeared ready to thank the woman for her help. Instead, he drew back. The woman smiled and her eyes lingered on his father.

The strange woman turned to his mother and touched her arm. "I'm so glad I found him. This is a lonely stretch of forest. Poor child, he could have been trapped here for hours. It's a miracle that I discovered him." The woman's eyes scanned the forest. "It's the magic of this place. I was supposed to find your son."

His mother pulled away. "God protected our son, and we're grateful you helped us. But there's nothing magical about this place."

The woman's eyes narrowed. "Oh, you better believe in its power. If you don't…"

Dad cut her off with an abrupt goodbye. "We need to make our way home." Michael felt his father take his hand. It felt big and strong and eased his apprehension. "Kiddo, you're going to be okay." They started up the embankment, and although his father had placed himself between the family and the woman, Michael could still feel her stare. At the top of the rise, he turned and saw the woman walking away.

She stopped and, without turning, said in a voice that seemed to fill the forest, "Jacob Knight, there is a powerful force seeking control of your life. Beware." She spun and looked up the embankment at them, her eyes wild. "Leave this place. Leave while you still can."

The tone in her voice made Michael shiver. The family huddled close. "I'll take my chances. We don't scare easily. The force that lives in me and my family is the God of all creation. His power is greater than all the evil this world can contain. We belong to God and we'll stay until He tells us otherwise."

The woman's face darkened. She turned and walked away.

His father stood defiant, staring down the path until the woman was out of sight. "The brass of that woman!" Michael watched his parents exchange glances. "Remind me to tell you something about her."

"I will."

The clouds that had been threatening released big drops of rain and the darkness of early evening deepened.

"Let's get out of here before we're completely lost."

Michael agreed. He wanted nothing more than to be home.

CHAPTER TWELVE

—⚭—

Richard McGregor was about to blow a gasket. These religious fanatics intended to build some cathedral or temple thing opposite his house, and that fact didn't sit well. Fortunately, the public notice gave him a chance to fight. The council would meet January 10th.

Jean knew what was coming next. This would become another hobby horse for her husband. Richard had rambled on for the past half hour and was becoming quite a bore. They'd been sitting in front of the fireplace, and Jean was tired of his prattling. She watched the flames lick the logs and shoot sparks up the chimney.

"Richard, please give this church thing a rest. We don't need the added stress."

"That's just it, Jean. That's what they want. They want everyone to give up fighting."

"No one is fighting but you."

"Jean, if no one tries to stop this thing, we'll never have a moment of peace again. I can handle this. You don't need to worry at all. Soon, everything will be back to normal."

"And what's normal anymore?" She rubbed her eyes. "When you get like this, you're unbearable. Remember the last time?"

"What last time?"

"With Gerald. You almost lost your job over that incident. You made him look pretty foolish in front of the whole office staff."

"He had it coming."

"But he was your boss." She studied his face. "Please Richard, let go of this."

"Never mind, Jean. I know what I'm doing." He squeezed her and she melted. They kissed and the subject evaporated. Soon, the two of them headed for bed.

Jean picked out a silky nightgown and headed to the bathroom. *How did he do that? He manipulates me like putty.*

* * *

The allotted six months for renovation at Erindale had come and gone and Christmas was looming near. Jay was directing a Christmas musical. Nate was performing in a Christmas pageant at school. The lads kept asking when they were getting a tree; cards were still in their boxes and Lisa was frazzled. Lisa had made Nate's costume and signed up to help with food. At the moment she was packing boxes in the kitchen. Joey squirmed in his high chair and Lisa dropped a handful of Cheerios on the tray for him to eat.

Jay wanted to move in the cottage now. He'd done what he'd agreed to do: central heating, carpeting, new plumbing, and had painted everything that needed paint. Only the kitchen cabinets remained. They were on back order. To Jay that was simply an inconvenience; to Lisa, cabinets were essential.

Jay tried to comfort her. "Lisa, we've got lights, heat, water, phone, everything including the kitchen sink. We can manage without cupboards for a couple of weeks. We could make this a memorable Christmas by celebrating in our new home. It could be wonderful."

"Maybe wonderful for you, but certainly not for me."

They were really arguing over a couple of weeks, give or take a few days. "Lisa, payments begin now on the cottage whether we're in it or not. If we're out of the manse, the church is responsible for the mortgage payments. We can't afford double payments."

That was the clincher. They would move. But Lisa still had her concerns. In ten years of marriage, she'd never seen Jay so stressed. She'd watched his energy level drop as the work droned on. It had to finish soon. Not only had he continued his ministry with the usual vigor, but he had become a builder of dreams. He could instill a vision in the minds and hearts of the congregation. Perhaps even the community. Lisa finally agreed to put her differences aside and work with Jay instead of against him. There was little else she could do.

*   *   *

By midmorning the move turned into a catastrophe. The moving van got stuck trying to get up the new driveway. The tires spun in the gravel and dirt until they couldn't move in either direction. It had to be unloaded twenty yards away, forcing the fuming movers to trek up to the house with each piece of furniture. It had been raining for days and the ground was saturated. The new heating system developed air locks which stopped the circulation. The movers had tracked mud onto the new carpeting. At one point Lisa locked herself in the bathroom. When she came out, her eyes were red and puffy.

At about one in the afternoon, she got her second wind. She had never felt quite right about this place, but she couldn't put her finger on the reason. Now, she charged into the task.

Five days before Christmas, a fresh pine tree stood in the living room of Erindale cottage. Its lights sparkled, enchanting the boys. The family still had to circumnavigate between rows of boxes in every room. Jay's theology books were stacked along the wall upstairs. Six boxes sat in the kitchen with the tops open. That way Lisa could glance at their contents without tearing everything open. Nathan and Michael dug in the boxes for toys, but were soon playing with the cardboard instead. Their bedroom became a train station with box cars running from end to end.

*   *   *

McGregor decided it was time to put his strategy to work. He first selected key individuals in the community that showed leadership quality. He plied them with flattery and friendship. Second, he used trigger words to get results.

"A cult here in Kingsbridge? Of course we'll support you. If it comes from the States and it is religious, it's got to be questionable. We can never be too careful. Next thing we'll know, they'll be chanting on street corners and asking for money. What can we do to help?"

"You can start by coming to supper tomorrow night. Say around seven?" McGregor repeated for the umpteenth time. "We'll be outlining a course of community action to counter this proposal. I'm convinced that together we can quickly turn the decision around in our favor." McGregor finished with a firm handshake. "It's great to have you on board."

*   *   *

Jean was busy cooling her apple pies. She lined them along the window ledge and opened the window a crack. She was humming when Richard walked in. He told her he'd been out visiting some neighbors and that set off alarm bells for Jean. Her contentment evaporated in a second. She had a feeling Richard was up to no good.

"I've invited some neighbors over for supper tomorrow night. I figured it's about time we get acquainted."

"Thanks for including me in this decision. We've been here for two years, why invite the neighbors over now?" She studied Richard's eyes. "What's going on?"

"Nothing. Nothing at all. They'll be here around seven. Probably about fifteen people or so." He left the room.

Jean knew the drill. By tomorrow evening, their home would become a war room full of strangers with one growing passion; to eradicate a menace from their community. Jean felt sick.

Later that night, as she climbed into bed, Jean found no comfort in her soul. Once again, an all-consuming passion would control her husband like it had so many times before. Each time, his activities wounded her. Each time, she felt the distance between them grow. Choked with silent sobs, she closed her eyes and tried to erase her pain, but it would not go away. Her attempts at contenting her husband always proved futile. She felt imprisoned, her life a tangle of regret and growing fear. She closed her eyes and tried desperately to put her fears aside and sleep.

She failed.

* * *

At the stroke of seven, strangers appeared at the McGregor's front door. Jean put on a smile and welcomed them, knowing that Richard had handpicked these people as part of his agenda. They would oppose, defy, and defeat the plans for the church proposal. A new church had not been erected in this village for the past one hundred years. The several edifices that housed any form of worship were close to empty.

Jean was surprised to discover Richard had invited a clergyman. He wore a frayed clerical collar. Mr. Madlaw introduced himself as a reverend and moved into the living room. He seemed eager to join in. The house was full of strangers. Jean was furious but hid her emotions from all but Richard, who ignored her glares.

McGregor clinked his glass and gave a warm welcome. "Thanks for coming tonight. I know it's a busy time getting ready for Christmas celebrations, and we appreciate you taking time from your busy schedule." A few people offered polite smiles. "The weather hasn't been very kind. But is it ever? Good ol' Bob Hope once said about our country's weather, England is the only place on earth where you can have four seasons in the swing of a golf club." The comment brought chuckles. "Here's what we're up against."

Richard handed out sheets of paper, which contained grievances against the proposed plans for a church building. He pointed out that the lane adjacent could not handle heavy traffic. There was no traffic light at the end of the lane, and it could cause serious overload. A further point included the green belt zoning. It would require major changes and could open the door for all kinds of industry if allowed.

A fidgety man asked, "What about services to that property? Do you know if there are sanitation services there?"

"Absolutely not! Sewerage and water mains are not available on that piece of land. The disruption would be significant."

Reverend Madlaw spoke. "But far more important is the type of people we are dealing with here. This Mr. Knight is a peculiar man, you know. I have seen him talking to people on the streets and preaching on the corners. One would think this were a pagan village the way he goes about recruiting. I'm quite sure he's teaching strange doctrines. It's a religious cult. He attracts teenagers in town. He holds little clandestine meetings in people's homes. My wife discovered one being held on our street."

A timid woman spoke, "But this man is a reverend just like you."

The minister flushed. "I don't belong to the same faith as that man. He preaches about sacrifice, blood, and death. We took such theology out of our books years ago." His voice rose. "They actually sing about blood and death. How twisted is that?" Madlaw gave an exaggerated shudder. "He teaches myths and superstitions. He says that Jesus was divine. Please, don't classify me with a man like Knight."

"I'm so sorry. I didn't mean to make you look bad." The woman blanched.

An older woman sat in the corner of the room, her thick dark hair braided and wrapped tightly around her head. She spoke with a heavy Baltic dialect. "This man has a strange power over the youth of Kingsbridge. I know. I know personally." She became emotional. "He got to my son." She began to sob. "He comes home from these meetings, very troubled, very upset. I can't talk to him for hours after. He just goes into his room and locks the door." She dabbed her eyes.

McGregor wrapped up the evening with some closing remarks, and then set a time for the next meeting.

One man had never entered the room, but listened from the hallway. He appeared ambivalent and slipped away before the evening finished. Dungess worked alone and needed no one.

CHAPTER THIRTEEN

——∿∿——

Jay felt the bed move; the motion dragged him from his slumber like a ship pulls an anchor from the deep. He rolled onto his back and noticed Lisa sitting upright.

"Jay, wake up." She slipped from the bed and padded to the bedroom door.

"What is it?"

She paused before shouting, "It's Michael!"

Jay tossed the covers back and followed her toward to the boy's room. They found Michael sitting in bed, gasping for breath. His small hand clutched at his chest. He struggled to draw a breath, but could only manage short wheezes. His crying came out as croaks, and his eyes were round with fear.

Lisa scooped him up in her arms in an effort to calm him to ease his breathing.

"Hang in there, cowboy," Jay said. "We're going to get you to the hospital. I'm calling the ambulance right now." He sprinted down the stairs to get the phone. An eternity of seconds slipped by while he waited for someone to pick up.

Jay gave instructions to the dispatcher and headed back up the stairs. Nathan and Joey woke from the commotion and the bedroom became pandemonium. "The ambulance is on the way. Nathan, help get Joey dressed. We're taking Mikey to the hospital." Jay prayed out loud as he rushed from one room to another. "Jesus, help us. Help Mikey right now!" He moved Lisa and Michael to the bathroom. "Steam, Lisa, he needs steam." He turned on the hot water.

Lisa carried Michael into the bathroom. She could feel his body stiffen. "The lights Jay, they're too harsh."

Jay flicked the switch but left the hall light on. "Michael, the Lord will help you." Steam billowed into the air as the tub filled with hot water. A radiant electric heater blazed warmth into the room. When the water was right, Lisa stripped his clothing from him and lowered Michael into the bathtub. The boy's rasping grew worse.

Minutes passed like hours. Finally, Jay heard the sound of the ambulance arriving. The medics took charge in a calm, quiet manner. Soon Michael lay on a stretcher, an oxygen mask covering his nose and mouth. His eyes dimmed to a helpless stare. His wheezing grew louder. His skin had gone from pink to putty gray, and Jay feared the worst.

Lisa rode in the ambulance as Jay bundled Joey and Nathan in the car and followed. Red and blue lights flashed arcs of color against the trees but the sirens were silent. Everyone was sleeping. Jay functioned on instinct as he sped down the highway toward Chester's Children's Hospital, his mind muddled by the suddenness of the attack. What had triggered it this time?

All was silent as the ambulance glided out into the open countryside, racing through intersections and warning lights. Jay could picture Lisa hunched over Michael's little body, praying desperately for help. His prayer became a jumble of fears, and his heart begged for hope. "Lord, spare Mikey. Help us through this."

The emergency room was an antiseptic hive filled with coughs and moans and scurrying nurses. Overhead lights illuminated everything with sterile florescence. They wheeled Michael into a waiting cubicle. Immediately a swarm of medical personnel gathered around his bed, poking and prodding.

"Please stand back," a nurse said as she pushed herself between parents and child. Lisa choked up as Michael's hand slipped from her grip.

"Come on." Jay took Lisa's hand. "We need to let them work and Nathan and Joey need us." He led her from the ER, the image of Michael lying as limp as a rag, scratching and wheezing for every breath branded on his brain.

The night passed slowly, one agonizing hour after another. The new day traded a bitter gray sky for the blackness of night. The family was exhausted; Nate and Joey finally fell asleep, curled up in chairs. Lisa's eyes were red rimmed and her hair was a frazzle. Slumped over a plastic chair, staring at the floor, Jay noticed he wore no socks. He rubbed his face and felt the stubble. He didn't care. He was pleading for his son's life and nothing else mattered.

The medical staff allowed Jay and Lisa a few moments to visit their son. Michael lay inside a plastic oxygen tent. He looked so frail. Jay watched as Lisa slipped her hand in to touch Michael.

It was nearly noon when Dr. Andrews stopped at Michael's bed. With only a flashing glance at the patient, he studied his chart and turned to the anxious parents. "Your son has an acute case of epiglottisises. It's a bacterial infection that inflames the pharynx and causes the epiglottis to swell, restricting his breathing. I see from his records that he had a similar episode about two years ago." They nodded. "He's obviously prone to respiratory problems." The doctor pushed his glasses on his forehead. "The good news is that this is bacterial and antibiotics usually cure it." He looked at the chart and flipped his glasses down. "I see the ER doctor had considered a tracheotomy but decided against it."

Lisa looked as if she might faint. "But he's only six years old."

"Whatever it takes to help him live through this." He paused. "Let's keep our fingers crossed."

"A lot of good that will do," Lisa protested. "Since prayer got us this far, I think we're better off sticking with what we know works."

The doctor shrugged and started to turn.

"What could have brought this on? We didn't have any warning," Jay asked.

"No idea. I'd suggest an allergic reaction." Dr. Andrews checked the equipment but made little eye contact with Michael. He turned and left.

"He seemed helpful," Jay said.

Lisa frowned. "Helpful?" She wrung her hands. "His bedside manners are pathetic."

* * *

It was the worst time of the year for a hospital stay. Nursing stations were decorated with ornaments and baubles, and nurses wore glitter in their hair. The cheerful ornamentation did little for the sick sequestered in rooms off the long corridor. Patients lay ill with little sign of celebrating. Only the fortunate would smile and look forward to Christmas at home. Outside, traffic snarled to a crawl while the city streets were crowded with commercial chaos. Only seven days remained before Christmas.

Lisa stayed by Michael's side all week long. In times like these she displayed a remarkable resilience to sleep deprivation and mental fatigue. Nothing wore her down. When Michael coughed, she came to attention and caressed his brow; always gentle, always hopeful, always with a prayer.

* * *

Jay had Joey and Nathan at home. He fixed meals, changed diapers, and taxied Nathan back and forth to school. In between, he did his pastoral work. He still needed to put the finishing touches on Christmas messages and had a musical ready to perform. At night, when all was quiet, Jay would climb the stairs to his waiting desk where he would attempt to put the puzzled pieces of their lives back together. Why had life become so crushing? Each morning, Nathan would find his dad asleep at his desk.

"Dad, Dad, wake up. I'm late for school."

* * *

Four days before Christmas, Dr. Andrews removed Michael's oxygen tent. Michael's breathing sounded healthy. Either the antibiotics were working, or it was the power of prayer, or both. When Michael's cheeks flushed and his mischievous grin returned, Lisa knew he was well.

"Mum, can we go home now?" His release papers came at 4:00 p.m. that day.

* * *

Christmas approached like a freight train and forced the Knights back into their busy schedule with family, school, and church. The musical had brought in crowds of visitors. Nate's school performance turned out to be exceptional, and Jay dutifully saved it on film. Lisa scrubbed the house clean and welcomed friends who came with gifts and goodies. But in all this, something had changed. Jay and Lisa were viewing the activities less seriously and their family with greater joy. So what if someone forgot their lines in the musical, or some presents went unwrapped? They had what mattered most—faith and family.

On Christmas Eve, the congregation of Kingsbridge Fellowship celebrated with a simple candlelight ceremony, commemorating the coming of Christ as the true light of the world. Afterward, people hugged one another, exchanged Christmas blessing, and lingered until their coats warmed them enough to head into the winter night.

After cookies and milk around the fire, the boys reluctantly climbed into bed. Jay led the family in a prayer of thanks. Lisa was content knowing her children were all safe.

* * *

Christmas morning, Lisa and Jay awoke to the squeals of excitement. The lads had discovered their Christmas stockings at the foot of their beds. With a yawn, Lisa pulled back the bedroom curtains and gasped with delight. The trees shimmered with a fine layer of new fallen snow. The winter sun had illuminated a forest of diamonds. The air shimmered as tiny avalanches of white powder fell and floated down. She turned her head, "Jay, you've got to see this." In the midst of their struggles, God reminded them of His faithfulness. Lisa whispered, "Thank you, Lord." Mesmerized by the wonderland, they held each other tight, not wanting the moment to slip away.

Soon the kids rumbled down the stairs, eager to discover what surprises lay hidden beneath the tree. After the gifts were unwrapped, there came the family's annual dramatization of the nativity. It always brought Jay and Lisa to tears. Overlooking the giggling that came because Michael was cast as Mary, the family felt touched by the reality of a plan far greater than anything in their little world. Jesus came to rescue sinners just like them.

The grand finale of the day was Lisa's scrumptious meal fit for royalty. Michael wanted to pray. "Hello Jesus. Happy birthday!" He paused. "Thanks for helping me breathe better. I love You. Amen." That prayer made the day perfect.

Nathan got a set of miniature racing cars, and Jay couldn't wait to play with them. The boys took the set upstairs and started assembling the tracks. Jay wired up the transformer and the boys set the five inch cars racing each other. They all lay on their stomachs, except Joey, who wanted to grab the cars and throw them. Jay monitored Joey carefully as the older boys won lap after lap.

Nate cheered, "We win, Dad. Hah, you and Joey are the losers."

A loud banging from below interrupted the joy. It vibrated against their tummies and Nate scrambled to his feet. Someone below was angry. Nate was jittery, "Dad, I don't like that. What are we doing wrong?"

"We are doing nothing wrong, son. Let's just keep playing and cheer softly."

Jay had designed a suspended floor that floated four inches above the existing hardwood flooring. He lined the cavity with insulation to absorb sounds and Lisa chose a heavy duty carpet and padding.

The night was drawing in and the room lay in shadows. Jay and the boys were having fun. Michael snuggled close to Jay. "Thanks Daddy, you're the best." It was a fleeting moment of seriousness. With a sly grin he pounced on his dad and Nathan and Joey piled on top. But before it got started, the laughter faded like an echo.

Nathan stopped playing and stood facing the window. His body had gone rigid. Unable to make a sound, he stumbled backward. Michael pulled away from the tangle and jumped to his feet, staring in the same direction. Instantly, his breathing became raspy like the scraping of metal. "Dad..." He stepped backward. "It's him. He's coming after us." He grabbed his dad's hand, but kept his eyes fixed on the image.

"What's the matter?" His voice trailed off as he saw what the boys were staring at. He got up slowly and pulled the boys away from the window. "Get behind me kids. Now." His voice was croaky. "Lisa! Lisa, call the police." The kids whimpered and Jay felt their bodies tremble.

Lisa rushed to the bottom of the stairs. "What's wrong?"

"Just call the police. Do it now. It's him."

Only inches from where they stood, a face had appeared outside their upstairs window. It seemed to be floating, with eyes so cold it made the children shiver. The face raged and raised arms with clawed-like fingers. He slammed himself against the glass. The glass flexed inward until a long shard broke free and fell to the floor. The terror that had paralyzed the boys finally erupted from their throats in a series of shrieks. They jumped backward, each grabbing at Jay's clothes for dear life.

"I'll get you. I'll get all of you." The face snarled.

Jay's reaction was instant. He rushed to the window and unlatched it, shoving it open and prepared to knock the man off the ladder. "Get off our property. Get down or I'll knock you down."

"The police are on the way." Lisa burst into the room. The children ran to her.

By the time she'd gotten to the window, the man was back on the ground. Something had sent the intruder sprinting for safety.

* * *

Ian and June Langley lived around the corner from Erindale Cottage. Ian was reading the *Daily Telegraph* in the lounge when he heard the noise. June was in the kitchen cleaning up from the evening meal when the sound made her stop. Ian and June met in the doorway. June said, "It sounds like a child's scream. We've got to do something." Ian rushed out the kitchen door and into the shadows of his neighbor's yard. He could hardly believe his eyes. To his horror, he saw Dungess perched on the top of his painter's ladder screaming obscenities and threats at someone. It had to be the Knight children. "He's going to kill someone. He must be out of his mind." Ian rushed toward the ladder.

"Get down you crazy fool. What's the matter with you?" Ian shook the ladder and Dungess wobbled, grabbing the window ledge with only his left hand. The children kept screaming. "Dungess, you're an idiot. You've gone too far."

Ian rattled the ladder and suddenly Dungess' foot slipped. He cursed the world as he dangled there with only a window ledge to hold on to. Ian waited a while longer and then moved the ladder close enough for the man to grab hold. He was shaking when he touched ground.

"Don't you ever do a stunt like that again, Dungess, or you'll have to answer to me." By the time the police had arrived, the man had put his ladder out of sight and disappeared. Officer Jones took down the information and seemed to have little patience over the incident.

CHAPTER FOURTEEN

—◦◦◦—

McGregor's office towered twelve stories above the dirty city of Manchester overlooking a myriad of uneven rooftops and crowded pedestrian walkways. Directly below, he could see a run down shopping center, cold and tagged by gangs. In the distance, three tall industrial smokestacks belched thick vapor into the air.

McGregor forced his mind to focus on the Kingsbridge project. In the outer office, the phone rang and Richard's secretary answered. Her voice carried through the open door.

"Mr. McGregor's office. Can I help you?" He heard Margaret pause. "Yes, Mr. Roberts, please hold a moment." The intercom sounded.

"Mr. McGregor, Mr. Roberts from the Cheshire County Planning Department is on line three." Margaret went back to her nail observation.

Richard grabbed the receiver. "Hello, Mr. Roberts. Thank you for returning my call. I know you're a busy man, and I won't detain you. I have some documentation here that will interest you. It concerns Proposal 375. I believe it is coming up next week at your council meeting."

"Proposal 375? Can you enlighten me on which one that is? We have twenty-four recommendations currently pending."

"It's the proposal seeking planning permission for the construction of a church facility in Kingsbridge. It's Councilman Clary's old farm property."

"Ah yes, I remember now. It's so rare to have a recommendation for a new church these days, how could I have forgotten?"

"Yes, well I have a few—"

Roberts broke in. "We have reviewed their proposal along with the architect's drawings and were really quite impressed. I believe the architect hales from the United States."

"Yes sir, probably so, but—"

"Yet the design is impressively suited for the local Cheshire area. He even intends to incorporate the local sandstone into the design. It really inspired me. I guess I expected some gaudy American rendition of St. Paul's cathedral with golden arches." He chuckled.

McGregor's face flushed with annoyance. "That's all very interesting Mr. Roberts, but I represent a substantial group of local residents in Kingsbridge. And frankly, there is a strong opposition to the plans for this church proposal. These residents have some legitimate concerns. I've taken the liberty to address these issues and have sent a copy to your office. I would also like to represent the concerned residents of Kingsbridge at that council meeting."

"Well, I'm sorry to hear that Mr…"

"McGregor. Richard McGregor."

"Yes, Mr. McGregor. You are welcome to attend and present your case. What are the main objections?"

"Well," Richard switched the phone to his other ear. "Item one and two expresses concern for the heavy use of Sandy Lane, which runs between the original farmhouse and the property in consideration. At present, the entrance to the property in question comes off Sandy Lane, directly opposite a substantial residence. There could be a conflict of use. The lane is definitely not adequate for heavy traffic and officially it is only one lane wide. We feel this could cause serious congestion. Sandy Lane meets the main road with only a stop sign at the T-junction. If it would be necessary to put a traffic light there, it could create traffic backup all the way into town. No one would be happy to see a traffic light installed there, simply for the sake of a church." Richard moved quickly to the next item.

"Item three is concerned with sanitation requirements and item four with parking. We have twelve objections to bring before the council."

"Well Mr..."

"McGregor, sir."

"Yes, McGregor, of course. You can address these issues, but I have to tell you, the council is probably going to give them the green light. I can imagine that Clary himself will not be pleased if something slows this down." He paused. "It's obvious you've spent some time on this. So, you plan to attend?"

"I owe it to the residents of Kingsbridge to represent them."

"You're welcome to address these issues when 375 comes up for discussion. The meeting is at the Town Hall next Thursday evening at seven-thirty p.m. See you there."

"One more thing Mr. Roberts, for information only." He hesitated. "All of the Kingsbridge churches have their own burial grounds surrounding them."

"You mean cemetery, Mr. McGregor? Indians have burial grounds, Englishmen have cemeteries."

"Thank you, sir. Has the council considered them wanting a burial ground?"

"Cemetery!" corrected Roberts.

"Yes, cemetery."

Roberts chuckled. "I assure you Mr. McGregor, there are no such plans for a cemetery. Besides, they need all the space they can get for their living members who drive cars. I don't foresee that as a problem. Of course, you can present your burial ground theory if you feel so inclined."

"No, no need, thank you for your time. Good day, sir."

Richard hung up and glanced down at his notes. *I need a convincing delegation at that meeting. I'll call that priest. He'll come. He won't be afraid to speak.*

* * *

Lisa picked up the phone on the third ring. She and Jenny were having a chat over a cup of tea and strawberry jam scones.

"Knight's residence, can I help you?" A man's voice unfamiliar to Lisa asked to speak with the vicar.

She replied, "My husband's out right now, but he will be glad to return your call."

"If he would, please. In fact, I would prefer to meet him in person if that would work. I live in the big white house just off of Sandy Lane. My name is Richard McGregor."

"I am sure my husband would be happy to visit you. Would you like him to come today?"

"Yes, anytime after 7:30 tonight. I'll look forward to meeting Vicar Knight."

Lisa hung up and scribbled a note. She turned to Jenny, "It seems a Mr. McGregor wants Jay to pay him a visit tonight. It must be urgent. He lives over by Fox Hill. He asked to speak to the vicar."

"God must be working on him. Wouldn't that be just the thing? Neighbor's finding Christ before the church is built."

* * *

Jay drove up Sandy Lane at seven-thirty sharp. Only now had it dawned on him that this might not be an altogether joyous occasion. He parked his car, grabbed his Bible and headed toward the big white house.

Jean McGregor answered the door and seemed surprised to see Jay standing there. "Hello, I'm Jacob Knight. Mr. McGregor has asked me to stop by this evening to meet with him."

"Oh, he did? I'm sorry, I wasn't aware of that. But, that is not unusual. Please come in and I'll get my husband." She led him into the living room where a fire roared. "My name is Jean, by the way. Have a seat. I'll get Richard."

Jay was admiring a large collection of horse brasses which hung on the wall. He turned and was startled to find McGregor standing there in silence.

"Hello, thanks for coming. I'm Richard McGregor," he said with an amiable smile.

"I'm Jay Knight. You've got a great collection here."

"Thanks. Jean and I have collected those over the years." He explained, "Horse brasses are worn only on the tack of draft horse's. Shire horses." He pointed to a framed photograph. "See, they're attached to a strap called the martingale."

"Yes, I've got a couple from a team of Clydesdales."

"Have a seat." Richard motioned for Jay to sit opposite him. "I see you came prepared." He nodded toward the Bible.

"Oh, yes," Jay smiled. "It's the tool of the trade. He laid it on the coffee table and focused on McGregor.

"You won't be needing that tonight." His voice suddenly chilled. "Let me get right to the point, Mr. Knight. I've heard of the plans you have to build a church next door."

The sudden change in McGregor's demeanor startled Jay. "Yes, we are. It seems an ideal location for a worship center. We're very excited about the prospects. We've searched for a long time." He paused before adding, "Obviously, you have some concerns."

"Let me be as direct as I can, Vicar." McGregor's face hardened.

"Jay. Just call me Jay."

"I want you to know that I have no malice toward you or your parishioners. But there are a number of local residents who see this as an unwelcome invasion in our quiet community."

"Our congregation is made up of residents from Kingsbridge. Several of our members live along this very road. This is their home, too. You should meet some of them. We've got a really great group of people. And I think you'd be impressed if you saw the architect's drawings. I have them in the car. Let me get them."

"Not interested. Our concern is not with the visual appearance of the structure. It's the congestion it will bring. And the consensus of opinion is that Kingsbridge does not need another church."

"We have a growing congregation and our people have been giving sacrificially so they can build a house for the Lord. We want to do everything necessary to comply with the wishes of the community. We will carefully consider your objections. But we have spent time, money, and great effort to get this far. My people have been raising funds for four years to get to this point. So, naturally, we are very hopeful the council will approve our application."

"Your people, huh? Your people? Well, our people, who live right here, have also spent much time considering this church and we intend to defeat your plans."

"I'm surprised. Three weeks ago, our proposal wasn't public knowledge. But thanks for being candid with me. We are dependent upon God to guide us. If He wishes, He can block our plans at any time. He can cause these plans to succeed with or without your approval. Nothing can thwart God's plans."

"All's fair in love and war, Mr. Knight. You use your resources and I'll use mine. I will see you on Thursday night, seven-thirty sharp."

"I'll probably be there early." Jay smiled politely and stood to leave. At that same moment, Jean walked in with a tray of freshly baked scones, still hot from the oven. The smell was enticing. She sat the tray down between the two men.

"Oh, you can't leave now, Reverend Knight. I have some supper ready for us."

"Mr. Knight is just leaving. He won't be staying for supper." Richard's tone was icy.

Jean's face fell. "But you just arrived."

Jay smiled again. "Thank you, Jean, they look absolutely delicious. But I think it best that I leave now. I'm really touched by your hospitality."

Richard walked the visitor to the front door and opened it. "Good night."

* * *

Jean looked at her husband with disgust. "What was that all about? First, you failed to tell me you had invited someone and second, it's obvious that the conversation wasn't very pleasant for him. It's about the property next door isn't it?"

Before he had time to shake his head, a knock came at the door. Richard pulled it open to find Jay standing there with the roll of architect's drawings in hand. He was still smiling.

"Since I have these drawings with me, I thought you might appreciate looking them over before the meeting next week. You can return them to me then." He handed them to Richard, nodded courteously toward Jean, and left.

McGregor stood there staring as the man got into his car and drove away.

141

Jean's fury flared. "What is wrong with you?" She carried the scones back into the kitchen, and in one swift move, dumped them in the trash. Half a dozen scones were still cooling. With a single swipe of her arm, she sent the cooling scones flying across the room.

Jean untied her apron, turned off the kitchen light, and marched into the dining room. Richard sat studying the plans he had rolled out on the table.

"How about those scones?" He didn't bother to raise his head. "I'm famished."

"I'll bet you are." She threw the apron in his face. "The oven is pre-heated. All the ingredients are in the kitchen. Bake your own scones, I'm going to bed." She pounded the stairs and slammed the bedroom door. A few minutes later, Jean crawled into bed and sobbed into her pillow. She felt so empty and didn't know why. All she knew was that something in her life had to change. She had grown tired of enduring Richard's battles.

* * *

Richard watched dumbfounded as she moved to the bedroom. "What's got into her?" He grabbed the apron, headed to the kitchen, and turned on the light. Jean had trashed the whole supper. Scones were scattered across the floor. Others were in the trash. *What a waste. She knows I can't cook scones.* His hunger still gnawing at him, he rummaged through the trash and rescued two scones. He dusted off tea grounds. He was annoyed with his wife.

Richard sat up long into the night studying the drawings with intense interest. He scribbled pages of notes on a yellow legal pad. When weariness pressed him to sleep, he chose the sofa over his own bed. He decided it would be safer.

* * *

Jay arrived home with a heaviness he had not antici-
pated. He paced the floors in prayer for hours. He prayed
for Richard McGregor and for God's people in Kingsbridge
and the plans for God's house. He was feeling overwhelmed
at the mounting opposition against him. Where was all this
coming from?

* * *

The night of the town council meeting, the weather had
dropped at least ten degrees after nightfall. The car heater
was a lost cause. Jay picked up David and they headed to
the town hall. As Jay pulled out on the main road, he rolled
down his window to help defrost the windows. Using his
sleeve, he cleared a spot on the windshield.

Dave watched Jay and grinned. "It's hard to find good
mechanics these days."

Jay shivered. "I guess it depends on what you're driving.
I've heard there's a great mechanic in town for all Mercedes
owners."

"I'll pick up your car in the morning."

"That would be fantastic."

Jay and David arrived at the town hall at seven fifteen.
McGregor landed five minutes after the meeting had begun.
He was not alone. A fifteen member delegation crowded into
the room, disrupting the meeting. Several carried placards
protesting the church plans. There was a third element which
Jay had not considered; the landowner, Councilman Clary.
He sat glaring at the protestors.

Jay scratched his head. "Who are these people, David?
Where'd they come from?"

David shook his head and shrugged. "I'm baffled."

The last person seated was a man wearing a clerical
collar. But it was his wife who startled Jay the most. "Oh

143

no," he moaned, rolling his eyes at David. "It's Madlaw and his wife."

"Sounds like you've had some personal time with them."

"Not him." Jay nodded. "Her. She chased me down the street with her broom.

"She did what?"

"She gave my head a pretty good whack." He touched the side of his face recalling the scratches left by the insane attack. "Look at all this. It is a ploy to draw attention to themselves." Jay nodded toward the chairman. "Roberts is steaming mad. I should have seen this coming. Did you have any idea?"

David shook his head. "No idea. This McGregor guy seems to have a lot of clout."

Jay whispered, "We don't stand a chance."

"Surely, you don't mean that, Pastor. 'If God is for us...'"

"Point well taken."

The meeting adjourned at ten and when the final gavel came down, the plans had been defeated. The church could appeal the decision after modifying their plans. The entrance was the issue. The property bordered only one stretch of a country lane and the council had just blocked its use. A field separated the proposed church property from the main road that led into town. As the meeting adjourned, Councilman Clary stood and motioned for Jay to wait as he made his way toward them. "Let's talk outside."

CHAPTER FIFTEEN

England's spring arrived in all its usual grandeur. Everywhere there were splashes of the most dazzling colors and luxuriant fragrances that made the countryside sing. The world was a better place when England was in full bloom.

In two days, Kingsbridge Fellowship would make its final pitch to the Town Council. The debate had dragged on for months, and skirmishes kept threatening to blow sky high. Somehow everyone backed off just in time to regroup. So far, only Councilman Clary's suggestion worked. He offered a strip of land that would run alongside his field and open onto the main road. The final proposal recommended blocking off the original entrance from Sandy Lane. This new entrance would give the church major visibility and a long grand entrance from the main road. Clary would sell the strip of land for a mere two hundred pounds.

The elders were committed to prayer and fasting. Jay preached on accountability. Even the local newspaper had fun playing one group against the other. The church refused to show malice and believed they would find vindication.

* * *

It was a brilliant Sunday morning, the church was full, and the service had gone well. Jay gave the benediction and made his way to the door to greet people. A coffee time always followed the service and allowed time for visitors to get acquainted with church members. Someone slipped from behind Jay and sauntered toward the door.

"Trevor, what a surprise. I didn't realize you were in the service. Where were you sitting?"

"Who cares? I don't believe in all this rubbish anyway."

"Then why did you come? Why bother if it's so meaningless to you?"

"I like to watch all you chumps who think you've got something special."

"You're right; we do have something very special: a relationship with the eternal God. Something you need." Jay moved closer. "Trevor, you're welcome anytime, just as long as you don't disrupt others in their worship. These people come because they believe in something beyond themselves. We're convinced that Jesus is the answer to our lives. And I think that's why you come. You're looking for God because you know you need Him.

"Sounds like another sermon coming on. I'm out of here!" He took some quick steps toward the door. "This stuff is not for me."

"I think you want to believe in God, but are afraid." Jay raised his voice as Trevor walked away from the building. "You don't need to be afraid, Trevor."

Trevor ran.

* * *

Richard McGregor usually spent his Sundays gardening, rain or shine. He believed that the males of the human species bore some primal instinct to capture and dominate. It seemed right to cut the grass today.

Jean was busy in the kitchen with clean up. Richard pulled out the lawn mower, filled the tank with a mixture of petrol and oil, and rolled it to the top of the garden. One yank and the engine roared to life. He cut the first row and returned the mower with a quarter inch overlap. His fifth row looked the same as the first with meticulous precision. On his sixth row he became distracted as he glanced at the old barns across the road. The sight of them triggered a flush of anxiety.

"Good riddance to bad rubbish," He mumbled over the motor's roar.

What about those Christians, Richard?

Richard swung his head in both directions but saw no one.

You've obsessed over them. Why?

Richard stopped cutting and stared straight ahead. "Who said that?" But no one answered. Certain that his mind was playing tricks on him, he went back to cutting the grass. On his return pass, he noticed the line was no longer straight. He cursed.

That land doesn't belong to you. Who made you its caretaker?

Richard stopped again. "What's going on here? Where are you? Show yourself." He gripped the mower to steady himself. A cold sweat broke out on his forehead. He caught a glimpse of Jean staring at him through the kitchen window.

Richard felt irritated. This was nuts. Something stroked his face; a touch from something he couldn't see. He took a step back waved his arms at the invisible force. By the time he noticed it, the mower had crept down the slope on its own, rolling toward the house and chewing everything in its path. It finally ground to a halt and sputtered out.

Someone ran past the mower and headed toward him. "Richard?"

Why are you doing this to My people, Richard? They're good people, doing what I've asked them to do. You cannot thwart My plans.

"But, I mean…"

"Richard. What's wrong? Richard?"

Jean's voice irritated him. "I'm okay, Jean. Don't worry. Go back to the kitchen. Put the kettle on."

She held her place.

"I said, go away. Leave me alone."

Tears filled her eyes and her lip quivered. Slowly, she turned and walked back to the house.

Richard addressed the voice. "It's You isn't it? So You do exist."

Did you ever really doubt? You've always pretended not to believe in Me, but you've always known, haven't you? You've lived your life manipulating people to get your own way.

"Well, no, I mean yes, I guess. Where are you?" No clouds shifted or shapes formed in the grass cuttings. He studied the trees and watched for moving shadows, but saw no one. The voice was impossible to deny. His hands began to tremble. He walked up a slight incline toward the rear of the garden and grabbed the fence to steady himself. God was following him, he could feel it. Staring toward Fox Hill, he spoke with the One he'd always rejected.

God spoke.

And for the first time, Richard listened.

I finally have your attention. The voice drew so close he could almost feel His breath. *I've left clues for you since you were a child, but you always seem to ignore them.*

"Clues? What kind of clues?"

When your father passed away. You were only ten. I held you in My arms for hours, but you wouldn't cry. Instead I felt your anger.

"I remember. I blamed you for my dad's death." He leaned heavily on the fence. "I tossed my room."

That rage has simmered in your heart ever since.

"I know, and I can't seem to get beyond it."

You can't without me. When you rejected my comfort, I reached out in other ways. Jean was part of my plan. I knew she would be perfect for you.

His voice lowered. A caldron of emotion and scalding memories boiled in him. "I don't deserve her."

You take her for granted, so I put a business obstacle in your way: the Sainsbury account.

McGregor shook his head. "So, You arranged for me to lose that account? It would have been huge."

I've arranged your entire life, so you would depend on Me. I've influenced everything in your life to bring you to this moment. And not only for you.

Richard turned and saw Jean standing at the kitchen door. He could see tears stream down her cheeks. "Jean?" Richard knew.

You've stood in Jean's way. She calls to Me for help.

"I've stood in Jean's way? I never thought of that."

Now's the time to start thinking. You've made life lonely for her. She needs to feel loved. But you're ambition is consuming.

"I am so ashamed. How have I missed seeing You all these years?" He looked up. "What do I do now?"

"First, call Jacob Knight and get him over here. He will tell you everything you need to know about surrender.

Richard thought about Jay Knight. "How can I face him again? I've been his worst nightmare."

You're right, but he's forgiving. He will tell you how to find peace.

He felt empty, cored out, and left a mere husk of himself.

He felt filled. Changed.

Richard ran to the house.

"Richard? What's happening to you? Are you okay?"

"Never better, Jean." He paused a moment to look in her eyes. "Man, have I got a lot to tell you. But first, I've got to make a phone call." He headed to the phone, then stopped. "Jean have I told you lately that I love you?" He kissed her passionately on the lips and then rushed to pick up the phone.

CHAPTER SIXTEEN

—⚒—

Noel Dungess staggered out of the Bear's Paw. He gripped the door frame for an instant to steady himself, then let go. His body stumbled forward until he slammed into the side of his work van. He felt nothing. The last few hours had left him self-anesthetized. He struggled into the van and cranked the engine. It coughed to life. Dungess pulled out onto the main road and shot into oncoming traffic then jerked the vehicle into the proper lane. A car swerved. Tires screeched as if in pain.

It took a moment for him to get his bearings, but when he did he recognized a familiar car. "Well, what do ya know, it's that stupid American." Dungess shoved his foot on the accelerator and rammed the back of the car. "Just a little bump," he slurred. The car fishtailed and then straightened. Dungess howled and rammed it again. "What's wrong with him? The idiot just keeps driving." He ground his teeth. "Maybe you need a harder knock—like this." Bumpers collided and a piece of the cars tailpipe fell off. "Oops." Dungess chuckled and finally pulled off the road. He watched the American's car until it was out of sight. A minute later, he passed out.

The sound of rain pelting the metal skin of the van jolted Dungess awake. He wiped drool from his chin and looked at his watch. It was one o'clock in the morning. Somehow he'd steered his van into a shrub along the side of the road. He started the motor and drove the last mile home. He climbed out of the van, shoved a big screwdriver in his back pocket, and pushed through a hedgerow toward Erindale Cottage. The American had parked his car at the front gate. Dungess staggered forward and cursed the man as he made long swipes on every panel of the car with his screwdriver, leaving long scars in the paint.

Elda was standing in the doorway when he returned. Her bellowing made his head throb. He slapped the old witch and it knocked her backward. She fell backward, disappeared into the kitchen, then returned with a fry pan in her hand. She wielded it with precision. One whack and he crumpled to his knees. He managed to crawl into the garage before he collapsed.

The concussion stupefied Dungess and his mind conjured up a voice that had been dead for years. "Noel, you're a worthless piece of sewer. You were supposed to be a priest, but you failed. Look at you now. You're a dirty little bugger. I should have tossed you in the river the day you were born." The wind moaned and blew in under the garage door. Outside, rain hit the ground in jagged sheets.

* * *

McGregor had called the vicar several times that evening, but the line was always busy. He decided to try later. By night fall, his head buzzed with burning questions. Where does evil come from? Why do people suffer? What about Buddhists? The voice of God was now a soft whisper but still as clear as a bell. As some new truth emerged, Richard would confess his failure to God and then to Jean.

He wondered if his wife felt like a priest in a confessional. Each time he confessed something, he felt lighter. What was this power? By one in the morning, he felt ten years younger. By two thirty, twenty years of stress and guilt had slipped away.

Around four o'clock, Jean fell asleep in an overstuffed chair. Richard covered her with a tartan throw and kissed her on the forehead. His eyes burned and his clothes were disheveled, but he felt great. The sound of heavy rain splashing could not distract him; he was in another realm. At one point Richard stopped and rummaged through a box in the hall closet. He pulled out the McGregor family Bible under a pile of books. He thumbed through it and discovered the names of six generations of the McGregor clan. Richard began reading the first chapter of Genesis then decided he needed help. In spite of the ancient text, bits of truth revealed themselves, and he felt his faith grow.

By five o'clock, fatigue had settled in so he headed to the kitchen to brew a cup of tea and to wait for daylight to come. Two questions puzzled him, "Why come all the way to Kingsbridge to build a church, and why had he, himself been so hostile?"

He came to tell people like you about Me. You've been kicking at the door of heaven for quite a while.

* * *

The telephone jangled downstairs. Jay opened his eyes to the darkness. *What's wrong? I hope it's not Bryan again. He's been doing so well.* He'd put himself into rehab and had stayed the course. Kate said she had not seen such determination in Bryan since they were first married.

Jay dragged himself from the bed and plodded downstairs complaining to himself for not putting a phone jack in the bedroom. "Hello?" He cleared his throat and tried again. "Jacob Knight speaking—"

"Hello, Father Knight?" The voice was enthusiastic.

"This is Jacob Knight, can I help you? Who is this? Are you calling from America? You do know it is still night here in England, don't you?"

"Sorry, Father. This is Richard McGregor. I know it's a wee bit early, and I'm just up the road here in Kingsbridge, but I had some urgent business to discuss with you."

Jay straightened. "Don't apologize, Mr. McGregor. Sorry I was confused. We often get American friends who call without checking the UK time zone. They think the rest of the world revolves around them." He laughed. "I was just about to get up anyway." He swung his head around to look at the clock and winced.

"This is rather important. It's in regard to the property and me. I've done some serious thinking and well, could we get together today?"

Jay was definitely awake now. He ran his fingers through his rumpled hair. "I'd be happy to stop by your place today, say around ten?"

"Thank you Father, but could it be a wee bit sooner. I have to be at my office by nine. I commute to Manchester."

"No problem. How about seven? Would that work?"

"Absolutely. I'll have the kettle on. See you then. Cheers."

"Cheers." Jay put the receiver down and moaned, "So much for a day off." He bolted up the stairs as the adrenaline kicked in. Suspicion replaced the short lived sense of euphoria. *When your adversary calls for a little chat just hours before the big showdown makes a man nervous. This could be a setup.* Jay didn't want to step into a trap.

* * *

Clanging pots and pans woke Jean. She was stiff from sleeping in a chair all night. Slowly, the events of last night retuned to mind. She remembered Richard's transformation.

"Richard, what's going on in the kitchen?" She stood in the doorway with the tartan wrapped around her shoulders.

Richard was trying to make scones, but flour and goopy paste were everywhere. "I'm hopeless without you."

"I know you are." Jean shook her head and smiled. "Should I be expecting this every day? Is this all a part of the new Richard?"

They grinned at each other and Richard gave her a peck on the cheek. It left a flour mark behind. "I've invited the Vicar over for breakfast."

Jean let the throw fall from her shoulders as she rushed into the kitchen. "Oh no Richard, you're impossible. When is he coming?" She scrambled to pick up the mess.

"In about thirty minutes." He looked at the clock on the wall. "Or less."

Just then the doorbell rang. Jean shoved Richard out of the kitchen and closed the door behind him. "Stall him while I clean up your mess. I'll call when breakfast is ready."

* * *

Lisa found a note on the bedside table: *Got a call to meet McGregor. Not sure what's up, so pray. Love ya, Jay. PS. Someone keyed our car. I'll be back soon.* "Keyed? What does that mean? He's finally had a car key made for me. That was sweet."

She fretted over Jay's visit and wished she knew what was happening. The more she knew of McGregor, the more he seemed like a wild cannon. Whatever Jay was heading into, she knew he would not back down—not where the gospel is challenged.

* * *

Jay knocked on McGregor's door three minutes late. Clusters of budding daffodils surrounded the house. High overhead, crows floated in circles cawing to each other.

"Thank you for coming, Father. Please come in."

"Good morning, Mr. McGregor. And please, call me Jay."

The two men walked into the lounge and Jean poked her head through the doorway.

"You remember my wife Jean?"

Jean smiled broadly, "So glad to have you here. Being it's so early, Richard thought you might like to join us for a hot English breakfast."

Jay looked apprehensive. "It sounds great, but—"

"Don't worry, it was Richard's idea this time. We promise." Jean grinned. "I won't be long."

Jay and Richard made small talk until Jean announced breakfast. Jay waited for a bombshell to strike. In the kitchen, plates were laden with fried eggs, thick Danish bacon, fried tomatoes, and mushrooms, and crispy fried bread wedged on a porcelain toast rack. Richard stared at Jean with wonder, and she beamed.

After they sat, Richard seemed at a loss of what to do next. Finally he nodded to Jay. "Isn't there something you're supposed to do before we eat, Reverend?"

"Yes. I'd be honored to pray.'"

They bowed their heads and Jay spoke to God as a son to his father. Jay's prayer poured easily from his heart. He prayed for the McGregor's, their concerns, their future, their family, and finally the food in front of them. When he finished, Jean was wiping tears from her eyes and Richard looked emotionally fragile. Were these the same people Jay visited only a couple months ago?

Jay had just taken a bite of a warm scone when Richard blurted out, "I think I actually heard God's voice yesterday. I mean, does God talk to us like that?"

Jay choked on his food. He grabbed a glass of orange juice and washed it down.

"Are you all right?" Jean asked.

Jay nodded. "I'm fine thanks." When his airway was clear he replied, "God can do anything He wants. And yes, at times, He surprises us with a visit. He speaks to everyone who listens and He speaks in many different ways."

"What ways?" Richard had not taken a bite yet.

"Well, He speaks to us through our waking thoughts, our conscience, even through creation. But it's important that we test everything by comparing it with what he says in the Bible." Jay studied their faces. "Something's happened hasn't it?" Jean's eyes welled up as she nodded. "It's Richard. He's not the same man he was yesterday."

The meal had taken a backseat to the conversation. Richard looked pensive. "Does God ever speak to people, like a man talking to a friend?"

Jay smiled and pointed to his Bible.

Richard blushed. "I'm so glad you brought your Bible again. Please tell us what we need to know."

Jay's heart thumped wildly as he turned to Acts and began the story of a rebel named Saul. "This guy reminds me of you."

With stops and starts, they ate the meal and the discussion was heavenly. Richard leaned forward eager to discover the mystery of God. It took little effort on Jay's part to lead the couple to Christ. In the gentleness of their trembling prayers, Jay imagined the cheering angels in heaven.

After the prayer and another round of tea, Richard spoke up. "I'm sorry about being such a jerk over the church proposal." He paused to formulate his words. "I've changed my mind entirely. I hope you'll forgive me."

"Certainly." Jay was flabbergasted. "Certainly."

"I want to do whatever it takes to turn this proposal around for the church."

Jay hardly knew how to respond. "But Richard, the council meeting is only forty-eight hours away. There is hardly enough time to convince so many people to withdraw their objection."

"I realize that." McGregor smiled. "But it can't be too hard for God."

"Of course not."

"Last night, I put together a counter-petition opposing my original complaints." Richard continued, "This afternoon, I intend, with your permission, to knock on every door that signed the original petition. I intend to change their minds about this property. I can do that. If I've got God on my side, I can convince people to do right. I'd like to join you at the council meeting tomorrow evening."

Jay shook his head in wonder. "Of course, but how can you be so certain that you can change the minds of all those people?"

"Because God told me what I must do. And besides, I'm a pretty darn good salesman."

Jay wanted to jump up and hug the man, but he contained his emotions. Once again, he was speechless at the good things God was doing. So surprising. So unexpected. So wonderful. So like God!

Richard arranged to pick Jay up at six o'clock the next night.

* * *

Excited chatter filled the council room. Jay entered, surrounded by a group of his elders on one side and Richard McGregor on the other. Ray and Jenny had arrived late and slipped into two chairs at the back of the room. Jay felt their presence and knew they were there to intercede with prayer.

Jay fidgeted while the council dealt with routine matters and other items on the docket. After long minutes, Proposal

375 came to the floor for discussion. The architect had made adjustments to the entrance, so that it now came from the main road. The drawings sat upon an easel for everyone to view. McGregor rose and waited for acknowledgement. The chair nodded and McGregor began his defense.

"After reconsidering this entire proposal, I've concluded that my objections were prejudiced, and I am withdrawing my complaint." Richard produced a list of all the signatures on a counter petition and handed them to the chairman. The chairman sat speechless. He flipped through his notes and pulled out the original petition. He reviewed both and looked up dumbfounded. Name for name, the lists were identical. Not one neighbor refused to sign the counter. According to the list, each one had recanted their objections and voted in favor of having a church built on Fox Hill. When Richard was satisfied that they understood his current view, he returned to his seat.

The crowd sat in silence. The ticking of the wall clock filled the room. No discussion followed. No one on the council bothered to ask why. When they voted, the approval was unanimous. Thunderous applause roared through the room as the crowd stood cheering.

Richard pumped his fist in the air. "Yes!" A second later he took Jay in his arms. That night's victory went uncontested; a landslide for the Kingdom of God.

*   *   *

As they drove home, Jay asked McGregor about the list. "Did you ask everyone to sign the counter petition who had signed the original?"

"Everyone. Absolutely. And they did."

Jay was puzzled. "I remember a couple of people who came to the last town council meeting who were very hostile to our plans. I didn't see them there tonight, but I wondered what happened to them, like Reverend Madlaw and his wife."

Richard nodded with a knowing smile. "Yup, and then there was another woman who looked rather like a gypsy, right?"

"Oh yes, I remember her well," he paused. "She has a dog named Randolph."

"I don't know about Randolph, but her name is Chernik, a peculiar woman. She really got excited about something. They didn't want to go the conventional way, she said they had bigger plans to block this church. I'm not sure what she meant, but I saw her cozy up to the Madlaws after, and they were concocting something in secret. "Nope, they never signed a thing." He looked bemused. "They just made a lot of noise."

"And your positive?" Jay shook his head.

"Absolutely."

They rode in silence, listening to the rhythm of the wipers working against the rain. Jay was lost in thought.

"What were they up to?"

Richard shrugged and concentrated on the dark road ahead. "I wouldn't worry if I were you. Your biggest nightmare is over."

"You were my biggest nightmare, Mr. McGregor."

"Yes I was." Richard nodded.

In spite of the victory, Jay was troubled. Richard's words rattled Jay's mind. *They were concocting something in secret. What would they try?*

The victory was real tonight, and Jay would celebrate it. But an uncomfortable tangle of fear formed in his gut, an all too-familiar sensation. He squeezed his eyes shut, willing the feelings to leave, angry that this fear could rob him of the joy of the night's victory.

* * *

The following evening, Jay and Lisa sat with the McGregor's in their lounge celebrating the victory of the previous evening. The fire crackled as tiny chunks of coal exploded, shooting fireworks up the chimney, leaving little wisps of smoke in the air. The pungent smell mingled with the fragrance of Jean's freshly baked apple pie topped with melted cheese. Fresh scones and strawberries with whipped cream rested on fine china. She had made small fancy-cut sandwiches, and a rich variety of fruit, meats, and cheeses.

Jay could see that Jean was doing what she loved best. The foursome talked through the evening speaking of eternal hope and what God's Word promised to those who love Him. Jean was teary. "I finally found the peace I'd craved my whole life."

Lisa smiled at her. "God knew the right moment."

"He's brilliant," boomed Richard. "He cornered me in the back garden this week. I couldn't get away from him. And I know for certain, that God speaks to us directly. No doubt. He let me have it right between the eyes." His eyes shifted to images only he could see. A moment later he added, "And Jay, I've still got a lot to change. I'll need some guidance."

"You've got it. It will be my privilege."

*   *   *

The following week, *The Cheshire Sentinel* did a full-page spread with headlines declaring, Council Approves New Church Plans with Unanimous Vote. There was a quarter-page photo of Jay, Lisa and the lads standing on the promised land of Fox Hill. Jay wore his clerical collar and had Joey in his arms. Lisa had her arms around Michael and Nathan and a happy family smiled through newsprint at the twelve thousand residents of Kingsbridge. A photo insert of a beaming Richard and Jean was off to the right of the article. Richard's grin reminded Jay of the Cheshire cat.

Richard's story had gone public.

*   *   *

On the most prominent elevation in the center of Kingsbridge stood the ruins of a once magnificent church; its roof gone, leaving only great stone arches and a bell tower. Built to inspire hope and defend Christianity, it had fallen in battle, declaring the Christian message out dated. Now it proclaimed a neglected faith and rejected Savior.

The new church proposal was the hottest topic of the decade. Many doubted that it would ever come about. Some thought it was just the big dreams of a crazy American cowboy. Others waited and watched before casting judgment. The news even spread to the city.

One day, "Bones," a popular DJ from the radio station, Atlantic 252, read the headlines and, intrigued by the story of the American preacher, had gone to his sources at the *Manchester Sun*. It was arranged that a brief service would be conducted, filled with interviews and music. Before long, a van with basic broadcasting equipment arrived and a two man crew scurried about setting up. The dusty barnyard was going live across the county's airwaves. People sat on bales of hay and a portable generator gave temporary light. The people gathered to sing and give testimony, orchestrated by Jay, and watched by curious Bones.

With microphone in hand, Bones shot tricky questions at various church members, eager to stir emotions. Instead, they simply shared their faith in Jesus Christ and told how their lives had changed. Bones seemed impressed. The people possessed a fire that caught the imagination. He interviewed teens, and broadcast their testimonies uncut and uncensored. One teen sang a solo that was show stopping. As a finale, he asked Richard McGregor to tell his story. McGregor was quick to declare his unequivocal allegiance to Jesus Christ.

Time would tell if a church would be built. Bones promised his listeners that they would follow the story to the end.

* * *

It was spring and daylight was stretching out as darkness folded into short hours. Impatient for night to arrive, a man stepped through his back door and headed into the forest. Most of the village was asleep. A dirt path led him toward his future. Chilled more by the deed of the hour than the cool night air, the man pulled his jacket tight around his neck and headed deep into the unbridled darkness.

CHAPTER SEVENTEEN

—⟋⟍—

The night turned spectral under a canopy of tall pines. The wind swelled, causing branches to groan and creak. The forest floor felt soft under his feet silencing each step. He moved toward Mason's Lake to wait as instructed. The posted letter was encrypted with an alphanumeric code. The numbers represented date, time, places, and attendees. Each attendee had a numeric identification. The circle never used names except to pronounce a curse upon an outsider. And only the Co/rrguinech, Druid crane magicians, held authority to pronounce a curse.

The initiate had memorized the codes and then burned the evidence. As he counted his paces, he was startled to discover how well he could see in the dark. He stopped and studied the path. A light emanated just ahead. It had a faint green flicker to it. He smiled, already feeling an inner power rise within his soul. He had become a part of something bigger than he had ever known. His religious upbringing had never prepared him for such power.

Within twenty minutes, the man reached the perimeter of Mason's Lake. He stood beneath an old oak and waited. The lake gave off a faint luminescence. He recalled the fable of the lake's ancient curse. The lake was dead, unable to sustain life because deep beneath its waters laid the bones of a child. Human sacrifices to Teutates were always drowned.

The man shivered and carefully pulled a robe over his head, drawing the hood around his face. The dark green robe, symbolizing the "People of the Trees," draped in heavy folds around his ankles. Gold cord, braided in the traditional Celtic weave of three strands, trimmed the border of the garment. On both sides of the lapel was the emblem of the solar wheel in shimmering material. Two panels ran vertically along the front of the robe, each a silver streak of lightening. Together, these symbols venerated the Celtic god Taranis, the dreaded god whose spirit dwelt within the ancient oaks of Britannia; a demon god described by the Romans as merciless and whose demand for human sacrifice matched their own Scythian god Diana.

He felt protected.

*   *   *

Normally, he reserved this night for Lughnasadh, one of four fire festivals. They would usually celebrate a Druid rite of passage for a couple contemplating a trial marriage. But tonight, there were no couples, and the agenda instead took a dark and sinister tone. Angry land spirits were seeking revenge. Taranis intended to destroy anyone who laid claim to his land.

The man slipped from behind the tree and walked soundlessly to the water's edge. Others took their places alongside him. A chill washed through him to realize these people were good at what they do. The Wiccans and Druids made deception an art. Without their cloaks, they would know each other as ordinary citizens, bankers, lawyers, and housewives of Kingsbridge. But tonight, they were a force of spiritual power.

Centuries ago, Druids marked their ritual sites with columns of stone with astronomical alignments. They built altars to make human sacrifices meant to appease the gods. Tonight Taranis himself was stirring, the territorial spirit of the land. Someone had challenged his power.

The initiate followed like a lamb as the procession moved steadily into the undergrowth until they reached a clearing known as Celtic Grove. The smell of sulfur hung in the night air; the presence of evil draped every branch and shrub. The power of Christianity had to be neutralized in Kingsbridge.

Soon some of the participants had kindled an immense fire in the center of the circle. Its flames flicked high into the night sky.

The man waited.

A figure emerged from the shadows singing an intoxicating melody. This gypsy was Elena Chernik, a Romany who was well practiced in the Wiccan arts. Her chants were low and dreamy and repetitious. The sound of it was hypnotic.

"Ceridwen, oh great Ceridwen,
crooked woman, the bent white one,
send yourAwen, your flowing spirit to meet us now,
this night of Ludhadsadh.
Be our guide and be our teacher, oh Awen."

Another female voice sang out, the voice of the Banfha/ith, the seer. Her high-pitched notes chilled the night. They called upon spirits to come and work their power. The two voiced separate songs creating a mournful divergence. The sound of a reed instrument added to voices until the night reverberated with a haunting vibration. The banfha/ith sang ballads of past heroic victories.

"Mighty Nemetona, powerful Taranis.
Lord Esus, strong Teutates, you have driven
the enemies out of Ierne
and Albion
and deadened their power, throughout the history
of this Isle.
You have long since been the ruler of the Isles of Pretani
and caused our ancestors to stand strong.
Tonight a battle begins, tonight the enemy will be routed,
and Druidry shall flourish.
Tonight the Wiccans join us in defense of your power.
Tonight the witches of Wicca become the witches
of the Celts,
and the two become one.
We surrender to your power.
Send your Awen now."

Gradually her song rose to a fevered pitch and the tempo increased. The sounds were mesmerizing. Someone pulled the initiate into the center and a presence settled over him.

In a single moment, the music hushed immersing the circle in a chilling silence. The celebrants breathed heavily and their silent plumes billowed and drifted into the night air. The ritual began. Reverend Madlaw stood helpless in the circle. He felt childish yet excited. Three men surrounded him. One was a Bard, the other an Ofydd and the third a Derwydd. They represented the three-fold path of the Druidic religion. Madlaw had been on a spiritual quest for most of his life. His Christian religion seemed powerless and his soul empty. He despised himself, feeling like an unfilled vessel with nothing to give or draw from. To him, Christianity had been a great disappointment. Doubts had followed his thirst for more meaning and where the vacuum of disbelief existed, drudic power took hold.

The Bard spoke with hands raised over Madlaw, "Tonight, we celebrate the Gorsedd of Bards of Caer Abiri. Our companion and brother seeks a more powerful presence to be his mentor-guide. Tonight, he brings his Christian call to the eastern quarter, joined by a follower to the South, a witch to the West and a follower of the Northern traditions. We welcome our multi-faith brother within the stone circle."

The Ofydd raised his hands over the preacher and called down a spirit upon him; "Goddess Ceridwen, we invite you to bestow your spirit on this man. Brew your cauldron of inspiration and give us the three drops from which the gifts of poetic inspiration, prophecy and shape-shifting come. This new brother joins with the Bards of Wales to welcome you as his patroness of this order."

Madlaw felt something move inside him. It jolted him like an electric current. His mind grew heavy as if he had just eaten a feast. He wanted to sleep. Memories and desires swirled in chaotic flashes in his head. He felt faint and began to sway. His eyes rolled back in his head, and consciousness fled as he fell to the ground. The preacher collapsed in a trance. Events around him moved in slow motion. The Derwydd held up a young squealing pig and slashed it with a knife. Blood spurted in the air and oozed down the hands of the Derwydd. Madlaw's eyes glazed as blood dropped onto his face. His body jerked and convulsed as something tore through him, seeking a place to rest. Something alive moved within him.

A moment later, Madlaw lay as still as a corpse.

* * *

Another initiate was pulled into the inner circle. The gypsy woman came close and brushed her lips across his face, whispering in his ear. Boldly, Dungess threw back his hood and raised his arms into the air. This was the power for which he was born, his mother would be proud, his wife would bow, and his world would shake in terror. The Druids evoked the spirit Taranis to empower Dungess. A loud clap of thunder shook the forest and a blade of lightening lit the night sky. The high Priestess groaned. Dungess dropped to his knees, his arms still raised skyward. Instantly, forces ransacked his body demanding control.

Dungess screamed, "More, more." He collapsed, his body flat against the ground. Noel Dungess awoke as hot blood dripped on his face and body. He lapped it hungrily and turned for more. The gypsy woman stared into his eyes until he surrendered. He would do her bidding.

The circle swayed and chanted.

Rain pelted the earth, and thunder rolled through the air. Another searing blade shot across the sky. Madlaw and Dungess rose and stood in the clearing letting the rain wash the blood stains from their bodies.

Dungess felt more alive and more powerful than ever before.

* * *

Jay woke with a start. His body snapped upright; his heart pounding. *Was that thunder?* He couldn't say why, but he felt something was wrong—very wrong. He strained his ears, but heard nothing but rain on the roof and windows. Lisa laid still, her face serene. He leaned close until he felt her breath against his face and relaxed. Slipping from bed, he grabbed his robe and put it on as he walked down the hall toward the children's room. He paused and peered out the window through the sheets of driving rain. Nothing seemed unusual except Dungess' work van was gone. *Where would he be at two in the morning?* He gave it a moment's thought then headed to the children's room.

Jay checked on the lads and sighed in relief. Nathan was sprawled across his bed with his toes hanging out from under the covers. Michael was bundled under his blankets like a muffin. Joey was in his crib curled tight, one hand clutching his blanket and the other with his thumb in his mouth. All three children were breathing evenly, unruffled.

Seeing his family safe brought some relief, yet Jay still felt troubled. He was certain something terrible was about to happen. He had experienced such premeditations before, but they had been fleeting. This was persistent. Usually when he woke, his dreams would dissolve; this time they seemed more real than ever. He whispered a promise of hope, "Greater is He that is in you, then he that is in the world." *I believe that God. No one can thwart Your plans. Help me believe it wholeheartedly.*

In a few hours dawn would come. He stood in the hallway mulling over what he should do. He decided to grab a blanket and head downstairs. Jay lit a fire, and flames leapt up, quickly igniting the lumps of coal and wood shavings. Wrapped in a blanket, Jay sat on the sofa and stared at the yellow flames. The unsettled feeling grew like a malignant lump in his gut. *Lord, help me stay steady. Why do I have this feeling something terrible is about to happen? Help me to trust in You. I'm scared.*

The room grew warm; Jay picked up his Bible, and turned to Psalms 56. "When I am afraid, I will trust in you. In God, whose Word I praise, In God I trust; I will not be afraid. What can mortal man do to me?"

He thought those words through. *The worst anyone can do is kill me. No one can take God from my life.* But it was a lot to trust, and he wondered if he could hold on if something should happen to his family. The passage gave him comfort. After half an hour, Jay put the fire guard around the flames, turned off the light and headed back to bed.

* * *

Dungess had received instructions. He must drive to Fox Hill and hide his van inside a large stone barn one mile from his home. The barnyard gate rolled open without a sound. He had turned his headlights off and was inside within thirty seconds. He cut the engine and sat unmoving for a full minute to make sure his arrival had raised no one's suspicion. A bat swooped down to investigate, flapping in circles, then disappeared into a crack. It was three-thirty in the morning. Three other cars hid in the shadows of the massive barn.

Finally satisfied, Dungess emerged from the barn's entrance and using a flashlight he found the second barn where he was to meet the other members. The shaft of light darted across the barns surface until he located a small door where a faint flicker of light could be seen.

He felt comfortable in this semi-darkness. It empowered him. In the dark, he could feel tall, taller and stronger than everyone else. He could look down on his enemies and do whatever he wanted to them, and they couldn't stop him.

He pulled the hood of his robe up around his face and went through the doorway. It smelled dry and musty. Stale hay covered the floor. The barn was mostly empty accept for a few cobwebs and dried bird droppings that crunched beneath his feet.

Dungess stood just inside the barn entrance for a moment. In the dirt, a circle had been drawn on the floor. Within the circle was the five-pointed star. In the center of the circle was a metal cage, which held three ill tempered ferrets. They were agitated, running along the edge of the cage, hissing at each other. A larger ferret claimed dominance by attacking the other two with his front claws. He could hear their teeth gnashing at each other.

Dungess moved slowly toward the center of the circle. A lit torch stood in the center of the circle with the base driven into the ground. The torch gave enough light to perform the ritual and offer the blood sacrifices. Around the edge of the circle stood three people robed in green, hoods covering their faces. Dungess did not recognize them, but he knew they were the Crane magicians, the Co/rrguinech. Druidic Coven assigned them to offer up a curse on this building, and he felt privileged to participate. He was a willing subject, the chosen instrument to deliver its decree. One of the men directed him to stand at the center of the circle beside the cage.

The three magicians began the ritual. Dungess understood very little of what they said. They spoke in Gaelic. Even though he did not understand the words, he felt its driving force override his emotions. Nothing else mattered. This was it. This is what he had craved all his life, and now he was a part of something more powerful than he could have imagined. He was the chosen one. He wanted to shout it out. He wished he could get acquainted with the three blokes around the circle.

As the Co/rrguinech called upon the demon gods, a presence entered the barn. Dungess could not see it, but he felt it. It raced through the building, stirred up dust from the floor and tore the air like a tornado, nearly extinguishing the torch at times. Then it would stop and produce a spray of green light that moved about the room, giving off a putrid smell of decay. Once released, the barn became alive with a horde of spirits.

Dungess gasped for air. Something would touch his shoulder, whisper obscenities, and jab him. Once in a while, a shadow or partial image would appear and he could see as though he were looking through a distorted mirror. The image never lasted more than a moment.

Dungess felt his head buzzing and his limbs tingled. He gave a crazy laugh until one of the men growled for him to shut up. The chanting chilled him to the bone.

A magician picked up the cage and opened the door. All three vermin were bleeding from attacks on each other. He grabbed one by its neck. It hissed and clawed, letting out a high pitched screech. The ferret writhed in his hand as the men chanted. The magician looped his second finger and thumb around the animal's neck and held up a black-boned knife. The Gaelic curse sounded like gibberish to Dungess, but the words he could identify, "Fox Hill" and "farm" sent a sudden thrill through him.

The Co/rreiguch pierced the writhing ferret. A spray of blood hit Dungess in the face. Instinctively he jerked back and his eyes widened. A moment later, he grabbed a silver chalice and caught the blood.

The next magician pulled out the second ferret. It shrieked and hissed. The jumble of words cursed the builders and congregation. The blade split the animal. Blood spurt everywhere as the animal kicked to its death. Blood covered everyone; the rest they caught in the chalice.

The third magician grabbed the largest ferret and held it near his face. He repeated the chant. The ferret clawed the magician's cheek. Surprised, the man dropped the animal. It sprung to its feet and attacked. It charged the man until someone slammed a boot hard on its hind end. Taking hold of the animal again, the man raged and squeezed it with both hands. The animal gave a terrible scream as the man slashed it with the black-boned knife. His curse came out in English. "Take your fury and your rage and use it on the preacher Jacob Knight. Destroy him with your cunning art and let fear rule. Make him despised by all who look on him. Bring division between him and his wife. Bring ruin to all his efforts in life. Scatter his family to the four corners of the earth. We spit on him. Blessed be Taranis."

The three animals were skinned and their naked bodies hung from the rafters of the newly purchased barn, the future church home of Kingsbridge. The Co/rrguinech passed the chalice around for each to drink of it. Dungess held it to his lips, hesitated for a moment and then drank it dry. Was Taranis pleased with the sacrifice?

The reply came without delay. A violent vortex of spirits swirled through the building, spiraling upward and then down, lapping up the last drops of blood spilt on the ground, licking the skinned carcasses as they passed, causing them to spin. As the vortex increased, the demons penetrated the material world, briefly becoming visible. Dust and dirt spun through the air whipping the killer's robes and throwing dirt in their faces.

Dungess stared in awe. The demon's translucent bodies were bloody and cancerous, covered in human diseases; oozing lesions, cancerous lumps, deformed limbs, and gouged eye sockets. They carried with them the curses of humanity. Dripping mucus, their saber sharp teeth snapped viciously as their jaws mechanically moved back and forth. The vortex tightened into a thin line that spun itself out through the roof.

The dust settled and the curse became a part of its new surroundings. Without uttering a word, the four participants took straw and disbursed it over the circle and star, covering their marks. They extinguished the torch and put away the implements of sacrifice. Silently, the vehicles emerged from the barn and drove away.

Chapter Eighteen

———〰———

Lisa finished the last touches of make-up in front of the mirror. Blonde curls hung loosely on each side of her cameo face. After considerable indecision, she hung a pearl drop earring on each ear and surveyed her work. She sighed and called, "Lads, I hope you're ready for school."

The familiar sound of Nate's chair scraping the floor as he jumped up from the table rolled up the stairs. "I'm ready. Gotta brush my teeth." He nearly ran into Lisa at the foot of the stairs.

"Slow down, Poppet. Don't get so anxious. You won't be late."

When Lisa entered the kitchen she found Michael poking at his food and Jay packing their lunches into blue and red Superman lunch boxes. Joey clung to his father's pant leg while Jay tried to move about the kitchen. As Jay walked, Joey's bottom slid across the kitchen floor like a dust mop. Jay gave a loud laugh and Joey giggled.

Lisa had been in the kitchen less than two minutes when Nate reappeared.

"Mum, I can't be late. Mrs. Lawson would be very upset if I came in late."

"Nate, you still have twenty-five minutes before the bell rings. Dad always gets you there on time. Don't be so anxious sweetheart." Lisa gave him a big hug.

Lisa fretted over the lads at times. Nate was only nine, but he hoisted unnecessary weight on his young shoulders. He was more excitable than his brothers, yet all three carried an extraordinary sensitivity to the world around them. They loved each other and monitored one another's moods cautiously. Regardless of their stair-step ages they were almost inseparable.

"Nate, Daddy will pray with you and Michael before you go to school," her voice was reassuring. "I'll pick you up after school."

"Promise?" Nate looked into her eyes.

"Promise. Now scoot."

Comforted, Nate finally smiled. "Thanks, Mum. Don't forget! Love you, Mum."

Michael shouted as he moved outdoors, "Bye, Mum. Love you, Mum."

"Bye, sweetheart." Lisa picked up Joey and held him.

"Bye gorgeous. I'll be back in a jiff and the car is yours."

Lisa watched as Jay cranked the engine. It surprised her by starting immediately. A cloud of blue smoke rumbled out the tailpipe. Through the car windows, Lisa could see Jay pray with the lads as the car warmed. Fifteen minutes later, Jay returned and they switched over. Lisa kissed Jay, handed Joey to him, and climbed in the car.

"What a nice way to start the day. Getting a kiss from a blonde bombshell who just happens to be the pastor's wife."

"I won't tell if you won't," she winked. "We're meeting at Jen's house for the ladies prayer and praise time—just in case you need me for anything. And I will be picking the lads up from school. I already told Nate, so don't worry. I hope you get a lot of studying done this morning, after Joey takes his nap, of course." Joey was reaching for his mother.

"Right." Jay rolled his eyes. "Maybe while Joey gets to sleep."

Lisa waved good-bye and drove down the narrow lane. The leaves were a cool green and the spring morning was brisk and vibrant. Steel-gray clouds filled the sky, making colors more intense. She passed a blanket of blue bells and smiled.

Lisa swung the car into a right-hand turn, the tires crunching loose gravel. Carriage Drive was narrow with deep ditches on both sides. Two cars could never pass each other. To let someone pass, a car would have to back up and reverse into a driveway. A car pulled out and Lisa slowed, letting Ian Langley have the right of way. They both waved and Ian soon disappeared.

A moment later, Lisa continued down the hill. A flicker of movement ahead caught her attention. A vehicle of some kind was speeding in her direction. Instinctively, she braked, bringing the car to a crawl. The oncoming vehicle didn't slow. Adrenaline kicked her heart into high gear. "Lord, help me."

She looked in her rearview mirror to see if she could back up. Before she could decide, there was a sickening thud and clash of metal. Her body shot forward against the steering wheel, then back against the seat. Her head bobbed. Dials on the dashboard burst free, disgorging springs and gauges everywhere. The windshield shattered, showering glass over her body. The driver's side window burst into shards. A second thud shoved the car sideways. There was a brief moment that Lisa felt airborne. She called to God.

She heard the roar of an engine, then felt her car slip off the asphalt and slide down a six-foot gully. The car came to rest on its side. Lisa tried to move but her leg was pinned between the seat and the console. Something warm trickled from a gash on her head. Water seeped into the wreckage and bubbled up around her body. Lisa's face was now scratched and bleeding; her hair caked in filth. Mud oozed in through every side. The car lurched forward once more and then thumped to a stop.

The threatening sky finally tipped the bucket and poured a deluge of water onto the scene below. Lisa lay still struggling to breathe. Rain fell through the broken window and pattered against her face. A moment later, she lost consciousness.

* * *

A crumpled van inched its way into a garage and parked. The driver wasted no time in throwing a tarp over the vehicle. He locked the garage as he left.

* * *

Jay lay sprawled out on the living room floor playing with Joey when he first heard the siren. *That sounds close.* But Joey wanted no distractions. "Okay, okay, you want to keep playing don't you?" Jay went back to building block towers so Joey could knock them down.

Jay glanced up again when he heard a sudden downpour of rain. "Wow, that's a lot of rain. Look Joey." Joey only wanted to play. Jay was frustrated because he had a mountain of work upstairs. This could go on all day.

The siren's started again. Jay went to the window and peered through the gray rain. *What a miserable day for a crisis.* The sirens bellowed and Jay opened the front door, trying to detect where the sirens were coming from. He closed the door and shivered. *Somebody needs help. Lord, watch over whoever's in trouble.*

A few moments later the phone rang.

"Hello Mr. Knight, this is April Langley, your neighbor from around the corner."

"Hi April, how are you on this wet day?"

"I am afraid I've got some bad news. It seems your wife has been in an accident on Carriage Lane."

The news froze Jay in place. The room tipped and blurred. "An accident? Are you sure it was Lisa? Where is she? What happened?" The throbbing in his chest grew deafening.

"I passed the accident on my way home. She must have lost control. I couldn't see another vehicle. I called the authorities. They were on the spot soon after. They're taking her to Countess of Chester Hospital, but that's all I know. I am so sorry."

"I must go to her."

She paused. "I wish I could tell you more. Skid marks were everywhere. I'm sure the police will investigate everything."

"My wife needs me, but I've got the baby here—"

"Let me watch the baby for you. I'll be over in a tick."

"Thanks, I—" April had already hung up.

Since Lisa was on her way to Jenny's house, Jay called and blurted the story in a flood of emotion. "I've got to get to the hospital. I've got to find a way there."

"I'll take you. I'll be there as fast as I can."

April arrived within minutes. Her take-charge ability was exactly what Jay needed. She shooed him up the stairs to get ready. When he came down again Joey was playing happily on the floor and Jenny stood in the door. Jay followed her out through the downpour and into the car. He was now in a daze.

"Pastor, we'll have to pass the accident and I really don't think it's wise for you to see it. It would just make you feel worse."

"How can I feel worse than I do right now? My wife's in the hospital and I'm not there."

Jenny headed down Carriage Drive until activity on the road forced her to stop. A tow truck had hoisted the mangled car up from the mud hole. It dangled, suspended by cables as water poured from gaps in the frame. Mud oozed from the smashed windshield. The front bumper, now only twisted metal, dangled precariously and finally broke free and fell back into the ditch. Jay was sickened at the sight and it was all he could do not to vomit. He shuddered.

Jenny rolled down her window and shouted to a Policeman directing traffic. "We need to get past. Were in a hurry to get to the hospital."

Jay jumped out of the car and into the cold rain. "That's *my* car. Is my wife okay? How did the accident happen?" His teeth rattled like ice.

"I'm sorry, sir. We don't know much. There had to be another car, but no one can figure where it is. Apparently, there were no witnesses." Flares flickered in the rain sending out plumes of pink smoke. Jenny motioned for Jay to climb back in. She turned to the man again, "Sir, we're in a hurry. We need to get to the hospital. Can you help us get around this mess?"

The man nodded and whistled for the truck to halt. Jenny inched her way past the growing mud hole.

"Let's get out of here fast." Jenny sped away and was soon on the M53 heading north.

The landscape blurred as Jay pleaded. *Lord, not again. First, it was Michael and now my Lisa.* A flash of Lisa made him choke up. *Lord, please. I can't face this again. I can't.* Jay wiped his eyes as he stared through the rain seeing nothing but the mental image of his wife.

"We'll be there soon."

"I know." Jay's voice was low. "Thanks for doing this."

Jenny sped across the parking lot and screeched to a halt in front of the ER entrance. "I'll park the car and meet you inside."

The ER was crowded. A pimple faced guy slouched in a chair trying to sleep. A man paced nervously. Somewhere a child cried and a baby fretted. A teen stood holding a cloth to his bleeding head. Nurses were busy taking information or temperatures. The queue snaked through the room and nearly out the door. In desperation Jay called out, "Can someone help me?"

"We all need help," the kid with the bleeding head snapped. "I've been here for an hour. What's your problem?"

"My wife…I'm trying to find my wife, Lisa Knight. She's been in an accident."

A nurse raised her head from studying insurance forms. "Who just called for Lisa Knight?" The nurse surveyed the milling crowd.

"I did." Jay raised his hand. "I'm her husband. Where can I find her?"

"She's been moved to third floor, Room 322. Take the lift to your right."

"Thank you so much." He rushed to the elevator just as the door began to close. Jay wedged his foot in the opening and pried the doors apart. As he walked in a hand touched his shoulder. It was Jenny. She was breathless from running.

"Sorry Pastor. I had to park at the back of the lot. It's chock-o-block out there. What's the news?" She was soaked to the skin.

"She's on the third in Room 322. I don't know anything more."

"We'll find out soon enough." Jenny's confidence was calming and Jay let her take the lead. The lift stopped at the third floor and the doors creaked open. "Pastor, I know this is hard for you. You'd rather be the one helping. Today, God's allowed me to help you." She squeezed his hand. "God is helping us. Let's go."

Jay followed Jenny to the nurse's station. Her words seemed to go through Jay's heart and get lost. Accepting comfort from others took an unfamiliar skill.

A nurse spoke. "Lisa Knight? Yes, they're just making her comfy." She nodded. "And here comes Dr. Griffith now."

"Dr. Griffith?" Jay rushed toward the man. "I'm Mr. Knight, Lisa Knight's husband. Is she going to be okay?"

The doctor nodded, then took hold of Jay's elbow and walked him slowly down the hall. He spoke in hushed tones.

"Your wife has had a severe concussion, which we're monitoring now. But the scans look good." He straightened his sagging posture and smiled. She'll be sore from head to toe and I'm having her wear a neck brace for awhile. "She's suffered a nasty cut to the scalp. It took eight stitches. I think she's going to be fine. You'll just need to be patient."

Jay felt a wash of relief. "Thank you, Lord."

Jenny nodded with a smile.

Dr. Griffith said, "You may go in, but let her rest. She has a lot of healing to do." He shook Jay's hand and turned away.

"Thank you, Dr. Griffith. Thank you so much."

* * *

Lisa stared at a blurred circle straight ahead. *What is that?* She tried to reach for it, but her arms felt like lead. *What's wrong with me? Where am I?* She blinked, and tried to focus. Her head ached and her body protested any movement. She tried to speak, but her words sounded like gibberish. Fear filled her mind and she closed her eyes for a minute trying to calm herself. When she opened them again, the amorphous circle took shape. It was a clock. It read three-thirty. *Three thirty! Oh no! I'm late to pick up the lads from school. Nate must be frantic.* She made another attempt to move but the pain sent waves of nausea roiling through her. She wished she could vomit. Her eyes darted around the room seeking something that made sense. *What happened to me?*

"She's waking. Mrs. Knight, can you hear me? Mrs. Knight, open your eyes, love. Come on, open your eyes."

Lisa blinked. A nurse stood by her bed. "What happened?"

"You've been in an accident, love, but you're going to recover just fine." She moistened Lisa's lips with a swab. "You're in the Countess of Chester Hospital. You were brought here by ambulance today, Mrs. Knight. Do you remember the accident?"

Lisa's brow wrinkled. "Accident? What accident?" She tried to sit up but a new wave of pain put an end to the idea. "My boys. I have to pick up my children from school."

"There, there, Mrs. Knight, stay calm." The nurse spoke softly. "Your husband has made arrangements."

"Jay?" Lisa's eyes searched the room for her husband.

"I'm right here, babe." Jay stepped into the room, bent down, and kissed her. Tears filled his eyes. "I was stretching my legs in the hall. I'm so sorry, babe. You've been through a terrible accident." He kissed her again on her forehead. "I love you so much."

"What happened?" Lisa searched her mind for the event that landed her in a hospital bed, but found nothing.

She began to cry.

*   *   *

The rain had slowed to a spit. The angry clouds had gone yet the sky remained a slab of gray. Michael and Nathan stood by the school gate, shivering. The playground was deserted, with the exception of Tony. Tony was always last, waiting for his mother, the headmistress. He kicked a muddy soccer ball around the field.

Nate was growing anxious. Something had to be wrong. He pulled his collar up around his neck. It would soon get dark and that meant more cold. He peered down the street. *Mum promised. Where is she? What's happened?*

Michael kicked a stone. "I'm hungry, Nate. Where's Mum? Maybe we should start walking home."

"No, we can't. Mum promised." It was too far to walk home unless they went through the woods, and his parents had forbidden them to go that way alone. "Mum will be here soon."

Mrs. Lawson, the headmistress, finally appeared. "Nathan, what's happened? Did you miss your ride?"

He shook his head. "Mum promised to pick us up today. She'll be here soon."

"Maybe she's been delayed. Why don't I give you a lift home?"

"No thank you. Mum will be here soon." Nate glanced down the empty road.

"I shouldn't leave you two here alone." She looked at her watch.

Michael said, "We don't live far away. We could walk."

The headmistress seemed relieved. "Right you are then lads, hurry along before it gets dark." She waved and headed to her car with Tony and a muddy soccer ball.

"Why did you say that, Michael? You know Mum and Dad won't let us walk through the woods alone."

Michael shrugged. "We got to get home, don't we? Let's go."

Pushing against the wind and darkening sky, the boys headed toward the wooded entrance. Nate felt sick with worry.

Michael led the way toward the woods. The entrance to the footpath was dark and yawning. "Hurry, Nate." He was already yards ahead and into the shadows. Nate rushed to catch up. Something terrible was going to happen—he just knew it.

* * *

A blue Ford sedan sped past the wooded entrance and headed toward the school. Jenny made a quick U-turn in front of the schoolyard and tooted her horn. The grounds were empty and the school dark. She jumped from the car and called, but no one answered. She looked at her watch: a half-hour late. She drove to a shop on the corner. "Have you seen two lads walk past here recently?" she asked the attendant.

"Sure have, probably two dozen since school let out. They stop to buy sweets and sodas."

"One is blond, the other has dark hair. They're wearing Overton jackets."

"Sorry, love. They all look the same to me." He gave change to a boy for a bag of chips. A bell jangled as the boy walked out the door.

Jenny felt frantic. She spotted a kid at the back reading a sports magazine. "Excuse me, but do you know Nathan or Michael Knight from Overton?"

"Nate's in my class. Why?"

"I'm trying to find them. Did you see them after school today?"

"Only at the gate. Maybe they took a hike through the woods round the corner."

"Where would that take them?"

"Carriage Drive."

Jenny rushed out the door and turned the corner where the woods began. "God, help me find those lads before anything happens." One step into the woods and daylight disappeared. Jenny ran along the path shouting their names, but the woods were silent.

* * *

David and Rachel Thatcher sat at the kitchen table pouring over bills when the news came of Lisa's accident. David immediately called the towing company and had the

Knight's car rerouted to his yard. Rachel got the prayer chain rolling. She organized meals for the family and made sure there were volunteers to watch the children.

Early that afternoon, David made his way to the hospital and found Jay pacing in the corridor. "I'm so sorry."

When Jay looked up he smiled. "Hi Dave, thanks so much for coming." They embraced. "Lisa is sleeping now. The doctor says she'll recover fine. It was pretty scary for a while."

"That's good to hear." David felt greatly relieved. He listened as Jay described her injuries.

"Jenny told us she had brought you here. She also said she'd pick up the lads from school. I'll stay with you until you're ready to go home."

"I should be there when the lads arrive—they'll need their father. I know how much this has frightened me. I can't imagine what it'll do to them."

"They'll be fine, Pastor. Scared, but fine. Their good boys; strong like their father."

"I don't feel strong."

David's heart went out to Jay. "It's not how you feel, Pastor. It's how you act."

Jay nodded but said nothing. David could see tears rising in his friend's eyes. He put a hand on Jay's shoulder. "If you're going to be at the house when your sons arrive, then we had better leave soon."

"Yes. I'll just say goodbye." Jay moved from the corridor into Lisa's room. David followed but stopped at the threshold. He watched as Jay leaned over Lisa and kissed her.

The two men walked to the elevator.

"I've got your car at my place, but don't expect to drive it again." The wind was icy and howled around the corners of the building. Jay shivered and pulled his collar up.

"Here, you'll need these." David jangled a set of car keys on his index finger.

Jay looked puzzled. "What do you mean?"

"They go to that little VW bug over there." He nodded. "It's filled and ready to go."

"Whose is it?"

"Well, it's yours now. I've been fixing it up in the shop as a surprise for you. Of course I had no idea you'd need it this soon."

"David!" Jay stopped in astonishment. "No, I can't accept that."

"Come on, Pastor. It's cold out here."

"But, David..." Jay shook his head in wonder. "What can I say?"

"Absolutely nothing. Hurry and unlock it. I'm freezing." He stamped his feet.

* * *

Nate and Michael had lost their way. The woods had grown dark so fast and now the wailing wind shook the trees limbs.

"I can't see the path anymore, Nate. What do we do?" Michael's bravado had fizzled.

Nate was terrified. He grabbed Michael's jacket. "Which way is the shop?"

"I don't know." Michael's breathing was raspy and thin. Nearby branches clacked together like dry bones. They crouched together hoping someone would find them.

CHAPTER NINETEEN

—∿∿—

J ay's world had turned inside out. After dropping David off at his home, he checked his watch. Jenny should have the boys by now. Earlier she had said that she'd give them supper and then bring them home around six-thirty. He had an hour to spare. He needed some answers. A cold darkness had fallen quickly. The car's headlights made two long cones of illumination on the lane ahead. He headed to the church site for a few minutes to pray and make sense of it all. He parked his car by the gate and fished around until he found a flashlight in the glove compartment. David thought of everything. Jay grabbed it and climbed out. A street lamp washed the farmyard in an eerie orange glow. Jay unlatched the gate and walked through, closing it behind him. As he approached the barn door, several bats flapped from the entrance, missing his head by inches, and then swirled into the sky. He hated those things. The hair on his neck prickled. He stepped into the darkened doorway and shown the beam of light into the room.

* * *

The boys huddled close to a tree. The little light that remained cast ominous, crawling shadows. Tree roots seemed to slither around them. Holding on to each other's jackets, they whimpered softly. A gust of wind whipped leaves that rose and fell, swirling around the children, stirring fear in their hearts.

"Nathan, I'm scared. Why didn't Mum or Dad come get us?"

"Don't know. Something's wrong." His voice was shaky.

Somewhere in the distance, they heard a woman's voice.

"Did you hear that?" Michael said. "It's Mum."

"We're over here," they shouted.

A tiny light glowed in the distance. The voice grew louder.

"Help. Help. Over here." The children were now sobbing.

"Michael, Nathan." Suddenly, the voice found them. "It's me, Auntie Jenny." The tiny light shone on their faces. "Michael and Nathan, I've come to take you lads home. You're safe now." She held a small penlight that gave a weak flickering glow.

"Lads, I'm so sorry." Jenny knelt down beside them. "I'm so sorry I wasn't there when you got out of school. I told your dad I'd pick you up but I was too late."

"Where's Mum? She promised to pick us up today." Nathan blurted.

"I'll tell you everything, but first, let's find our way back to my car." Jenny took their hands and stumbled through the darkness until they reached the road and Jenny's car. After checking them over carefully, she said, "Hop in the car, lads. I'll make us some supper."

"I want to go home. Where's Mum?" Nathan persisted. "Is she okay?"

Jenny caught her breath. "Your mum's had a little car accident, but she's—"

"Is she hurt? What happened? Where is she?"

"Your dad called earlier. You're mum's going to be all right. Her car tumbled into a ditch and she had some bangs and bumps. She's at the hospital right now, but the doctor said she's going to be just fine."

Nathan finally began to sob. It came in waves. "I knew something was wrong."

"Where's my dad?" Michael choked up.

"You're dad will meet us soon. He's been at the hospital. Let's get some supper and then I'll take you home."

*   *   *

Night brought a new blanket of black clouds that that roiled overhead on a westerly wind. One minute darkness ruled; the next, moon poked through breaks in the clouds and cast a silvery sheen across the landscape. Jay stepped into the barn doorway and frowned when the light hit something glistening on the floor.

He felt uneasy. The already cold air took on a strange and deeper chill. Something stung the lining of his nose. His light zigzagged around the room. Had kids been messing around in here? Something wasn't right. What were those markings? Jay squatted to study the lines. His heart thumped hard. The wind swept through the doorway and blew a cloud of dirt in his face. There were scorch marks, a discarded candle, and dark spots of liquid on the floor. That's what was glistening. Goose bumps ran up and down his arms.

"What's going on here?" Something cold and sticky dropped on his head. He instinctively jerked back and looked up. A second drop splattered on his forehead and ran down his face. It was thick and smelled like—blood.

Frantically, he slapped at his hair, smearing the blood across his forehead. He heard a noise. His light flashed along the beams. He was horrified to see skinned animals dangling from the rafters over head. A swarm of flies circled the carcasses creating a low buzzing sound. Jay stood there nauseated and frozen by the sight. He heard a loud swoosh and a bat swooped low and brushed his hair. Jay slowly backed out of the building. Sudden fear weakened his limbs. His movements must have disturbed the bats which took to flight like a black cloud. They turned on Jay swooping down nipping at his hair.

"Get off me. Get off me!" He covered his head and ran into the open field. The sound of flapping wings and high pitched screeching chased him to the car. The bats swooped around him attacking his face and hair. He flailed his arms in a vain attempt to ward off the creatures. Jay fought his way to the car, jumped in, and slammed the door. The door caught one of the bats by the wing. It flopped wildly, releasing a piercing screech. Others continued the attack striking the windshield and sliding off.

Jay turned on the ignition and pressed the accelerator to the floor. The car sped down the road until he brought it to an abrupt stop at David's garage. No live bats had followed. When Jay opened the door, the pinned and now dead creature fell to the ground. Jay kicked it and hurried to David's house.

"David, we've got a serious problem." Jay struggled to control his breathing. "Someone has performed a blood ritual in the church building. There're skinned animals hanging from the rafters. And…" He gasped for breath. "I was attacked by a swarm of bats. I hate those things. I can't deal with this on my own David. I need your help."

David's face paled. "Maybe it's a hoax or prank of some kind."

"Trust me, it's no hoax. It's too gruesome to be wasted on a prank."

David looked uncomfortable but agreed to go. "You'll have to tell me what to do."

Jay nodded. He wished he'd paid more attention to his studies of satanic cults. He had read about missionaries encountering the demonic, but never expected it could happen to him.

* * *

David stood in the doorway and swallowed hard. He was an instant believer. He shone his flashlight up at the weasel faces.

David paused. "I guess you scared off the bats."

Jay shivered. "They scared me off."

"What do we do first, Pastor?" His voice trembled.

"I believe that this ritual represents a claim on this land. Like territorial spirits. They meant for us to find this. It's as blatant an attack against Christianity as I've ever seen." He pointed his flashlight into the rafters. We must pray against the power of this curse. Obviously, our work has posed a serious threat to the spirits that dominate this region."

"How do these spirits work?"

"I don't understand how they work, but one thing is for sure: they are intelligent beings that patrol this territory and we are a threat to their reign. We might be in the center of a stronghold."

David looked at Jay. "We must be doing something right."

"We're telling people about Jesus Christ and that will never change."

Fifteen minutes later the two had cut down and burned the sacrifices. In prayer, they claimed the building, the community, and the church for God, and denounced satanic rulers as impotent.

Jay led the prayer. "In the name of Jesus Christ, I now break the power of any occult spirit that has attached itself to this place. We break the powers of chants and spilled blood and curses on this building in the name of Jesus. We bind the spirits of darkness, death, and destruction that seek to destroy this ministry, this congregation, and this community. We do this in the Almighty name of Jesus. Amen."

Jay and David opened their eyes and looked around. Everything looked the same. Jay, however, felt different, weak, worn.

David said, "Are you sure it worked?"

"Yes."

"Then, why hasn't anything changed?" David paused. "It would be nice, just once to see the real battle going on where the good guys win."

"I guess because belief is our weapon, not a sword. That's a dimension we only see through faith."

"I know, but it wouldn't hurt just once."

"Well, I'm not Elisha, but the principle still applies. Those who are with us are more than those who are with them." Jay turned to leave. "Let's go. I can't think of anything else the enemy can take."

* * *

Elena Chernik had dozed in her worn, overstuffed chair by a cold fireplace. Something from another dimension startled her. She bolted upright and glanced around the room. Something was happening. A chunk of burnt coal fell from the grate and turned to ashes as it hit the hearth. The woman croaked out a curse, went to the window and stared into the darkness. She snapped her curtains closed, grabbed a throw, and wrapped it around her shoulders. She shuffled toward the kitchen while a twisted smile grew on her face. "Jacob Knight, I'm coming for you." She put the kettle on and headed toward the toilet, cackling softly.

* * *

It took several hours before Jay could comfort the boys while shielding them from the worst of the events. At midnight, he lay in a lonely bed and wept. He'd nearly lost his wife today. He was horrified at what his boys went through. And then there was the ritual. How could Satan be allowed to hatch such evil against him? What kind of person would walk into a place consecrated to God and be so bare-faced as to shake their fist at Him. He squeezed his eyes tight, but all he could see where the hideous sacrifices, those bloody things swinging from the rafters. Had he come face to face with evil? He felt targeted, as if Satan had him in his cross-hairs ready to shoot. Jay prayed until exhaustion took hold. He finally slept.

CHAPTER TWENTY

—⁕—

Richard McGregor's overnight conversion became town talk for weeks. The man whom everyone knew as loud, flashy and bombastic now was more agreeable, patient and often apologetic. "Hello Mr. Worrel," McGregor would say, "I noticed that crunch on your front fender is still there. That was my fault. I ask for your forgiveness. Here, take my card. Call me with your estimate and I'll pay your mechanic in cash." Then he would stuff a fifty pound note in the man's hand. "Please take this as a gesture of my earnestness to right my wrongs. I want you to know that I'm no longer the same guy. God forgave me."

The townspeople were baffled. There had been a number of sightings of Richard leaving notes and cash on car windshields and stuffed through letter boxes. The electric company discovered that someone fitting his description had paid six residential electric bills all in cash. Someone had left three bags of groceries on a widow's front stoop. A group of teens appeared at Mr. Andrew's front door with paint brushes ready. Someone was paying them to paint the pensioners house inside and out.

First, people were surprised. Eventually people became suspicious. What does he want this time? What's really behind this new façade? A man who had the charisma to sway public opinion in either direction made people question his intent. Some of his harshest critics were church members.

"I'm sorry Pastor, but this McGregor thing makes me nervous." Nigel was the youngest man elected to the board of elders, which, in itself, seemed an anomaly. "How can we be certain Mr. McGregor is genuine?"

Jay had responded, "Maybe we're no better than the early Christians who doubted Saul's conversion when he became Paul. The church doubted his authenticity too."

* * *

Jay was exhausted from juggling his responsibilities to his children, wife, and ministry. It seemed like a year since Lisa's accident. The lads moped around not really excited about anything. Dad's meals were usually burnt and crispy except for the one that caught fire. They had more peanut butter sandwiches that week than Lisa had made in a month. And every day the boys came home with grass stains on their knees. Jay gave up. Of course Michael's shoelace would break just as they rushed out the door. Jay found some white string in a drawer which worked. With shirt tail flying and a crooked tie, the boys made it to school each day, always in the nick of time.

By Sunday, the grapevine had wound itself across town. The church folk offered their prayers, expressed concern, wrote flowery get well letters, and brought dishes of food for the family.

* * *

Sunday morning was always hectic. Without Lisa, it was inevitable that something would go wrong.

"Hurry lads. We're late. Follow me to the front of the church. Quick." Jay scurried Michael and Nathan up the side aisle and sat them on the front row. Joey was in the nursery. He knew he looked more disheveled than the children, but he wore a smile and greeted everyone. "You folks have been so supportive of me and my family. What a blessing you've been to us. The world should be envious of the great love that we have for one another. Thanks for standing beside us through our crisis."

Jay gave them an update, and then turned to Nigel who wanted to speak. He filled in the gaps Jay had missed and then asked the people to pray for Lisa's full recovery.

"If some of you would like to gather up at the front, we can join together in faith." Two elders came forward. Then others joined. Suddenly the room seemed congested as they gathered around Jay and his sons. When the praying began, it started with a trickle and soon accelerated like a rumbling freight train that had no brakes. God must have heard the prayers. The people wouldn't stop until they'd penetrated heaven's rafters and were certain God had listened. These spiritual babes seemed to be catching on quickly.

Jay felt energized and began preaching from John 15. The theme was simple: God expected all followers of Christ to bear fruit and that fruit would remain.

McGregor sat seated somewhere on the left, scribbling notes on page after page. About midway through the sermon, Richard raised his hand. He interrupted Jay to ask him to explain something he'd said. Some were annoyed, but most smiled at his obvious thirst for truth and ignorance of decorum. As Jay gave the call to preach the good news, he could see something in Richard stir. When the service finished, he rushed to the front.

"Wow. What a great time we've had. And that message was just for me today, Pastor. I want to learn how to share my faith. I know lots of people that need what we have. Will you teach me how?"

"Absolutely." Jay gave Richard an affectionate jab. "Remember, faith comes from God. The more you share it with others, the stronger it grows in your heart."

"I want that. When can we meet? How about today?" Richard stood close and Jay stepped back. It was a habit of northerners and it left Jay gasping for air.

"How about later in the week when things settle at my house? If all goes well, Lisa should to be released tomorrow."

"Of course, Pastor. I didn't mean to be pushy."

"You're not being pushy. You're just eager to grow. I'll give you a call maybe on Wednesday and we can decide then. Does that sound okay?"

"Sounds brilliant."

The last person to leave was Kate. She smiled big when she shook Jay's hand.

"Hi, Kate. How's it going at home?"

"Bryan is still on the wagon. He's gone to every AA meeting there is in town. He's a changed man, Pastor."

"So where is he today?"

"The youngest has the flu. Bryan has become devoted to those lads. He's made up for the years that alcohol had robbed from us."

"God is restoring the years that the locust have eaten."

"Thanks again, Pastor." She gave Jay a quick hug and then headed to her car.

* * *

Monday, around noon, the doctors gave Lisa her discharge papers. She had to wear a neck brace, which hampered her movements. Her stitches were healing nicely, and her bruises were turning a mottled yellow.

Lisa had asked Jay to bring her red cotton dress with small floral print and tailored collar. She couldn't wait to get out of the open-backed hospital gown and her peach colored robe. He also brought her make-up bag and curling tongs. As she put on her makeup, she flashbacked to the last time she had done her makeup. She looked at herself in the mirror. What's missing? Earrings! She was wearing her pearl earrings when she set off. The hospital had taken her personal items when they admitted her to ER. They had put her watch and wedding band in a plastic bag. It lay on the bathroom sink in front of her. She looked in the bag again and found a single pearl drop earring. *Where is the other one?* She looked through her clothes and handbag, but couldn't find it.

Jay would be there any minute. She gave up the search for the moment, and finished dressing. A short time later, she checked herself in the mirror. "Ready."

She walked cautiously back to her bed and sat on the edge. She was still bothered that a period of time was missing from her memory. And so was her earring.

As a nurse wheeled Lisa toward the hospital entrance, she spied Joey squirming in his daddy's arms. He'd seen her from a distance and wanted her to hold him.

She stood, trying to ignore the nagging pains of her injuries. "Oh Joey, I've missed you so much, but I can't hold you right now, sweetie." She gave Joey a hug and kissed him. He wasn't satisfied. "I can't hold you now, sweetheart." He fussed and wriggled.

"Come on, buddy. Let's get in the car and Mum can hold your hand." Joey kept squirming. "Come on Lis, I've got something to show you."

Jay led her into the parking lot and turned the corner.

"A bug? I love those cars."

"Good, because you'll be driving this a lot."

"What?" She felt a wave of excitement. "Oh Jay—" She put her hands to her mouth.

"It's a gift from David and Rachel. He'd been working on it to surprise us. I told him you'd like it. Shall we go for a spin?"

"I can't wait. What a wonderful thing for them to do." With painful caution, Lisa slid in while Jay fastened Joey in his car seat.

"Where would you like to go, dear?" Jay gave her a wink.

Lisa's eyes brightened and she raised an eyebrow. "Do I look too silly in this collar thingy to be out in public?"

"Not at all. Everyone's used to seeing the pastor wear a collar. I'm sure they would have no problem seeing the pastor's wife wearing one too. They'll just think you've gotten a higher calling." He grinned. "But, be careful because the Bible warns about stiff necked people. Should I be fearful of you?"

"Funny, funny. You know what I would love to do? Let's go into Chester and have lunch at some little cafe. I'm so tired of hospital food and I'm afraid your meals are no more appetizing. No offense."

"I can tell you're feeling better. You're feisty again."

"I'm just plain hungry."

Jay pulled onto the A41 toward Christleton. He followed the ring road and turned right onto St. Oswald's Way. They passed St. Mary on the Hill. As they neared Pepper Street, Jay eased into a multi-story-parking garage and parked near the pedestrian entrance.

Lisa watched as Jay belted Joey into his stroller. "I've missed my boys. I can't wait to see Nathan and Michael."

Jay nodded in the direction they were headed. "You'll need to be careful. The lads will want to hang on to you for a long time. It's really been hard on them." He smiled. "And me."

"Me, too. We belong together and it hurts when we're not. Thanks for being so strong through all this."

"Me? Strong? I sure haven't felt strong. Besides, I'd never make a good housewife. I'm afraid I've failed miserably." He leaned over and kissed her. "God knows that I can't live without you." She let him take her in a soft embrace.

"You do choose some of the most romantic places to express your undying love." Lisa said with bit of sarcasm.

"Let's go eat." He grinned. "I know just the place."

Taking Lisa's hand and pushing Joey's stroller with the other, they headed toward the shops. They crossed over the Bridge of Sighs, and along the Roman wall. They followed the steps down from the Eastgate Clock tower and through the narrow archways of the wall along cobbled paths. The Cathedral bells chimed the hour as they passed by little antique shops and busy market stalls.

"Hey, I read up on the history of Chester during my spare time. It's fascinating. Did you know that Earl Hugh Lupus of Chester owned much of the city?"

"I had no idea." Lisa grinned. "What an odd name."

"Yeah, but everybody called him 'The Wolf.'"

"If I were known as Earl Lupus, I'd find a nickname too." She laughed. "By the way, where are we going?"

"You'll see. We're almost there." They passed the Roman baths and amphitheater and continued toward a set of steps that led below ground.

"Jay, this is perfect. 'The Crypt.' I love this place." Lisa stepped down carefully into the cool underground where limestone arches married roof and floor. The smell of aged limestone mingled with freshly baked bread. Rich tapestries hung from stone walls and small tables were tucked into corners lit only by candlelight. A waiter led them to a table where Jay parked Joey's stroller against the wall and put him into a high chair.

Jay glanced at the menu and then studied the room's architecture. He said, "Did you know that several battles were fought right here in Chester."

Lisa furrowed her brow. "What brought that up? I thought we came here to eat, not study history."

"It's this place. It's full of history. Here we are touching the same stone walls that medieval warriors once touched." He looked back at his menu. "What sounds good?"

"The Plowman's Lunch sounds good to me. I'm famished. How about you?"

"There, you see, we can't get away from the past. How many plowmen do you know?" He rubbed his chin. "I think I'll have a steak and kidney pie."

"And where did that come from?"

"A cow and a donor, of course." He closed the menu and glanced around for someone to take their order. "Someone will eventually come, I suppose. Hey look." He pointed to an inscription carved into the wall. "It's written in Gaelic, so there's no telling what it says."

"You probably don't want to know." Lisa grinned leaned to the side to talk to Joey while Jay stared into space, with his mind obviously on another planet.

A server, a lanky young woman, appeared at their table and asked what they would like to drink.

Jay spoke first. "Coffee please. Make it white."

"And I'll have a cup of tea please."

"What would you like for the bonnie laddie?"

"A cheese sandwich on white please, cut in wedges." Lisa said, "And a small glass of milk." Joey clapped his hands with only his tiny palms touching each other. Lisa and Jay added their orders which the waitress jotted down on her order pad.

When the waitress left, Jay leaned over the table. "Lisa, what do you remember of the accident?"

"It's rather vague. I remember seeing someone I knew in front of me. Who was that? Someone drove out in front of me. It was . . . um . . .Ian. It was Ian Langley."

"Ian Langley hit you?" Jay looked shock.

"No. He had come out of his lane in front of me and we waved." Lisa struggled to remember. "Wasn't there another car there when the ambulance came?"

"I'm told there was only your car at the scene. I didn't know anything about the accident until you were already in the hospital. Can you remember anything else?"

"Not much."

"Thank God." Jay touched her hand.

"Yes, I guess He is protecting me from whatever happened." She furrowed her brow. "I do remember a car headed my way. I think it was coming fast." She shuddered.

"The paramedics say it was a miracle you survived."

"Have you seen the car?"

"Only briefly while they were trying to lift it out of the mud. David had it towed back to his place. There's nothing left of it. I'm sick that I didn't drive you that day. I should have."

"Don't be silly. You had no way of knowing."

"Lis, I could never live without you. I tried this week and it didn't work." He paused as if reliving the week. "So, you don't remember any details?"

Lisa shook her head. "No. It's like there's a blank spot during whatever happened that sent me over the edge." Lisa touched her ear. "Jay, did the hospital give you anything of mine after the accident?"

"They gave me your Bible, but it was so muddy and torn you wouldn't be able to read it. It's at home. Why?"

"I'm missing a pearl earring."

"If that's all, then you're okay. I'll buy you another pair."

"Thanks, but those were special. My grandmother left them to me in her will. They're genuine pearl." Lisa looked up and noticed the waitress carrying three plates of food.

"There you are. Can I get you anything else?"

Jay studied the plates for a moment. "It looks like we're good to go. Thanks."

"Enjoy." The waitress moved to the next table.

Jay gave thanks and they began to eat. "I'm really sorry about the earring," he said. "I can't replace their worth, but I can replace their looks until I become rich and famous."

"Tell me what you have been up to since I've been gone — besides making cheese sandwiches?"

"Peanut butter sandwiches." He swallowed a bite of steak. "Well, I've learned how to use a needle and thread, improvise with string when Michael's shoelace broke, wash diapers in the bathtub, and stay up all night and still preach in the morning."

"You have been busy. I knew you could be domesticated."

"Oh Lis, I'm useless. I could never replace you. The kids reminded me every day. Mum does this better. Mum does that."

"There must have been some good this week." She ate slowly, savoring not only the food but the moment.

"Sunday was good. The place was full. Richard McGregor is growing like a weed. He interrupted me in the middle of my sermon. It was hilarious." He paused. "Something else happened earlier in the week."

"What?"

Jay hesitated and Lisa detected a change in his mood. "Nothing really. Never mind. It's not really appropriate table talk. I'll tell you later."

"Later? Don't do that to me, Jacob Knight. Don't start and then stop."

"Sorry. Since it's my only flaw, I do hope you'll forgive me."

Lisa decided not to press the issue — at least not at the moment. They continued to chit-chat until their meal was done. Lisa enjoyed every morsel and every minute. Finally, she leaned back and took a deep breath. "Jay, I'm beginning to fade. I think I overdid this trip. Can we go soon?"

"Absolutely. I'm finished and Joey is a total mess as usual, so I guess we are ready to take off."

Joey had squashed his cheese sandwich to death and made holes in the bread. Jay was surprised that Joey's hair had successfully escaped any trauma.

The trip home was quiet.

Lisa closed her eyes to rest.

CHAPTER TWENTY-ONE

—〰—

Coming home brought an emotional release for Lisa. She was now safe in her own home, surrounded by the familiar. "I'm so glad to be home." A tear escaped a flooded eye. Jay caught it with his finger, and then kissed her forehead.

"You need to rest. Go lay down while I pick up the lads at school." He checked his watch and reached down to pick up Joey.

"Leave Joey with me. He won't be any trouble. I've missed him so much." She stroked the boy's hair. "I've been alone in a room for a whole week. Joey can just play here. But before you go, let me give you a shopping list." She wrote a few items down after glancing through the cupboards. "No wonder you only fixed peanut butter sandwiches. There is nothing else in the pantry."

"I can't run this ship like you can. I did well to make sure the lads got off to school with their clothes on straight and Joey wearing clean nappies."

"You've done fine, except…" She studied Joey. "I think you've put his diaper on backwards." She looked at the back-side of Joey's diaper. "I know you have."

"I think it's time to exit. I'll be about an hour. You sure you can manage?"

"Yes, sure, …poor baby. Daddy put your diaper on backwards." She suppressed a snicker.

"I'll be back soon." He waved and climbed into the VW. She watched as he drove down the lane.

*   *   *

A hand released a branch and let it spring back into place. Eyes had been watching the home coming. The man sank back into the foliage and returned to his home. In his garage, he shuffled through a wood stack and pulled out a post made of pine. He hefted it and felt satisfied. Carrying it, he positioned himself alongside of the Knight's kitchen window careful to remain out of sight. This was the only place at ground level where the preacher's window looked out onto Dungess' courtyard. He had a right to be here. If the woman came into her kitchen and looked out, he'd attack. The post was a good weapon and it could do a lot of damage to that pretty little face. He waited patiently.

After a while he grew fidgety. He mumbled a curse. Finally from somewhere in the house he heard a phone ring but couldn't pick up a line of conversation. Where was she? Where's the bawling kid?

Dungess glanced around him. It was broad daylight, and the early afternoon sun broke through the cloud layer and then vanished again in a shroud of gray. Dungess felt brazen. He owned his own house. No one can stop him. Dungess heard the woman's voice. She was close, very close. He shivered.

*   *   *

"Joey, would you like mummy to read a story?" Joey jabbered long sentences of baby talk. Lisa smiled. "I've missed you so much Joey. You're my sweetie. I'm going to put you in your high chair while I fix a cup of tea." Lisa grunted as she lifted him up and settled him in his highchair. "You're getting so big." She showed him a Dr. Seuss book. "Do you want to look at a book?"

"Book, book." Joey mimicked.

BOOM.

A thud jolted the kitchen wall and window frame. A second later, splinters of glass exploded into the room. Shards flew in all directions. Needles of glass struck Lisa's face and arms. She was terrified.

She screamed and raised her hands to protect her face. Joey began to wail. She staggered back then caught herself. It was him. Through the broken glass, she saw the face of Dungess. He was in a rage and held a wood post in his fist.

"Leave us alone!"

His face was contorted. "I'll get you and that bugger husband of yours."

Lisa shook. She rushed to grab Joey from his chair, but skidded and lost her footing on the splintered glass that covered the floor. She dropped to the floor cutting her hands and knees. The fall jarred her body and she screamed in pain. She struggled to her feet and moved to Joey.

Joey screamed, kicking hard to escape the confines of the highchair. Lisa yanked him from the chair and ran from the room. Every move added more pain. Adrenaline pumped through her as she headed for the stairs with Joey on her hip. "Help me Lord, help me."

As she climbed the stairs large black spots filled her vision. She knew she could black out at any moment, but she had to get up the stairs. "Help me Lord, I need to..."

Blackness settled around her and sounds grew distant. Somewhere Joey was screaming. She groped for the handrail. Her head whirled and her skin prickled with clammy sweat. "No, Lord." She pleaded. "I can't let go. I've got Joey."

At the bottom of the stairs the front door rattled in its frame. The sound of it filled the house as if it were a bass drum.

* * *

Dungess saw the woman flee the kitchen. He dropped the post and sprinted to the front door and hammered it with his fist. When his fist didn't do the job, he kicked the oak slab. The door creaked and shook. With each kick, he cursed. "I'll destroy you—you and that bloody preacher." He delivered another series of kicks. "You're as good as dead. Do you hear me? Dead."

Lord, make him go away. Somewhere between the landing and the bathroom, Lisa blacked out. Joey's screaming and the mad man's ranting faded.

Her pain dulled.

Blackness descended like a curtain.

* * *

She began to stir. Voices. Far away. Distorted but familiar. Someone was calling her, rousing her from the sea of blackness.

"Mum, Mum, wake up."

Her children's voices pulled her back from the abyss. She blinked, but didn't move. Her boys knelt beside her, tears streaming, faces washed with relief that she was alive. Jay was kneeling too, with Joey in his arms. She and Joey were alive.

Tears came.

* * *

Dungess tossed the post back into the woodpile and headed for the kitchen. He liked this new feeling of power, especially over women. He washed his face and hands in cold water and dried them with a towel and sat down in the living room to watch television.

* * *

Jay helped Lisa sit up.

"Is Joey okay?"

"He's fine, Lis. He was sitting right here in the hall like a little pumpkin." He studied her eyes. "What happened?"

"I guess I fainted."

"That's an understatement. You've got small cuts over your face and the stitches are bleeding." Jay dabbed her forehead with a tissue. "Your hands are cut, too."

"It was Dungess. For no reason, he shoved a board through the window. He's evil. He tried to kill us. I know he did." She trembled at the memory. "He could have killed me. He could have killed both of us."

"He's got to be stopped."

Lisa groaned. Her collar chaffed. She looked at her hands and noticed a sliver of glass embedded in her left palm. "Joey was in his high chair, and I was fixing myself a cup of tea." She picked at the glass until it came out.

Jay felt rage well up in his belly. His face flushed hot. "What is wrong with that man? He must be mad!" Jay's anger began to swell. "I'm going to call the police. We are not going to let him get away with this."

He studied Lisa for a moment. "Can you stand?"

"Yes, I'm okay." She rose, using Jay's arm to steady herself.

"No Lis, you're not okay. Nate, help your mum get to her bed."

Nathan and Michael fussed over their mum wanting to help. "Michael and Nathan, I've missed you both so much." They walked beside her until she got to her bed.

Jay's hand shook as he dialed 999.

"Kingsbridge Constabulary. Constable Davis here."

"Hello yes, we have just had someone throw a board at our kitchen window and try to break down our front door. Can you send someone to us right away?"

"Your name and address sir?"

"Jacob Knight. Erindale Cottage." There was a long pause. "Hello? My wife has been injured. We are at the top of Carriage Drive, just before the woods. Please hurry."

"Be patient sir. Your telephone number please?"

"788 205." Jay paced. "Can someone come out right away? This is urgent."

"Thank you, Mr. Knight. We'll send out a patrol car right away."

After hanging up, Jay walked into the kitchen and saw splintered glass across the floor. The sight of it stoked the fire of his anger. He wanted to punch this crazy man.

Twenty minutes later, two uniformed officers arrived. As Jay opened the door, a queasy feeling ran through his stomach. Never before had he needed to call for police assistance in their home. Jay wondered if this was the start of something sinister. He opened the door and invited the officers in. They introduced themselves and began to interrogate Jay.

Constable Jones asked the questions while Constable Mercer took notes.

"Tell me precisely what happened, sir."

"Well, my wife was in the kitchen making a cup of tea when out of the blue a board hit the wall or window frame. It shattered the glass."

"May I see the window?"

"Yes." He led them into the kitchen.

"Where were you when this happened?"

"I was buying groceries. When I arrived a short time ago, I found my wife passed out on the landing."

"So you didn't see anyone throw the board?"

"No I didn't, but my wife did."

"Can we speak to her please?"

"She's lying down. She hadn't been home from hospital more than an hour."

"But we need her statement. We need to speak with her."

"Okay. I'll get her."

Jay rushed up the stairs leaving the two police officers standing in the kitchen staring at the damage. He brought her down the stairs. She looked pale and fragile. Her eyes were puffy and red.

Jones and Mercer introduced themselves to Lisa. "We just need to ask you a few questions, please. Would you care to sit down?"

"I think I'd better. I'm not feeling the greatest." She tried to give a weak smile but her mouth merely quivered. Jay put his arm around her and led her to a chair.

"Can you tell us what happened here?"

"Yes. I had only been home about 20 minutes, maybe less. I decided to make a cup of tea, so I put Joey, the baby, in his highchair and came over here and turned on a burner to heat the water." She shook a little. "I am so thankful that Joey was on the opposite side of the room in his chair. It would have killed him." She trembled and pools of tears formed in her eyes.

"Please continue."

"The man next door slammed a board through our window. It didn't come through, but you can see the damage it did. I think he was trying to hit me."

"How big was the board?"

"I don't know. Maybe five or six feet long. It was like a fence post."

"Where is the board now?" asked Jones.

Lisa looked puzzled. "I don't know. I guess he still has it. His name is... What's his name, Jay?"

"Dungess. Noel Dungess."

"Hmmm." A knowing look passed between the officers. "Very interesting. We'll have to make a visit to Mr. Dungess' home. How do you get to his house?"

"He's next door," Jay pointed, "but around the back."

"One last question, Mrs. Knight. Can you think of anything that might have provoked this man to violence?" Lisa looked at Jay with a puzzled expression.

"I wouldn't have a clue. The house had been empty all morning until we arrived home from the hospital. No one had been here to provoke him."

Jay added, "He tried to kick the door down. You can see the boot prints on the door."

"We noticed that when we arrived," Mercer said.

"Will you let us know what's going to happen, Constable?"

"Yes. Hold on until we return."

* * *

Mercer knocked several times, but no one answered. Finally, he took the end of his night stick and banged it on the door. An old woman answered. She was tall with thinning gray hair that seemed to float around her face. She forced a polite smile and asked what she could do for the officers.

"May we speak with Mr. Dungess, please?"

"I'm sorry. He's still at work." She closed the door behind her and moved away from the house. "He usually gets home around five-ish. Is there a problem?"

"Yes, we've received a complaint by your neighbors the Knights. They are claiming that Mr. Dungess threw a board at their kitchen window. We see that their window is broken. Can you give us any information concerning this?"

The woman looked mystified. "My husband couldn't do anything like that because he's not here."

"Why don't you come out here and take a look at this window a moment." Jones asked. She shrugged and complied, but only smiled when she saw the damage. She spoke in a hushed tone.

"They're a crazy family. They must have broken the window themselves."

"Why would they do that? Besides, Mrs. Dungess, the glass had to be shattered from the outside. It is all over their floor. And there is none on the ground out here."

"Exactly. They had to have done it themselves."

Mercer scratched his head and looked at his partner. "Mrs. Dungess, you're missing the point. It is impossible for them to break the window from their side and not have glass here on the ground.

"Not for them. They practice weird religious stuff." She leaned closer. "It's got to be some American cult. You know, like those Normans who have lots of wives."

Mercer tried to suppress a grin.

"I've already reported them to the local council," the woman boasted.

"For what?" Mercer stopped grinning.

"That man put up a light outside his front door and leaves it on at night."

"There's nothing illegal about that. It has to be dark in these woods at night. What was the problem?"

"Well, he keeps the birds awake at night with that crazy light. It's totally inhumane. If the council doesn't do anything, I'm planning to contact Greenpeace. I know they'll take action."

"Where is Mr. Dungess right now?"

She looked at her watch. "Why, I think he's finishing up a job in Warrington. It's quite obvious that he's not here. He drives a work van and the Volvo over there is my car."

"I'd like to take a look in both of your garages." The woman looked surprised but quickly recovered.

"Sure. The door on the right is chock-o-block with old furniture. There's an old van that hasn't run in years. I don't have the key for that padlock anyway. Noel keeps them. But I can let you look in the first one." Elda heaved the door open with a dramatic flair causing her large breasts to wobble.

Mercer and Jones nosed around as though they were at a garage sale. "Where does that door lead?" He pointed to a closed off wall that seemed to lead right into the Knight's living room. "What's happened here?"

"It was an entrance to their living room at one time. But contractors blocked it off to make two houses instead of one. The greedy buzzards."

Mercer raised his eyebrows.

"Of course, the doorway from the cottage has been bricked up. My husband just uses this area for his workbench. He keeps paints and brushes and so forth along this wall. It's his secret place to hide from me."

Mercer moved on, continuing to look around, poking through tools, ladders, old tires, and stacks of rope. A strong smell of tar reached his nose. Jones had walked to the other side of the garage when he discovered a six-foot post from a woodpile.

"This is interesting." Jones hoisted it up.

Elda rolled her eyes. "Constable, my husband keeps all kinds of pieces of timber about, just in case he might need it for a job. That board proves nothing. I could show you ten other pieces just like that one."

"Will you tell your husband, that we will return later when he is home? We would like to talk with him concerning this problem." Jones looked at his partner and motioned for them to wrap it up. "Let's go Mercer, there's nothing here." The officers exited the garage. The woman closed the door looking rather smug.

As the officers turned to leave, Mercer stopped.

"I want to check one more thing." He walked to the locked door. "You say you don't have a key to this half?"

"That's right. We haven't gone into there for years."

Mercer wiped the glass with his shirtsleeve and peered into the room. He cupped his hands against the glare. The room was filled with old furniture stacked and stuffed in every direction. Sure enough there was a van of some sort covered with a tarp. He pulled out his flashlight and shone it back and forth across the tarp. He saw something that interested him.

"Come on Mercer, we're wasting our time."

"Hold on, one more tic." The cone of light crisscrossed along the floor at the edge of the tarp. Finally Mercer snapped off the flashlight, straightened and turned to Jones. "Let's go, we've got all we need."

Jones shrugged and turned to the woman. "Listen Mrs. Dungess, I must warn you. Neither you nor your husband must do anything to incite these neighbors of yours. They have a right to their own privacy and their own beliefs. Do you understand?"

"Of course. I guess even foreigners have some rights. Come back another time and I'll brew a pot of tea for you both. Cheerio." She stood in the doorway with her hands hitched to her hips. Her faded blue housedress flapped in the breeze. When they were out of sight, she marched into the house like a shot. "Noel, where are you?"

* * *

Jay boarded the window with cardboard and tape. Lisa swept up the glass and vacuumed every corner to be certain the children were safe from stray splinters. When the officers returned to say they had no conclusive evidence tying Dungess to any vandalism or threats, they were dumbfounded. The window repair was easily fixed. But the families shattered emotions were left to fester. And what about next time? If this could happen without the slightest provocation, what could happen if the children annoyed them for some reason? Lisa wondered why the law couldn't protect them from people like Dungess.

Jay and Lisa prayed long hours over the situation, but found no peace.

CHAPTER TWENTY-TWO

—∿∿—

Richard weaved in and out of rush hour traffic on the M55 heading north. Rain pelted the pavement, washing the grime off the congested city into clogged sewers. The clock on the car's dash read 5:48 and he still had twenty miles to go. He'd promised to help Jean prepare supper for their guests, Jay and Lisa. They were to arrive at seven. After fifteen years of marriage, this was a first, and Jean let him know that she was still holding her breath, just in case the balloon burst. Of course, Richard was not the same man he used to be.

Two months earlier, he wouldn't have thought it important to help his wife. But, his male chauvinistic bullheadedness died when he'd met God's irresistible love. Now Richard's world had turned upside down and he knew he had a lot of catching up to do. He found himself doing things he'd never done before. He wanted to change the world. He wanted everyone to discover what he had discovered—*who* he had discovered: Jesus.

He pulled into the fast lane and his tires slipped on the soaked road. The rain had raised oil to the surface, making the driving hazardous. His wipers drummed back and forth providing cadence for his prayers. *Help me to be a man of God, O Lord. Help me to change what needs to be changed and to learn how I can live the Christian life. Help me to make a difference in my world. Thank You for showing me the way.*

Richard zoomed into his driveway at six-twenty, give or take. The rain had slowed to a drizzle. His headlights winked out as he scooted out of the car and into the kitchen. Jean was busy baking fresh scones. The smell of them made Richard's stomach growl.

"I'm home, love. I've missed you all day. These are for you." He gave her a hug and kiss, and held out a bouquet of spring flowers.

Jean started to cry. "Richard, this is so wonderful."

Richard squeezed her. "What can I do to help?" He whipped off his tie and rolled up his sleeves. Rubbing his hands together with excitement, he prepared himself to face whatever culinary challenge Jean threw his way.

"I'm still not sure you're really my husband. Sometimes you scare me."

"I scare me too, love. That's okay. Because if things go back to the way they were, then we're both in real trouble. Controlling my own life is scarier than letting God have control. I don't ever want to be in that position again. And as a Christian, I don't want to mistake what God is trying to tell me. Of course I still have a lot to learn."

"Well, I did leave a few things for you to do, just in case you were serious. Here, put this pinny on." She grinned as she slid the apron over his head.

Richard scowled at having to wear an apron with three-inch ruffles.

"Don't worry, nobody will see you. I'll make sure the apron is put away before the pastor and Lisa arrive." Jean tied the ribbons in the back and then patted him on the backside.

"Do we have to go this far? I mean, wearing a pink pinafore, is a bit over the top."

"It helps you get in the mood." Her eyes sparkled with mischief.

Richard followed instructions. He was to cut small sandwiches and stack them into neat piles. Jean chuckled.

Around ten minutes to seven, they heard a knock at the front door. Richard's eyes flashed to the kitchen clock.

"Oh no, they're early. I can't go out like this."

"Fly up the stairs and I'll get the door. I'll tell them you'll be right down."

* * *

When Richard was out of sight, Jean opened the door.

"Welcome Pastor and Lisa. Come in."

"Hello, Jean," Jay said as they walked over the threshold. "Just Jay and Lisa is fine."

"But you know we have never had a pastor before. It is very special to have a friend who is also our very own pastor. You wouldn't want to deny us that privilege would you?"

Jay shrugged, "I guess I never thought of it like that. Sure. You can call me whatever you'd like, just as long as you call me for supper."

Lisa had brought a bunch of daffodils for Jean which Jean rewarded with a hug. "Let me take your coats."

"Go on in and have a seat. Richard is upstairs changing his clothes. He had a little extra job to do when he got in, but he'll be down in a moment."

From the top of the stairs Richard called out to his wife in a loud whisper. "Jean! I need your help."

"What is it, love? Our guests have arrived. Are you coming down soon?"

"Yes." He stood at the top of the stairs in his boxers and black calf-length socks, still wearing the pink pinny with the ruffles bouncing over his shoulders. "I can't figure out how to get out of this thing. You must have double knotted it."

Jean covered her mouth and giggled.

Jay shouted, "Need some help, old buddy?" He got a laugh.

Jean started up the stairs. "I almost like it better than your tartan; no one can tell what's under them."

Richard stood like a statue and tried to look indignant. A moment later he erupted into laughter.

"See if I offer to help you in the kitchen again, Mrs. McGregor."

*   *   *

The evening was full of joy. They laughed at each other's faux pas and basked in the growing friendship.

Jay kept a watchful eye on Lisa, but she appeared comfortable and caught up in Jean's stories. It had been a fortnight since she'd returned home and her first night out without the lads. Watching Lisa interact with Jean made Jay feel good. He knew she longed for a friendship that was genuine right down to the bone.

After lots of laughter, Richard edged on his seat and shot a question to Jay. "Tell me how to share my faith. There are a lot of non-believers in my universe."

"Richard, you're a natural salesman. You know how to get people's attention, grab their interest, and whet their appetite to buy your products. The skills you already have, which I think are God given, can be used to tell people about Christ. But that's where our human ability stops and God takes over. People already see changes in you and they want to know why."

Jay could see the admiration on Jean's face as she turned to her husband. "I keep pinching myself to see if I'm dreaming. He's changed so much."

"It's no dream. The transformation in both of you is something only God could do. It's greater than any dream, because everything changes when you turned to Christ." Jay leaned forward. "We need to let people know that this new life comes from God and not us."

"Life powered by Jesus Christ," Richard said. "What a great tag line."

"He's always thinking about marketing." Jean rolled her eyes.

"'Life lived by McGregor; powered by Jesus Christ.' That would make a great bumper sticker don't you think?"

"You've got it right, Richard. We could use some-body with good marketing skills. We'll have to brainstorm sometime."

"It's a deal. But back to our discussion, I want to help people find God. Where do I begin?"

"You simply have to tell your story. Your story should not point to you but to—"

"Jesus Christ." Richard looked almost childlike.

"Right. Many feel empty and hopeless. They fear the unknown. Your story shows that God loved you before you believed in Him. You needed someone to save you from your sins." Jay scooted closer to the edge of his seat. "Only Jesus can forgive us because he paid the price with his own life."

"That's the key isn't it?"

"Absolutely. But remember, it's the Holy Spirit who teaches us to reach out to people. He will do the work of showing them their sins and giving them a longing to accept Christ. This means that the people that come your way have been prepared beforehand by the Spirit of God." Jay leaned back and studied their faces.

Richard nodded. "That's for sure. When God first spoke to me, He smacked me between the eyes. That left quite an impression."

"So I've been told," Jay said. "But God has been working on you from the moment you were born. He let you experience everything that life threw at you. Eventually you became hungry for God. What about you Jean?"

"Oh, Pastor, I was ready from the get-go. I just didn't understand what was missing. I always felt empty, but I couldn't explain it, not even to Rich. I knew there had to be more to life than what I was getting. When Richard walked in the kitchen that day, I could see that he had found what I had been looking for. The rest was easy. It didn't take me long to know that Jesus was the one I had left out for all these years. I just never knew. No one had ever told me about Him before."

"I'll give you a list of Scripture verses which will help you both share your faith. Stay regular in worship and Bible study. This new life in you needs constant watering and nourishment. Never let it wither."

"We can't get enough, Pastor." Jean stopped, then popped to her feet. "Excuse me, please. I forgot all about supper." A minute later, she rolled a pastry trolley loaded with fancy sandwiches, homemade soup, tea and biscuits into the lounge. Then she returned to the kitchen for one more item. Before she rounded the corner she announced, "I wanted to do something special for tonight. So here it is."

She carried out a pizza-sized pavlova.

"What is that?" Lisa said, amazed. "It looks gorgeous."

Jean set it down on the hearth for everyone to admire. She beamed with pride. The dessert was a layer of crispy, white meringue covered in a layer of fresh whipped cream, with another layer of strawberries on top.

"Jean," Lisa said, "you're a master chef. Have you ever done catering before?"

"Never, but I absolutely love creating new dishes in the kitchen."

"You know, Jean." Lisa said thoughtfully. "Next month we are having a team of builders come from Canada and the U.S. to begin the construction of our church."

"You are?" Richard said.

"I told them they needed to bring along a cook because they will spend most of their daylight hours on the construction site. Would you be interested in helping organize the food for meals?"

"I would love to do that." Jean made no effort to hide her excitement.

Richard's eyebrows rose slightly. "When are they are coming?"

Jay answered. "Four weeks from now. The team will be here for a month. We're housing them with some of the congregation."

"I'll take those four weeks as my holiday time from work. I would be happy to do whatever I can to help build. I have some experience in several of the building trades like brick-laying and joinery. I've also done some electrical work." But Richard had something else to offer. "I've been thinking about the upcoming street mission, but I don't know much about it. How does it work?"

"It's an exciting time. We set up a portable puppet theater with a full sound system. Usually the youth help a lot and we gather around and sing and share our personal story of conversion to anyone who will listen. We also hand out leaflets with the message of the gospel on them. People always crowd around."

"We actually speak to the public about our faith?"

"Absolutely. Are you game?"

"Why not? I'm going to invite some of my neighbors to come around. They might as well see the real me—the new me. They better get used to it, because I'm not going to stop."

Jay believed that God could change anyone, but the remarkable turnaround in Richard amazed him beyond words.

* * *

Jay and Lisa headed home, buoyed by the evening's events. The night air felt fresh and Lisa lowered the window slightly, allowing the cool breeze to touch her face. She smiled as she took Jay's hand in hers.

Jay noticed tears on her cheeks. "You okay, babe?"

She nodded and leaned against the headrest. Their little car headed up the hill beneath a canopy of trees. Jay turned on the high beams, but darkness seemed to envelop them. Lisa's hand went cold. Jay glanced and saw fear in her eyes.

"What's wrong, Lisa?"

"I don't know. I suddenly feel afraid." He heard a tremor in her voice. "It's silly."

Jay whispered a prayer as he drove toward home. When they turned up Carriage Drive toward their cottage, Jay felt the temperature turn icy and Lisa's grip on his hand tightened. She shivered but wouldn't let go. The windows fogged and shapes seemed to form and morph on the windshield. Fear rumbled in Jay's belly as he fought off panic.

* * *

It was three in the morning and Jay lay still, desperate for sleep to come. He'd tried to pray, but answers seemed too elusive and his brain felt muddled. Weary of waiting for sleep, he climbed out of bed, went to the window, and looked between the curtains. Outside, the darkness seemed almost sentient. He heard Michael cough, and he froze, fearing a return of that appalling croup. Michael coughed again and wheezed. "Lord, no, please no. Deliver us from this evil."

The coughing stopped as quickly as it started.

Jay turned back to the window, studying the night's blackness. From the children's bedroom he heard a weak whimper. One of the boys was having a nightmare. Jay slipped into their room and waited.

It was Nathan. "No! No! Go away, go away." He tossed his head back and forth.

Jay knelt beside him and rubbed his back. "Shhhh, Nate. Daddy's right here. No one's going to hurt you. The Lord is watching over you." He kept rubbing his back.

Jay stayed beside Nate's bed until his legs went numb. "I love you, kiddo." He kissed Nathan's head and stood. The children were finally sleeping peacefully.

He returned to bed and eventually slept. Somewhere before daylight, a muffled scream awoke him. It was his scream. In his nightmare he'd seen himself in a mirror and he had no mouth.

CHAPTER TWENTY-THREE

—ᴍ—

There were procedures to follow in conducting a street mission in Kingsbridge. Jay parked his car in a visitor's space and walked up the steps to the Kingsbridge Police Precinct. He'd done this many times before. The post-modern building looked run down, and smelled of stale coffee and grime. Jay walked to the desk where two police officers were chatting. It was Jones and Mercer. Seeing them brought back the emotions of Dungess' attack. He reminded himself he was here on church business.

"Can I help you, Vicar?" Jones asked.

"Hello, Constable Jones." He gave a polite nod and smiled, "Constable Mercer."

Jones' words had a barbed edge. "Is this a friendly visit or are you here today to lodge another complaint?"

Jay was startled. "Not at all. I am just asking permission to set up our puppet theater on Main Street again. We plan to have our usual stories and music for the shoppers on Thursday, during the hours the market stalls are operating. Is that all right?"

Jones studied the request log in front of him. "I don't see any reason why not. We haven't had a problem before. You know the rules." He wrote something down.

"Thanks, Constable." Jay headed for the door but stopped. Something had been eating at him and now was a good time to ask his questions. "Before I go, could I ask you a question?"

Jones' expression cooled further, but Mercer moved closer to the counter.

"Has anything more been investigated regarding the incident at our house?"

"I'm afraid not. We have no further information."

"So, he gets away with it, just like that?"

"It's their word against yours." Jones seemed to have already judged the case.

Jay scratched his head. "But, you saw the damage. Someone had to do it." Jay returned to the counter. "It seems a fairly simple conclusion."

Jones dodged the question. "We could not interview Mr. Dungess. He wasn't home from work."

"He had to be. My wife can testify that he was there." Jay felt agitated. "He was home all right, probably hiding in a corner somewhere. Besides, you saw the footprints on the door. Do you think I did that?" Jay frowned and shook his head. "Who knows what he was planning or what he's capable of?"

"Let's not jump to extremes, sir. Once again, I repeat, we had no proof."

"You had proof, plenty of it. Shoe prints, broken glass, maybe a post stashed somewhere. How much more evidence do you need? Maybe you chose not to believe it."

"Listen Mr. Knight, you might be accustomed to the thrills and spills of Hollywood."

"I'm not accustomed to being victimized at all. I've never met someone like Dungess. He has such penchant for hatred."

"Regardless of what you may think, we do know our job. I've logged your complaints and given suitable warning."

Jay lowered his head. "I apologize. I was completely out of line. Certainly you know your job. I'm just at my wits end. We don't know what to do. Every few days he's up to something new to harass us. My family lives on pins and needles. We feel like no one understands our dilemma." Jay stared at Jones as a thought formed. "Is it because we are Americans?"

Jones looked down at the desk. He started to speak and then stopped. Finally, he stuttered, "If there is nothing else I can help you with, then good day."

"Good day, Constable Jones." Jay left the station and headed for his car. He felt impotent, frustrated, and angry. As he unlocked his door, someone came up from behind.

"Excuse me, Mr. Knight. Can I have a word with you?" It was Constable Mercer.

"Certainly. And I apologize again for my strong words. It's so frustrating."

"I understand. Officer Jones can sometimes be a bit stubborn. I wanted to ask you if you know what kind of vehicles Dungess drives."

"Yes, he drives a blue Volvo station wagon. I don't remember the license."

"What about for his work?"

"Well, recently he puts ladders on the roof rack of his Volvo and takes that to work. Why do you ask?"

"So there are no other vehicles? No van or truck or—"

"He has an orange van that he usually drives, but it must be in for repairs. I haven't seen it for several weeks." Jay frowned. "What is this about?"

Mercer moved closer and lowered his voice. "So the van disappeared, say, right around the time of your wife's accident? Can you recall seeing it since then?"

Jay was surprised. "Do you think...I hadn't put any of that together. I was more focused on my wife's condition than the neighbor's van." He thought for a moment. "It does seem rather coincidental." He looked at Mercer. "How stupid of me."

Mercer's radio squawked and he answered, "Mercer here." Jones wanted him back inside pronto. "Be there in just a tic." Jones growled that a tic wasn't good enough. "I'm sorry about this, Mr. Knight. You've helped me a lot. I'll get in touch later. Don't concern yourself over this. I'm just formulating some thoughts."

Jay thanked him and added, "Hey come by our little group on Thursday. You'll be glad you did." He climbed into his car and pulled onto Main Street. A wave of exhaustion rolled over him. At the traffic light he waited and flipped the visor down and looked at his own reflection. *I look so old today.* A car pulled up behind him and Jay caught the reflection of Dungess in the rearview mirror. Jay groaned. *I can't get away from this guy.*

The red light seemed to last forever. Dungess crept forward until their bumpers connected. *He's trying to intimidate me,* Jay thought. Finally the light changed and Jay shoved his car into gear but it stalled.

Dungess laid on his horn and rolled down his window. "Move it you stupid monkey. Get off the street if you can't drive."

Jay's hand shook and he broke out in a cold sweat. He turned the ignition. "God, help me stay calm." After a second try his car came to life and Jay paced himself as he drove down the main street. The car rumbled behind him like a bulldog. Jay refused to speed up.

The next red light brought a second nudge from the Volvo. Jay ignored it, determined not to surrender to the intimidation.

He'd planned to visit George Evans who lived down Marsh Lane. The man was seeking truth and had lots of questions. Jay tried to concentrate. Where was that turn? The light turned green and Dungess' blasted his horn. He rolled down his window and shouted, "Move it you parasite."

Jay made an abrupt right turn onto Marsh Lane. The old Volvo followed him close enough to fill his rear view mirror. Panic squeezed Jay's throat as he realized this could be a showdown. Will he follow him to Evan's house? Will he get violent or just embarrass him? *That guy is determined.*

"Lord, what do I do? Help me." Sweat ran down Jay's neck and the air in the car seemed to thicken. A few hundred yards further on the road would end. Then he saw it. There was a Y junction straight ahead: one road dead ended and the other circled back round. He'd forgotten this turn. He made a hard right. The tires squealed. The Volvo followed, spitting out gravel.

He saw the house coming up fast on his right. "Thank you, Lord." Without braking, Jay sped into the driveway and down shifted to slow the car. The sudden turn must have caught Dungess off guard. He sailed past and then screeched to a stop. Jay grabbed his Bible and hoofed it to the man's front door. The Volvo backed up two hundred feet, swerving wildly. Jay reached the door and knocked. His knees nearly buckled under him.

Dungess backed up until he was at the driveway then shot forward. Jay knocked again. *Come on Evans, be home?* The Volvo rolled forward crunching gravel as it came closer. Dungess had Jay trapped.

Lord, keep me calm.

Dungess' car sat idling in the driveway only five yards from Jay. Slowly, the car door opened and Dungess stepped out.

The front door of the house opened and Jay nearly melted in relief.

"Hello?" The man looked first at Jay and then curiously at the man next to the Volvo.

"Hello, Mr. Evans."

"Ah yes, Pastor Knight. What a delight to see you. Come in. Come in." Evans peered over Jay's shoulder. "Is that man in the Volvo with you?"

"No sir. It's a bit embarrassing but he's been following me through the village."

"Shall I call the police for you? They might just come out and talk to him."

"Oh thank you Mr. Evans, but that shouldn't be necessary. I think he'll go away on his own soon enough."

Evans seemed so delighted to see Jay, that the incident didn't seem to faze him. They went in and shut the door. "Thanks so much for coming. No minister has ever visited our house before. You'd better sit down; you look like you could use a good cup of tea."

He led Jay to a French style sofa with gray and blue pinstripes. The sound of squealing tires crept into the house.

"My wife is out at the shops right now. So, I'll make us a brew."

"Thank you, Mr. Evans. That sounds great." Jay settled and felt his anxiety slowly leak away. The relief was sweet.

"Please call me George," the host called from the kitchen. "Sugar?"

"Please. And call me Jay." He waited for George to reappear.

George appeared with a tray of biscuits and two mugs and set it down in front of Jay. "The sugar was hiding." The man had salt and pepper hair with a matching goatee. He had a professorial look about him. He sat opposite Jay. "Well now Jay, tell me all about yourself." And he added, "Before you start, you should know that I'm a salesman myself, so you've got my undivided attention."

Jay's adrenaline was still pumping from the chase. Now faced with eternal matters, Jay used this energy and plunged into a creative presentation of the gospel. "Well George, what I have to offer you is absolutely revolutionary. It's life altering.

"It's more than a concept or philosophical persuasion; more than a wish or dream. It's life with a capital L and carries an eternal lifetime guarantee, direct from the makers."

George sat mesmerized and scooted an inch closer.

"It has global market potential and could transform life as we know it. Every human alive has wanted it, dreamed about it, and some have died trying in vain to get the same results without the original product. As you can imagine, the world is insanely jealous of the maker. Some have tried to clone it, replicate it, eradicate it, and even deny it, but all have failed.

"This thing you speak of is…what?"

"The chance to live forever, forgiven, and complete."

"Ah, you've discovered the fountain of youth."

"Eternal life."

George had played along. "Let's get to the price. What will it cost me?" George's face tightened.

"You couldn't afford it. Not in a million lifetimes. It's priceless."

"Why offer me something I can't buy?" George haggled. "That's cruel."

"You can't buy it, but you can have it for free."

"What's the catch?"

"There is no catch."

"There has to be a catch. You and I both know that nothing that's worth anything is free." George leaned forward. "Right?"

"Absolutely. It's free to those who accept it by faith, but at the price of the death of God's only Son. The contract was signed and sealed in God's own blood."

George Evans took no notice of the kettle screaming in the kitchen.

"Do you need to get that?" Jay pointed to the kitchen.

"Huh? Oh yes. Crumbs." George said. "Don't go anywhere." Tea brewed in record time while the two talked about the world's condition and humanity's need for rescue.

After a half hour of listening, George said, "I never understood the purpose of the cross. Now, I wonder how I ever missed its significance."

George was ready. Gently, Jay led George Evans to the cross where he surrendered a lifetime of struggle, in exchange for eternity. That day George's name was written in blood in the Lamb's Book of Life.

"Thank you my friend. I'm so glad you came. I want my wife Laura to listen to your sales pitch. Would you be willing to talk with her too?"

"Absolutely."

CHAPTER TWENTY-FOUR

—⚬—

It was a brilliant, sunny morning with billowy clouds that floated across a sapphire sky. Sun worshippers filled the sidewalk cafes. The street market was already crowded with vendors calling out their wares. The smell of freshly baked bread lingered outside the bakery.

Today was Richard and Jean's introduction to street evangelism. They were excited, but also nervous. They'd attended the prayer meetings and worked on their stories and now the day had arrived.

A group of teens helped Jay assemble the puppet theater. It stood six feet tall and four feet wide. Bright colors covered its surface and the image of two puppets posed to resemble the Greek masks of drama caught the eyes of every passerby. Volunteer actors had recorded the scripts with musical scores and sound effects. The short plays contained dry, poker-faced humor designed to make the audience think, and then laugh at the absurdity of it all.

The set up included a portable sound system designed to connect to Jay's car battery. It carried the good news throughout town. The team, supplied with leaflets, huddled in a corner to pray before the ministry began.

By nine, the market stalls were bustling, and apart from the modern clothing and vehicles whizzing past, Jay could easily imagine the scene as purely medieval. People haggled with vendors. Shoppers delighted to save a penny. It was a happy crowd.

It was in this marketplace that Jay and Lisa first stood in Kingsbridge to tell the good news to people. It was here where the kernel of hope sprung forth in hungry hearts and where the foundations of a new church had formed. Jay felt he was standing on sacred ground.

Nathan and Michael had started their lives cradled in a world of evangelism. Before they could speak, they'd heard the Gospel countless times and witnessed conversions. Truth had taken root in their young minds. Today they were more than observers. They helped assemble the theater, hand out leaflets, and laugh at the stories the puppets told. Joey sat in his stroller or rode on daddy's shoulders as he witnessed.

As before, a few adults stopped to ask challenging questions. With the English propensity to debate, Jay was certain to get a response. The ministry team worked together, supporting a newcomer and stepping in with relevant responses. Ray and Jenny were experts in this field and helped train others in sharing Scripture.

The outreach included more than puppets, several church members had promised to give their testimonies. Jay whispered to Jean, "Are you ready?"

She shook her head. "I don't think I can do this."

"Just tell your story."

Richard stood close as Jean reached for the microphone. Her hand trembled as she began.

"Hello." The microphone screeched. "My name is Jean McGregor and I have a story to tell." People gathered to listen. Jean looked at Richard with pleading eyes, then shifted her gaze across the street. She hesitated.

Jay followed her gaze and saw a slack-jawed woman staring back. "Do you know her?" he asked Richard.

"Her name's Dottie. She's a neighbor."

Jean took a deep breath and let the words tumble out.

"I have a story to tell. It is a story about my search for the meaning of life; my life." A little white haired woman waved, and Jean waved back. "Hello, Mavis." Jean's voice grew stronger. "I thought life consisted of a good marriage, a great family, and all the material wealth I could accumulate. But there was always an emptiness inside me that I couldn't shake. I used to cry a lot at night because I felt so frustrated.

"Two months ago, I met a person who told me all that I had ever done, and yet loved me just the same. He wanted to be my friend. He wanted to be a part of my life forever. He told me that I could be forgiven of my sins. Jesus Christ has become my best friend and he is the one who now fills that emptiness with the greatest satisfaction."

Jean was on a roll. She used her hands to encourage listeners to respond. Her courage brought excitement to the entire team. Motivated by her example, others lined up to share their testimony.

"It's time for you to receive Jesus Christ. Come and talk with us." She finished and handed the microphone to Jay. Before he could do anything, Jean grabbed it back. "Don't be afraid to come to Him. It will be the best choice you ever made."

* * *

Across the street, hidden between two stalls, the gypsy woman stood in a trance-like stare. Elena Chernik pointed toward the crowd of Christians and growled a curse. "I curse you and your family, you stupid preacher."

* * *

The witnessing team continued with their upbeat songs and challenging testimonies. The crowd grew. A gang of bikers roared past and then circled round to see what was going on. They pulled up and sat on their machines, letting them rumble and cough fumes into the crowd. Jay made no response. They laughed and jeered at the Christians, but the program continued. Finally, the leader cut his engine and signaled for the rest to do the same. A few pub crawlers came out carrying pints of Guinness. As the singers continued, Jay spotted one man who seemed somewhat interested. "Hi, I'm Jay. Thanks for coming to listen. What's your name?"

The man stumbled slightly but caught himself. "Flannigan, Patrick Flannigan, but you can call me, Paddy." He wiped his mouth on his coat sleeve and reached out to shake Jay's hand.

"I never heard nothin' like what you been sayin' before. And my mum told me that my great, great granddaddy was an Irish priest, only no one s'posed ta know." He held up a finger to his mouth. "Shhhh, now don't tell. He done wrong, I know that, but we can't do nothin' about it now, can we? We can't change the past." He cocked his head at a tilt.

Jay believed the story because he recognized pain in Paddy's eyes.

"No Paddy, we can't change the past, but Jesus can forgive us from our past. As far as the east is from the west, so far does He remove our sins from us when we repent. Isn't that wonderful news?"

Paddy's eyes filled up. His leathery, lined face softened.

Jay signaled Ray to join him and help Paddy find God. The music continued as the three men prayed for heaven to come down.

Paddy sobbed with remorse over his broken life. He'd failed his wife and children. His drinking had kept them nearly destitute.

Ray took Paddy's name, address and phone number and arranged to take him to church Sunday morning. Ray would work well with Paddy. He'd been on the wagon for ten years, so he understood the challenges that awaited Paddy.

To Jay's left he saw Richard single out a man he knew. The two of them talked for a long time.

Jenny was praying with a woman and her daughter in one corner of the crowd while David and Rachel were sharing the Good News with a young family.

Lisa had the three lads, but was talking in earnest to a woman with shopping bags in her hands. The woman was crying.

Several teens latched onto the bikers and sat on the ground sharing their faith.

By day's end, there were four new believers added to the Kingdom of God.

Just before the team disbanded, an older man walked to Jay and asked to speak with him privately. Jay agreed and directed him towards a park bench away from the crowd. The man looked familiar to Jay.

The old fellow was dressed in worn tweed and rumpled trousers. It was when the man tugged at his collar that Jay knew — Madlaw, the minister of the United Church. But he'd changed.

"As you know, I'm the minister of The United Church in Kingsbridge and have been for the past twelve years. There really isn't sufficient population in this community for another church. We've already closed down one and amalgamated two congregations to keep the other alive. Since the United Church has been here for at least a century, we ask that you give us all your contacts from these . . . these…" He waved his arm around in a circle pointing to the ministry team, "Missions, or whatever this distraction is called. We can provide all new recruits with a nice chapel, you can't. We can offer the services of marriage, baptism and burials which people wouldn't want to be performed in a community center, or a barn for that matter." He chuckled and his laughter rattled like ice cubes in a glass.

Jay listened in silence for a moment. When he spoke, his voice was low and steady. "I hope you were as thrilled as I was to see people respond to the gospel today. I'm appointed here by my church, my denomination. I am accountable to them for the new congregation under my care. I have no authority to pass these precious new believers to anyone else." Madlaw tried to interrupt. Jay held up his hand and continued, "Certainly there is nothing stopping you and your congregation, logistically, from holding a mission here in this same place anytime you desire. All contacts you make would be your own, and we would honor that."

The man bristled. "Who do you think you are?"

"Just a guy with a desire to help people find God. We did our research before we came. Kingsbridge has a population of approximately 12,000. Out of that, less than 500 people attend Christian services on a regular basis. I'd say that the majority of the population is unchurched." Jay stood. "It looks like we both have a lot of work ahead of us. I must get back to my people. Good day, Mr. Madlaw." Jay turned to leave.

"Curse you; you're nothing but an American cult." He stood blocking Jay's path. "You're a charlatan, Knight. You're a con." He shoved his chest out and slammed into Jay like a school yard bully.

"This conversation is over."

The man shoved Jay again, knocking him onto the bench.

Jay caught himself and stood. "I'm sorry for you, Mr. Madlaw."

The man's eyes grew black. He lunged at Jay but fell short and stumbled.

Jay headed back to the event where there was safety in numbers. Hopefully, Madlaw had finished making his point. Jay shook the incident from his thoughts and focused on the fruit of the work. "This is what we're here for. This is where

God wants us to be at this particular moment." Jay needed the reminder. Otherwise, the attacks would dominate his thoughts and he wouldn't let that happen.

He turned to see Madlaw walking away, talking to himself.

The team had been tearing down the equipment and packing it away when suddenly, the heavens opened up, delivering sheets of driving rain upon Kingsbridge. Lisa and the children were in the car. By the time Jay finished, he was soaked to the bone. As the family headed home, Lisa studied Jay's face. "That was great today."

"Yes, it was." Jay turned the wipers higher. "It was incredible."

Lisa asked, "Are you okay?"

"Sure. Why wouldn't I be?" He studied the road ahead a bit too hard. "I'm just tired, like the rest of us."

The children were close to dozing, crunched together in the backseat. The windows steamed over and Nate drew happy faces on the glass.

Once the car was parked and the engine off, Jay said, "I was reminded of a verse from Isaiah. God said, "I have put my words in your mouth and covered you with the shadow of My hand."

Lisa raised her eyebrows. "Has something else happened Jay? Something I don't know about?"

"Nothing significant, all things considered." Jay said.

"You disappeared for a while. Where were you?"

"Everything is fine, I told you before." Jay started to open the door.

"We can't take anymore, Jay. At least I can't." She wouldn't let go. "I can't take this conflict. I hate those neighbors..."

Jay put his finger to his lips. "Shhh. The lads." He rolled his eyes to the backseat.

Lisa softened her voice but continued speaking. "I just wish we had some support here. You, me, we both need support. This work is too hard on our own."

Rain was hammering away at the car's roof and hood. Jay nodded toward the front door. "Let's get inside the ark before we're washed away."

CHAPTER TWENTY-FIVE

—⁓—

The day finally came for the builders to arrive. Jay stood waiting in Terminal Four at Heathrow Airport just outside London. Thirty-three people from Canada and the U.S. were meeting for the first time; some of whom had never stepped foot outside of their homeland. The volunteer workers had responded to a need paying their own way and using their skills to build God's house. There were stonemasons, carpenters, electricians, and cabinetmakers, roofers, and an army chef.

Jay weaved his way through restless crowds. The cavernous terminal was noisy, filled with a constant hum of travelers. Jay had set up a rendezvous point identified by a sign that read "Kingsbridge Temple Builders." Team members traveled on Air Canada, United Airlines, and British Airways coming from places that spanned a three hour time difference. Thirteen hours before, they'd left their homes and families to land in the world's loneliest city. They would experience a cultural jolt.

*   *   *

Back home, McGregor had some plans of his own. In the early morning fog, Richard drove his SUV between the old barns and parked in the open field. He'd gotten some steel cable from a scrap yard. After tying one end around the top of one of the colossal stone columns, he affixed the other end to his vehicle. Once the cable was in place and taut, he began chiseling a line around the base of one of the columns. Huge beams and a slate roof tied the columns together. It took two hours to chisel all four columns. Already the structure creaked and groaned. Richard knew this would be a great surprise to Jay when he returned with the builders. It would save a lot of time.

* * *

The first to arrive were two brothers, both stonemasons from Oregon. Thirty minutes later, carpenters arrived from Arizona and Kansas. Others came from Washington, California, New York, Ontario and Alberta, Canada. Three university students were the last to arrive due to a customs delay in Greenland.

* * *

Richard wiped sweat from his forehead as he stood to survey his work. With a sense of accomplishment, he climbed into his vehicle and started the engine. He watched from his rear view mirror as the cable twanged and jittered under the pressure. The Mercedes lurched forward and fragments of stone and dust sprayed from various pressure points on the columns. He leaned out the window to watch dust billow as shingles broke and slid down the roof. Roosting pigeons flapped into the sky. The structure twisted at an angle and began to slope downward. One beam teetered precariously as the stones loosened from their century old moorings.

The Mercedes strained forward while the building trembled and groaned. "This is really working." He felt like a kid.

A charge of adrenaline made Richard shout, "Hallelujah. Whoopee."

* * *

Once the group had gathered, Jay flipped his sign around which read, "Follow Me," and pointed to a bus outside the terminal. The rumpled travelers were weary but excited and followed their leader outside and beneath an overcast sky. A long line of taxis rumbled at the curbside belching plumes of diesel exhaust into the air. One by one, the recruits climbed onto the bus for the last leg of their journey.

* * *

The structure collapsed like matchsticks. The ground trembled as one ton stones hit the earth and tumbled toward the SUV. Richard's heart thumped so hard it hurt his chest. He realized too late that this could be dangerous. The cable was too short. He watched in horror as an avalanche of small stones pelted his vehicle. He floored the accelerator, but the cable kept the SUV tethered to the pile of rubble that was thundering toward him. His windshield shattered into fragments spraying glass chips in his face. The back window imploded. Football sized rocks bounced on the roof, denting it like a soda can. Before he could breathe, a massive stone came hurtling toward him. He screamed as it hit the backend of the Mercedes, thrusting the front of the vehicle up in the air. His prayers came in bursts of stuttering syllables; "God... save... me!" To his surprise, the vehicle didn't fall back down. Apparently, the enormous stone had pinned the back end of his SUV to the ground and he sat there, suspended in the driver's seat like an astronaut ready for takeoff.

Richard froze in his seat as strained metal screeched around him. The glove compartment popped open spilling its contents everywhere. A half filled coffee mug poured cold liquid on him. He started to move but his seat slipped and thumped back a notch, causing the car to spasm and his heart to jack hammer. He glanced out his window. He hung five feet from earth. How would he escape without starting an avalanche of mangled metal and stone?

He decided he would have to jump and scramble away before the thing fell completely. He tried his door, but it was jammed. He considered the possibilities and determined that his only way out was through the shattered windshield. Slowly, he clawed his way through the opening. It was now or never. He pulled himself onto the hood and a moment later dropped to the ground. The wreck shook and groaned as Richard scrambled for his life on all fours. The Mercedes rumbled as the stone holding it in place yielded its grip. The vehicle crashed to the ground, landing on what used to be four good radial tires.

"Thank you, Jesus. I'm still alive!" He brushed the dirt from his face and clothes and checked his wounds. With one final look at the Mercedes he said, "There goes my bonus."

* * *

The bus followed London's Ring Road and headed north on the M6 motorway. Jay gave the team a quick overview of their assignment and a rough schedule. He'd prepared handouts for the group. The recruits were beyond exhaustion, yet too charged to sleep. So the last leg of their journey gave them an opportunity to get acquainted and plan. Around the time they reached Stratford, they had chosen a supervisor who began to formulate a schedule. When they hit the suburbs of Birmingham, there was still a lot of chatter and Jay had met everyone. As darkness fell, the travelers headed into a storm that had swept in from the North Sea. The driver slowed to a steady pace and soon the droning of tires and the rattle of rain lulled the travelers to sleep.

Jay kept vigil. He could not sleep with so much on his mind. His brain had hit overload long before this day arrived. Life, both good and bad, had suddenly become so intense that Jay wondered if he could sustain a healthy balance. With each slap of the wipers, his thoughts raced between hope and fear; possibilities and overwhelming dread. *I'm depending on You, God. I don't think I can hold it together on my own.*

* * *

During the next four weeks, the old farm yard turned into a construction site and finally transformed into a temple of worship. Each morning at daybreak the workers assembled for prayer and then swarmed over the work area and labored until a church began to rise from the rubble. This was no erector set construction. This was steel and brick and walls of hand-hewn stones carved a century before and waiting for this crowning moment to become part of God's house. Britain's great cathedrals took lifetimes to build. This one was built in a month.

The work seemed never to stop. The volunteers dug footings, poured concrete, raised steel arches, and laid stone walls. A two-story chancel appeared to rise overnight followed by an imposing bell tower with a slate roof. Carpenters built windows and doors and crafted pulpit furniture. Masons selected color and pattern in their stones to create a wall of beauty. Craftsman set a stained glass window in the center of the nave. Atop the tower the simple lines of a cross shadowed the earth. It seemed too that God was reclaiming the land. Once ruled by darkness, a group of Kingsbridge residents had seated the King of Peace in their midst. The soldiers of God had moved in, subdued and conquered the territory, and had done so in the name of Jesus Christ.

As their time came to a close, the builders and congregation had formed a marriage of hearts that stretched into eternity. The final night was an unforgettable celebration that would carry them through the uncharted waters still to come. Emotions were high. The mayor came, along with his entourage of council members, city planners, a few photographers, members of the press and Councilman Clary. These dignitaries insisted on having their photos taken with Richard and Jean, who endured a million questions about their new faith. Jay had invited his Supervisor, Vic Trinder, and his attorney, Philip Gentry. They seemed thrilled with the work accomplished in Kingsbridge.

Jay and Lisa took in everything, basking in the ecstasy of what God had done. It was a night like no other. They drank in the sights and sounds and feasted on the celebration.

Vic Trinder leaned close to Jay and whispered, "My son, what you've done in Kingsbridge is worth a lifetime of service to God." He studied Jay's face and added, "If you never do another thing for the Kingdom of God, you've done enough here." In spite of their intended praise, the words left Jay unsettled. As the two groups said their final goodbyes, a melancholy settled over Jay's heart, like the shadow of God's hand.

CHAPTER TWENTY-SIX

—⚇—

Lisa was ecstatic. "Jay, this envelop was left at our front door. Look." She almost danced into his office.

"What is it?"

"It's a letter and check from the McGregors. I can't believe it."

Jay looked up from his studies. "Well, what's it say?"

Lisa rolled Jay's chair out and sat on his lap. "They've arranged for us to take a weekend break in Stratford. And here's spending money." She waved a check in her hands. "They've booked a cottage for three days. And look," she held up two tickets, "we've got tickets to the Royal Shakespeare Theater to see *Macbeth*." Lisa squeezed Jay. "Can you believe it? And they'll take the lads while we're away."

"Cash the check before they change their minds," Jay laughed. "I guess you're not excited are you?"

"Never. I'll start packing now."

* * *

Following school on Friday, the lads were delivered, without incident, to the McGregor's and the couple set off heading south.

Lisa preferred that they head directly to Stratford-on-Avon and check into the bed and breakfast. Then they could eat and do some sightseeing or take a walk along the river Avon. The weather was wonderful and warm, and the drive went by effortlessly.

The Inn was perfect in Lisa's book. The thatched cottage displayed dormer windows which looked out over an English garden in full bloom. The front door of the cottage had climbing Constance Spry pink roses which had a sweet fragrance. A young girl greeted them and showed them to their room.

The bedroom had polished dark oak floorboards that had been doweled rather than nailed in place. The furniture was authentic Elizabethan, with a tall poster-bed in dark oak. The bedclothes were finished in gold brocade with satin pillows and sheets. There were ornate accent rugs dotted around the room, and in every corner Lisa noticed antique vases, wall hangings, and historic furniture. A rocking chair sat to one side of the bed.

Jay closed the bedroom door, raised his eyebrows, and smiled. "Well, what do you think? Pretty nice stuff. I think this will do." He walked toward Lisa and gave her a big hug lifting her feet off the ground.

She responded with a kiss. Jay held her tight and swung her in a circle. "Oh Jay, this is what every woman dreams about. This cottage couldn't be more perfect. It's like a fairy tale come true." She flung open the diamond leaded windows allowing the fragrance of the garden to permeate the room. She hugged herself with delight and swung around as she heard a knock at the door.

"Come in, please."

The hostess of the cottage was a tiny lady in her late sixties. She had gray hair, pulled back and pinned up. Dainty stones hung from her ears. Her dark purple dress with the high, white-laced collar seemed appropriate for the setting.

"Welcome. My name is Dorrey. I hope your journey was comfortable."

"It was just great," Lisa said beaming at the little lady.

"Dinner will be served at six-fifteen sharp. You have bath towels set out for you, but if you should need anything else, just give me a tinkle. We serve dinner in the dining room by the open fire. Following dinner there is coffee or tea along with cheese and biscuits. Do you have any questions?"

Lisa looked up at Jay with contentment. "I don't think so, Dorrey. You're place is lovely. Thank you for sharing it with others from time to time."

"Oh, I wouldn't do it any other way. This cottage has been in my family for three generations and it has always been open to weary travelers. If there is nothing more, I shall go. Remember six-fifteen sharp. We have ten other guests that will be dining together with you."

"Certainly. Thank you."

Jay flopped on the bed. He heard the Westminster chimes in the hallway ring out five o'clock and suddenly felt very tired.

Lisa quietly shut the door and locked the bolt. "What a sweet lady."

"Come and lay down beside me for forty-five minutes. We'll be more refreshed for the evening." He patted her side of the bed.

Lisa slid down beside her husband, set the alarm, and then snuggled close.

*   *   *

Dinner was a feast of roast beef, Yorkshire pudding, roasted potatoes, veggies and lots of gravy. There was hot cider to drink and a rich trifle for the sweet. Coffee beside the fire, finished off with cheddar cheese and biscuits, made the meal fit for royalty.

The fire roared and crackled in front of them. The stresses of the world seemed to fade. It was a time of refreshment, a time to forget that there were bad people in the world; a time to love each other and be refreshed. After the meal, they slipped into the early evening to enjoy a walk along the riverbanks of Avon.

They walked in silence for a while. The willow trees along the banks swayed in the breeze and caressed the water's edge. They stopped to watch two magnificent swans glide along the river. The summer days were shortening and daylight faded into eventide. Slowly gas streetlamps came on one by one.

Lisa felt her world gradually become tranquil and serene. She sensed feelings she had not experienced in several months. She held her husband's hand, but then let go so she could put her arm around his waist and draw him closer. She wanted to hold on to this moment forever, to feel secure and know that the world still offered promise.

The path led them over an arched wooden bridge where they paused to listen to the sounds of the night. They heard the water lap against the bank's edge and above, the flutter of wings as birds settled in for the night.

Tonight, the world offered magic for Lisa, yet, she knew it was fragile. She looked up at Jay and kissed his lips, then laid her head on his chest, holding him tight. She could hear the gentle beating of his heart. His heartbeat was the sound of life and love. She smiled in the growing darkness. In spite of her husband's impetuous ways, in spite of his blundering words, his heart was good. His heart wanted to please God and his heart loved Lisa and the lads. Silently, she thanked God that she had a man with a good heart.

"I love you, Jay. Our lives are like a whirlwind some-times, but it hasn't changed my love for you."

"I love you too, babe." Although she tried to hide it, he noticed her tear. "What's wrong, Lis?"

"I'm not sure." She paused. "Why is life so hard at times? Why do we have to fight to survive?"

Jay held her close. "Isn't that what we signed up for?"

"We signed up to tell the good news." Lisa's voice was muffled. "I just forgot to read the fine print." She hesitated. "I just wish—"

"What?"

"Nothing. I promised I wouldn't bring up this stuff. I'm sorry. Let's not discuss it now. Not here. Not on this trip."

"It's a deal." They strolled back to the cottage. Before going to their room, they sat in front of the fire and sipped steaming mugs of hot chocolate. Flames danced in the hearth and soon they were spellbound. Around eleven, they went to their room.

Behind the bedroom door, they allowed their passion to grow; passion that had been stifled by too many distractions. With the building of the church, the demands of three boys, and the madman next door, there didn't seem time for, or interest in lovemaking.

Now there was.

She turned to look at him. She loved the features of his face, features that revealed kindness and confidence. She liked the way his lips parted when he smiled at her. She liked the way they felt against hers. She kissed him again.

They let the moment build slowly, kissing, caressing, touching and holding.

"You smell good."

"You feel good."

"Is it getting warm in here, or is it just me?" she asked.

"I hope it's just you."

She whispered, "Why don't you turn out the lights."

"Certainly ma'am."

* * *

Lisa looked exquisite in a Sapphire gown that fit like a glove. The lines were pure yet simple, accentuating her shapeliness. The gown gave elegance to Lisa's natural beauty in a way that took Jay's breath. A single strand of pearls around her neck and a replacement set of pearl drop earrings made her stunning.

Jay studied his princess for a moment. "You are not merely stunning my lady, you are ravishing. You're the most beautiful woman on the planet. May I offer you my arm?"

Lisa's demure smile made Jay want to do a double flip as they walked arm in arm toward the Royal Shakespeare Theatre.

The orchestration soared to create drama as the house-lights dimmed. Actors strutted on stage in luxurious attire. The powerful strains of music and the intensity of the script were captivating. Lisa was caught up in the tragedy of Macbeth.

> "To-morrow, and to-morrow, and to-morrow,
> Creeps in this petty pace from day to day
> to the last syllable of recorded time,
> and all our yesterdays have lighted fools
> The way to dusty death. Out, out, brief candle!
> Life's but a walking shadow, a poor player
> That struts and frets his hour upon the stage
> And then is heard no more: it is a tale
> Told by an idiot, full of sound and fury,
> Signifying nothing."

In the closing scene, Macduff entered with the head of Macbeth in his hands. The witches' prophecies were fulfilled and Malcolm was hailed as King of Scotland. The players bowed and the curtain closed. The music rose in crescendo then ended dramatically. Through the play, the audience faced a tragedy that has rolled through the ages.

"Shakespeare certainly was the master of tragedies, wasn't he?" Jay said. He and Lisa watched as others began to leave. Men dressed in tuxes and women in satin gowns rose and moved into the aisles, each discussing some element of the plot, the depth of the story, or the intensity of the violence and betrayal.

"I haven't read Shakespeare since university. I'd forgotten how bloody it was." Lisa paused as a couple slid past them. "I wished we could have seen a more romantic play like Romeo and Juliet."

"Ah yes, but there was tragedy in that story too. Tragedy is more a part of our lives than we care to admit. It is a good thing that in real life, God uses tragedy to bring about good."

Lisa shuddered.

"Are you okay?" Jay put his arm around her as they walked out of the theater doors and into the night air.

"It's chilly out." She paused and looked at him. "The conflict in the story reminds me of us."

"You mean that someone wants my head?" Jay tried to lighten Lisa's sudden mood change.

"Be serious a minute, Jay. Why can't God take away the things that hurt us?" She stopped walking. "God could send the Dungess family to another town. He could turn them into…"

"A family of frogs?"

"Stop it. I'm serious. If God loves us so much, why can't He protect us from them?"

"Do you really want to talk about this tonight? I'll do it if you want, but it could ruin the evening."

Lisa studied Jay's eyes. "You're right. I've broken my promise twice." She gave him a quick kiss. "Sorry."

They walked arm in arm beneath trees that framed each lamplight. Across the lawn, Jay spotted a pub called the Dirty Duck. The outside patio was filling with some of the younger theatergoers. "Want to go to the Dirty Duck?"

"Let's head back, Jay. It's not very appealing. People get loud when they drink."

Just beyond the theater, they entered the secluded New Place Garden. They strolled down the lane and watched other couples do the same. They stopped by a huge Mulberry tree.

"Lisa." He looked into her eyes. "You were the most beautiful woman there tonight. I was proud to be by your side. You are the best thing that ever happened to me."

She blushed. "Thanks," she whispered in his ear. Then she kissed it.

They walked again, heading toward the cottage and the comfort of a roaring fire.

CHAPTER TWENTY-SEVEN

—⟋⟋⟋—

October arrived with a gray mist and a biting chill in the air. The warmth of summer had quickly faded, and the cold days of winter had already pulled autumn into its grip. The leaves changed colors, withered, and dropped almost in a single motion. The days shortened, and the darkness of night deepened.

Jay left the car with Lisa and walked using short cuts across town to make his pastoral visits. First, Jay visited Bryan and Kate. With only two slip-ups in his sobriety, Bryan had made real spiritual strides, taking responsibility for his family. He'd taken training for another job that gave him more time with his wife and kids. Kate was happy when he put away his butcher knives for good. He attended AA meetings twice a week and brought other members to church. He and Kate decided to get marriage counseling to deal with Bryan's past. During Bryan's low moments, he would call Jay and weep over what he almost did, and reassure his pastor that he was a new man in Christ. When Jay left their house, it was four in the afternoon and the street lights were coming on. Across the horizon, Jay could see a thin sliver of gold as the sun dipped below the cloud layer.

Jay slipped through a snicket and down an alleyway to get to Main Street. From there he headed north, turned down a cul-de-sac, and arrived at the Raines house on the other edge of town. Geoff and Brenda had never given up hope for Maria. Over time, they learned to leave her in God's hands. They'd received a letter from her six months earlier saying she was living in Wales with her baby and some guy. But Maria had given no forwarding address.

Jay made it a point to visit the Raines at least once a week. He could only imagine what it must be like to have their only child runaway. They had never met their only grandson. They needed reassurance that God was working on their behalf. Jay reminded them that God's timing is different than ours, but He's never late.

It was well after five when Jay left their house and day had given way to darkness. He walked quickly through the alternating puddles of light from street lamps.

The streetlamps ended at the entrance to Carriage Drive leaving only the lights from distant houses to guide him. Thunder rumbled but offered no rain. Jay hurried along when a vehicle swung onto the road behind him and started up the hill. Only one headlight glowed, and the parking lights flickered. The driver had put on his high beams. The one-eyed van traveled up the hill dragging its exhaust pipe along the ground. At first, Jay was glad for the added light. But as it came closer he stopped, fearing the driver might not see him in the dark. He knew the road had deep gullies on either side. Ground mist hung low and swirled around his feet giving a false sense that the ground was flat. The vehicle was coming closer. Jay turned and waved wildly, but the van kept coming. The driver's dome light flicked on and Jay felt a wave of nausea when he saw Dungess' face. He seemed to be enjoying some kind of twisted pleasure in finding Jay in the dark. Jay stepped back, but the van kept tracking him like a hunter.

Dungess jerked the steering wheel and Jay jumped backward certain he was about to be hit. The loose ground at the road's edge gave way. Grasping for a handhold, he slid and

tumbled down into the gully. The van roared past and disappeared into the fog. Jay had no light to see, but he felt the
oozing mud suck him down. He reached for anything that
would hold his weight, but each move caused him to sink
deeper into the mud. His legs felt like lead.

He prayed for help as he grabbed clumps of grass and
weeds. His hand touched what felt like a root of a tree and
he grasped it with both hands. His hands were slick with
mud, but he fought to keep hold of it. Slowly, he pulled one
leg from the stubborn muck, but his hands slipped and he
fell back into the ditch. He tried again. This time his foot
found something firm to stand on and he pushed himself up.
Reaching with his left hand, he grabbed at another root close
to the road surface.

Something sharp jabbed Jay's hand, but he wasn't about
to let go. He held on tight, slowly pulling himself out of the
ditch. He drew himself onto the road and lay face down until
he could catch his breath. His hands still grasped clumps of
dirt and grass. Rain began to fall. Whatever jabbed him felt
like a fish hook, but it was the least of his concern. He was
glad to be out of the ditch. Minutes passed as he calmed
himself. Rising from the ground, he trudged home.

When Lisa opened the door and saw Jay covered in mud,
she gasped. "What in the world happened to you?"

"It's a long story. Can you help me get out of these muddy
clothes?"

She started pulling his shirt over his head when Jay
yelped. "Stop. I've got something stuck in my hand. Go
slowly."

Carefully, she peeled his shirt and pants off at the front
door leaving him standing in his boxers. He shivered while
she got buckets of hot water and doused him from head to
toe. "You poor baby. Who did this to you?"

"One guess." He stepped inside and Lisa wrapped him
with a bath towel while the boys snickered behind her. "You

think it's funny, huh?" He sat down in the kitchen. "I guess I do look kind of silly."

"Were you playing in the mud, Dad?" Nathan teased. Jay shook his wet hair at the boys and they all squealed with delight.

"Jay, you're bleeding. Open your hand." Lisa dabbed at the mud. "What's this?" Her eyes widened. "You found it! I can't believe it. You found my missing pearl earring?"

"Earring? So I've been wearing an earring all this time? I'll never live this down."

"Hold still while I unhook it." She was amazed. "Where did you find it?"

"I didn't. It found me. It must have been on the side of the road somewhere or in the ditch. I felt it when Dungess tried to run me down." Jay's voice halted and he stared at Lisa. "Are you thinking what I'm thinking?"

Lisa put her hand over her mouth and gasped.

"The police never did figure who ran you off the road did they?" Jay said. "One of his headlights was smashed and the van was banged up pretty bad. You have to hit something for that to happen."

A flush of anger rose in Lisa. "That man is homicidal."

"I'm calling Mercer. I think he suspected him all along." Jay stood.

"You can do that later, first, you need a shower and some dry clothes. I need to clean out that wound so it won't get infected."

* * *

Heavy thudding woke Jay from a sound sleep. Lisa bolted upright. The windows were rattling and the house shook as if someone were ramming a truck against it.

"What's happening? It feels like an earthquake."

"It's more than an earthquake." The rhythmic thump continued. It was still dark outside and the house was cold. Jay was already down the hall when screams erupted from the children's room. Lisa rushed behind him as the children tumbled out, nearly colliding in the hall.

Nate screamed. "Daddy, the house is falling. We're going to die. That man is hammering our walls."

"Hey cowboy, help me get your brothers downstairs." Jay flicked on the children's light and watched in shock as fissures appeared on the plastered walls, shooting out puffs of plaster dust into the air. "Quick, let's go." He grabbed Joey and headed down the stairs. "Lis, get a blanket."

Lisa didn't move. She stood in the children's doorway riveted by what she was seeing.

Jay turned and looked back up. "Lisa, quickly."

Lisa didn't seem to hear. Slowly, she backed away from the children's door.

"Lisa, come on!" Why wasn't she moving? Jay noticed she was trembling. "Lisa, get down here, I'm calling the police." Lisa balled her fists and let out a blood curdling scream. "Stop it, you crazy man. Leave us alone. Stop it. Stop it." She pounded the door and stomped on the floor. "Stop it, you evil man." She slumped to the floor and sobbed.

Jay had Nate take his brothers into the living room while he went back up to get Lisa. "Lisa, I need you down stairs." He lifted her up from the floor. "Quick, I need you to calm the children while I call the police."

She stared straight ahead. Her eyes no longer focused. "We're not safe here. Not in this house; not in this town; not in this ministry. God has abandoned us."

Jay guided her down the stairs and into the living room.

"Enough is enough. This crazy man is going to kill us. I know it."

"Don't talk that way, Lisa. Not in front of the kids." Jay found a throw and wrapped it around the three boys. The children were hysterical.

"Come on, boys. Sit close together until the room warms up." Jay flicked on the thermostat. His family was in chaos.

Lisa looked up. She suddenly came out of her stupor and ran into the kitchen. "It's in here Jay. He's trying to break through our kitchen." She grabbed an iron skillet and began banging it against the wall. The clanging turned chaos into pandemonium. "Stop it you fool. Stop terrorizing us. Leave us alone." She banged frantically until Jay took the skillet out of her hands and wrapped his arms around her.

"Lisa, calm down. This doesn't help anyone. I'm calling the police. I need you to get a hold of yourself so you can help with the kids." She fought with him and pushed him away. "Will you help me?"

"Call the police. They won't do anything. They haven't done anything in the past. They're spineless." She'd wrapped her arms around herself and turned her back on her husband.

Jay dialed 999 and gave details to the dispatcher. "Please hurry." He shouted into the phone. "Please hurry."

"I can't take any more of this. This house is our prison. This town is our prison." She ran into the living room and grabbed a sofa pillow and held it to her face. She screamed and sobbed, muffled by the pillow until her breathing became erratic. The boys put their hands over their ears and cried all the more.

Jay sat beside Lisa and held her. "Calm down, Lis. The police are coming. Try to calm yourself. You're scaring the boys." Jay felt helpless.

"*I'm* scaring the boys?" She screamed. "*I'm* scaring them? That's ridiculous. That idiot next door is scaring them and you're doing nothing to stop him." The children wailed.

"Lisa, please Lisa. Try to calm down."

She grabbed at her hair. "You were determined to buy this stupid house and move here. It's your fault. You've put your family's lives in peril. You need to stop him."

"How do I stop him?"

"I don't know; you figure it out." She curled up in the corner of the living room and covered her head with her hands.

Jay felt powerless to quiet the chaos. Lisa was beyond reasoning. He turned to Nate and squatted in front of him. "Nate, listen to me." He turned his son's face to get his attention. "Nate, look at me. Hush. The police are coming and they'll make the man stop."

Nate's cry's quieted as long as Jay held his gaze. "Look at me, Nate the banging is down here, not upstairs. I want you to take your brothers back up into our bedroom and close the door and lock it. I want all three of you lads to get in our bed. You'll be safe there. Maybe you could read to your brothers until I come up." Jay kept his eyes fixed on Nate. "Look at me Nate. Do you understand what I need you to do?"

Nate nodded.

"Good boy. Go." Jay motioned toward the stairs and watched as Nate led his younger brothers up the stairs. "That's right. Good lad. Now stay there until we've finished talking to the police. When it's over I'll come get you."

A police car drove up in silence; its blue lights swept through the trees and flashed against the dark house. Jay opened the door before the two officers could knock. When they stepped inside, the house still throbbed with its hideous heartbeat.

"Thanks for coming Officers." Jay was surprised it was Jones and Mercer again. "Do you guys ever sleep?"

Mercer smiled but Jones looked annoyed. "So what's going on tonight?"

"Let me show you." Jay led them into the kitchen. With each crash, the walls trembled; dishes fell and shattered on the floor. Pots and pans that sat on the drain board jittered until they tumbled into the sink.

"When did this start?" Jones shouted.

"Around four thirty and it's been non-stop ever since." Jay ran his fingers through his hair. "Officer Jones," he lowered his voice. "I fear for my wife's sanity." Jay nodded toward the living room. "This can't be acceptable behavior in any society."

Jones said, "Not to worry, sir. We'll get to the bottom of this. He's probably doing some remodeling and so absorbed that he isn't even aware of the time."

"It's too late not to worry. My family is exhausted from this man's erratic behavior. Last night he ran me off the road. He's threatened to kill me. He makes threats on my wife and children. He hunts me down around town."

"Calm down, Mr. Knight, one thing at a time. Let's deal with the business at hand and then we can talk about the other claims." Jones remained unrattled.

Desperate, Jay turned to Mercer who scribbled on a pad. "This man has to be stopped. Maybe we could go over there together and reason with him." Jay worried for his wife who seemed to be unaware that the police were in the house.

The two officers discussed it and agreed to let Jay come. Jones added, "Don't say anything that would inflame the situation. Let us do the talking."

"Thank you both." Jay went over to Lisa and stroked her hair. "Lisa, I'm going next door with the police. The boys are upstairs in our room. Will you be okay while I'm gone?"

Lisa didn't look up. "Do whatever you have to." Her tone was flat.

Jay went with the officers to Dungess' front door. The pounding continued unabated.

Jones rapped on the door with his nightstick but the pounding continued. He banged harder and finally the pounding stopped and Dungess shouted, "Who is it?"

"It's the police. Open it." Jones now appeared irritated.

Dungess opened the door. He was covered with dust and had a sledgehammer in his hand. "Yes sir. Is there some problem officer?"

"Yes. I'm afraid you're the problem. It seems you have been hammering for quite a while now and it's still not yet six o'clock. Do you realize that other people might be sleeping?"

"Sleeping? Huh. Well, some of us have to work around here. We can't all have cushy jobs like him." He started to close the door but the officer put his foot in the doorway and grabbed the door handle.

"Hold it. Not so fast. What are you doing?"

"I'm remodeling the kitchen. Is there a law against that?"

"Exactly what kind of remodeling?" Jones asked as Mercer peered into the kitchen.

"I'm installing a wood burning stove. I have to make an opening into my chimney in the kitchen. The hammering is nearly finished." He brushed the dust from his clothes.

Suddenly, Mercer spoke up. "Where is your permit?"

"It's my house. Why do I need a permit to remodel my own kitchen?"

"Because you're altering the structure. All structural changes must be done to code."

Jones looked at Mercer with surprise.

Mercer tapped his clipboard. "Show us your permit and show us your certification to do structural work. If you can't produce those documents, then you must cease and desist until a building inspector approves your plans and you have a qualified builder. Furthermore, you are not to cause such a disturbance at this time of the night. Do you understand?"

Dungess nodded and smirked.

"If you can't judge what is reasonable, we can spell it out for you."

"I understand."

"If we have to come out again, we'll have you arrested. Is that clear enough for you, Mr. Dungess?"

"Yeah. Sure, mate." Dungess shrugged but his jaw was grinding hard. He slammed the door.

"And I'm not your mate," Mercer shouted. "You can call me, 'Sir.'"

Jones grinned. "Well, well. He does have a tongue."

Jay walked back to the vehicle with Jones and Mercer. "Thank you for your support, Officers. As you can see, my wife is pretty close to a nervous breakdown over all this."

Jones said, "Please don't do anything to irritate this bloke. Try to get along with him. Okay?"

"Yes, of course." The men climbed in their car and Jay leaned in through the open window. "Thanks again. I'll walk back. There's a snicket by my fence."

The police vehicle reversed out of Dungess, driveway and disappeared down the road. Jay turned toward the fence. Dawn began to push back the darkness. Jay felt exhausted.

"Going somewhere you little snitch?"

Jay jumped at the sight of the man who now blocked his path. Ignoring his question, Jay turned to his right and Dungess blocked him again. "Hey idiot, I asked you a question. Where do you think you're going?"

"I'm going home."

"Good. Because you're just a parasite in this country."

Jay's shoulders suddenly ached with heaviness. He had no energy to challenge this man.

Dungess moved closer, his sour breath blasting Jay's face. "If you take one step on my property I'll smash your face in. And your police buddies will never know what happened."

"They know quite a bit already. They know more about you than you realize." Jay turned to his left and Dungess blocked him again. "Why do you hate us so much?"

"Because you exist and breathe my air. I hate you and everything you represent. I hate you're little Christian God because He's powerless."

"How do you know He's powerless?"

"I know, because He failed me."

"It must have been a different God than the one I know, because my God cannot fail and no one can stop His plans."

Dungess' face puffed out. "Let's put Him to the test. Let's see if He can protect you from me." Dungess made a fake lunge at Jay. "Get out of here before I do something permanent to your face."

When Jay got home he was shaking, but relieved to see Lisa working in the kitchen. Upstairs, he heard Nate reading a storybook to his brothers. He took several deep breaths to calm himself and then headed to the kitchen.

Jay wrapped his arms around Lisa and held her. She had tears in her eyes and she was pale. "I love you and I'm sorry this is happening. The police promised to take action against Dungess if he doesn't comply with building regulations and permits. They told him he'd be arrested if he doesn't stop harassing us."

Lisa turned and held onto Jay as if she was afraid to let go. For a while she sobbed into his shoulder. With a muffled voice she said. "I'm sorry I lost it this morning. I just had had it with these neighbors and couldn't face another thing."

"I know. I know. I'm going to the realtors to find a place to rent until we can get this sold."

"You would do that?" Lisa stopped and studied Jay's eyes. "But you love this place. You've worked so hard—"

"We've both worked hard, but if we can't live in peace, it's not worth it. You and the lads are more important to me then this pile of bricks."

"Then he wins." Frustration came into her eyes. "No matter what we do, he wins."

"He'll never really win. It might look like it, but in the end, he's the loser. God's word promises that." Jay wiped a tear from Lisa's cheek. "Besides, I think this is a lot bigger than Dungess."

"What do you mean? Like a conspiracy?"

"Yeah, something like that." Jay hesitated for a moment. "Remember Amber?"

"The girl with the dreams? You think she has something to do with this?" Lisa furrowed her brow.

"In a roundabout way, yes."

Lisa seemed doubtful. "I can't imagine she even knows Dungess. That girl was just a wannabe witch with a vivid imagination. It's obvious her message was wrong."

"Was it?"

"Of course it was, think about it. We're still here in Kingsbridge, we've built a church and the congregation is growing. People are still coming to Christ." Lisa pulled out of Jay's arms to fill the kettle and turn on the heat.

"What if it was a real warning? There've been too many other coincidences." Jay leaned against the counter.

"What are you talking about?"

"There was that gypsy woman in the woods and your accident, and what happened in the—" He had already said too much.

"What? And what?" Lisa studied Jay's face. "Tell me."

"Never mind." Jay wiped his hand over his face in exhaustion. "I have this terrible feeling that a bigger battle is going on." Jay peered out the window. "I still think I should try to find another place, at least to rent."

"Jay, please don't rush into this. The thought of moving is overwhelming to me."

"But I thought you'd be thrilled to get away from this."

The kettle screeched and Lisa dropped tea bags into the pot. "I know I've said a lot of things, but please wait a little while anyway." She filled the pot and left it to brew.

She leaned close to Jay and studied his eyes. "Please wait. Maybe this whole thing will die down soon. He can't pound the wall forever."

"I'm confused. I don't know what you want." Jay sat down and sipped his tea. Fatigue settled over him. His neck and back ached.

"I've grown to love this cottage. I just want to live in peace and quiet and for us to feel safe."

"If we stay here, I can't guarantee that." They sat at the table sipping their tea.

CRASH. BANG.

"I can't believe this guy. It's like he knows what we're thinking." Lisa's hand shook and she stared helplessly at Jay.

"Dad, he's started again." Nate shouted from the bedroom.

He looked at Lisa. "We're going on a trip, right now. Can you grab some warm clothes for everyone'? Let's get in the car as fast as we can."

"Thanks." Lisa bolted upstairs calling after the children. "Come on lads. We're going on a trip."

A short time later, the family huddled in the car as it sped toward the Welsh border. Jay had a twenty pound note in his pocket and nothing more, but there was gas in the tank and they could share a bag of fish and chips and pretend they were on vacation. As the Welsh Mountains began to rise on the horizon and the Cheshire plains receded, his anxiety melted away. By half past eight, the children were playing a guessing game as Jay followed the hairpin turns through the slate mountains of Wales.

Lisa rode with her eyes closed.

* * *

A month had passed since the last crash of the hammer. Sightings of Dungess had diminished to a handful. Although the kids seemed happier than they'd been in a long time, Nate frequently complained that he didn't feel well often complaining of headaches. He was also convinced that their bedroom floor would cave in at anytime.

Jay had been building a tree house among the branches of a huge oak. This seemed like a perfect time to finish it so the kids could get fresh air and play. In spite of low temperatures, the skies had been crystal clear. Nate and Michael helped sort through boards and pound in a few nails. They helped rig up a hoist so that one of them could fill a bucket on the ground and the other could pull it up through an opening in the floor. A load of Mum's homemade cookies arrived first and then juice packets and sandwiches. Another load brought toys; a plastic light saber, a Viking helmet, plastic body armor and a Superman cape. Once fully stocked, they named the fort Erindale Castle. Each day after school they played in their fantasy world of knights and dragons. They told each other secrets about a wicked witch that lived somewhere among the trees.

*　*　*

It was another Monday. Jay was reading a novel in front of the fire and Joey played at his feet. With the chilling temperatures and damp days, Lisa kept the house closed up and the thermostat hovering around 70 degrees. After making the children's beds, she checked their windows. One window was open a crack and a strong draft sucked in cold air. She drew her fingers along the sill and they came up black. She chastised herself for not keeping it cleaner.

CHAPTER TWENTY-EIGHT

—⟋⟋⟋⟋—

From the inception of the church, the people met in homes. The congregation was now too large for any one home. That was good news. Still, many missed the earlier days. So when the new heating system malfunctioned one week, the people were quick to hold their midweek Bible study in someone's house. Jean jumped at the chance to open her home.

People gathered in her lounge taking every available seat. Younger members of the group sat on the floor and filled every corner. In the fireplace, flames crackled. The next wave to arrive sat on the steps of the staircase. By seven-fifteen the house was jammed and latecomers had to stand along the walls and in the hallways. The place buzzed with excitement. When the music started, the crowd belted out their praises.

A young woman named Christina Woodward came in with her mother. Christina had searched for purpose in life after she'd watched her father die after an excruciating battle with lung cancer. Only five days before, she'd surrendered her heartache to God. Now she wanted her mother to find the same peace. People were so delighted to see her that several offered their seats. The congregation treated young faith with special honor. New believers were spiritual infants in God's family. Jay had taught them that they were like parents with a new born. New faith kept them young at heart.

An hour into the meeting, the group began to pray. They interceded for the people of Kingsbridge with honest and raw emotion. Prayers ascended to Heaven for neighbors, families, and employers.

* * *

Outside, across the lane, an old green Vauxhall crept up the drive toward the empty church. A gust of wind blew a dust cloud across its path as the driver pulled in front of the church and idled. Its headlights cut through the night and cast a glare against the building. A moment later, the car door opened and a woman stepped onto the gravel driveway. She studied the structure then slowly made her way to the door. The wind whipped the edges of her tweed coat and tossed her gray hair in all directions.

She turned the handle. Locked. She studied her watch, then peered through the windows. Seeing no one, she turned to make her way back to her car when she saw a slip of paper flutter near her feet. She bent to pick it up but wind snatched it away. Several quick steps later she caught it and squinted through the dark to read it aloud.

"Due to heating problems, our usual midweek Bible study is being held at the McGregor's house across the lane. Everyone's welcome, so come and join us. It starts at 7:30."

The woman looked at her watch again. The meeting had been going for at least an hour. She turned her attention to the house across the lane. Light poured from the windows and cars filled the driveway and lined the lane. Parking would be impossible. She shivered at the cold and pulled her collar around her neck. The woman reached a decision: she started toward the fence, hoisted up her skirt and coat, scaled the fence, and walked briskly across the lane to the McGregor's house. At the door, she heard friendly voices. She took a chance and knocked.

* * *

When Jean heard another knock, she answered the door immediately. A gray haired woman stood there shivering. "Hello, come on in."

Gerri Jones stepped inside the house and saw a room full of people gazing back and smiling.

Gerri whispered to Jean, "Is this the place where you study the Bible?"

"Absolutely, love. We're glad you joined us." Jean led her into the lounge and someone stood immediately to give her a seat.

"I've come to study the Bible. I read the church sign out by the road that said you study the Bible every week. Can I study it too?"

"Certainly." Jay replied. "Here's an extra Bible for you." He handed it to her. "I'm Jay. Welcome to Kingsbridge Fellowship."

"Well, hello Jay. This is all so new to me. I don't really know what I'm doing."

"If you're on a search to find answers for your life, then you've come to the right place. That's why all of us are here. Now Gerri, tell us about yourself."

With a little encouragement, Gerri began to tell her story. Gerri's strong midland accent flavored her speech. "I live down the road near Tarnum. I've never been what ya call a churchgoer. I dunno why. But after retirin' from the refinery we decided—John and me—to go on hols. Well, we went to Crete and had a grand time. The weather was fantastic and all them hotels was good for me husband, because he is dyin' of cancer and so this was an important trip for us both."

Gerri shifted in the chair and continued. "We visited lots of places on the island and that's when I noticed the sign."

"What sign was that?" Jay asked.

"It said 'Saint Paul visited this place.'"

She pulled a folded piece of paper from her coat pocket and opened it carefully. "I copied this from the sign. It's recorded in the Bible in Acts, chapter twenty seven and verse eight, that Paul visited Fair Haven. Well, you could o' bowled me over. I never knew the Bible was for real. Thought it was a book of fairy tales. But now I found a historical place where somebody named Paul had visited. Well, that was good enough for me. We got home yesterday and I said to me husband that I was goin' to find out more about this Bible thing. I gotta know. 'Cause if it's true, then me and John have to know about it. He's got only a few days left. As I was driven' down Kingsbridge Road tonight I saw's your church sign invitin' people to come on Wednesday nights to study the Bible. I said to meself, That's for me."

The group was spellbound. Finally Gerri folded her hands in her lap. "So's I'm here and ready to be told all about the Bible." She looked expectantly at the crowd and then at Jay. Everyone turned to him waiting for an answer.

After recovering from surprise, Jay began to share the good news of Jesus Christ. Together with a room full of witnesses, Gerri Jones listened to what the Bible had to say.

"So, what's next?" Gerri asked. "I believe every word you said tonight. It all makes so much sense. How does this faith thing work?"

The attentive crowd sat in awe as they witnessed the workings of the Holy Spirit. Jay led this plucky woman to Christ before her newfound friends. She confessed her sins and declared her faith in Jesus Christ.

Someone started up a song of praise and the crowd joined in. "It's all about Jesus. It's all about Him."

When the singing stopped, Gerri asked Jay a question. "Could you come tomorrow and tell my John about Jesus? He's wantin' to know before he dies."

"I'll come tomorrow morning if that is all right with you."

"That's fantastic. I'll have John up and ready. He knows he's missed somethin' important and now we know what it is." She stood. "Nine in the mornin'?"

"Nine in the morning," Jay said with a wink. "Let's all stand and sing *Amazing Grace* together. We have seen it demonstrated so clearly tonight. Thank God for Gerri's hungry heart. Praise the Lord."

Together, fifty-two believers linked arms and sang through their tears. Gerri Jones stood in the middle and raised her hands in the air as though she had done it a thousand times.

"Thank you Jesus, for that wee note that brought me here tonight."

"And thank you for the Crete tourist board," added Jay.

"Aye," said Gerri. "Aye."

* * *

At nine the next day, Gerri's door opened as Jay walked up the path. She had been waiting. As soon as he crossed the threshold, she led him to John's bedside.

"John, this here is our pastor, Jay. He's going to tell you how to get to Heaven. Are you comfy, John?"

John nodded and tried to smile. His skin was gray and his flesh draped over his bones like a loose grave cloth. "Thank you for comin'." He tried to sit up but failed. "Gerri says you can help me find my way home."

"Yes, I can. Let me introduce you to a friend of mine. His name is Jesus."

The two men spoke in hushed tones. Minutes later John offered a simple prayer. When he looked up his face radiated joy. "It's so easy a child could find Him." A flush of pink came to his cheeks. "I wasted a lifetime running away from God. Why would He want me now?"

"God has used everything in your life to bring you to this moment. He's always loved you. Nothing is ever wasted with God." Jay held on to John's bony hand. "God has prepared a place for you in Heaven and He's been waiting for this very moment." Jay kept his voice gentle.

At around five o'clock the next morning, before daylight washed over the Cheshire plains, John stepped across the border into another world. His last words came to his wife as a whisper, "Goodbye for now my love. I'll be waiting for you on the other side."

CHAPTER TWENTY-NINE

—⁓—

Lisa woke with a start. It was 8:00 and she'd overslept. Jay's supervisor Vic Trinder had come by at 7:00 and the two had headed out to Chester for a meeting and lunch. He must have turned the alarm off. She leapt from bed and rushed into the children's room. "Nate, Michael, wake up, we're late for school." Their room smelled foul and she wrinkled her nose. It smelled like smoke, but she saw nothing unusual. "Nate, Michael, wake up."

The boys were groggy and barely responded to her voice.

"Nate, wake up. You're going to be late for school." Lisa shook him.

He looked anxious the moment he opened his eyes. "I don't feel good today, Mum. Can I stay home?"

"Still? What hurts, sweetheart?" Lisa pulled the blankets back.

"I don't know. I just don't feel good."

"It's not much of an excuse to stay home." She brushed his hair back. "Come on now, kiddo, everyone overslept. So help me by getting yourself ready."

Lisa shook Michael. "Why are you boys so groggy this morning? Did you guys go back to playing after I turned out the light?" She shook Michael again. He finally woke and sat up. Lisa noticed his labored breathing. "Oh Michael, you're wheezing again. What brought it on this time?"

Michael rolled out of bed and stumbled into the bathroom where Nathan was brushing his teeth. Joey was still asleep peacefully sucking his thumb. Lisa would take him in his pajamas. She pulled the curtains open and peered down at the courtyard below, but saw nothing unusual. "I've got to find out what that smell is. It's probably your stinky socks."

After the kids were in motion, she threw on some clothes, brushed her hair, and ran down to the kitchen to make sandwiches and get breakfast on the table.

By the time she dropped the boys off at school, they had only five minutes to spare. "You boys did great. I'm so proud of you both."

Michael waved goodbye and ran to catch up with a friend.

Nathan complained, "My head really hurts, Mum."

"I'm sorry, sweetheart. If it gets any worse, go to the school nurse and I'll come pick you up. I've made a doctor's appointment for Friday. I'm praying you'll feel better soon. I love you."

"I love you too, Mum." He slipped from the car and moved slowly through the schoolyard.

Lisa drove into the village to buy a few groceries. Joey was awake and seemed content enough to watch everybody. She put him in the child's seat in her shopping cart. Lisa hated for others to see her in public like this, but the pantry was bare and she didn't want to make an additional trip into town. When she saw Jean McGregor heading her way, she grinned and pretended to hide her face. "Hi Jean, I'm so embarrassed to be seen in public like this. No makeup—"

"You're always a delight to see." She gave Lisa a hug and talked with Joey for a minute. "Everything okay?"

"Sure. We woke up late today and Nathan gets so worked up if he thinks there's a remote chance that he'll be late. He panics just thinking about it."

"Sounds like my Richard. I wish I could say he'll outgrow it, but…" She shrugged and grinned. "Some boys never grow up."

Lisa laughed. "Maybe that's our cross to bear." She picked up a loaf of white bread and put it in her cart. "I'm worried about Nathan. He's been complaining about not feeling well for weeks now." She picked up a box of cereal and let Joey put it in the cart. "He never used to complain at all."

"What kind of complaints?"

"Oh, headaches, sore throat, you know, normal things that children get. I still think it's stress."

"Have you taken him to the doctor?"

"I made an appointment for this Friday."

"Good. Let me know what he says. And remember to call if you ever need help." Jean studied Lisa's eyes. "I mean it. Okay?"

"Okay. Thanks Jean. That means so much. And thanks for your concern."

Lisa returned home and parked the car. She carried a bag of groceries in one arm and Joey in the other. "Joey, you're getting so big now." She trudged up the slope and stopped twice to catch her breath. "Joey, you wear me out."

When she got to the gate she stopped. "Oh no, no, no." The bag of groceries slipped from her arm and tumbled, spilling cereal, butter, cooking oil and a bottle of orange concentrate down the steps and on her shoes.

Slime of overly ripened eggs covered the front of the cottage; dozens of fractured eggs dotted the face of the home. A sulfuric stench caused Lisa's stomach to heave. Slime dripped from window ledges, slid down brickwork, smeared across glass, and stuck to everything. The glistening trail held shattered egg shells. Joey cried.

* * *

"We just need a break from it all, just a couple months to get away where we can think more clearly." Jay said to his Superintendent, Vic Trinder. "The church is doing well—"

"I know that. I've tracked your church's growth patterns from the day you arrived in Kingsbridge. Considering that you and Lisa started with nothing, I'd say the work has been rather phenomenal." He beamed like a proud father.

"Thank you, Vic, but I didn't come here for praise." Jay shifted uncomfortably in his seat. "I feel we're under some kind of spiritual attack, and I'm worried about the well being of my family."

"Of course you're under attack. You're on the front line of the battle. You're leading the charge." He lowered his voice. "But warriors don't give up in the middle of the fight."

"I'm not giving up. I would never do that. But sometimes I feel I'm alone in this battle. Soldiers should never fight alone." Leaning closer he said, "It's Lisa. I worry about her."

"How is she doing?" Vic sipped his coffee while his eyes focused on Jay.

"Not well. Not well at all." Jay traced the edge of his cup. "We're a team and I can't let anything happen that could hurt her." Jay looked up. "You know we came to the U.K. right after we married. She was committed to me and to this assignment. I loved her for that."

"So, what's changed?"

"She doesn't feel safe anymore." Jay stared at Vic. "And I don't know if I can protect her."

"Protect her from what?"

"Well, this guy next door for one. He's threatened to destroy us, and I think he's crazy enough to try."

"He sounds like a nutter. Just let the police take care of it."

"I wish they would, but they seem rather passive. But that's not all." Jay lowered his voice to a whisper. "There was some kind of blood ritual performed in the middle of the sanctuary. I found the remains of animal sacrifices hanging from the rafters. It had to be some Satanist group. It was such a blatant attack against the Christian gospel and God Himself. Lisa would freak out if she knew."

Victor leaned back and fell silent. Finally he turned. "Jay, my dear fellow, it sounds like a scare tactic. Someone is trying to frighten you off. Don't believe their threats."

"You don't believe it's real?" Jay blinked.

"I believe Satan is real, but something like this ritual? I don't think so. It sounds more like a Hollywood stunt to me."

Jay stared at his friend. He hadn't expected an answer like that. "You mean you don't believe there is such a thing as spiritual warfare?"

"Of course, I do. But nothing is that simple. Yes, I believe in spiritual warfare, but Satan doesn't need spells and curses to do his dark work. It's more effective for him to cause us to doubt God, to fear his threats and defeat us with discouragement."

"Oh, I get all that too, but what I saw in the church building wasn't done by kids. It was pretty spooky stuff. I have no doubt they wanted us to find it. It was a deliberate act of defiance."

"Jay, how much do your supporters know about all this mess?"

"I send out a newsletter each month. I ask for prayer for the church and our family."

"Have you told them anything about this sacrifice?"

"Not yet, but I plan to. They need to know how severe the attacks are against us."

"I wouldn't say anything about the stunt done at the church. People might get the wrong idea."

"I don't understand. What wrong idea?"

"Right or wrong, some theology can become divisive. Your supporters love you. They believe in the Knight family, in your ministry. Many give sacrificially."

"I know that and it humbles me." Jay frowned. "But people want to hear the truth, good or bad, so they can pray effectively."

"Just be careful. Remember that many of your supporters are very conservative. You don't want them to think you've gone…" He seemed to fish around for a word. "…Pentecostal." His voice lowered. "You could lose support…"

Jay was stunned. "I only write the truth. I know what I saw and know that my family is being targeted. Evil is evil." Jay kept going. "Our salary is usually stretched pretty thin. But I would still tell the truth even if it stopped our support altogether." Jay studied Vic's eyes hoping for reassurance, but finding none. "Two months ago, I contacted Don at headquarters and told him how desperate our situation had become. I told them that our lives were in danger. I'd sent a letter with all the details. We've been counting on their prayers. But we didn't hear from anyone. So, last week I called Don again and asked about the letter." Jay shook his head. "He'd forgotten all about it. It had never been sent out to our supporters because he lost it." Jay became agitated. "It's our lives at stake."

"That is really disappointing. It's not like Don to be so careless." He took a sip of his coffee. "I'll need to address that when I'm back at General Conference."

Jay's voice broke. "Vic, the letter still has not been sent. We really feel they've let us down."

"No doubt you do." Vic straightened in his chair. "That should never have happened. Jay, you and Lisa have shown great courage in your trials."

"That's why we need a sabbatical. Just a short one before we crack. Do you realize that we've ministered in England for over fifteen years now?"

"I know you're overdue for a break." Victor weighed his words. "I know it's tough and I've agonized over this for days. But, if you leave now, you'll never be able to pastor the Kingsbridge church again."

Jay couldn't speak. His mouth went dry and his throat seized. "Why?"

"The logistics are the problem. You filled a ministry gap for us. I had no one else with your set of gifts to begin a work like Kingsbridge. It was tailor made just for you. And if you leave, I'd be hard pressed to find someone, anyone who could replace you. As you know, some of our Irish pastors, Seamus and Fergus have a circuit with two or three churches to care for. We're all so busy in our own ministries that Kingsbridge would suffer greatly if you were gone."

"Just a break, that's all I'm asking."

"That's the hardest to fill. I have no one who would leave their pastorate for two months to care for Kingsbridge. And even if I did find someone, it would never work to have a temp here until you returned. The church would flounder."

"I'm not that important. I've worked hard to build this church on Christ, not me. I've heard of churches collapsing when the founding pastor leaves. Ours is different. I've purposely safeguarded against that. This is not an American church or a Jacob Knight church. It's God's church and He can take care of it with or without me."

"Well said, well said. I know your heart. Kingsbridge has not experienced such a great evangelistic thrust for decades. Maybe even back to the Welsh Revival. In fact, what has happened here is nothing short of a miracle. I know you and your family need a break, but I have no one who could step in at this time. No one."

Jay stared out the restaurant window at a colorless sky. He watched a barren oak branch shaken by the invisible force of the wind. Like the limb, he felt shaken. "So, I guess that's that."

"Remember, you're not alone, Jay. There's a great cloud of witnesses watching you."

"I wish just for once, one of them would stop watching and offer a little help."

"Perseverance is the key. Perseverance, remember that."

"I've tried so hard to hold on." Jay felt desperate. A wave of fatigue hit him.

Victor's pager beeped. "Ah, it must be your wife trying to reach you. Your number just came up." He waved at their server to bring the bill. "We should be on our way." He put his credit card on the table. "There've been many missionaries that have suffered loss for the sake of the Gospel. It comes with our calling." He leaned close. "Jay, God is using you mightily."

With the bill paid, the two men walked out into the cold. A chill rattled through Jay's bones and he rushed to keep up with Victor's long strides.

"I'm prepared to sacrifice and if that means suffering, so be it. But I can't make that decision for Lisa."

"She did that when she accepted the call to come here."

The two walked with heads down against the bitter wind. Before they reached the parking lot, Jay made one last effort. He stopped and turned to Vic. "What would you do if your ministry put the lives of Margaret and your daughters in danger?"

Victor said nothing until they reached his car. "If we would have to make such a decision, God would give us grace to do so. But Jay, I don't believe it would ever come to that, not these days, not here in Kingsbridge. Not for you or for me."

"Vic, we're already getting death threats. How much more do we have to endure before the church realizes this is real warfare?"

The men climbed into Victor's car and headed back home. The discussion slowed to a stop as though the two travelers had come to a fork in the road and decided to follow a different path. The soft strains of classical music filled the car and Jay withdrew into silence as they traveled. A growing despair chewed at his insides. He'd asked for help and got nothing. He felt alone and trapped in a stronghold that seemed impossible to break. How would he tell Lisa?

* * *

When Jay got home, Lisa had already gone through several bottles of cleansers and her knuckles were bleeding and swollen. After she told Jay the details, she went back to work, sullen and clearly discouraged.

"I'm so sorry, Lisa." He reached out to hold her but she pulled away.

"Forget it Jay. I'm finished discussing it because nothing ever changes. I'm fed up with all this." She scrubbed harder than ever until her knuckles were bone white.

"Lisa, you've got to stop. You're hurting yourself. Let me finish."

"So what? Who cares anyway? The denomination doesn't care, the church doesn't care. I wonder if God cares." In spite of blinding tears she scrubbed the walls in a fury. They worked side by side in silence until the job was done. Jay knew that a fire was smoldering beneath Lisa's exterior. It wouldn't take much for the embers to erupt into a wild fire. If that happened, there would be nothing left. He shuddered. "Lord, help us."

Long after Lisa had fallen asleep, Jay listened as she ground her teeth. He wanted to comfort her and hold her close, but even in sleep she flinched and withered at his touch.

CHAPTER THIRTY

—〰—

On Friday at nine o'clock, Jay and Lisa waited in the doctor's office while Dr. Hutchison examined Nate. Jean McGregor offered to take Michael and Joey for the morning. The sterile room with its antiseptic smell made Jay queasy. He and Lisa had suspended their differences so they could focus on Nate's health. Jay grew more anxious as Dr. Hutchison made copious notes in Nate's file without saying a word. He tried to read the doctor's expressions but couldn't. Nate looked so small, sitting alone on the examining table. Jay wanted to hold him tight and reassure him that everything was going to be okay, but, he wasn't sure himself. No one but God knew the future.

Jay glanced at Lisa but she avoided his eyes. He feared what she was thinking. She tied every hardship to him. If he'd only stayed put. If he had only been content living in a rental. If he'd only followed the normal route of an American pastor they'd be in a lot better situation. They would be a normal family.

If only...

When he finished the examination, Dr. Hutchison asked Nate to wait in the lobby while he talked to his parents. The doctor spoke in quiet tones. "I believe that Nathan is suffering from cyanosis. It's a condition that comes when the body has limited oxygen intake. You can see it in his skin. His skin has a bluish tint and he's got dark circles under his eyes. I need to do some blood tests. If they confirm my suspicions, then it would indicate carbon monoxide poisoning, which can cause brain damage in some cases. If left unchecked it can be fatal."

Lisa gasped. "What have we done to our children?" She looked at Jay for a moment. Her eyes revealed a torrent of emotions.

"Don't start blaming yourselves. Carbon monoxide fumes are hard to detect, sometimes impossible. It's often called the 'silent killer.'"

Tears pooled in Lisa's eyes, spilling down her cheeks like water over the top of a dam.

"We caught this thing in time. You did the right thing to bring Nathan in today." The doctor gave a reassuring smile. "We'll run your son through these blood tests to determine what action we must take." The doctor looked over the rim of his glasses. "I want all of you to be tested. Tomorrow. My receptionist will arrange everything." He waited for them to nod. "Good."

The doctor looked down at his chart. "Now, back to Nathan. My assistant will administer the tests and we should have the results back in a couple of days." He turned to Jay. "Mr. Knight, you can begin by having your home tested for toxic chemicals."

"How do I do that?"

"The Shell Oil refinery down the road is required to test toxic levels on their shop floors. Give their administrative office a call. They might be able to advise you."

"Thanks. I'll do that immediately." Jay felt hollow.

The Doctor turned to Lisa. "Mrs. Knight, you'll need to teach Nathan how to use this inhaler." He handed a package to her. "He needs to use this three times a day for the next week." The doctor scribbled instructions on a prescription pad. "You can start with this sampler inhaler. It should last for a couple of days." He tore the prescription off the pad and handed it to her. "I'll need one of you to sign the consent form to do blood work on Nathan."

The parents nodded.

The doctor sent them down the hall to the lab. Shaken from yet another blow to their lives, Jay and Lisa left the building with Nathan and headed to the car. Lisa's hands trembled.

"What's wrong, Mum?" Nathan asked. "Did I do something wrong?"

Lisa made no attempt to hide her tears. Jay knew it would have been impossible. "No love, you've done nothing wrong." She wiped her nose with a tissue. "We just..." she started again. "I just love you so much and I'm sorry this has happened."

"It's not your fault, Mum." He patted her arm. "Don't cry."

Her son's concern made her cry all the more. "I'm fine, Nate. I'm just sorry I didn't listen when you kept telling me you weren't feeling well."

"That's okay. God heard me and He made everything okay."

"Listen, big guy," Jay chimed in. "Mum and I are a little stressed and we're concerned for your health. The doctor gave us an inhaler and we'll show you how to use it when we get home. That might help relieve some of your headaches. You're going to be fine."

They drove back home. Tension mounted like an electrical charge.

When they arrived, Nathan climbed out of the car and rushed toward the house. Lisa and Jay sat there for a minute. Lisa finally spoke, "Jay, I feel like we're on a roller coaster ride and we're plunging toward destruction. I'm scared to death."

"I know." He reached out to comfort her. She pulled away. "Lisa, don't do this. We need each other now more than ever." His voice broke. "Somehow in all of this, God is going to come to our rescue."

"What if He doesn't?" Her tone suddenly cooled as anger rushed in. "What if God decides to leave us here in this mess?"

"*Life* is messy. You know that. But we've made it this far. God just asks us to trust Him no matter what happens." Jay paused. "I don't know why all this has happened, but I know He hasn't changed."

"Why did we come to this God-forsaken place anyway?" Her tears had dried, her face hardened. "I really don't think God cares about what happens to us."

"God cares about everything in our lives. And He's never too late, Lis. Don't believe those lies. We just don't know His timing. He simply asks us to trust in Him."

"We did trust God and looked what happened. I'm fresh out of trust these days." Lisa studied Jay's eyes, demanding an answer.

Jay had none.

* * *

Jay dialed the Shell Oil refinery's administrative office. After ten minutes on hold, his call bounced from one department to another, until he reached a woman who gave him the information he needed. She'd given him names and numbers for three people who were qualified to do the testing. Jay said thank you and hung up.

The first number was a man who lived in Chester and was on holiday until the end of the month. His voice mailbox was so full that it cut off before Jay could leave a message. He tried the second number only to find the man had moved.

The last number was local. Jay dialed and waited for another disappointment.

"Hello, this is Jacob Knight and I'm—"

"Jay, it's me, Ian Langley, your neighbor." He laughed at Jay's confusion. "How can I help you?"

"How silly of me," Jay said with embarrassment. "Nathan has been showing symptoms of carbon monoxide poisoning. The doctor is running blood tests to confirm it. He suggested we test the house for toxic fumes. We've got to find the source and stop it before it kills us all." Jay tried to hide his stress. "I don't know where to begin or what to look for."

"That's not something to mess with. I'll be happy to check it out for you."

"I can't thank you enough, Ian. What exactly do you do?"

"I measure air levels to identify airborne toxins. I check for carbon monoxide, carbon monoxide-acrolein mixtures and hydrogen cyanide. I make calculations to determine time-to-incapacitation for any combination of CO and HCN concentrations." Ian laughed. "That's the technical jargon. Basically, I make sure the air quality is safe for employees."

"Ian, you're an answer to prayer. Thank you so much."

"I wish I could tell you it's free, but it's not. A testing kit costs about eighty quid."

"We'll pay whatever it costs."

"I'll see how fast I can get the kit. Let's shoot for Friday evening."

"That would be great. I can't thank you enough for your help."

"You know we worry about your family. We can't let anything bad happen to you." He paused. "Until Friday, I'd advise you to leave until we know it's safe."

"I don't know where we'd go." Jay felt a weight pushing down on him. "We don't have family near by." Jay scratched his head. "We've already moved our bedding into the family room until this fiasco is over. But that doesn't seem safe either."

"Can you go to a hotel for a couple nights?"

"We really don't have the resources to do that, but..." Jay was thinking. "Maybe one of our church families could put us up for a few nights."

"I wish we could help you Jay. We just have the bungalow with no room to spare."

"Don't even think about that Ian. We'll find something."

"You've certainly had your fill of bad luck since you've moved into that place. I couldn't have survived it."

"We're no different, Ian. But I know that God sees all that happens and He's merciful. He loves us more than we can comprehend."

"I can't see how a merciful God would stand by and let bad things happen to good people."

"When you get to know Him intimately, you'll understand better just how He views things. He knows what He's doing, even if we don't."

Ian went quiet on the phone.

"Ian? You still there?"

"Sorry. I'm still here, just pondering your words." He paused again. "I really admire your faith and courage."

"I'm a very weak man and full of flaws. Just ask Lisa." He laughed. "It's God who holds us up and keeps us going. Any good that I have comes from Him. I'll be seeing you on Friday evening."

"Friday it is. Take care."

* * *

"I'm sorry to have to ask Vic, but we need a place to sleep for a few nights. So far, no one can spare the room. Everyone is sympathetic, but no one is used to opening their home like that. Especially to a family of five." As he talked on the phone, Jay flipped through the yellow pages, frantic to find someplace for tonight. "I'm sure you understand Vic. You're nearly half and half internationally." Jay tried to be humorous. It was so embarrassing to ask for help like this.

"Jay, I'm sorry. We've got a professor friend from Edinburgh staying with us right now. You know Anthony and Sharon."

"Sure. No problem. I'll find something." Jay was growing more anxious by the minute.

By ten o'clock that night, Jay's youngest elder Nigel was eager to help. "Pastor, you know I'm always ready for an adventure. And it's just the two of us here, so why not! Besides, I love kids."

"I'm so grateful Nigel. Hopefully, it won't be forever. I'm going to stay in the house. Keep an eye on things you know. But I'll feel so much better knowing that Lisa and the lads are safe for now."

"Absolutely. I'll have my wife make arrangements with Lisa."

Jay was drained, but at least his family would be safe until the cottage was clear of all things dangerous. Lisa accepted the offer. She didn't argue with Jay anymore. She was too weary. When would this nightmare ever end?

* * *

By Friday, the tests confirmed their greatest fears. The house had dangerous levels of carbon monoxide in every room, but the most lethal concentration was in the children's bedroom. There was enough carbon monoxide to asphyxiate the entire family. After three hours, Langley was able to pinpoint the origin of the deadly fumes within a three foot section of the shared party wall that backed onto Dungess' kitchen. He traced it passing through a clogged chimney shaft where it seeped through loose mortar and filtered unnoticed through a web of hairline cracks into the children's bedroom. But that wasn't all.

Ian took Jay and Lisa outside and pointed to the roof. "The intensity of smoke gathers close to the roof top. When you open any upstairs window smoke gets sucked directly into the room. It's like second hand smoke. It's more deadly than what the stove emits in your neighbor's kitchen."

"He must be burning something more than wood or coal. Sometimes the smell is so foul."

"Who knows what he burns. I've given up trying to understand this man. They don't even need to burn solid fuel. They've got gas central heating. I remember when it was installed." Ian offered. "Dungess seems to have a grudge with the world."

"He's got a grudge with God Ian.'

The news was devastating. Every effort to live peacefully had failed. Now the iron beast in the Dungess' kitchen was belching lethal doses of harmful gas into the Knight's house. Jay wondered if the legal system would fail them again.

Jay held the official report in his hand and pondered the potential horror of it all. Would they survive this? He wondered how much damage had already been done to their children's health? He shuddered at the thought and prayed for God to sustain him.

* * *

Elena Chernik sat in front of her fire with a poker in her hand. She leaned forward, resting her elbows on her knees and studied the dwindling flames. With a quick flick of her wrist, she jabbed the poker into the glowing coals and stirred them back to life. She chuckled as flames leapt high sending a spray of sparks up and out into the night sky. "Keep it up, Dungess. Give em' a taste of the pit."

* * *

As gracious as any family could be the stress of living out of a suitcase in someone's home had warn thin. The courts had given Dungess a court order to stop burning rubbish until the chimney was fixed. Late Saturday night, the family moved back in trusting against hope that the neighbor's would obey the courts. The family slept in their home for the first time in three weeks. They decided to stay together in one room until they were sure.

A bone chilling blast of winter swept down from the Scottish Isles known as the Outer Hebrides. Just before dawn, temperatures plummeted along the English coast sending Kingsbridge and its surrounding communities into a deep freeze.

Just before six, Jay woke to the cold and knew he had better get moving. Lisa lay curled tight against him and the boys slept heaped together in sleeping bags at the foot of their bed. Jay kissed Lisa's forehead and slipped from under the covers. He grabbed some clothes and headed to the bathroom. Slipping into his jeans, shirt, and a wool jacket, he drove to the church. Within minutes, he had the furnace on and cranked the thermostat to eighty. By eleven, the church would be a comfortable sixty-nine degrees.

Just before he exited the church, the office phone rang. Startled to get a call so early, he rushed back and grabbed it.

"Hello, this is Pastor Knight. Can I help you?"

"Oh yes, please Pastor. This is Christina Woodward. I need your help."

"What's wrong? Is your mum ill?"

"She's fine and we're all okay. It's just that my fiancé Michael is asking a lot of questions about my new faith. He says he's been an atheist his whole life, but now he's not so sure. He wants to talk to you. Can we come over right now?"

Jay was startled. "Christina, I'd be pleased to talk with Michael, but do you realize just what time it is? It's only six fifteen."

"It is?" She paused. "Oh, I'm so sorry, Pastor. We've been talking for hours. I guess we lost track of time."

"No need to be sorry. It's wonderful that Michael is thinking this seriously." Jay paused to think. "Can you both meet me here in about an hour?"

"That'd be brilliant. Hang on a sec." A moment later, she said, "Michael says he's been reading a guy named Bertrand Russell and he was not very impressed with his line of reasoning."

"Well, you can tell him that I've read Russell's work too, and I wasn't impressed either. There are some great British writers that will help Michael understand his journey to faith. Even some former atheists."

"That's wonderful. We can't wait. See you in a few."

Christina's excitement brought a smile to Jay's face. *Such hope for young believers.* This was his reason for being here. He loved leading people to Christ. He appreciated their impassioned quest for truth. They understood their need for God and their need for forgiveness. Jay headed for his car. Dawn had washed the earth in a million shades of gray. He hurried. He had little time to waste.

* * *

Worshipers packed the morning service in spite of the chilling temperature. As the opening song began, Jay noticed Victor had slipped in the back. The superintendent had brought his wife Margaret. Jay nodded in their direction. When Victor wasn't traveling, he often chose Kingsbridge as his local place of worship.

The worship band played several upbeat tunes while the people clapped and sang. When the music stopped, a young

Welsh girl stood and began to sing. Her voice was so stunningly beautiful and her words so passionate that silence was the only appropriate response.

From his place at the front, Jay could see the singing had captured Christina's fiancé's attention. Only an hour before the worship began, Michael had argued, debated, and finally surrendered his life to God. Christina could hardly contain her joy. She wept and laughed all at once. Before the service, she introduced her fiancé to everyone. Richard McGregor latched onto Michael and within minutes he had opened his Bible, pointing out verses that had guided him to the Truth.

The spontaneity of the worshippers lifted Jay's spirit and he felt he was riding a wave. Lisa, on the other hand, seemed distracted during the service and Jay expected nothing different. She'd been through so much. His heart ached for her.

When the service finished and people were talking, Jay watched Lisa from the corner of his eye. She seemed genuinely happy for Christina. They embraced more than once while they talked. She chatted with Michael for several minutes and patted his arm. He could almost imagine her words: "You've made a wonderful decision to follow Christ." When Jay caught her attention, he gave her a smile and wink and she smiled back. It warmed his heart like summer sunshine.

Eventually, the crowd dispersed and headed home to their Sunday meals. Lisa and the lads always helped Jay tidy up before leaving. Jay locked the door and they headed home to their dinner. The kids were hungry and eager to get out of their church clothes. Lisa was quiet.

"That was great news about Michael," Lisa said. "I'm glad you got to talk to him."

Jay touched her hand affectionately. "Me too. He seems to be a pretty sharp thinker."

Lisa didn't pull her hand away. "And that was just this morning that he made his decision?"

"Amazing isn't it?" He turned right and accelerated up Carriage Drive. He parked the car but didn't get out. "I sure love you, Lis. I know things have been hard on us, but nothing is going to stop me from loving you."

"I know." She gazed out the windscreen. "I have no doubt about that."

"Dad," Nate pleaded. "Let us out. I'm hungry. Can I unlock the door?"

The kids were getting jumpy in the back and Joey started whining.

"Sure." Jay exited and pulled the driver's seat forward so the children could make their escape. He handed the house key to Nathan. He and Michael rushed to the front door pushing to see which one can get in first. "Don't fight, lads."

When Nate got the door unlocked, they spilled into the living room. Jay and Lisa followed behind. Dark, noxious smoke forced them back outside, choking and gasping. Plumes billowed from the doorway. On instinct, Lisa pulled the children together and herded them back into the car while everyone gasped for breath.

She slammed the car door and whirled around at Jay. "I can't take another thing, Jay. I can't." Her voice was shrill. "I've had enough. Where is God when we need Him? We must be doing something wrong because we keep getting attacked."

Jay didn't take the time to respond, but raced around the house, peering in every window. Smoke blanketed the entire downstairs but he saw no flames. Where was the fire?

"I'm going in. I can't see any fire." Jay covered his mouth with his hand and ducked inside, but exited immediately. "It's impossible. I can't breathe. I can't see a thing. I think we better call the fire department."

"Look," Lisa shouted. She pointed toward the rooftop. "There're flames coming out of the chimney."

Jay ran down the driveway so he could see the roofline from a distance. Sure enough, six foot flames were leaping out of one of the chimneys and sparks showered across the roof.

The sound of an approaching siren filled the air. Jay felt the ground vibrate as the monstrous fire engine rumbled up their drive. "Thank God. Someone else must have called the fire department."

A crew jumped from the truck and surrounded the house. Jay noticed smoke seeping out of their upstairs windows. Curls of smoke escaped from between the roof tiles. Firemen in breathing gear ran into the house, pulling hoses with them. Someone flung open an upstairs window and called down, "Nothing live up here, Chief." A radio burped, "Hey Chief, send Kramer on the roof. There's a fire in here somewhere. It's either in the attic or one of the chimneys."

The Chief bellowed into the radio, "Kramer, take two men to the roof. Madison, find an attic entrance and send in your team." Chief Walker finally saw a flame in the chimney. He turned to Jay. "There's your fire. What are you burning?"

"That's not my chimney. It belongs to the house next door. We only share part of the roofline."

The Chief barked out several orders, and three fire fighters jumped the fence and rushed up to Dungess' house. As they hammered on his door, Kramer's team was already clambering across the roof slope. Once they gave the signal, a stream of water shot out the fire hose sending gallons of water down into the throat of the belching chimney. Only when the smoke turned white did they stop.

* * *

Chaos erupted at Dungess' front door. The man came out like a wild boar on a rampage. He cursed and threatened payback. The water that had subdued the fire now flooded

Dungess' kitchen floor, leaving a residue of wet soot and ash. Mrs. Dungess was in a rage over the state of her kitchen and she promised to sue Kingsbridge fire department for trashing her house.

Chief Walker needed to inspect their kitchen, but Dungess blocked the doorway.

"If you don't let me in to inspect your property, I'll make sure the authorities slap arson charges on you."

Dungess refused. "You're not coming in. This is my house."

Walker had had enough. "I'm coming in whether you like it or not." He elbowed past. "Now, get out of my way!"

Dungess turned crimson, his nostrils flared. He cursed and sputtered.

"Where's your stove?" Walker snapped.

"Over there against the wall," the woman answered.

The Chief inspected the face of the chimney and found hot spots. "Here's your problem. You've had a fire burning inside the chimney wall."

"There's nothing wrong with that chimney," Dungess insisted.

"Then why is this—" Walker took hold of Dungess' hand and forced it flat against the wall, "—so hot?"

Dungess yelped as he yanked his hand away.

The fire Chief took a clipboard and wrote comments on an inspection form. He studied the chimney and cooker. He checked the cooker's connection and scribbled more notes. "Nothing is installed to code here. You're lucky you haven't asphyxiated yourself." He wrote a series of numbers. "You've violated building regulations and public health codes, and created an environmental hazard. You've put your neighbor's lives in great danger because of your stupidity."

"How dare you call me stupid. I'll sue you for—"

"Sue away. You'll only waste your money. If you refuse to get this stove and chimney up to code, I promise you that a full investigation will be done and you'll find yourself paying some heavy fines just to keep your rear-end out of jail." He handed Dungess a copy of the warning and slapped a red tag on the stove. This contraption cannot be used until the Council inspects it." Walker headed out the door.

"Wait, you can't leave yet. Who's going to clean up this mess?"

"You should have thought about that before you lit the fire." Walker turned back. "Your mess isn't half as bad as what you've done to your neighbor's home."

Holding his hand like a wounded paw, Dungess stopped and mulled over the news. A grin widened on his face and his voice lightened. "Have a good day, Chief Walker." He mocked in an American accent. "Thanks for your help."

*   *   *

Jay and his family stood in the driveway staring at the fire truck as it disappeared in the distance. A sudden down draft stirred dust around them and the air felt colder. The children huddled together and asked the obvious question, "What do we do now, Daddy?"

"Yes, Jay, what do *we* do now?" Lisa threw her hands up. "Why can't someone stop this evil man from destroying us?"

Jay couldn't argue at a time like this. His family was hungry and cold. Smoke and soot had damaged their house. They had no resources to get away for a while. Their bank account always hovered close to nothing.

"I'm going in to see the damages. I'll bring the kids something to eat."

*   *   *

Numb and disoriented, Lisa and the children headed back to the car where they could get out of the cold. The children squabbled over who sat where.

Lisa raised her voice. "Boys stop your argument right now."

"But Mum," Nathan said. "Michael won't move over. He's hogging the seat."

"Stop it, I said."

"It's Nathan's fault."

"I said, shut up!" Lisa screamed. Immediately her shoulders slumped and her body shook with sobs.

The children fell silent.

Through sobs, Lisa said, "I'm so sorry, boys, I shouldn't have said that." She reached back with one hand and patted them on the knees. "I'm really sorry. I'm just at my wit's end."

Nathan sniffled. "I'm sorry too, Mum."

* * *

Jay stepped into the living room and stared at the damage. Most things were where they had left them that morning, but what he saw looked more like a faded photograph of what had once been. All color had drained from the room. From the walls to the sofa and down to the carpet, the room had turned gray. Jay touched a small lamp table against the wall. A thin layer of ash covered it. The walls were smudged and dirty where the firemen had pulled their equipment through in search of a flame. Jay brushed a cushion and dust billowed and caught in his throat.

Soot floated in midair. Jay stepped into the kitchen and groaned. His movements stirred up more ash until it stung his eyes and burned his throat. "God help me. What do I do now?"

From the window he could see the VW and the family inside. Lisa was leaning back talking to the kids. He knew they were hungry. Pulling a dish towel from a drawer, Jay covered his nose and mouth and brushed the counter of soot with his other hand. He coughed and gagged, but he found peanut butter in the pantry and a loaf of bread in the breadbox. After he cleaned an area of counter, he made sandwiches and dropped them into a plastic shopping bag.

Jay grabbed a few more items. Right now would be a good time to be back in the states. They'd just go to a fast food restaurant. But they were here and there was nothing close and nothing cheap. With his hands full of sandwiches, a bag of chips and a carton of milk, Jay headed for the car.

The children devoured the chips and started on their sandwiches until they gagged. "Dad, these taste bad."

Lisa turned to see. "Jay, what have you given them? Are you trying to make them sick?" She stretched back and grabbed the sandwiches and stuffed them back into the plastic bag.

"No I'm not. And it's not fair to say that. I'm as stressed out as you. We're all stressed." Jay turned to the children. "I'm sorry, kids. I just grabbed what I could. Must be the bread wasn't sealed tight. I'm going to call the McGregor's. Maybe they could let us stay there for the night until I can get the place cleaned up."

"This is crazy," Lisa said. "Why, why, why can't you stop this madness?"

It was then that they noticed him. From an upstairs window, the man stood staring down at their little drama. Dungess appeared amused that they were fighting.

* * *

Jean had just finished cooking when she got the call. On the counter, a fruit pie sat cooling. A big roast rested in the oven and a pile of homemade scones cooled on a rack. Serving dinner guests was her specialty and today she was glad she'd made more than enough. "Richard, don't touch anything in the kitchen until they arrive." She hurried up the stairs to finish the guest room with fresh towels and a bouquet of flowers on the night stand.

"Jean, they're here. They just pulled up." Richard stood at the door with a big smile and open arms. "Come in, come in everyone." No matter the problem, Richard made people feel good.

* * *

Once the family had cleaned up and sat down to Jean's great cooking, the crisis seemed to lighten. They could survive this ordeal. God had sent Richard and Jean to support them. Jay was relieved to see Lisa laugh at one of Richard's jokes. Thank God for humor.

"You'll stay with us until the chimney is repaired." Jean stated. "No arguing. I've got the rooms all set up for you."

Lisa wept.

After eating, Richard and Jay went to the cottage dressed in work clothes and armed with cleansers. The job was messy and bigger than they had expected. By midnight, they'd cleared out the closets and loaded them in Richard's car. They pulled the linens from the beds, removed the curtains, and took them to Jean for cleaning. They wiped down and disinfected all hard surfaces. The house was put into mothballs until it could be inhabitable again.

CHAPTER THIRTY-ONE

—⟋⟋⟍—

On Thursday, Jay called their attorney, Philip Gentry.
"I need your advice about my neighbor. He's been
terrorizing my family continually. He's got to be stopped."

Gentry said, "Do you remember what I told you about
the history of darkness in that region?"

"Yes, I remember. I just didn't expect it to be this way."

"This is exactly what I was talking about. Does Victor
know?"

"Victor knows some of it, but not all."

"And your church back home?"

"Headquarters knows, but so far our supporters have not
been notified. It's a long story and it makes me angry to think
about it. Supposedly, they lost the original letter and forgot
all about it. They promised the letter would be sent to our
supporters by now."

"You shouldn't have to carry this all on your own."

"Lisa feels like we've been abandoned. She's more honest
with her feelings than I am. But I don't think the denomination is taking us seriously." Jay felt he'd finally found a
sympathetic audience. "I've asked Victor if we could take a
sabbatical, but he said it's not possible."

"Jay, you're an anomaly. You don't fit the typical description of most pastors or missionaries."

"How is that?"

"If you were a missionary in Africa, you'd expect to take a sabbatical every five or six years, no question about it. But they're not seeing you as a missionary. And you're not the typical British pastor either. Your family support structures are half way around the world. And more than likely, your success feeds jealously in some British circles. All of those together could cause a major alienation from the support you should have."

"Why should that matter? As long as the work gets done, it shouldn't matter where we've come from."

"It *shouldn't* matter, but it does. I imagine that Lisa understands this better than you do. Women are usually more perceptive than men."

"I appreciate your honesty, but what should we do? This guy behaves like a lunatic and nothing seems to stop him."

"Let me get moving on this. First, I'll call Kingsbridge town council and find out if the authorities have filed any charges against Dungess. I'll need the council's ruling on environmental hazards and building codes for resident structures. When I get some answers, I'll be in touch." Gentry's voice softened. "I'll give Victor a call to discuss this with him. You and Lisa are in my prayers."

* * *

On a Monday in February, Jay and Lisa sat at the hallway of the Cheshire county courthouse. Lisa had lost weight and her complexion was pale. She fidgeted with her necklace and kept her eye on the clock. Jay wore a sports coat and an opened collar shirt. He felt old, as though he'd aged ten years in a day. Stress had etched furrows on his brow and chiseled the contours of his face.

Noel and Elda Dungess sat across the corridor. Noel looked uncomfortable in his shiny polyester suit. Elda wore a green cotton housedress that hung limp on her frame. Her black shoes were sturdy and unstylish. The couple glared down the hallway, ready for a duel.

In another room, attorney's Gentry and Milford where battling it out in hushed polite tones. After twenty minutes, both lawyers emerged from the anteroom and approached their respective clients.

Gentry sat beside the Knights. "I've discussed the details and charges against Milford's clients. It could be long and drawn out. Dungess has not been cooperative."

Lisa commented, "That isn't surprising."

"I've also been notified that the hearing is delayed by two weeks because court cases are backed up. We can either wait or settle out of court."

"What do you recommend?" Jay asked.

"Dungess has already been forced to comply with the council ordinances on an environmental ruling. He must comply. If we wait, it could be another two months of your current condition before any action is taken. Or, if you and Dungess agree to settle out of court, there would be equal sharing of costs and it gets done immediately. I'd suggest that you take the deal."

"So, in essence, we're paying Dungess to install a flue in his house, so we can breathe normal air," Lisa questioned. "Where is the justice in that?"

"There is none. Unfortunately, waiting for the courts to force him to respond could put your family in more jeopardy."

"Lisa, it's not worth the hassle to fight this. In the end, the most important thing is our family's safety."

Lisa nodded in resignation then turned her head away in disgust.

"We'll do whatever it takes to protect our family. Will Dungess agree?"

Milford nodded yes.

Dungess agreed on one condition: That he be allowed to select the installation company himself.

Costs could start at a thousand pounds and go up from there. It had to be installed using a crane and inspected by the County Health Department before use. The installation would take place within a fortnight. The Knights left the courthouse too tired to fight. They were desperate for some peace.

Two weeks drifted into three, but eventually, the flue was installed, the fumes abated and the family finally moved back into their home.

CHAPTER THIRTY-TWO

—〰—

The skies were gray with dark clouds overhead. The lads were at school and Lisa had wanted some space, so she took Joey for a long ride into the country. Jay offered to watch Joey or even ride along, but she declined both offers. Jay built a fire and watched as the flames grew slowly, warming the darkness. A single lamp lit a corner. Everything else was in deep shadows. Alone, Jay pleaded with God.

"Lord, what's the point of all this suffering? I'm losing Lisa and I don't know what to do. No woman should have to live in these stressful conditions." He thumbed through his Bible until his gaze fell on John 15. "If the world hates you, keep in mind that it hated me first. If you belonged to the world, it would love you as its own." He read the words but couldn't accept them for himself. He'd made selfish choices. He'd gotten in the way of God's will. So, how could he align his sufferings with that of Jesus Christ? "They will treat you this way because of My name, for they do not know the One who sent Me." He could never be worthy of suffering for the sake of the cross. Too much of him stood in the way. "They hated me without reason."

No answer came, only a quickening sense of personal fear. Despite every attempt to keep control of his life, it seemed to be slipping from his grasp.

He agonized with his thoughts without resolve. When he got up he was surprised to hear rain pummel the ground, pinging against the window, soaking the earth. He hadn't noticed that a storm was brewing.

The phone jangled, startling Jay. It was a call from the States.

Lisa's mother was returning her call. They'd been away at a conference.

"Oh, I hadn't realized Lisa had called you. She probably wanted to tell you about our court experience. It wasn't much fun, that's for sure."

Her folks had finally received the letter from headquarters, but they'd known the story long before this notice arrived. Perhaps now, the church will be praying for a breakthrough in Kingsbridge. Jay chatted for a while and he tried to sound upbeat.

"I'll leave Lisa a note that you called. She'll probably be back in a couple hours. If it's not too late, I'll have her call. Thanks for your prayers."

When he hung up, he felt worse. Jay put on a wool jacket and a pair of old leather boots. He grabbed an umbrella and headed into the storm.

* * *

Marianne White had been watching the downpour from her desk in the real estate office. She'd just prepared the disclosures on a house she'd sold a week ago. She allowed herself a minute's reprieve to watch the rain. She loved its mesmerizing patter. Marianne hadn't even heard the door open until Jacob Knight stood in front of her desk. He looked distraught; certainly not like the enthusiastic man she'd remembered several years ago. He looked hassled, distracted, and damp.

"Hello, Marianne. It's been a long time since we've chatted." Jay closed his umbrella and leaned it against the doorframe. How are you?"

"I'm fine thanks. What a nice surprise." She stood to greet him. "How is the Knight family doing?" Before Jay could answer she continued. "My mum just loves attending your church. She tells me everything, and your new building is beautiful she says."

Jay ran his hand through his dripping hair. "I'm embarrassed to say that I didn't know your mother attended our services. What's her name?"

"She's probably the only lady in your congregation with a South African accent."

"Oh, Mrs. Kenton. She's your mum?"

"She is. My father was of Dutch decent and reared in South Africa. When he died, she vowed to retire there. We finally persuaded her to come back here to be around her children. Your church makes her feel at home. Similar to her church back in Johannesburg. She loves the easy way you preach."

"You should come along with your mum sometime. What's stopping you?"

Marianne finally stalled. "Well, I uh, I should, I guess, sometime."

"You just might find you like it."

"I'm sure you're right. Now, what can I do for you today?"

"Where would I go to find a listing of house rentals or flats in the area?"

"Right here, but why? Aren't you happy with Erindale Cottage?"

"Oh, the cottage isn't the problem. There are some safety reasons."

"I know the cottage is a bit isolated there in the woods, but Kingsbridge is a very safe place. The incidents of crime are so low, that I can't remember the last time a crime was reported in Kingsbridge." Marianne paused to think. "I lie, there was an incident several years ago up in your part of Kingsbridge."

"What happened?"

"Domestic violence."

"And?"

"The man attempted to strangle his wife as she tried to get out of her car."

"Really? Was he arrested?"

"He was. But the woman decided not to press charges. It was big news around Kingsbridge. Scandalous. It even hit the London tabloids."

"Who was it?"

"A man by the name of Dungess, Noel Dungess."

Jay had a strange sensation of vertigo. He grabbed the corner of Marianne's desk to steady himself.

"Are you all right, Pastor Knight?" She offered a chair.

Jay was glad to sit down. "Thanks. I'm just a little dizzy. It will pass."

"Taking care of all those people has to be a big responsibility. What you need is a good holiday away."

"Sounds great." Jay forced a smile. "But…"

"Maybe next year." She encouraged. "Now, we were talking about a rental. Did you want to put your name on a list?"

"A list? What kind of a list?" Jay rubbed his forehead.

"Well, rental properties are scarce in Britain. There is always a long waiting list, even for government housing. People qualify for Council housing based on economic reasons. But I doubt you'd qualify because you're not a subject of the Queen."

"I pay British taxes and they're always eager to take it. Isn't that enough?"

"Ironic isn't it?" Marianne shook her head as she handed him a form. "You're welcome to submit an application, but I'd hate for you to waste your time on it."

Jay despaired and lowered his head. He wasn't feeling well. When he looked up he saw black spots and Marianne had gone out of focus. Jay shook his head and blinked. The room appeared distorted. He tried to concentrate on why he'd come here. "What about a private rental property? Surely, there must be something."

"Are you sure you're okay? You don't look well."

"I guess I'm not so hot after all. I apologize, but I am desperate to find a place as soon as possible."

Marianne's face softened. "I can check for you right now." She swiveled her chair to face her computer and typed in a command. She scrolled through a file and then turned the screen around so Jay could see. "I'm really sorry Mr. Knight, but you can see for yourself. There's nothing." She clicked to the next screen and a file appeared with two columns of names. "And here is the waiting list just for this region." She paused. "That represents about a two year wait."

Jay tried to understand what Marianne was saying. *What's wrong with me?* His breathing became erratic. A wave of claustrophobia washed over him. His worst fears were happening: he had no control over his life anymore—not even his mind.

"I'm sorry Mr. Knight. I wish I could offer you something." Marianne said.

"Thanks for checking." He gasped for air. His left cheek twitched. He hoped he could walk out the door without collapsing. With one step his vision blurred and his world went silent. His heart felt like it might explode.

Everything went dark.

* * *

Jay tried to pull himself out of the dark cocoon that surrounded him. His mind was cluttered with incomplete thoughts; questions with no answers. Voices coaxed him to consciousness.

"Jay, open your eyes." Lisa caressed his forehead.

"What happened?" His voice sounded weak and foreign in his ears.

"You collapsed at the real estate office."

Jay blinked. "Where am I?" he croaked. His eyes darted around in fear.

"An ambulance brought you here to the hospital." Lisa stood by his bed. "I've brought some friends."

Richard and David moved to the bedside.

"Hi, Jacob," David said. "We heard what happened and rushed straight over."

Richard spoke up. "We're all concerned for your health, Pastor. You've led our church like a shepherd and we all love you. You've given us hope and taught us so much about God. You've become a spiritual father to so many in Kingsbridge. We owe you and Lisa so much."

"No one owes us a thing. God brought us here. It's His story and His church." Jay pulled himself up in bed. He turned to Lisa. "What has the doctor said?"

"They thought it was a heart attack, but they're beginning to think it was some kind of stress related attack. Like a panic attack."

"That's nonsense." He started to get out of bed.

"Hold on, Jay." Lisa laid a firm hand on his shoulder. "Let's wait until the doctor arrives."

David moved toward the bed. "Jacob, your family needs you and your congregation needs you. That's why you *must* take it easy for once in your life."

Within the hour, the doctor arrived and flipped through Jay's charts. "How are you feeling, Mr. Knight?"

"I feel okay. A little while back I was afraid that I might lose my mind." Jay grinned. "Will I live through this?"

"You will survive, no doubt. Such attacks are very scary for the patients."

"How serious are these attacks, Doctor?" Lisa asked. "Can they be stopped?"

"It is serious to the person having one, but they won't die from one, although they feel like they will. There is still a lot we don't know about panic disorders. It's physiological and very real. It's usually associated with something that at one time had caused genuine panic. It might be the location that you're in or a smell or sensation that can trigger panic when there is really nothing to panic over. Your brain makes an association and fires a signal, which sends you into panic mode."

Lisa asked, "What can we do to stop them?"

"I'm giving your husband a mild antidepressant. They'll take a week or so to kick in, but they'll take the edge off the anxiety. Also, I've got some deep breathing exercises that can help during a crisis moment." He turned to Lisa and spoke softly. "I'll sign the discharge papers and your husband can be ready to go within the hour. Keep an eye on this man."

"Thank you, Doctor. I will."

CHAPTER THIRTY-THREE

—〰—

Regardless of the drama in the Knight household, there seemed to be no impact on the church. Christina's fiancé Michael was still gaining new understanding that challenged his old way of thinking. He'd lived his whole life in the dungeons of unbelief. His new faith was unstoppable. Instead of taking steps of maturity, he took leaps. He wondered how he allowed himself to be duped into believing there was no God. He had the razor-sharp mind of an engineer and he understood absolutes. If there is no God, there is no purpose, reducing life to meaningless existence. He saw too much value in what he now knew was truth. It gave hope and he reveled in it.

When Michael first read the story of the centurion trusting Jesus to heal his servant, he questioned the pastor more specifically about God's desire to heal. From then on, he prayed that God would allow him to see and believe for someone else.

The Sunday following Jay's collapse, he was back in the pulpit. Lisa opposed it, but in the end it seemed more stressful to find someone to preach than for him to preach himself. One of the elders announced that there would be a special prayer time for a child with leukemia. Michael and Christina arrived late and slipped in the back. Michael was eager to watch and believe for this child's healing. Four-year-old John looked small as he sat between his parents Joyce and Derek. They allowed him to wear his Mickey Mouse baseball cap to church because his treatment had left him bald. Chemo had stolen what the cancer had not eaten, but the boy's bright eyes were full of hope.

John's prognosis was not good. Each week his healthy blood cell count dipped lower as the cancer destroyed his blood, marrow, and bones. At low points, John hovered just over the chasm between life and death.

After the worship music, the children left for their classes. John went with his friends while the congregation prayed for his healing. The doctor had made it clear that his body couldn't stand another round of chemo. It was only a matter of time before the four-year-old died. That's when John's parents asked the church to pray.

After John had gone to class, Joyce told the congregation how John had suffered with this incurable disease. She told of his faith in God and his courage as he faced hospitalization over and over. Tomorrow, he would go in for his regular blood work. Derek and Joyce were convinced God could do what doctors couldn't. Joyce wanted to come forward in proxy for John. She would stand in on her son's behalf.

Derek and Joyce stood in the front. A sense of promise hung in the air. There was no emotionalism, no hocus-pocus. Jay announced the purpose of faith on John's behalf and he invited the elders and anyone who would like to join in faith to move forward as he anointed Joyce with oil.

Jay took the small vial of olive oil and put a drop on her forehead. A handful of men and women surrounded her, each putting a hand of faith on the person in front of them. A lattice-work of prayers was knit together from one hand to another, from one heart to another, until the entire room was as one.

Joyce remained still. This was a holy moment. Jay's prayer was simple. He prayed for John's complete healing from the ravages of disease. He prayed that his blood cells would be restored overnight. He prayed that John would not have to face chemotherapy any longer and that God would receive all the glory for the healing.

Others prayed, then they sang, "Jesus Loves Me" and finished with prayer. Joyce promised to call the pastor the next morning after John's blood work returned. As the church cleared and most had left, Michael waited behind to speak to Jay. Like the rest of the congregation, Michael's faith was simple and pure.

Michael said, "Pastor, I've never seen a service like that before. Is that what you call a healing service?"

"No Michael. I call it an anointing service." Jay read James 5:14-15 to him: "Is any one of you sick? He should call the elders of the church to pray over him and anoint him with oil in the name of the Lord. And the prayer offered in faith will make the sick person well; the Lord will raise him up."

"But it was so calm and quiet."

"We aren't asked to do anything else but that. God is the healer, not us."

Michael moved closer and lowered his voice. "We weren't alone today. He was here."

"Who was here?"

"Jesus. You know me, Pastor, I'm an engineer. I was at the very back and the last one in the room to stand and place my hand on the person in front of me."

"And?"

"And another hand was placed on my shoulder. I swear!"

"Don't swear, Michael. What do you mean?"

Michael whispered. "I felt a man's hand on my shoulder, and when I turned around, no one was there, but I still felt the weight of His hand. You probably think I'm crazy, but it's true."

"I believe you, Michael."

* * *

All Monday morning, Jay's mind returned to John and his results. Then the phone rang and Joyce was talking. Her voice was calm and firm.

"The doctor said to me, 'John's blood cells are as healthy as yours Mrs. Davis.' Those where his exact words. There was no sign of leukemia. Both his white and red blood counts were perfect. How about that, Pastor? Healing by proxy, God did a miraculous transfusion."

Jay and Lisa were amazed at the detail of God's handiwork. It was like a stand-in healing, a miraculous blood transfusion from mother to son and the doctor's words confirmed it.

The nagging question at the dinner table that night was "Why?" If God could perform a miracle in one family then why not theirs? Why didn't He at least give them a break? Why wouldn't He release them from this burdensome situation? He had to know their limits. It seemed so unfair. Scripture reminded them that the same God that gives is the same God who takes away. Jay and Lisa wondered why they did not see God intervene in their personal crisis. Would God choose one over the other? Could it be that God's ways were so complex that they need only trust Him, even when they couldn't understand what He was doing?

The answers did not come easily.

CHAPTER THIRTY-FOUR

—ﻬ—

Night closed on the home enveloping it in darkness. The air within Erindale Cottage felt compressed. Jay sat at his desk trying to study. His breathing felt labored. He sensed something was wrong but didn't want to alarm the family. Upstairs, the children were building a toy fort with LEGOs on their bedroom floor. They chattered and laughed as usual. Lisa sat in the family room working on a tapestry.

Something hit the side of the house. The children screamed.

It happened again. The sound of the impact reverberated through the home. Jay heard Lisa running up the stairs. The house throbbed as crash after crash continued. A picture fell from the wall. A light fixture tilted and swung back and forth. A porcelain vase shattered and the children became hysterical.

Jay almost collided with Lisa as he bolted from his office.

"Jay—the boys."

Jay grabbed Joey and pushed Nathan and Michael ahead of him. "What is that crazy man doing now?" The pounding came from the closet beneath the stairs. Handing Joey to his wife, Jay flung open the closet door and screamed at the wall. "Dungess, you're insane!"

Crash! Boom! Plaster snapped and popped off the wall. "Dad, it's him. He's going to get us this time. Look," Nate had followed his dad downstairs. He screamed. "He's going to kill us!"

"No he's not, Nathan. I'm not going to let anything happen to you." He pulled the boys away from the closet. "He's a scary man, but God is tougher than he is and God will protect us." Jay turned to Lisa. "Hurry, call the police. I'll stay here in case he breaks through."

Lisa ran to the phone, but someone was banging on the front door. "Jay, someone's here. What should I do?"

Jay shouted, "Who's at the door?"

It was Ian and April Langley from next door. Relieved, Lisa opened it. "Come in quickly. It's finally happening."

"You poor love, what is the problem with this man?" April hugged Lisa. "We could hear the banging all the way from the back of our house. That man is mad."

"Thanks for coming, you two." Jay stuck his head around the corner. "This has gone too far."

"I need to call the police." Lisa's hand trembled as she picked up the phone.

April turned to her husband. "Ian, make the call for her?" She looked at Lisa. "You poor girl. This is horrifying."

"Let me do it, Mrs. Knight." Ian took the phone and dialed 999. He gave an urgent report as the hammering continued in the background. "The police are on their way." He headed for the door. "I'm going to wait down the drive for the police to arrive. You're place is hard to find in the dark."

The pounding was relentless. New cracks formed like fissures, tearing the plaster into crooked roads and inter-sections. Dungess' curses grew louder as the dividing wall began to crumble.

Jay shouted. "Lisa, get out of here. Now! Run! Take the kids and go to the McGregor's house."

April said, "Let me take you there. We can come back later and get some clothes if you want. I'll get the lads in the car." April herded the children out the front door while Lisa stood sobbing.

"Lisa, you must go now." Jay turned back to the wall. A chink of mortar popped, spraying his face with grit. "Go Lisa. I'll come as soon as this is over."

Lisa continued sobbing. "Jay, what if... I'm afraid."

Jay pulled her into his arms. Her body shook with great sobs as dust billowed around them from the hits. "Take the children and go." He added. "No matter what happens, I love you."

"I know you do. That's why it's so hard."

"What are you talking about?"

"I'm sorry, Jay. I'm so sorry." She gasped for breath. "I know you've tried so hard. I know you didn't mean for any of this to happen."

Jay stared at her without understanding. "Lisa, not now."

"I'm just not strong enough to put up with this." She stared into Jay's eyes. "I can't do this anymore." Sobs overcame her. "I hope that one day I'll see forgiveness in your eyes. I'm so sorry. Goodbye, Jay." She turned and ran for the car.

Jay's eyes darted around the room. He could not comprehend her words. Nothing made sense, except that he was losing his wife. He ran to the door. "No. No Lisa don't leave. I beg you, don't leave me. The children—" He ran to the idling car. Inside, the children huddled in fear, crying for their father.

Jay took Lisa's arm. "How can you do this now?"

Between sobs, she said, "I'm sorry. I can't live like this anymore. Someday, that man will kill someone. Maybe one of us."

"I wouldn't let that happen." Jay frantically tried to slow his breathing, to think clearly, to stall the inevitable. Inside the house, the walls shuddered. The noise sounded like a jack hammer and Dungess was screaming like a wild man.

"You can't stop any of this from happening. It's out of your control. Only God can do that and He seems to have other plans."

The children were crying. Michael held out his arms for Jay. "I want Daddy."

Jay's heart ached to see his children reach for him. He broke. "Please, Lisa. I beg you not to do this."

"Jay, we need to go."

"Where are you going? What about the kids? How can I find you?"

"My parents. They've already made arrangements. I'll get in touch after we settle."

The revelation rocked Jay. This decision was made before tonight ever began. Suddenly she was gone. The car sped off into the night and the preacher stood alone as his world crumbled.

Jay no longer heard the throbbing walls. He didn't care what Dungess did anymore. He didn't care about the house. Dungess had won and Jay's life would never be the same. What he cared about most was heading into the night without him.

Far below, swirling blue lights were approaching. The night quickly turned into a bizarre dreamscape. Jay's legs went wobbly. He swayed then fell to his knees. His mind refused to process what he saw, what he heard. Police vehicles pulled up in front of him and officers got out, but Jay didn't move.

"Mr. Knight?" Constable Mercer called out. "Are you okay?"

Jay stared straight ahead. He heard someone talking but it was garbled. He couldn't understand the words.

"We need to ask you some questions, Mr. Knight."

Jay's head throbbed and his thoughts muddled.

"Mr. Knight. Can you hear me? I'm Constable Mercer. Do you remember me?" Jay stared through him and gave only the slightest nod of recognition. The officer reached down and helped Jay to his feet. "Let's go inside so we can talk." Mercer guided Jay down the steps and up to his front door. House lights blazed and dust hung in the air.

"Mr. Langley is with Officer Jones at the Dungess property. He's giving a statement." Suddenly the policeman's radio squawked. "Very good Sir." Mercer answered and then turned back to Jay. "They're arresting Noel Dungess now. They've found the sledge hammer and damaged wall. I guess he was pretty determined. Langley has agreed to testify on your behalf. We'll need statements from you and the Misses. From the looks of things, Dungess had no intention of stopping until he'd gotten you. He's been after you for a very long time."

Jay finally stirred. Looking at Mercer he said, "What happens now?"

"I expect there'll be a trial. Hopefully, this man will be stopped for good. For now Reverend Knight, you're family is safe. You don't need to fear this man anymore." Mercer cleared his throat. "I want you to know Reverend Knight that I've always believed in you after that first incident. I have some doubts about our British system, but I know there's been a grave injustice done to you and your family. I'm truly sorry." He paused. "I just wanted you to know that Sir."

Jay turned away and faced the wall. A sob suddenly erupted and Jay could no longer hold in the grief and rage inside.

*   *   *

Jay lay in the darkness for hours. He must have dozed, because just before dawn, he was roused, yet he heard nothing. He reached out for Lisa, but she was not there.

"Oh God, it can't be true." He crawled from bed and groped along the hallway. He pushed open the children's bedroom door and stared at their empty beds.

"Oh God, what have I done?" He collapsed onto Nathan's bed and hugged his son's pillow. "No God, no. I can't bear this. My life is nothing without my family. What purpose could there be in all this loss?"

Slowly, dawn crept across the horizon until daylight lanced the darkness, stinging Jay's eyes.

* * *

Night and day had become a blur. Downstairs, the phone rang at various times. Mercifully it stopped. Jay was vaguely aware of knocking at his front door, but that too eventually stopped. He went into the bathroom and found the bottle of pills the doctor had prescribed. He stared at it and finally poured out two and washed them down with water. He felt sick. He gagged and wished he could vomit all the pain that churned in his stomach.

The phone rang again. Jay groaned and put a pillow over his head. It was incessant. "Stop it." He bellowed. "Leave me alone." He'd disconnect the phone. Jay headed down the stairs when it occurred to him that it might be Lisa. He picked it up. "Lisa?"

"Pastor, this is Steve Hayes. I'm sorry to have to call you like this, but my father is dying. He's suffered a massive heart attack and they don't give him long at all. He's on life support now. Please Pastor, please visit him, and pray with him."

"I'm sorry Steve, but I've had some serious complications of my own."

"Pastor, I don't know who else to turn to. You're my only hope. My father's dying and he doesn't know God."

Jay had never turned a request down, but more than anything he wanted to now. He was in no shape to reach out to someone else. He regretted answering the phone.

"Your father doesn't know me. There might be a hospital chaplain who could pray with him." Jay paused. "Steve, this is the worst time of my life and I have nothing to give."

"You've got God and my father doesn't. Please."

Jay slumped against the wall and fought off panic. "Okay, I'll be there in half an hour. Wait for me at the entrance."

Jay had no choice. Duty forced his hand, but God prompted Steve's words. How could he do otherwise? He showered and changed and looked at himself in the mirror. "Knight, you're a pathetic mess." Downstairs, he heard a clank as mail dropped through the letter slot. Picking it up on his way out, Jay put a sealed envelope on a table beside the phone and headed to the hospital. He thought only of Lisa and the boys and his heart ached so much he thought it might rupture. He was useless. Driving recklessly across town, he spoke to God. His prayer felt distant and bitter.

"Lord, why am I doing this? My life has been destroyed by someone who sought only evil. I'm empty. I'm only going because I know I should. If You want to do anything for this man, you'll have to do it Yourself."

Steve waited just outside the hospital doors, pacing. Jay parked and met the grieving son. Steve led him to ICU.

Steve's father lay shrouded in a death-like state; his breath, dead air; his mind lost in unconsciousness. Entangled with tubes and wires, Ken breathed with the aid of a machine: first the clicking sound, followed by a rasping gasp.

Without the ventilator, he would die. A man without God was being sucked into another world from where he could not return. Jay touched his pasty hand. Dark blue veins protruded like three-dimensional road maps. Jay tried to pray, but his words dried in his throat. He started again and prayed for Ken. He mouthed the words, but they came from beyond his spirit. The words challenged death and called forth life. But Jay could not own the prayer. He had no right to offer what he considered false hope.

The doctor waited silently in the doorway. Following prayer, Ken's vital signs dipped dangerously. Still not flat lined, the nurse pulled the plug and rolled Ken away to die naturally. Obviously, the prayer had little impact on Ken's condition. He would soon meet his Maker.

Jay chided himself for offering such a weak prayer. He promised Steve he would visit the hospital the next day. Meanwhile, Jay's own trauma, as great as life and death to him, had to be stuffed inside, hidden from those who needed a fearless shepherd. He doubted he could pull it off.

Back at home, Jay immediately fell back into a pit of despair. He closed the shades, locked the door, and paced the floors, praying, begging, pleading that God would rescue him. How could he face another day without his family? He'd called Lisa's parents time after time, only to get their answering machine.

Jay could not be consoled. He poured through the Scriptures. He read the Psalms and pleaded along with David. He questioned God like Job and found no comfort. Somewhere in the middle of the night, he succumbed to exhaustion and drifted into a fitful sleep. He woke before daylight and dragged himself out of bed and into the shower. After dressing, Jay brewed a pot of coffee and poured himself a cup.

The kitchen wasn't right without Lisa. He wanted to see her smile again, to hear her laughter. How could she have left him? How had she endured this so long?

Jay wanted to hear his children laugh and play. He remembered them playing in the tree fort. They loved playing knights and castles or cars and trains in their bedroom. He remembered the many nights he'd listened to their prayers, praying for each other and even for Dungess. Jay choked and sobbed. The house was eerie without their laughter and giggles. "Oh God, how can I live another day like this?"

Overwhelmed again, Jay got his coat and headed to the front door. There on the phone table was the letter that had come the day before. It was from his Superintendent, Victor Trinder. Jay sat down to read it through.

Dear Jay and Lisa,

I know this has been a terribly difficult time for you both. I've agonized over your request for a sabbatical. You both deserve it and it's long overdue. My difficulty was in finding a replacement in your absence. You both have been an invaluable couple to lead this great work in Kingsbridge. What you've done in Kingsbridge is beyond what others would do in a lifetime. You've sacrificed, borne great persecution, and still stood strong against the opposition.

God has rebuked me for the way I've handled your request. I ask forgiveness for my failure. I should have allowed you to take a needed sabbatical long ago. Please forgive me. I am therefore releasing you both to take some necessary time away so you and your family can be strengthened again. And, after you've recovered, I welcome you to come back to Kingsbridge and take up your charge once again.

Your brother and friend,
Victor Trinder

Jay groaned at the news, so long hoped for and now too late. He slumped back in his seat. "Why God, why now?" He balled up the letter and threw it across the room. "You're too late Victor." He got up and headed to the hospital.

At 10:00, Jacob Knight entered the hospital ward again as he'd promised. There was a pervasive antiseptic smell, mingled with the remains of institutional breakfast. A different patient rested in the ICU bed. He wandered through the ward and scanned the patient's faces. There was no sign of Steve's father. He expected as much.

He probably died within minutes of me leaving. I'll need to call Steve. I should never have offered such a prayer of hope. I've got nothing left to give.

Ken's doctor leaned beside the nurse's station. He'd been studying the pastor's movements. Ashamed to make eye contact Jay lowered his head and headed out the door.

"Excuse me, Pastor." The doctor hurried after him. "I'm Dr. Nichols, Kenneth Brock's physician."

Jay stopped dead.

"I was here yesterday and I watched as you prayed with my patient."

"Yes. I'm so sorry. Has the family been notified yet?"

"Absolutely. They're ecstatic."

"About what?" Jay felt a bit foolish.

The doctor smiled. "Obviously, you haven't heard. Mr. Brock is in the bed to your right. He's our Lazarus."

"But how?" Jay struggled for words.

"I wouldn't have recognized him either if I hadn't pulled two shifts and saw his recovery with my own eyes. We're going to keep an eye on him for awhile but it looks like he'll be discharged soon."

Jay was flabbergasted. He followed the doctor to Kenneth Brock's bed. He'd just finished a hot breakfast and was reading the morning paper.

Jay suddenly felt shy as he approached Mr. Brock. The physician moved to Ken's side.

"Ken, you should meet this man. He visited you last night and prayed for you."

Ken sat up. "So, you're the man that saved me from the jaws of death?" Ken shook Jay's hand and his eyes conveyed gratitude.

"Not me. What God did, He did on His own. We're all lost without Him."

The doctor leaned in closer to Ken's bed. His voice was a whisper. "Medically speaking, you should be dead. We used the ventilator in hopes that you might survive, but your vital signs dropped rapidly around ten o'clock. Between you and me, you're alive because God intervened when this man prayed."

No one felt more surprise than Jay. In his utmost weakness, God came through in power and worked an unexpected miracle. Somewhere between his extreme human frailty and God's overwhelming compassion, a rift opened for God's power to disrupt natural laws, do the impossible, and raise Ken to life. He was indeed a Lazarus.

Jay drove home to his empty house. His heart ached but it had not stopped loving. His life was in shreds, but he would go on believing. His family needed him and God proved He would meet him at every turn, no matter where in the world he'd find himself.

EPILOGUE

—∿—

Several years later in Santa Maria, California.

A warm breeze rippled through the palms and chased the scent of jasmine into every corner of the garden. On the sun-warmed patio a man sat alone, his head bowed.

"You okay, Dad?"

Slowly, the father lifted his head and smiled, while his eyes told the story. Behind those cerulean eyes lay a mystery of a man who'd plumbed the depths of the unknown and finally found a deep settled peace. "I'm okay, kiddo. Just thanking the Lord for my boys." Finally he stood and the two men embraced. The father whispered in his ear. "I'm a man greatly blessed." He paused. "I am blessed because all my sons love Jesus Christ."

The son held on tight and whispered back, "You both showed us how to love Him." He paused. "We just followed your example."

A sea gull soared high overhead, circling slowly in the sun. Jay finally let Nate go. "I'm so proud of you Nate. And Katie is a jewel with a godly heart." He looked at his watch and then at the assembling crowd. "Has your mum arrived?" Jay searched the sea of faces.

"Yes. She's sitting in the shade waiting for Joey. He's her escort."

Jay finally spotted her and his eyes glistened. "Ah, there she is. She's as gorgeous as ever. She looks so happy today."

Michael walked around the corner and joined the two men.

"Michael, any news on Joey?"

"Yes, he just called. He's only a minute away." Michael patted his dad's shoulder. "Don't worry, Dad, he'll be here on time. You know our Joey."

A guitarist began to play a quiet medley of hymns and the crowd hushed to listen. A few moments later Joey appeared and slipped around the seated guests toward Jay. "I made it, Dad." Joey gave his father a hug and grabbed both brothers and wrapped his arms around their necks in a single embrace.

"We have ten minutes. Michael do you have the ring?"

"I got it." Michael grinned and turned toward Nate. "Good choice, bro."

Jay reached into his jacket pocket and pulled out an unsealed envelop. "Joey, you're escorting your mother to her seat. Do you remember where to seat her?"

Joey nodded.

"I have one small favor, Joey. Can you give this to your mum after the wedding?" He held out the worn envelope. "It's important to me."

"Sure, what is it?"

"It's a letter and photos from the McGregor's in Kingsbridge. A lot of our old friends are there. I promised I'd pass them on to your mum. They say the church is doing great." Jay hesitated. "I thought…" He couldn't complete the sentence. He stuffed the envelope into Joey's pocket. "I thought she'd like to know."

"Sure, I'll do that."

"Dad, it's time. Will you pray with us?"

* * *

Beneath the veranda Lisa watched the four men standing in a huddle. They bowed their heads and draped their arms across each other's shoulders. Her sons were praying together, each well seasoned in their life with God.

Lisa studied Jay's lips as he prayed. She was so accustomed to his prayers, so familiar with his worship. When he finished she breathed an "Amen." She quickly grabbed a tissue and dabbed her eyes. Tears pooled so easily these days.

* * *

When the last of the guests took their seats, Jay said, "Okay lads, I think we're ready." He squeezed Nate's shoulder affectionately. "You and Michael follow me." Jay stopped beside a white trellis laden with clusters of Wisteria blossoms.

At the back, Lisa rose and took Joey's arm.

"Are you ready, Mum?" Joey beamed.

She looked for a fleeting moment at Jay, her gaze forgiving and forgiven. "I'm ready," she whispered. Then, smiling up at her son she walked with the grace of royalty. Once seated, Joey bent and kissed her cheek. "Mum, I love you so much."

The bride appeared at the garden gate. The guitarist began an acoustic version of Mendelssohn's *Wedding March*. The crowd rose and craned their necks to see the bride. Katie was dazzling in a bronze gown of satin and lace, her hair woven with orange blossoms.

With his brothers at his side, Nate turned to watch his bride meet him at the altar. Katie and Nathan would trust

God to pen the lines of their future with perfect wisdom and grace. They trusted God explicitly. They had no reason to doubt Him.

THE END

Printed in the United States
80551LV00003B/1-87

9 781602 664340